I0562035

VASILY MAHANENKO

START THE GAME

*Books are the lives
we don't have
time to live,
Vasily Mahanenko*

GALACTOGON
BOOK #1

MAGIC DOME BOOKS

START THE GAME
GALACTOGON, BOOK ONE
COPYRIGHT © VASILY MAHANENKO 2015
COVER ART © VLADIMIR MANYUKHIN 2015
ENGLISH TRANSLATION COPYRIGHT ©
BORIS SMIRNOV 2015
PUBLISHED BY MAGIC DOME BOOKS
FIRST PAPERBACK EDITION 2018
ALL RIGHTS RESERVED
ISBN: 978-80-7619-015-3

ALL BOOKS BY VASILY MAHANENKO:

The Way of the Shaman LitRPG Series
Survival Quest
The Kartoss Gambit
The Secret of the Dark Forest
The Phantom Castle
The Karmadont Chess Set
Shaman's Revenge
Clans War

The Alchemist LiTRPG series by Vasily Mahanenko:
City of the Dead
Forest of Desire
Tears of Alron

Dark Paladin LitRPG Series
The Beginning
The Quest
Restart

Galactogon LitRPG Series
Start the Game!
In Search of the Uldans
A Check for a Billion

Invasion LitRPG Series
A Second Chance
An Equation with One Unknown

World of the Changed LitRPG Series
No Mistakes
Pearl of the South

**The Bard from Barliona LitRPG series
(with Eugenia Dmitrieva)**
The Renegades
A Song of Shadow

You're in Game!
(LitRPG Stories from Bestselling Authors)

You're in Game-2!
(More LitRPG stories set in your favorite worlds)

TABLE OF CONTENTS:

PROLOGUE

"**W**HAT SAY YOU, NERPS—shall we go out with a boom? Who's got what?" asked our guild leader merrily and, without waiting for a reply, used his scroll of *Withering Fog*.

At once, an ashen cloud descended on the immense forest that, with its rare creatures and plants, represented the extent of our in-game empire. If memory served, there would be nothing left of it all within the hour—save a scorched barren that even the mobs would shun. As the guild leader's spell did its work, the imperial palace nearby became the target for every rare and powerful spell that had accumulated in our guild's coffers. Actually, some of these spells were more than rare— they were legendary, one-of-a-kind. Though, then again, a spell like *Black Death*, which will instantly lay waste to an entire city, isn't exactly suitable for public circulation. The *Black Death* doesn't take population into account, you see: It doesn't matter if it's cast on a hovel with two or a megalopolis of millions— everything dies.

GALACTOGON BOOK ONE

Though most of our group seemed perfectly merry destroying what we had spent several years defending (from hordes of demons, monsters or just ordinary players looking to make some coin), personally, I saw nothing worth celebrating. Everything I had—right down to my pants—I had already sold to the merchants, who went on doing business as usual, zealously coveting their hard-earned coppers despite the imminent apocalypse.

To our chagrin, the merchants were not interested in spell scrolls, so the only thing we could do was either throw the parchments away or...

Or use them to raise a franchise of hell right outside the Emperor's Palace.

The game's admins had declared today the darkest day in the fifteen-year history of Runlustia. Today would see the official endgame—played out in-game as a meteor falling from the sky. Today the final cataclysm would take place and neither new expansions, nor free trial periods, nor new scenarios or unique items would reverse it. The game owners had done everything they could, but no one can compete with Galactogon at the moment. And so, even the monster that was Runlustia's game world was forced to exit the stage. The present is no place for dinosaurs...

You were killed by the Black Death spell. You cannot be resurrected because the game is shutting down. We wish you all the best and thank you for the time you have spent with us!

START THE GAME

And that was that...

Eight beautiful years of life as an Elf Paladin (one of the top Tanks—I am not a humble man—in the history of Runlustia) had reached their end. Eight years of dashing about sword-in-hand all over this virtual world, grinding my Strength, Dexterity, Intelligence and forty or so other stats. Eight years—of which I had spent five supporting myself entirely through this game, guiding low-level players through dungeons, dominating PvP arenas and tournaments, signing sponsorship deals...There were neither sponsors, nor deals, nor players now...I had enough money theoretically, but there'd hardly be enough for another six months of the kind of life I'd grown accustomed to. I had not yet figured out what I'd do next. The last month in general had turned out to be a month of cataclysmic changes—I lost my job, I lost my favorite game (in which I'd become used to spending up to twelve hours a day) and I lost my girlfriend who suddenly decided that there was no future with me after all. There were no words for it all—only feels.

"Welcome back to reality, Master!" Emerging from my gaming capsule, I was greeted by my smart home. Literally like that: "Master"—you could hear the capitalization and all. The cocoon's cover closed behind me, switching the capsule into a state of hibernation and me into a state of contemplation. To be one of the best takes more than being in the best guild or having the best weapons and armor—you have to have the right equipment in real life too: equipment that's tailored to the needs of the game. This is exactly the kind of equipment I had outfitted my house with and yet, today, it had already become a mere monument to itself. Customized specifically to Runlustia, my cocoon was no good for anything else. I could of course update the software and chisel and hammer the cocoon to fit another game's requirements; but I also understood that attempting this kind of refit was likely beyond my powers. If I ever did decide to dive into another virtual game world, I wouldn't feel right without a new cocoon customized specifically for the game in question anyway. If you're going to do something...

"Alex, what's up!" A call from one of the few people who qualify for the vaunted title of "my friend" tore me away from my mandatory evening jog. The habit is many years old—my father forced me to run, claiming that no cocoon in the world with all your simulators and gizmos can replace good old physical exertion (a controversial claim, nowadays, considering modern advancements in cocoon construction). He nonetheless managed to instill in me the habit of torturing myself on a treadmill. And I am grateful, I guess—the jogging helps me think.

"Nada. What's up with you?" I replied, toweling off my sweat and pausing the machine. "What are you getting into?"

"Nothing at the moment—but I've been thinking...Do you want to hold a wake for our characters? I mean, we were inseparable for seven years."

"Eight," I corrected Alonso.

"What's the difference—let's go drink!"

"Will Lucy let you go out?"

Lucille was Alonso's wife. How that meathead managed

to wangle one of the city's prettiest girls, no one knew, including he himself. But—no use arguing with facts—the two had been a full-fledged family unit for four years now and were raising a son just as feckless as his daddy. In his paltry three years, this little wonder had managed to brick the family smart home three times already. It reached the point that Alonso began carrying the boy constantly in his arms, proudly explaining that the family was raising a future master hacker...who, according to me, was just another blockhead with his hands sprouting from the wrong place. Then again, no one asked my opinion, Lucille least of all. She and I have had more than our share of disagreements— we've had everything short of armed hostilities.

"Nothing doing. I got her permission before I called," came Alonso's self-satisfied reply. "D'you see Qi Wen cast the *Black Death*? It wasted the entire city all to hell—hold on...What sweetie? I'm not swearing! Okay, okay, 'hell's' a bad word too, I get it...Anyway, what was I talking about?" The captive of connubial life returned to me finally (and they try to tell me that THAT is a good thing? Love, comfort, security?) "I wish we had that scroll when we were taking Landir Keep! Remember? Alright, we'll meet up at the bar at six. We can talk about it then. Later!"

The siege of Landir Keep was one of Runlustia's most memorable scenarios. The unapproachable citadel had been occupied by a dark necromancer who began sending his undead armies into all four empires of the realm. It took the players seven weeks just to break the keep's defenses and another three to clear the citadel entirely. And all this happened live, 24/7—the players never stopped their assault, periodically substituting each other. It was a good time...

"Alexis Panzer?" The next phone call caught me at a very inconvenient moment.

"That's right," I muttered from my half-full bath, angrily looking where the warming current of water had just been. One dumb feature of the smart home is that if someone calls you, the house automatically adjusts all the settings necessary to take the call. I made a mental note to block all incoming calls during bath time—I like my baths. "Pardon me, who am I speaking to?"

"You can call me John. Would it be possible to meet with you this evening at six? I have a business proposition for you."

"Excuse me, John, but Runlustia has been shut down." Realizing what the caller was getting at, I quickly dotted my i's and crossed my t's. Considering that the website advertising my services had not yet been taken down, John was either a player wishing to skip the early level grind with my help or a sponsor wanting to place some advertisement on my character.

"I am aware of Runlustia's closure. I am likewise aware that you are now unemployed. I wish to offer you work for precisely these reasons—work that is related to your favorite pastime—computer games. What do you say?"

"You've piqued my interest," I replied, sitting up. John was completely correct—I was unemployed and so had to grab any offer involving games with both hands, legs and also teeth, just in case.

START THE GAME

"Before anything else, allow me to ask you one important question. Your answer will determine our subsequent conversation. What do you know about Galactogon?"

"Galactogon?" I echoed surprised. "As far as I understand it, Galactogon is a game set in space. The players have space ships—they fly around and try to destroy each other...Oh! There're also planets—that is, moons or asteroid belts—I can't remember the correct term—where you can mine resources. I'm sorry, I am not very familiar with that game world. I would need time to prepare myself better. About a week should do—then, I'll be able to tell you whatever you need to know about it."

"Are you saying that at the present moment you have absolutely no grasp of this game's nuances?"

"That is correct."

"I beg your pardon for the intrusive question, but would you be willing to aver this in front of a polygraph machine?"

"...?"

"I see. I propose we meet tonight at six. I will explain everything to you then. A car will come to pick you up. May I inquire as to your address? One major request: If you really don't know a thing about Galactogon and want to get the job, please don't read a single thing about it. This is very important. Have a good day!"

The tap water and the music came back on, as well as whatever movie I had been watching on the holograph...But my thoughts left this comfy situation far behind. One thing was clear—I wasn't going to make it to the bar this evening. Work was more important. My hands reflexively reached for the virtual keyboard—before I jerked them away. During my time as a Tank, I had learned a valuable lesson—if the clients want something, it's best to give it to them. This one had requested that I avoid any information about Galactogon, so no question about it. It's not that hard to survive without knowing something for eight hours. Better call Alonso and tell him that I won't make our meet up.

The main thing is not to think about the white elephant in the bath...Don't think about the white elephant in the bath, Alexis...

I had never imagined that our city had a real, full-blown palace just outside of it. But there it was—located in a sector that was closed to fliers and the general public. A portion of the compound was entirely covered with protective domes, so all you could do was wonder what lay beneath them—but that someone had built an authentic, real castle in there—from stone and wood and all...That—I definitely had not expected.

The conference room that I was ushered into reminded me somewhat of the Emperor's private chambers in Runlustia. It was just as beautiful, just as grandiose—and just as brainless from the perspective of defense. Although, what unwanted guest could make it to this room alive anyway? The massive oaken table, evoking the epoch of the first French Revolution, occupied half the office. Along the perimeter of this colossus stood five armchairs which, at first glance, conceded nothing to this table in style—but which on second glance must have begun their lives as furniture around the time the London Underground first opened to the public. The rest of the interior decoration lived up to these luxurious furnishings.

"Please have a seat," said the steward who had ushered me in, indicating an unoccupied armchair. "The masters will be here soon."

Two of the five chairs were occupied and, judging by the looks on their occupants' faces, I understood that these people were prospective employees just like me. If my logic didn't betray me, there was about to be a discussion. Hmm...I was beginning to like this situation more and more.

The first prospective hire I studied was a girl of about twenty-five. Even her roomy clothes couldn't conceal her well-toned body—she was one of my people. "My" meaning that she was a gamer like me, who spent most of her time in a virtual world, while her game capsule tended to her physique IRL. Based on her outward appearance I wouldn't have called her an amateur either. She had gray eyes, medium-length blonde hair, a slightly-turned up nose and thin lips. Most likely, I thought, this lovely person's discerning gaze had already processed the value of my clothes and shoes, my manner of walking and sitting and had arrived at its conclusions—which were clearly not in my favor. On the whole, the vibe I got from her seemed to say, "I am a woman, so the whole world owes me."

I liked the second applicant better—men are reasonable creatures in general, by and large. I liked him because, having cast me one fleeting glance, he gave me a friendly nod and closed his eyes, sinking back into slumber. I understood him very well. War is war, but war can wait—sleep, on the other hand, should happen whenever the opportunity presents itself. You never know when the chance will come again. By the look of him, the dark-haired guy also turned out to be a virtual aficionado but, unlike the girl, he wasn't afraid to show it—the tight black T-shirt pleasantly emphasized his body's athletic build. A mere two- or three-hour workout at the gym or in a gaming capsule wouldn't bring one's body into such condition—I know as much from my own experience. And so, there were currently three players sitting at the table including myself. All of us had come from Runlustia or some other MMO that had recently shut down. And all three of us had been offered work in Galactogon. Well, well—let's see how this turns out ...

After a ten minute wait the door opened and the Masters, as the steward had called them, entered the office. One rapid and discerning glance was enough for me to almost choke. I instantly jumped to my feet and greeted my seniors with the customary deference I had honed as an imperial courtier in Runlustia. Out of the corner of my eyes, I noticed that both the girl and the dozing guy jumped up along with me...So he wasn't sleeping at all but assessing the situation with eyes closed. This made me like him even more—it was too bad that only one of us would get the job.

"Please take your seats," said one of the newcomers, taking our reactions for granted. He was the owner of factories, ships, shopping malls, cinemas and whatever else one could own in our world. According to official and unofficial data, he had been the wealthiest man on our planet for going on ten years already, yearly increasing his net worth exponentially. It was he who owned Galactogon and it was he who was responsible for my current unemployment.

"Gentlemen and gentlewoman, please excuse the delay," said the second Master, the President of our long-suffering nation. "We needed to receive full confirmation that you met all our requirements. Now, we can safely say that all of you fit our needs."

All of us? Were they really going to give the job to all three of us instead of just one?

"And what is it about us that fits your needs?" the girl instantly jumped in, utterly unfazed by the newcomers' social status. Okay, I'll say something nice about her—this Iron Lady had a very pleasant voice.

"For the sake of the experiment, we need three volunteers who are utterly unfamiliar with the subtleties of Galactogon," explained the first Master. "After receiving your polygraph release forms, we ran a quick check and confirmed that you were telling the truth. My analysts investigated what you have studied over the past two years—please, no need to fret, Constantine—and confirmed your lack of experience with the game. In this manner, we've determined that you three, by virtue of your ignorance and your professionalism, are just who we need. All three of you are professional gamers who have until recently supported yourself through your craft: Alexis in Runlustia, Constantine and Eunice in *Draanmir*. By the way, why did you never consider my game?" the first Master suddenly asked. "I'm almost a bit insulted."

"Personally, I saw no point in it," the girl piped up first again. I made a point to remember her name, Eunice...some kind of ancient name. "If you want to be the best, you can't get distracted by other trifles. Besides, I had my hands full with *Draanmir*'s constantly evolving world."

"I agree," Constantine finally spoke up. There's truth in the observation that a long time spent playing as one particular class leaves its mark on the player—leaning back in his chair, Constantine had practically dissolved in it, as though he was unconsciously trying to seem less conspicuous. Then, it struck me: In *Draanmir*, he must've been a Thief, a Rogue, an Assassin, a Ninja...The title may vary game to game, but the idea remains the same—stealth multiplied by surprise. Interesting...and who was Eunice then? "I had no time to study anything that didn't seem useful to me."

I simply shrugged my shoulders, demonstrating that they wouldn't hear anything novel from me and I didn't much feel like repeating things.

"In that case, let me explain the gist of our proposal," the President began. "Perhaps you are familiar with the immortal

---

short story by Mark Twain called 'The £1,000,000 Bank Note?'"

Having received three nods to the affirmative, the head of our nation went on:

"Excellent. That makes my explanation much easier. My friend and I," the President nodded at the mogul beside him, "recently encountered a disagreement between us. Namely, I believe that it is impossible to achieve anything in his game without investing real money. He, on the other hand, claims the opposite—despite the fact that the media has already christened his project 'a cash vacuum,' which pumps the players for their last few coppers."

"You want us to establish ourselves in the game without any investment?" the girl popped up again.

"Patience, my dear," the mogul cracked a smile which, to be honest, made me cringe and try my best to dissolve into my chair too. Noticing that the girl's reaction was similar, I made a mental note never to butt into the conversations of the almighty of this world. Not good for your health that…

"As mentioned," the mogul went on, "we did not see eye to eye. And, because any mention of real people who had reached the apex of the game without investing a single real coin, was contested, we decided to conduct an experiment. To that end—"

"Ahem," the President coughed, drawing attention to himself. "I thought we agreed that I would be the one to outline the challenge? If you go on, you'll pile on a bunch of limitations and then good luck finding a way out. And so! We have created

---

a planet in Galactogon and on this planet we have hidden a single, unique item. Your task is to start playing from the very beginning, find this planet and, as a final touch, pick up this particular item. I should tell you right away that no one will be able to pick up this item without having the right skillset, but whoever does will receive a check in the sum of one billion pounds sterling."

"What's the catch?" this time, I couldn't help but blurt out. No one simply gives away presents like this—so logically, now should come the information that would put an end to any hope of winning this prize of prizes. One billion pounds is…well, it's everything! It would guarantee a carefree old age for my great-great-grandchildren. It was definitely worth fighting over.

"There is no catch, as such. The planet's location is known only to a select few of the game's locals—that's what we call non-player characters (or NPCs) in Galactogon. You will have to figure out who they are on your own. But even this is not the main thing. All three of you will start the game in specific circumstances. One of you will start without a credit in your pocket, just like all new players. Here, I must note that buying credits with real money is strictly forbidden and is grounds for disqualification. Another one of you will receive a monthly salary equivalent to a senior researcher's monthly salary. This will be credited to your in-game account. The third player will also receive monthly payments to their game account, but these will be equivalent to a senior researcher's *annual* salary. You can spend your funds as you see fit…Well, I mean the two of you that will have such funds. For all three of you though, the only objective is to reach the planet with the billion-pound check. We'll cast dice to determine who will play what role."

"But that can't be all the conditions, right?" I asked, understanding perfectly well that a player with unlimited money would be in the winning position from the get-go. In which case, how could such an experiment be considered objective?

"Yes, there are several further conditions. The player with the annual salary—or as we will call him, the unlimited player—can only play the game no more than four hours a day. One minute more and he will be disqualified. The semi-limited player can only play eight hours, while the third has no time limitations whatsoever and can play all he wants."

"Why would two individuals as famous as you decide to bet on three ordinary players?" I asked the question that probably should have been asked at the very beginning of the conversation. "I mean, something could happen to us. We could become depressed...or even, I don't know...come down with something serious and be unable to go on."

"This is precisely why there aren't just the three of you," the President smiled. "There are altogether twelve players, distributed evenly across the game's twelve empires: Three professional gamers who specialize in Galactogon; three professional gamers who don't know anything about the game (that's you three); three ordinary, as you call them, users who are merely familiar with Galactogon; and a further three ordinary users who have absolutely no experience with games at all.

That's twelve players, who shall tomorrow set out in search of our little scroll."

"What type of interface can we use to play?" Constantine asked.

"Despite the fact that your question is somewhat over my head, I will attempt a response," smiled the mogul. "You may play the game either in Third Person mode—that is, with a VR headset—or through the First Person somatic interface—that is, with a gaming capsule. I should mention that the game does not have...but no, you will discover the rest on your own. Now, I have a question for you. Do you agree with our proposed terms and do you agree to this job? By our calculations, the search could last several years, so we are prepared to offer you a monthly stipend in an amount that is, again, commensurate with that of a senior researcher. We don't want you to be worried about money during your quest. There are no strings attached to this—you can spend all two years lying around on your couch for all we care. All you have to do is make that first, initial log-in. That is, you must be in-game tomorrow by 6pm. The only limitation is that there can be no alliances or teamwork among the participants to the wager. Each one of you has to play for himself or herself alone. There are many empires in Galactogon and you will be starting your games in ones that are at war with each other. As I already mentioned, there are twelve of them altogether. If you are willing to set out on this journey and agree to all our terms, please place your palm on the screen."

A hologram of the contract materialized before our eyes.

START THE GAME

Getting comfortable and entirely forgetting the others' presence, I began to meticulously peruse the document. Regardless what piles of gold were glinting in the distance, it was mandatory to familiarize myself with my rights and obligations. Without that, forget it.

"I was sure that you would all agree," the mogul said with satisfaction as soon as all three of us had signed the contract. "In that case, let's cast the dice. Eunice, as the only lady, we will allow you to roll the dice first…"

Eunice rolled a 17, Constantine a 12 and Alexis (me, that is) a 9. Two 2s and a 5 isn't the luckiest throw and it put me firmly in the rearguard…Welp! No unlimited game for me, I guess.

"And so we have determined the order of selection. Eunice, which of the three games types do you choose?"

"Unlimited."

"Affirmed. Constantine?"

"The second—the semi-limited."

"Affirmed. And you, Alexis, will play the limited game type then. Affirmed. In that case," the President got up from his chair, leading us by example to stand up as well, "tomorrow morning all three of you will be visited by technicians who will install specialized Galactogon capsules and VR headsets. The game itself commences tomorrow precisely at six in the evening. Tonight you will be accommodated here in the palace. We want to ensure that you will set up your characters without any preliminary research. After that, no help is bad help, pardon the tautology. But not yet. Oh! One more thing: Please notify all your relatives that you will be unavailable until tomorrow evening. We don't want them to worry needlessly. All incoming calls are blocked in the palace. Best of luck to all of you and thank you for participating in our little experiment!"

"Please follow me," the steward from before appeared beside us. "I will take you to your chambers."

"Guys, since we'll be locked up here together for the next day, I propose we celebrate the sad, sad passing of our respective game worlds," I offered at our communal dinner. Thank god that the Masters had not forbidden us this essential tradition—odd, seeing as we had been accommodated in different rooms, even different floors, to prevent any chance of our interacting. They were a strange bunch, these Masters...A game, after all, is just a game—it shouldn't have any effect on real life! The fact that we might hate each other in the virtual world didn't mean that we should feel the same about each other in reality. I mean, this was like kindergarten!

"Agreed," Constantine upheld my proposal. "While we're at it, let's pool anything we know about Galactogon. It's silly to compete in real life—there's more than enough of that in-game."

Now didn't I say that men are a sufficiently reasonable bunch..?

"Oh no," Eunice instantly cut him off. "I don't see any point in sharing knowledge that could help me win...But I'm always down to hang out...Can I get some wine?"

START THE GAME

"And you and I will get into some scotch, okay?" Constantine glanced at me slyly. Hah! He thought he'd found himself a chump!

"Of course! If we're going to celebrate, than palace single-malt is the only proper way!"

(Three hours later.)

"...Hic! And then we came flying in on griffons when everyone was expecting an assault from the ground. Why, we darkened the skies!"

"...Alex, what class do you think is better—a Pal or an Assassin? Wanna bet I'd get you? I would show up with decoys and then..."

"...I was an officer in the toppest clan in all of Draanmir*! Why, the newbs would send me tribute daily..."*

"...All men are scum! You simply can't be trusted! Hic! Unreliable, unfair, weak..."

"...Tss! You'll wake him up! Hold onto me! Alright, leave him here—someone'll pick him up in the morning...Wanna come over to my place?"

"WHAT?! I am a respectable woman!...It's my place or no place!"

I can't see a thing—I hope this is it...At last, my own palatial chamber..."

GALACTOGON BOOK ONE

"Orders, Master?" asked my smart home upon my return.

"Block all calls. For the next several days, I don't exist. Make me dinner for tomorrow, the standard plate. And look up everything that has anything to do with the game Galactogon."

"It shall be done. Please note that you have missed your morning workout, which may negatively—"

"Turn off nagging-wife mode," I interrupted the program. "Get to work."

The specialized Galactogon cocoon—delivered as promised by the Masters—both stunned me and inspired my curiosity. The humongous box, stylized to look like a spaceship, occupied basically half of the room I dedicated to my gaming bells and whistles. Furthermore, the cocoon was a 2-in-1 monster of a device, including not only the gaming capsule but also the VR headset. Knowing that I simply wouldn't forgive myself later for starting the game in Third Person mode, I got into the spaceship cabin and closed the lid. A wonderful design! Regardless of how the experiment turned out, I would be asking them to let me keep this wonder.

A screen unfurled before my eyes and images began to flash upon it, submerging the player in a specific state—full immersion...

Welcome to Galactogon!
Character generation complete! Starting empire

START THE GAME

---

selected! Please choose your starting occupation ...

Okay...If I understand correctly, my character, just like the Empire, has already been chosen for me. Alright, that just means I'll have less to fret over. As I understand it, I've been assigned to the Qualian Empire. At the moment, I don't know what this means, so no point in bashing my head against it. Onwards—name. I've already been assigned one...Mmmkay...From here on out, I will be called "Surgeon." I'll have to see how many Surgeons there are running around this game already—as I understand it, in Galactogon, names don't have to be unique...But surely, someone else has picked this one already? Weird, I wonder how the mail and notification system works then...I mean, there must be some unique identifier!

Fine, I'll figure that out later too. Since it's asking me to pick an occupation, let's do that. What do we have?

...Marine, Engineer, Navigator, Gunner, Harvester, Scientist, Ship Commander...

I'll be damned! More than fifty classes, each of which has its own rank and skill-tree! Now I see why those two dear fogeys didn't want to give us a chance to study the FAQs.

I hate doing it, but it looks like I'll have to choose randomly—the strengths and weaknesses of this or that class are utterly unknown to me. I always thought that Galactogon was just about some kids flying around in spaceships, but here I see that a commander is just one of many possible jobs!

Tough choice this…

Not wanting to be too smart for my own good, I chose the one that I'd heard the most about.

You have chosen to develop as a Ship Commander.

Please note that you may change your character's occupation after you have graduated from basic training.

Have a good game!

A flash of light and I merged with my character…Hello, Surgeon!

CHAPTER ONE

GETTING TO KNOW GALACTOGON

WELCOME, RECRUIT!

The Qualian Empire has entrusted you with a great responsibility! Strive to be the best, purchase upgrades for your ship and...

A HUGE, SEMITRANSPARENT sheet appeared before my eyes, telling me how wonderful and carefree life for players in the empire was; however, I instantly waved it away. I hadn't the slightest interest in working for the Qualians and the word "purchase" made me instantly lose any and all interest in the text. The main thing for me at the moment was to play through the tutorial and then flee back to reality—where my educational resources awaited me.

The starting point for new players in Galactogon was not particularly astounding—a landing platform with a spaceship, from which the new recruits emerged. Who we were and how we appeared in this world wasn't important. A player stepping out onto the training planet of any empire became any ordinary recruit without any specific allegiance. At least that's what the helpful notification bobbing before my eyes told me. Kind of dumb, that...About two hundred yards ahead of me stood a large building in the direction of which, along sun-soaked pavement, trudged a stream of new recruits. Hardly had I gotten a good look at this building when a window popped up titled "Allocation Center."

And this window provided me with my first few tips about the game:

First—that each in-game item has its own attributes. For example, the allocation center had a Durability stat expressed as a percentage. There was probably some setting to show the absolute value in units, but for now this would do for me. And, it should be said that Durability was not the most interesting attribute of the building. More than anything else, I was happy to see among the attributes the line: "Building class: N/A." From this first window ran a line to point number two:

Objects in the game have their own levels, which meant that, logically, players did too. To make sure, I opened my character menu and...Oh boy. This was just getting better and better...What stood out most was the utter lack of stats and slots for clothes. In fact, the menu had nothing at all in it besides a brief description of the character's history (dating from my emergence from the spaceship) and a separate tab for inventory. That's all!

START THE GAME

Aside from that, this little panel, which to a Runlustian was the end-all-be-all, contained nothing at all! Though that's not true—there was also a 3-D projection of the character, which I could rotate from side to side and even use to correct my default posture—as well as a line which read 0.0 GC. Unless I was mistaken, this was an image of myself and a counter for how many Galactogon Credits I had.

Third—an object's or item's attributes will automatically pop up when you look at the object long enough. This was a bad thing. Looking closely at the players marching dutifully to the allocation center, I managed to confirm my hunch—extended attention indeed showed me the stats of nine recruits, utterly obscuring my field of view. What was worse was that none of the players' stats told me anything useful—just their names and occupations. And yet, this one panel took up a vast amount of space. Opening my notebook, I made a note to myself to look in the game settings for a way to turn off the attributes pop-ups. When I needed them, I would open the attributes panel myself.

Fourth—when in the somatic interface…

"What's the holdup?" someone yelled behind me and—rudely interrupting my contemplation of life, the universe and everything—landed a vicious kick to the small of my back, sending me flying several yards forward…

Damage taken: 5%. Health remaining: 95%.

Fourth—unlike Runlustia, the player is allowed to do

---

damage to another player using nothing but their own body. And again, in this case, the damage is reflected in percentages...

Somewhere, there's got to be a setting for this as well. But that isn't the main thing. The main thing is that I managed to stay on my feet, keeping my balance. This gave rise to a new tip:

Fifth—absent any character stats, the player's in-game capabilities are replaced with his capabilities in real life. So if I can do 200 pull-ups IRL, then that's how many pull-ups I can do in Galactogon...Or...If I know a martial art IRL, then I can use it just as well in the game...

Let's see how the developers have implemented this feature. Who wants to be my first victim?

The victim turned out to be a 6'5" bozo looking down at me from his great height. He had quite a body on him—I could see his six-pack through his shirt...Hmm...

Sixth—players wear clothes and clothes are effectively items, so they have their own specific attributes like all items. Considering that there weren't any slots to be seen, it followed the player could put on as much clothes as he could carry..? I need to make sure to figure that one out...

Recruit's Jersey. Durability: 20. Item class: F-1. Use: 0. Penetration Resistance: 0.1. Slashing Resistance: 0.2. Radiation Resistance: 0. Fire Resistance...

Seventh—items have their own levels which, logically, can also be increased. I was especially happy to see the long list of resistance stats that the jersey had.

And yet there seemed to be no buffs to Dexterity, Strength, Intellect, etc.

Only...

Damage taken: 25%. Health remaining: 70%.

Eighth (there are a lot of numbers in this game!)—tactile feedback is turned on in Galactogon. It's not very strong and feels like a light touch, but it's there. That's nothing to be happy about though! I shuddered, recalling the time and effort sunk into implementing this feature in Runlustia—the developers had resisted until the bitter end.

"Halt immediately!" one of the security guards shouted and—stripping me of the opportunity to respond to the bozo's blow with one of my own to his jaw—the bozo was suddenly lifted a dozen or so feet into the air by what seemed like a tractor beam. "Recruit! For assaulting another recruit you have been deemed unfit for service as Ship Commander!"

There was a flash and the big dude vanished. Oh boy!

Ninth—under no circumstances fight anyone during training. Although, wait! Why is it that I have the option to fight at all, if I'm not supposed to? Opening the settings menu, I found the replay tab and watched as, in a window right in front of me, a video of the past few minutes showed me emerging from the spaceship, stepping aside and standing quietly on my own, not bothering anyone. And here came that big bozo. Unlike all the other players, he made a beeline for me, yelled and kicked me.

And here was I, preserving my balance, followed by another kick that forced me down to one knee. Then the big dude flew up and vanished and that was it—the video ended. So then, he had gone for me on purpose? Why?

Literally a minute later I received an answer to this question. I watched as another player emerged, took a deep breath and stopped in place as if thinking about where he'd go next.

"What's the holdup?" The familiar bozo dude appeared once more from the ship and sent the tarrying player flying. Several moments later, this bozo (or his clone or whatever) was again sent to Kingdom Come by the guard, with no mention of his name. So this was simply a script in the game?! A way to set any players loitering at the entrance onto the one true path? Not bad. Something tells me that Galactogon will be a fun game…

Sign out.

"Master, I have not yet processed all of the information you requested. The job is 15% complete. Estimated time until completion is three hours." No sooner had the cocoon's lid moved aside, than Stan (as I sometimes referred to my smart home system) began reporting the work he had done over the past ten minutes. As the betting Masters had requested, I entered the game and set up my character without any further information. Now, however, I wouldn't be taking another step forward without first having learned all there was to know about Galactogon.

"Send requests to the top Qualian guilds or clans that are in the game, asking for any proprietary information they may have about leveling a ship captain without putting in real money. Offer them, let's say, fifty thousand dollars. I want to know everything—hidden missions, non-standard run-throughs and sequences and how to get them."

I couldn't invest real money into the game—the limitations of my agreement with the bettors weighed on me more than a winepress on a grape. The slightest, documented purchase of an in-game item in real life would count as grounds for disqualification. Information, however, had not been included in the list of prohibited aids. And that's exactly what I intended on using.

"Requests sent," Stan instantly replied. "What are your orders?"

"None. Like I told you, I'm not around until tomorrow," I repeated and sat down in my armchair. (It may not be as dramatic as the ones in the presidential palace, but it's mine and I love it.) "Let me see what you have at the moment—and keep updating the information every thirty minutes. It's time I did some reading…"

What can I say? Before creating this game, Galactogon's developers must have been under the influence of some controlled substances. For, never before in my gaming life have I encountered such wonders…

First of all, avatars in Galactogon really do not have any levels or experience points. The game designers decided that the player should not experience any discomfort upon transitioning into the game from reality. This was a famous dilemma, for in a game you could easily have a Strength of several million and could wipe out all the monsters in your path with one breath, while in the other place (real life, that is) all you had was a decently-fit body, and even that was only due to the capsule. This was especially painful for those players who spent the maximum-possible session in-game—two weeks without any connection to reality. Oh how you suffered when you had to adapt back to reality...I knew this firsthand.

The designers did not entirely give up the leveling mechanic, however. They simply transferred it to items and objects...

All the usable items in Galactogon have their own level, even your ordinary eating utensils. Each item type has its own form of leveling, which basically involves using the item constantly and successfully. For example, each time a spoon is used to successfully place food in your mouth, its experience level rises by a certain percentage. Once it reaches 100%, a new level is awarded and the XP counter is reset. The leveling is non-linear. Every new level requires more experience than the last, though the exact algorithm for this increment is kept secret. There is also, of course, an easier way to level up—through the in-game store. But that's not an option available to me, as I don't have the Galactogon Credits to buy upgrades and I'm not allowed to invest real money to do so.

Once an item reaches level 100, it either changes class or receives the "Legendary" attribute. The classes begin with "F," like the jersey on my character, and go up to "A." Only legendary

---

items, which are effectively at level 101 or higher, are better than A-class items.

Each item may have expansion slots—from none at all for F-class items to 23 for legendary class items. You can place other items into these slots, but there are certain limitations. You cannot combine two items that have three or more levels between them. For example, you can't equip a class-E ship with a legendary ship cannon. But you can equip it in a ship of class-B. It's very important to understand these nuances when operating or using any item or ship.

Getting back to our spoon, one curious thing is that almost all of them are legendary items. According to the forums, the first thing players do is get a legendary spoon, thereby earning the "Legend Owner" achievement. This legendary spoon isn't of much use—you can't use it to shoot down a ship or mine a bunch of raq (one of the most valuable in-game materials). However, any food eaten with this spoon will taste unforgettable: As you eat with it, nano-sensors determine your taste preferences, making even ordinary gruel taste amazing. The only requirement for this is that you play using the somatic interface.

Since I'm on the topic of nourishment, I should mention that food is not a pivotal resource in the game—with one slight condition. A player does not have to eat for the first six hours of his game session. Over the next six hours, however, the hungry player begins to feel discomfort, and after another six hours, there's a strong buzzing and the player "dies," heading to the respawn point. So, eating in the game is not a bad idea. Or, you could simply log-out of the game for a minute every six hours, since doing so resets the hunger counter.

The respawn point is also an interesting topic. The player cannot die until he has left the Training Sector. The allocation center, where each player must go upon first appearing in the game, is one of the facilities in this Sector. As soon as training ends—and training lasts at least one game month (that is, the player must spend one month in the game undergoing training)—the player is allocated: He gets to choose a homeworld on which he will continue playing his character. If the character is destroyed, some sort of Planetary Spirit or something (I haven't understood exactly what this is yet) will offer to resurrect the player for free. If the player agrees, he will get all his items back upon resurrection, but the items will have lost one class-worth of experience. It's worth noting, however, that this applies only to items on the player: Everything in the ship's cargo holds, for example, will remain drifting at the site of the ship's destruction.

If you refuse to be resurrected by your Planetary Spirit, you get the option of choosing any planet in the empire to respawn on, but for a fee. In this case, all your items and equipment remain where you died and your character respawns with nothing but the money he had at the time of death (which, presumably, was stored in some bank account somewhere all along).

As for the items dropped upon death, your enemy (or anyone else who comes along) can take these or destroy them. The only limitation is how much their ship can carry in her holds.

START THE GAME

Players who specialize in piracy plan their ship's future development very carefully—especially when it comes to cargo capacity. Pirates always need to make sure that they have enough space for their loot. According to the rules, a spaceship can be stolen, captured (in which case the defeated player is resurrected without anything) or destroyed. If she is destroyed, the ship's wreckage remains floating at the site of her destruction and another player may use it as material for repairs or may salvage it into a universal repair kit. This is why the first thing that fledgling ship-owners do is buy themselves a self-destruct device: It's better for your ship to be one class weaker, but still be your ship, than have to start all over again in an F-class tub.

Imperial Rapport...Leveling (which, it turned out, didn't exist for characters)...There was a lot of information, but I wasn't about to enter the game until I finished going through it all. My job was to find out everything about the game instead of running headlong into the fray hoping that everything would simply work out. I never did like players like that...

"Master, you have an incoming video-call from the leader of the Black Lightning guild. According to current rankings, this is the fourth-ranked Qualian guild. Would you like to accept the call?"

"Come on, throw it up on the screen."

"Hello!" a bearded face appeared on the screen. "Are you the one looking for information about Galagon?"

"Galactogon."

"Could be *Pygmalion* for all I care. What's your character

name?"

"Surgeon."

"Hmm," the leader of the Black Lightning frowned, looking somewhere off-camera. "There are about fifteen hundred Surgeons out there…Which one are you?"

"Fifteen hundred?" I asked surprised. "How'd you find that out?"

As I already figured out, a character name in Galactogon wasn't unique, so it was impossible to identify any player for certain. Mail as a category didn't even exist: If you wanted to communicate with other players, you had to acquire a communicator. And when I tried to look up how many Surgeons were running around just like I was, the system politely instructed me to consult the help menu—which told me that the number of players online was not subject to disclosure.

"Doesn't matter. What planet are you on? Our guide changes from planet to planet. And forgive me, I'm not about to give you all our guides for fifty thou."

"I haven't been assigned a homeworld yet," I replied honestly, since concealing this fact would have been pointless. After a little thought, I added, "I've started a new character. I haven't even entered the allocation center yet. Like I said in the email, I need information about leveling up without putting in real money."

"You started a new one? Why delete the old one? Why didn't you just go through retraining and become a commander without wasting an extra month?"

START THE GAME

"It didn't work out with my old one," I shrugged my shoulders vaguely, happy that I hadn't actually lied about anything. Let the bearded guild leader think that I already had some experience with the game and simply wanted to prove something to someone. At least then he wouldn't try to sell me any nonsense...Then again, he could still offer me something worthless and watch my reaction to see if I was just a fish that needed to be reeled in for all its money. You could sell anything to a newbie like that—from the "secret" number of the various ships in the game, to the location of a "simply unbelievable" planet brimming with raq (which was like gold) or elo (the game's universal energy resource).

"Whatever—your problem, your headache. If you want to relive training, that's your god-given right. In that case, for the sum you mentioned, I have a guide detailing non-standard events and how to find them in the Qualian Training Sector. What do you say?"

"For fifty thousand? You having a laugh?" I raised an eyebrow in surprise. "That's way too little to be worth fifty thousand."

"You asked for it," the beard instantly grew defensive. "You seem like a shrewd guy, so think about it: Why would I be offering you anything if I didn't know anything?"

"No, that's no good for me. I'm offering fifty thousand for information that's unique. The Training Sector isn't so big that I need to pay such a crazy amount of money for it. Like I told you, I'm interested in leveling a ship's captain. Do you have anything like that or not?"

"You know, Surgeon," the guild leader said after a little thought, "I could just as easily refuse. We sell guides quite frequently so customers aren't exactly hard to come by. But it's a funny coincidence. Just today, a highly respected player, who also decided to restart from scratch for whatever reason, contacted every clan in the game, including mine. He is offering to pay us one hundred thousand dollars if we keep our leveling guides secret for three months. What's more is that he wants us to let him know if a player comes looking for that kind of thing—and furnish him with that player's contact info. I'm guessing you sent your requests not just to us, but to all the other Qualian guilds as well—so you may be sure that Sergei Smolyanov is already well aware of your vidphone number and email. That bit of info is free by the way. If he weren't such a jerk—and from an enemy empire besides—I would absolutely be on board with his whole secrecy thing. A hundred thousand dollars is a very big sum, after all…Luckily for you, Serge smashed up my fleet last year, so…I'm not about to give you anything for free and I'd agree that the starting sector isn't quite the place to look for hidden goodies. Heck, I'd even say that there aren't goodies there at all—so the best I can do is give you our own in-house guide for how to level up your ship from F-class to C-class as quickly as possible. My goons use it all the time. Anything higher than C-class, you'll have to do yourself. What do you say?"

"The starting sector plus ship leveling?" I clarified, understanding perfectly well that this was better than nothing. The forums were bursting with a plethora of guides for leveling up, but the more I read, the less I believed that I would find anything acceptable. Even never having played Galactogon, I understood that they were a waste of time.

"Yup. And as a bonus, I won't be telling anyone that I sold anything to anyone. Especially what that second anyone may look like in real life. My friendly advice to you is, if you talk to other guild leaders, use an image scrambler."

"Give me your account info." I had had enough time to make up my mind. I can't say that I was much swayed by the beard's words, but when there are a billion pounds on the line…Well, that's a reason to give it a shot.

"Already sent. As soon as I get the money, I'll send you the guide you wanted. I've already got it ready. And—good luck to you! Who knows—maybe our paths will cross. Let me know as soon as you get a D-class ship. I'll send you an invite to my guild. No entrance exams or anything."

"Why such largess?" I asked surprised. As I had already managed to find out, guilds in Galactogon meant everything— home, family, money, resources, etc. The guild leaders and their officers were very careful when welcoming newcomers to their banners, seeking to weed out leeches and those who liked to dig around in others' coffers. A player gave quite a bit to his guild, but the guild itself did plenty for him in return too.

"Anyone who manages to get a ship to D-class without investing a single coin, even with the help of our guide, is already worth a closer look," smirked the beard. "When you get the

---

Workaholic Achievement—that's the one that'll show you've made it—I'll be happy to see you among my ranks. Until then, excuse me but I have to run... End call."

"Stan—panic mode," I uttered the code phrase that forced my smart home into emergency overdrive. Panic mode entailed the deletion of any online information that could lead someone back to my physical self. My name, my address, my description...I used to laugh about stuff like that, but then one day as I was coming home, I was rudely ambushed by a gang of imbeciles whom I had crossed in Runlustia. It seemed that they hadn't liked the leading role I had played in a raid on their castle. I paid for that with fractured arms, legs, ribs and—as a result—having to relocate to a new apartment. That was when I set up the panic mode command. Better safe than sorry. If the beard was right, a billion pounds was a large enough sum of money to justify a visit to a competitor in real life. A visit during which you would make sure that your competitor wouldn't want (or be able) to sign into the game for the next several years.

Two hours later, I had refused two incoming video calls—truthfully pointing out that I was taking a bath. Like I had figured after my conversation with the leader of the Black Lightning, the representatives calling from the top two Qualian guilds quickly lost an interest in talking to me without having the opportunity to see (or record) what I looked like. Constantly citing internal guild regulations, they kept asking me when would be a better time to call me back and whether we could maybe simply meet in real life and talk about my proposal like grown adults. They even offered to buy me dinner! Well, no wonder—for a hundred thousand dollars, I'd buy myself dinner too. Having received the information I needed from the Black Lightning, I ordered Stan to delete my vidphone number and mail account. Maybe I was being too careful, but it was better than getting bitten a second time.

When I finally delved into the beard's leveling guide, I couldn't help but crack a smile over having quit the game right away, before entering the allocation center. For, precisely in this lay the pivotal move that would give me a special reputation among the Training Sector's instructors—and not a very good reputation at that.

"What's the holdup?" yelled the local motivational speaker and kicked the air where my body had just been. Except of course I was already gone…The scenario hinged on being able to control your body and wanting to beat the bully, earning thereby a trip to jail even before you got into allocation. Fighting earned the player a bad reputation, allowing him to access an underground tournament that was held every few weeks. The specifics of the tournament (there were actually three tournaments altogether) varied each time. One would involve dueling, another item gathering and the third mining. Even if the player lost, he would still get pretty good money for someone just starting out. In my situation, this was a blessing from on high. According to the game manual, the only way to get money in the training sector was by investing real money.

Well…If I have to brawl a little, why not? Brawling can be fun…

"Feisty one, eh?" the bozo exclaimed and, scurrying faster than I expected, went for me with his giant arms akimbo. The ship behind me prevented any retreat and a jump to the side would land me in the embrace of the onrushing rhino. So I decided to do the one thing that the NPC's barebones AI would not anticipate—stepping back, I kicked off the ship's fuselage and launched myself into the bozo. Let's see who gets whom...

What's there to say about Galactogon's physics engine? It's almost perfect. What happens when a six-foot monster with a full head of steam meets an ordinary body? Jumping forward, I assumed that I'd at least stop him in his tracks. However, he didn't even seem to realize that I was trying to hit him and simply tossed me a dozen or so feet aside—right onto the pavement.

"What's this?" came the smug laugh. "Tough as a rock, but light as a feather, eh?"

The ground shook as the giant bozo vaulted from the gangway down to me. Strange, I wondered, where are the security guards? According to the guide, they should have already appeared to break us up and arrested me for fighting.

"Who dares mock Drill?"

Well, well, it turned out that this Frankenstein's monster had a name! Though, I couldn't figure out exactly when I had managed to mock him, but we could put that down to an oversight in the AI's scripting.

"Enjoy your stay in the medbay!" rhymed Drill, impressively managing to sound a little sinister. Raising his foot, he stomped it on the very place where my head had just been.

START THE GAME

Had he struck it, I would've lost a critical amount of health—maybe even been forced into resurrection. So I did something that the beard's guide never mentioned—I responded.

Rolling out of the way of the bozo's boot (stuffed to its seams with his trunk of a leg), I aimed a sweep at his supporting leg. It felt like I had kicked a pole buried deep in the ground. My health fell again. I whimpered something about how I couldn't care less about someone as insignificant as him—but my counterstrike had had its intended effect. Bellowing savagely the bozo began to keel over.

Ignoring the pain in my leg, I continued my roll, springing to my feet through inertia and then jumping—my intention being to land on Drill. Pointing my elbow in front of me and aiming it at his head, I managed to hear the welcome phrase "Halt immediately!" just as...

You have unlocked the "Murderer Rank I" Achievement. All weapons require 1% less experience to reach their next level.

Your rapport with the Qualian Empire has decreased. Current Rapport: -1.

"Surgeon!" I found myself lifted into the air and confronted by a security guard. Where were these guys all this time? "You are under arrest for the murder of another recruit. Your punishment is three weeks in jail! Next time you'll think twice before attacking our recruits!"

Now what did the tutorial say about how it's impossible to

kill other players in the Training Sector? Well, well, well, this is interesting. If I've already met my main goal of getting into jail, why not have a little more fun? Hasn't anyone ever tested this stuff before?

The guard was a member of the wonderful Qualian race—who are distinguished by their gray colored skin, the third eye in their foreheads, the suction cups on their fingertips and their serpentine hair. He was so seductively close to me that it seemed a graver crime not to attack him. Since I was already a criminal, why not go on and break the law a little more?

I was being held up in the air by means of a B-class manipulator wielded by the guard right beside me. This oddly-named rubber club emitted a bluish ray in my direction, forming some kind of force field which kept me suspended as if I weighed nothing at all. It did not, however, impair my ability to move—for example, my arms…

I felt a jerk and began to float toward the allocation center. The guard manipulating my body pulled its poor suffering mass even closer to him, wishing to turn me around so that he could just push me ahead of him. The two other guards had already turned away, deeming the incident to be resolved. I attacked silently. I don't know if Qualians have any weak points, but in Runlustia I got used to the fact that any NPC or local (as non-player characters are called in Galactogon) doesn't feel so hot when you karate chop him in the throat. Considering the attentive implementation of this game's physics, I had good reason to believe that guards here would be similarly affected…

START THE GAME

Once again, the physics engine didn't let me down. The strike to the throat turned out a doozy. The guard didn't even utter a groan but simply collapsed to the ground.

Critical hit!

You have unlocked the "Enemy of the Empire Rank I" Achievement. You have destroyed a subject of the Qualian Empire. All Qualian items require 10% more experience to reach next level.

Your rapport with the Qualian Empire has decreased. Current Rapport: -2.

What can I say? The physics engine in this game is quite impressive. Even a security guard with a class-B item died from a simple blow to the throat. It follows that you can't get very far in this game without a full set of armor—or, in my case, without a personal ship.

By the way, the guide I bought seemed to mention that it's impossible to have anything worse than -1 Rapport with the Empire, and yet I…Well, either way, my cell awaits me…

"Halt!" yelled one of the guards, alerted by the sound of me landing on the ground. As soon as the Qualian met his demise, the beam holding me vanished, releasing me. The fall wasn't a large one, but the sound it made was loud enough. To make matters worse, I landed right on the dead guard.

Search corpse?

GALACTOGON BOOK ONE

The shout, the notification and my fall (which twisted my arm a little) had all happened so quickly that I didn't think about the consequences when I clicked the "Yes" button. If you're going to be a marauder then go about it properly.

Acquired item: ZPEF-Manipulator. Item class: B-12. Weight: 2. Use: Lifts opponent of weight up to 2,000 lbs.

Acquired item: Qualian Guard Breastplate. Weight: 4. Durability: 100. Item class: C-44. Piercing Resistance: 33.2. Slashing Resistance: 33.2. Radiation Resistance: 0. Fire Resistance...

Acquired item: Qualian Guard Trousers. Weight: 3. Durability: 100. Item class: C-12...

Acquired credits: 23 GC.

Your rapport with the Qualian Empire has decreased. Current Rapport: -3.

Another rapport malus for marauding...This is fun...Clicking the "Yes" button three times, equipping the clothes and the weapon, I grabbed onto the body and instantly flew up into the air with it: The guards had recovered from their initial shock and used their manipulators to levitate me...Alright then, I've got nothing to lose now. According to our agreement with the betting Masters, I could restart from zero three times, deleting my character and making a new one. There were of course limitations: The new character started from scratch, lost all his equipment and money and reappeared in the same place where he started with the same exact occupation he had initially selected. So since I wasn't really risking anything at the moment, besides maybe time, I turned on the manipulator and pointed it at the guard. Two can play the "lift your enemy in the air" game.

Your rapport with the Qualian Empire has decreased. Current Rapport: -7.

You have unlocked the "Enemy of the Empire Rank II" Achievement. You have destroyed a subject of the Qualian Empire. All Qualian items require 20% more experience to reach next level.

It was evident that the AI couldn't much cope with human players. Having lifted me into the air, these two exemplars of the local fauna for some reason decided that they had triumphed and turned to go back to their allocation center. How naïve of them! Using my manipulator, I lifted the two guards just as effectively thirty feet into the air, after which I turned off the weapon. Two lifts—two bodies, enabling me to get some boots, gloves, two more manipulators and a bit of cash. I guess the locals weren't made for flying…While I was at it, I found out how long it took for a corpse to vanish: precisely one minute following death. By the time I finished robbing my latest victim, the first one had already disappeared.

I wonder—should I restart a new character or stay and find out what my punishment will be? It'd be useful to know, after all!

"Don't move," a menacing scream interrupted my

contemplation of "to be or not to be," so I decided to be a little more and turned my attention to this new Qualian approaching me. "Drop the manipulator!"

I was now facing a giant metal machine which, the description informed me, was a B-class Infantry Combat Mech. My manipulator's beam slipped harmlessly along its armor, after which my prize weapon beeped pitifully and disintegrated right in my hands. A notification popped up, helpfully informing me that the manipulator had been destroyed by the mech's active resistance. Well, I was definitely done for now…

"Remove your armor!" came the next command. Ignoring it was pointless. Even if I refused, this monster probably had some kind of special device that destroyed its opponent's armor without even having to touch him. All I'd get is another rapport malus and nothing more.

"Now, march!" This third order was welcome. No one had remembered the 67 credits that I had had the pleasure of pocketing. Likewise, no one had checked my inventory, which contained the other two manipulators. It had been too difficult to put the breastplate, boots and trousers in my inventory because all the items in Galactogon had three dimensions in addition to their weight. As a result I had only taken the manipulators. One was already broken, but the other two were still on me…

"Surgeon, in the name of the Qualian Empire, I find you guilty of the destruction of a recruit and three Training Sector guards. I therefore sentence you to twenty days of solitary confinement!"

START THE GAME

A brief trial took place as soon as I entered the allocation center. I was lifted into the air again to the surprise of several law-abiding players, who kept on popping up in the game, and literally a minute later found myself in a dark, windowless cell. The moist, stone walls and dripping water were already getting to me, so I instantly opened the main menu. Thanks everyone! I am indeed a bad person and have had enough fun in your lovely game for the moment.

Sign out!

"Stan, put me in touch with my bearded friend," I said, getting comfy in my armchair. Getting out of the capsule, I did my daily exercises, washed up and even had a little tea before deciding that it was time to have a chat with the leader of the Black Lightning. Of course from a legal standpoint our deal had been fair—he offered me a product and I had bought it—but from an ethical perspective, I believe he owed me one. So, I'd squeeze him for some more information for the money I had already paid him…After all, it's never good form to defraud a paladin, even if he's already a retired paladin.

The voicemail of the Black Lightning glibly informed me that the great leader was currently unavailable on account of being occupied with taking over the Universe and I was therefore welcome to tell him everything I thought after the beep—without of course any guarantee that the great leader would have any desire to listen to what the machine had recorded. That's what his voicemail literally said: "Can't promise that you'll be heard, but you can try." Suave guy, that one…

\#

The countdown on my sentence in solitary began as soon as I logged back into Galactogon. (It's impossible to delete your character from outside of the game.) The same dark moist walls and the water dripping from the ceiling—nothing resembling the advanced game in which players rocket about the vast reaches of space. I felt like I had found myself behind the walls of one of Runlustia's castles for yet another infraction. Not wishing to prolong my pleasure, I opened the main menu and clicked the "Delete Character" button. I had time to grin at the subsequent window asking me to confirm the deletion and provide a reason when suddenly…

"Ta-ta-ta, taa-taa-taa, ta-ta-ta…"

I froze inside. By that point I had already managed to describe my reason for deleting the character ("because refrigerator"), read two warnings about how all my items would be lost, agreed to these, battered my way through a cordon of confirmations and reached the "Delete" button and…

"Ta-ta-ta, taa-taa-taa, ta-ta-ta…"

The international SOS signal…An SOS signal in a computer game…A signal that could mean only one thing—either some player was goofing off in some nearby cell or…Instantly closing all the interface windows and returning to the game, I bated my breath waiting for the third signal. Considering that this is a game, then…

"Ta-ta-ta, taa-taa-taa, ta-ta-ta…"

START THE GAME

The authorities in Runlustia were very fond of snapping up players for various infractions and throwing them into prison—besides being a punishment, this was an excellent opportunity to level up certain skills and stats. Some of the more gutsy players used prison to get several missions which, once completed, would open previously hidden opportunities—for example, membership offers from the shadowy powers in the game. However, Runlustia had one very unpleasant mechanic—a cell's walls completely silenced a player's voice. Even if you could see a person through your grate, you couldn't talk to him—the game's magic prohibited direct communication. This led everyone to remember Q-codes and Morse code. To Runlustia's game magic, knock remained but a knock...

I knew very few Q-codes—only the most important ones. However, I knew where they were listed, structured and sorted by frequency of use. Switching out of the somatic interface to Third Person mode and thereby leaving the game (and noticing along the way that my solitary incarceration countdown paused), I ordered Stan to bring up the table of codes on my HUD. Let's have a chat, shall we? It's too bad I couldn't link Stan directly into the game—he could've communicated with the stranger much more efficiently than me.

I discounted the possibility that this was a human player immediately—you just couldn't create a tone like that with a shoe or a fist. Something hard and metallic was required, like, for example, this manipulator! The court had not conducted a full investigation of my belongings and sent me simply and directly to solitary. Equipping my manipulator, I began to knock on the part of the wall where the SOS was coming through loudest:

"Taa-taa-ta-taa ta-ta-ta ta-taa-ta-ta"

This was the Q-code "QSL," which in natural language meant: "I am acknowledging receipt." I had just let my unknown companion know that he had been heard and understood. The question now was whether he'd understand me—that is, whether the developers programmed a knowledge of Q-codes into the locals.

"Ta-a-a-a-a-a-a-a-a-taaaa-ta-ttaaaaaaa…"

All of a sudden, such a torrent of knocks began coming through that I simply didn't know what to do—any unprepared person would have had immense trouble understanding anything in this cacophony.

"QRS (Send more slowly)," I knocked out another ubiquitous Q-code, admitting in the process that I wasn't much of a radio operator.

"W A R N…P R E C I A N S…D A N G E R"

It turns out that it's pretty hard to decipher Morse code by ear. My unknown companion wasn't using codes, preferring plain text and pausing between the words.

"QSP (I will relay to) P R E C I A N S," I replied and then inquired, "W H O M…A N D…W H A T?"

I had never had to pound out such a long message before. Though, I hadn't done much shorter ones either. I wonder how people managed to communicate in Morse code in years gone by? Besides being incredibly inconvenient, the slightest mistake could flip the entire meaning of the message upside down.

"R R G O R D...S A Y...K R I E G...D O N E"

"QSL (I acknowledge receipt) K R I E G...D O N E"

"RRGORD...RRGOrd...RRgord...rrgord...rrg..."

The knocking grew quieter and quieter and finally fell silent. Either my companion had fallen asleep or, more likely, had left this world. Every game plot has the same trope: If you passed on the message, you may die with peace of mind. I on the other hand, needed to do some serious thinking...

And so!

First—in Galactogon, there is no such thing as a "mission." That is, the concept exists but not in the form that players of other games are used to: with a journal that contains a record of everything you need to do and how, and with a map of the locality and waypoints upon it designating any critters you haven't yet killed. There are no alerts, records or hints. Sometimes you won't even realize that you stumbled onto a unique mission at all. The locals simply ask you about this or that, after which they evaluate how you fulfilled their request—whether you did good or not—and thereby determine whether they'll maintain a relationship with you or not. In that sense, Galactogon is quite like the real world—the more influential the local asking you to do something, the greater the probability that not fulfilling his request will lead to negative consequences. It's very difficult to know when a request becomes an assignment, especially for a newbie who's used to neat mission descriptions popping up in front of his eyes.

Then again, there are exceptions. According to the forums, the Emperor may issue a call to action to all his subjects, asking them to perform some task he needs done. In the Qualian Empire, such a call has been issued six times over the six years of the game's existence, so when it comes, everyone drops whatever they're doing and runs to help the Emperor. Even perfunctory participation in the event, without performing any key functions, is rewarded with a huge bonus to rapport.

But this was obviously not one of those instances. Someone, most likely a local, had turned to me in the dungeons of the Training Sector with a request to let another Empire know that some kind of KRIEG or something had been completed. Moreover, I had to relay this message to some guy named Rrgord. Relations between these two empires were not strained—just the opposite: Officially, the Precians were allied with the Qualians, which made encountering one of them in prison all the more strange. Another notable thing about Galactogon's missions was that they had to be completed in-game. Even if, in real life, I asked some player familiar with Rrgord to pass on the message to this local—nothing would happen. Rrgord would simply not hear the messenger, even if he yelled it right into his ear and posted signs all around him. This was just another limitation in the game...And again, this was all under the assumption that this was a mission and not some ordinary request...Life in Galactogon sure was complicated.

I memorized the correct sequence to the question "Where

are you?" and switched back into the somatic interface where I continued my train of thought.

Let's assume this is a mission. Getting to the planet in question isn't too hard, especially with a ship. The main thing is not to get pulverized by the planetary defenses—about ten class-A orbital stations and one legendary-class Grand Arbiter. A Grand Arbiter is the apex of battle power in Galactogon. These ships are off limits to players, and each Empire only has about one thousand of them. They are used to combat piracy in the systems under imperial control. Not a single Grand Arbiter has ever been destroyed during the game's history. Many players have tried, organizing and launching raids targeted specifically at these ships. As such, more than ten thousand ships have challenged one Grand Arbiter before, and only a meager hundred managed to escape the meat grinder that the locals arranged for them.

But now I've gone and gotten distracted again…If this is indeed a mission, then I've received it in a very unconventional place. I doubt that players frequently find their way to these solitary cells. According to the guide the beard sent me, I was supposed to be thrown into a general holding cell where I was to approach some guard with a special insignia on his sleeve. But now…Switching again to Third Person mode, I told Stan to scan all Qualian forums for information about the prison in the training sector. I needed to know whether someone has been here or not…

My mysterious neighbor was no longer responding to the interrogative "Where are you?" which I went on tapping out at minute-long intervals. Having foisted on me the responsibility of passing on the danger warning, it seemed that he really had turned up his toes (or whatever it is that Precians have). Speaking of which, there was no guarantee that he was a Precian at all—he could just as easily have been a Qualian or some a citizen of some other Empire...But here I was thinking about utterly pointless things again...What I needed to figure out at the moment was whether I was ready to wait 20 days in this solitary cell, indefinitely putting off my search for the billion, or risk it and give into my great desire to fulfill this mission I'd stumbled across. If this Rrgord was a person of any note, then he could probably help my search quite a bit...Maybe he could even tell me where the planet I needed was.

It's decided then!

Switching out once more, I told Stan to yank me out of Galactogon only in the event of an emergency. Then, reentering the somatic interface again, I lay down right there on the floor and went to sleep. Twenty days of utter calm and solitude was not a bad price to pay for a chance to escape the utter bottom of the game's social pyramid...Well, that or find myself in even deeper difficulties...

CHAPTER TWO

THE TRAINING SECTOR

L YING AS COMFORTABLY on my mattress as my cell's cold, hard floor allowed, I began to study the details of *Galactogon*'s political world. A prison is a prison, but no one could forbid me from popping back into reality, gathering everything that Stan had prepared for me, sending it to my character's mail account and reading as much as I wished.

While I was at it, I figured out how the mail system worked. It was a very interesting system and could be best described as "there was no system." More precisely, players couldn't communicate with each other remotely without having specialized equipment to do so—transmitters, communicators etc. As a result, the beloved mail system that all games had and which could be used not only to send each other letters, but also to store things (quite a lot of things actually) did not exist in Galactogon at all.

However, the designers had made one concession to the player himself, which is precisely what I took advantage of now— and that was the player's personal PDA. This item, which the player could never lose even through death, was a device in which you could make various notes and things. These could then be synched with a special component of the gaming capsule and thereby receive textual information from the outside world.

And so, the political system of Galactogon...

There are a total twelve Empires, united unto three alliances, which are in a state of armed neutrality with one another. Officially, the Imperial armies remain at their bases or academies; however, mercenaries and players can do whatever they feel like. Trade routes exist both between and within the alliances; however, to prevent enemies from encroaching deep into their territory, each empire has specialized trade planets which are protected, at times, better than the governing planets. Money is critical in Galactogon because it can solve basically any problem. The Qualians have several trade centers: Adriada, Raydon and, the most popular—Shylak XIV, where more than 60% of commerce with other empires takes place.

The Qualian Empire is part of the Altan alliance, which includes the Precian and Anorxian empires, as well as Vraxis— not an empire, but a single enormous organism controlled by several individuals. Whereas the Qualians and Precians are humanoids (having two arms and legs and one head, all attached to one body), the Anorxians and Vraxis are robotic and insectoid respectively.

As a player who's started out playing for the Qualians, I can freely travel to any allied empire, having offered my services and requested to land on one of the hundreds of possible planets.

START THE GAME

The other alliances are closed to me, however. More precisely, they are open to all players except for me—travelling from one alliance to another costs money—real money. It's one of those things you just have to pay real money for in Galactogon.

The twenty days flew by almost unnoticeably, spent in reading and dividing my labors: I would spend my daytime in real life and my nighttime in solitary, rolled up in a ball on the tough mattress, observing yet another dream...On the whole, I had no difficulties serving my sentence. The only thing I regretted was that twenty game days ended up becoming a month of real life, during which the other eleven players were going through training and setting out on their quest for the billion-pound prize.

It seems that my mysterious neighbor really did depart this mortal coil—there were no further knocks during my remaining time in solitary. In fact, there were no other sounds at all, except for the daily buzzing of the dumbwaiter, lowering the next meal to my humble abode. At least the food here was plentiful...

Stan never managed to find a single mention of solitary confinement in the Training Sector. The jail reserved for rowdy recruits came up, as well as several references to underground tournaments held in it (thus bringing the value of the beard's information down to zip), but there was simply no mention of solitary. Not once—even in jest. It was as if the dripping walls didn't physically exist and the place I was in was some kind of febrile dream. No big deal. Judging by the description of jail, if a player ends up in it, then he is even prohibited from studying during his incarceration, whereas I will be able to understand all the basic aspects of life in Galactogon soon enough and from there set out to find that billion-pound check.

"Recruit Surgeon—step out!" Barely had the incarceration timer reached 00:00 when the door to my cell opened and I was paid a visit by a guard with a rubber club underarm. "Or do you like it so much here that you've decided to spend your entire training in isolation?"

Oh, but this guard has wit! I'm noticing that the developers endowed the locals with a decent intellect—not reserving it simply for the key NPCs. Sometimes in Runlustia, you'd start flirting with some servant girl and she'd just look at you with bovine eyes, totally missing your drift. Even a slight pinch below the waist would hurt her and summon the guards for attacking an NPC. In that game, the developers had not tried too hard to "humanize" each and every NPC, but focused only on the important ones. But here, your ordinary guard was capable of sarcasm—and pulled it off so well that you'd think he was simply created for the purpose. Recalling the local bozo-bully whose job it was to kickstart recruits into moving toward the allocation center, it became clear to me why players were gradually switching more and more to Galactogon. The realism here was an order of magnitude higher than in other games I'd played. In any case, that was my opinion in that moment, and only time would tell whether it was accurate or not.

New mission available: Deliver package to Qualian citizen

START THE GAME

Zaltoman located on the trade planet Shylak XIV (Coordinates: 7446244 x 3366181 x 4642990). Mission deadline: 2 hours.

My emergence from solitary was marked with some news. The first—the good news—was that I only had 10 game days remaining in the Training Sector. My twenty days of solitary had counted after all. Unfortunately, that was it for the good news. It turned out that the thirty days of training were divided into five units—repair, science, harvesting/mining, flight training and assault tactics. Each non-core unit entailed four days of instruction followed by an exam. If the player passed, he would earn a novice rank in that field. The rest of the time was reserved for teaching the player's core occupation—in my case, flight training. If the player failed his core exam, he had only two ways out—either switch his occupation to one in which he had passed the exam, or start all over and redo the Training Sector—another thirty days. In my situation, Repair, Science and Harvesting/Mining were already off limits—I could no longer get official work in these fields. I could let that go—but the most upsetting thing was that I had missed eight days of learning how to fly a ship! And, as though in deference to Murphy's Law, from solitary they sent me straight into a pop quiz that the instructors had arranged—cramming a bunch of us into some ship simulators…

One glance at the constellation of buttons speckling the ship's navigation panel was enough to bring me into utter despair. I had not the slightest idea of what to do. Any log-out into reality during training was strictly punished with an automatic Fail, so I hadn't much of a choice but to push anything that I came across, hoping that something would work. Damn! If someone were to ask me, for example, where Shylak XIV was and what role it played in Qualian trade policy, I could have replied without hesitation. But how to pilot this ship ...Well, I had purposefully skipped this topic in my time during solitary, naïvely assuming that I would start my training from scratch upon release.

"*Are you sure you wish to engage the Accelerator?*" No sooner had I pushed some blue button than the simulator replied with a notification on the ship's flight screen.

"*No,*" I declined, pressing the only button I understood, the one that said: "Abort." The inscriptions on the other buttons were utterly unintelligible, having nothing in common with human language. Instead, they were covered with some kind of squiggles, crosses and circles. I could have been mistaken, but, more than likely, this was the Qualian language. In that case, I'd have to study it too. So much fun...

"*Are you sure you wish to engage the stabilization system?*" another notification from the emulator brought me to despair. For eight days, the recruits were lectured on the principles of flight and ship instrumentation—the right buttons to press and the right order to press them in. And not just eight days, but 192 hours of training, during which you could—forget players—teach a monkey to fly a spaceship. No doubt, everyone except for me was already on Shylak trying to find Zaltoman.

"*Yes!*" If I understood correctly, the green button beside

START THE GAME

"Abort" would confirm the action—and the time had come to take a risk. Either I would fail my training now, or take off—logically speaking, one would probably want things to be stable before zooming off through the atmosphere.

"*Stabilization System has been engaged! Warning: No force field detected! Warning: Fuel pumps inactive!*—followed by ten more similar warnings. *"Your ship has been destroyed! Please leave the simulator—you have failed in your mission..."*

"Recruit Surgeon!" Scarcely had I tumbled out of the giant steel box that served as the model of a ship when one of the Qualians got in my face. "You have failed the mission and are disqualified from further piloting instruction! For the time remaining in this unit, you are being transferred to the logistics division! You will prepare the nourishment for those who place their education first."

Well, that's definitely it now. Since I'll have to start the Training Sector all over again either way, I can't afford the luxury of wasting time on becoming a marine. From what I've managed to glean about this occupation, the player becomes quickly bogged down in an immense hierarchy—Private to Sergeant to Lieutenant to so on. A marine can't go off to travel freely before his first battle. If he does so, he'll be listed as a deserter on all military bases and will suffer an imperial rapport malus that reflects this status. I don't need that and I definitely don't want to run around in an armor suit with blaster in hand terrifying the aborigines. I want to fly, therefore...

I was already familiar with the sequence of menus leading

to the delete character dialog, so it only took a few movements for the final delete confirmation to pop up, after which the Training Sector would welcome a new and somewhat wiser Surgeon, when suddenly:

"Move it!" the Qualian growled rudely and pushed me in the back, reminding me of his presence. Tripping over a step in the staircase, I stretched myself out the length of six stairs, triggering the laughter of my escort. "Only worthy recruits have the right to stay on their feet! The other chaff must crawl to the kitchen on their stomachs!"

The smirk on the Qualian's face was so irritating that a plan of revenge ripened in my mind. It's dumb, of course, to seek vengeance against a script, but to delete a character who suffered naught but humiliation in his short life…As a paladin, I could never brook such injustice!

"What's up kiddie? Are you upset?" the Qualian continued to sneer. It was precisely these words that finally pushed me to action. Producing the manipulator from my inventory, I aimed it right at his sneering mug and activated it.

If I have to leave this game, let my parting be a memorable one.

Like I managed to point out, the denizens of the Training Sector are not very fond of armor. Even the guards were wearing simple leather jerkins, which may as well have been cuirasses considering that almost all the instructors and recruits wore breezy clothes made of some light fabric. I had nothing to lose, since deleting my character would destroy all the items I had acquired, including my two manipulators. In fact, all that could happen now was a nice bit of entertainment.

And so, I smeared the Qualian's sneering mug across the ceiling, smashing him up over and over again. He tried to resist at first, splaying out his arms, but I quickly snapped them against the very stairs he had kicked me into not a minute ago. The nine-foot ceilings did not offer enough height to accelerate him properly, so it took me a while to hammer the Qualian to his death—about thirty seconds. Hardly had his formless mass crumpled to the floor (with, to my surprise, not a drop of blood escaping it) when I received another notification about decreased rapport with the empire and heard a siren begin to blare. To hell with it! I spent twenty days sitting around in full solitary and now have every right in the world to entertain myself!

I didn't bother searching the Qualian's body—it would do no good against the guy in the mech suit and the money would vanish upon deletion anyway. So I got out the second manipulator and returned to the hall with the flight simulators. As I recalled, the ceilings were much higher there.

After a little while, I confirmed a very important fact—you really can't destroy other players in the Training Sector. I didn't disrupt anyone's training, but whenever a player emerged from his "box," smiling triumphantly, I'd lift him 20 feet into the air and let him plummet. It took only two such flights to bring the recruits down to 1% health, but that was it. I couldn't finish them off beyond that. Laying around the floor and cursing at me, the players now looked unable to get back up—it seemed they needed medical assistance. This only made me happy, as now they couldn't get in my way.

"Drop the manipulator!" came the booming command. The hall's vaulted roof parted and a marine in a mech suit, accompanied by much dust and gravel, came flying in. Performing a pretty bank and thereby demonstrating his tight control of the jet engine strapped to his back, the marine stopped, hovering a few yards before me. Well, that's an end to my spree, I guess. The manipulator is useless against the active resistance attribute and isn't much of a weapon to begin with, seeing as how it's designed to lift things and…Hold on! Lift things?!

"I'm dropping it," I burbled, pointing the beam at one of the big simulator crates. Ample in its dimensions, this piece of equipment would weigh in at about a ton if not more. If the manipulator could do nothing against the active resistance, then we could try a different approach…

"I'm counting to five! One! Two! Three!"

A hit!

One manipulator was not capable of lifting an emulator. I established that much right away. Then again, I also established quite quickly that two manipulators work wonderfully swell in tandem, allowing you to lift what one cannot.

A hit!

New level reached: Your B-class ZPEF-Manipulator has reached level 13. Durability, number of charges and energy have been restored by 30%.

START THE GAME

It took a while to pound the marine into the floor—about a minute—and this pleasure cost me two simulators, the first breaking in half without having done any damage worth mentioning. I was lucky in that each blow would stun the marine for a few moments, allowing me time to lift the second simulator before he could point his weapon at me.

You have earned a new title: "Maniac." You have reached Rank III of the "Enemy of the Empire" and "Murderer" Achievements, without having left the Training Sector. The shadow guilds of Galactogon are now aware of you.

Smiling to myself, I dismissed the notification—quite a dubious achievement, or rather title. It'll sound very pretty along with my name—"Maniac Surgeon." Quite a ring to it! Having sent several other guards and instructors, who came running into the hall, to flight, I paused and waited, not wishing to leave such an advantageous place. If another marine shows up, I'll have several other compelling arguments for him in the form of simulators…as long as they show up one at a time and once a minute, otherwise…

Master, I'd like to inform you that news of your actions in the Training Sector has triggered a wave of outrage among the new players. The fora already bristle with demands to the administrators to get involved in the ongoing conflict and punish the perpetrator. That is, you. I will continue to monitor the news…

My desire to delete this character and forget this

nightmare ever happened was so great that it took all my willpower to take ahold of myself and approach the vanquished marine—my personal satisfaction indicator was not quite there yet. Bending over the pile of wreckage, once a handsome and self-assured Qualian, I touched the barrel of some black rifle when…

Qualian Marine Armor. Weight: 212. Durability: 23%. Item class: D-44. Resistance to all attacks: 112. Maximum weight to carried items: +400.

Qualian Assault Blaster. Weight: 12. Durability: 23%. Item class: D-44. Damage dealt: 60 (Radiation). Charges: 98 of 100.

Acquired credits: 588 GC.

Your rapport with the Qualian Empire has decreased. Current Rapport: -43.

It took only a moment for me to realize that my fun was just beginning! One or two hours won't change the things much and I'm morally compelled to try out such a miracle gift fallen from the heavens. Qualian Marine Armor plus a blaster with 98 shots…What could be better for a player who is consciously heading toward resurrection?

"I wrote down your name! You're dead meat! I'll find you IRL!" the players went on frothing helplessly. I paid them no attention, however. The suit of armor was much more important to me. Coming to grips with the realization that I had no idea how to pilot this piece of equipment and that I might cause harm to

---

myself doing so (by the way, what kind of injuries can a character suffer?) I pushed the "Engage" button. Let's see what happens…

The nice thing about the suit was that I didn't have to put it on piecemeal. It instantly embraced me, helpfully showing me its control interface. Crap! Once more, I found myself facing a bunch of buttons with strange inscriptions. Though, this time I wasn't hampered by the emulator's limitations and so, leaving the somatic interface, switched into Third Person mode.

"Master, I continue to receive messages about…"

"Don't panic! Stan, I need complete and, simultaneously, concise information about how to pilot Qualian Marine Armor. You have ten seconds, get on with it!"

"I have collected the requested information and sent it to your PDA. Master, I strongly advise you cease your aggression towards the Qualian Empire and…"

Stan's further advice remained a secret, as I switched back into First Person mode. Nothing had happened while I was gone. The players continued to strew the floor in a cursing heap. Marine reinforcements had not yet shown up and the guards and instructors were either dead or had decided that they had no business being there. Smart of them!

In Runlustia, I was used to the mechanic that even if the player hadn't the requisite skill to wear full plate armor, he could still don a steel cuirass and calmly head into the fray. Sure, he wouldn't benefit from the cuirass's special attributes—say, stat bonuses or magic resistance— but defense against physical attacks was enabled automatically. In Galactogon, this aspect turned out both more complicated and basic at the same time.

First of all, the player can use any item he finds in Galactogon's vastness, as long as this item doesn't require multiple players to control it at once.

Second of all, to use this stumbled-upon item, the player must know the correct combination of buttons to press—for, in Galactogon everything has buttons.

And third of all...The correct combination of button presses can be found in real life just as in the game—which is what I decided to do now.

The Qualian Marine Armor turned out to be a pretty interesting device. It was about eight feet long and made of some kind of alloy which fully covered the player, while moving him along the ground on two legs supported by powerful and clingy little paws. Judging by it all, a marine could even move vertically without much difficulty—as long as he could find places for the paws to cling to. The player's legs only reached down to the suit's hips, so losing an appendage did not actually hurt the player. The same applied to the arms. I could see several screens which showed everything that was happening around me. But even if the cameras were damaged, the cockpit surrounding me was transparent. This was probably to help you understand where you needed to flee to if it came to that...

According to the information Stan sent over, the instrumentation panel before me could be controlled with my eyes, allowing my arms and legs to focus on controlling the armor's movements. It followed that if I wanted to walk, I just needed to walk inside the suit—though only after finding a way to turn it on. And precisely this was what they spent four days of training on.

Red-green-blue-red—the armor vibrated palpably. This sequence activated the suit, allowing the player to start inputting commands. The screens went pitifully red, indicating that my suit's Durability was critically low, but at the moment this was meaningless—I only needed it for a few hours. Next, I needed to transfer control to my arms and legs in order to move...Activate vision...Microphone...Stabilizer...Shields...

Who cooked all this up?! To make the first step, I had to enter twenty different commands in sequence, adjusting the suit of armor to my body. Nevertheless, I persevered and got through the lot of them, knowing that next time this would be much easier. In fact, it was already clear what I had to do.

"Stan, I need instructions for how to use and reload a Qualian Assault Blaster!"

It took me about five minutes to absorb the principles behind the suit's operation and to get a handle on how to keep my balance without cracking up the crowd of fallen newbies around me. These were five minutes which were gifted to me by the instructors' and guards' unwillingness to disturb me with their presence. Aiming the primed blaster at the mess of newbies, I turned on the PA and said, "Nothing personal, you guys. This is just target practice."

I pulled the trigger. So I'll waste one shot—at least I'll be certain that the blaster works...

GALACTOGON BOOK ONE

You have earned a new title: "Destroyer." You have destroyed another player in the Training Sector. The shadow guilds of Galactogon are now curious about you. This title is logged and tracked officially. Number of players who have this title: 388.

The lights went out in the hall, submerging us in darkness. A single beam of light sliced through the opening above. The siren, which I had already become accustomed to, fell quiet for a moment and then erupted so loudly that the newbies on the floor began writhing, trying to stop their ears. Oh so this is how they want to play! An attempt to break my will with sound? How will the developers explain their use of this sonic weapon to the other players?

"Surgeon!" came a deafening roar, stifling the newbs' moans. "Put down your weapons and come out with your hands up! You have five minutes to make up your mind!"

What, am I no longer considered a recruit? Well, well...

The siren fell silent along with the other players' moans and, as I watched astounded, basically all of the recruits turned transparent and then vanished entirely. I'd guess they simply logged off into the real world—though a few remained.

"Hey, Surgeon, can you hear me? Wave your hand if you can!"

Waving my blaster at the remaining player to tell him to leave me alone, I continued to watch the doors with interest. I was wondering whether the assault would come through the roof or through the doors. I was still extremely insecure about my ability to pilot this craft—I sure wouldn't have tried to fly the way that marine had done it—so I knew that I needed to be prepared to resist without the benefit of maneuverability.

"Perfect," the prone recruit went on. "My name is Lestran. I'm a repairman but I also just passed the piloting exam. If you take me with you, I'll help you get off this planet! Better think fast—pretty soon you'll have no time for me."

"Getting out of here isn't possible! And even if we do, the Empire is closed to us," I replied neutrally, as if everything was under control and I knew exactly what I was doing.

"You don't trust me? Fine, but I know all about the pirates—if you doubt my abilities, check my status—I even won a local tournament. Do you even know how to get to it?"

"Through the jail with the guard who has the thingy on his sleeve," I ventured, growing more curious about this player. "Big deal...I've gotten myself a suit of armor—but you don't see me bragging about it—whereas you keep going on about some tourney..."

"Listen, I enrolled in training on purpose, so that I could get to the pirates. You, as I understand it, have already basically done it—but without my help, you'll never get off this planet! I spent seven months finding a way out of here. Without me, you're not going anywhere for at least as long! So make up your mind: Either you're about to delete and restart, in which case everyone is already pissed at you anyway, or you can trust me and take me with you. You got three minutes left!"

What else could I do? Trusting my experience, I made my decision: This player needed something and I could use that to my advantage. Anyway, as long as the current events didn't take up too much of my time, I could allow myself to go on playing. I could always delete Surgeon, but I was still curious what the Qualians would do and how Lestran wanted to escape the Training Sector.

"The armor has a medkit—first, you'll need to heal me. The button combination is gel-pax-pax-glar-kree."

"Let's speak human, okay? Qualian may as well be Greek to me."

"So how'd you manage to start the suit?" Lestran asked surprised.

"The buttons are color-coded—blue, red and so on."

"Bunch of nonsense...Alright, hang on a second...The medkit is blue-red-red-orange-green. I can't believe I'm even doing this...If anyone finds out, they'll laugh their..."

"If it works, it works," I replied, bending down over Lestran and putting my arm beside him. Barely had I entered the necessary combination when a needle extended from my suit's index finger and punctured the recruit's body. His health began to rise.

"Okay, now stay on my heels! We've got two minutes before they come!" yelled Lestran, jumping to his feet and running toward the doors. "Move it! We need to descend to the lower levels."

Lestran ran out of the hall so confidently that I had no

---

other choice but to follow him.

"Shoot it," I took thirty or so heavy, metal-clanging steps, when I almost ran into him, standing still and pointing with his hand at a niche in the wall. "You need to knock that down with your blaster."

"Knock what down?"

"The wall! What are you waiting for? The passage to the levels we need are on the other side!"

I didn't bother to ask how this player could be so sure of himself. Instead, I pressed myself to the opposite wall, aimed the weapon at the wall and pulled the trigger. Instantly, I hoped that Lestran had managed to dart behind a corner. Fragments of rubble flew everywhere, reducing the Durability of my armor by 1%. This was followed by my temporary ally's invective:

"You dingbat! You couldn't wait until I took cover? What are you standing around for? Heal me!"

Before I could administer another dose of the healing injection, I had to remove two large boulders that had pinned Lestran to the floor. The wall's demolition had turned out very realistic—there was so much dust that I even thought I was back in real life for a second. Typically, most games try to avoid taxing the capsule's system resources on rendering such insignificant details.

Bit by bit, the outlines of a passage began to flicker through the dust. Opening the instructions I had received from Stan, I entered the command to turn on the floodlights. Two bright beams split the murk and our eyes encountered a steep winding staircase, running both up and down.

"This way!" Lestran ordered joyously and deftly squeezed through the opening in the wall. "We need to go down!"

"One second," I replied, squeezing through the opening with some difficulty, after which I stuck my arm and blaster back through it and took several shots at the walls and ceiling of the hallway we had come from. In a few minutes, the assault would commence and I didn't want to leave an obvious trace of where we had gone. Let them suffer a bit removing the boulders, while I got to be Maniac for a bit longer. I needed to find out after all, how Lestran had learned about this secret passage.

"Right on!" the player agreed with me, descending several steps lower. "No one knows that you can bust through there and since it's all buried now, they'll think of looking in the hangar last of all."

"Do you know what's up there?" I pointed up the staircase.

"Sure. General Trank's office—he's in charge of all of Training Sector Alpha-332. I managed to find this stairwell during my last life, but they caught me in the office and sent me to jail—and boy did my imperial rapport suffer a hit. So I had to start all over…Otherwise, this is a very curious building, which I've managed to dig around in quite sufficiently by now…"

"So what's the deal? Do you think they'll look for us there?" I asked Lestran, pausing my descent. "Is it very far up?"

"Look for us?" Lestran also halted his descent and even climbed a few steps back toward me. "Doubt it. The office is three floors up and…Wait, don't tell me you want to go take a look?"

"Well what do you think would be better: If we approach the pirates with data we've stolen from the computer of the executive officer of the Training Sector or simply show up willy nilly saying 'take us as we are—we're so cute, after all?'" I said, applying pressure to Lestran's sore point. Why was he so set on getting in with the pirates? And why wouldn't I use that fact to my advantage? From my time in Runlustia, I could safely say that the offices of commanders typically had something worth stealing. At the very least, there would be some nice items up there.

"Let's go," Lestran made up his mind, squeezed past me and began to ascend. "Though, on second thought, wait here. If there's anyone in the office, we won't go in—we can't let them know where we are. If there's no one in there…I gotta say, I'm damn lucky to have met you! What's your guild anyway?"

"Let's do that later—the loot's getting cold!"

Lestran merely smiled and began climb the stairs.

Just then, a menacing and mighty voice shook the entire building: "Surgeon! You refuse to listen to reason and will therefore be placed under arrest until the investigation has been completed! Commence the assault!"

"It's clear up there." My partner said, returning. Then he nodded in the direction of the rubble, "D'you hear? They're looking for you already."

I could hear one of the Qualian commanders issuing orders through the wall: "First team take the rec area. Second team, you've got the exam hall. Third team—you take the mess.

Fifth team—lecture rooms."

"Those boys are not playing around," Lestran smiled again. "Come on. The general's office is empty."

"Why this is just paradise," whispered Lestran, as soon as he stepped into the office. "How things have changed in here!"

My new partner's astonishment was justified—we really had found a nice place. The ubiquitous gray walls of the Training Sector were covered bookcases. I could already see manipulators, blasters and energy cells strewn about their shelves. There weren't any force fields, so Lestran instantly dashed to the weapons rack and grabbed the first blaster he could get his hands on.

"Now we can play war for real," he said satisfied. I, however, stopped in my tracks: What if my partner decided to use his weapon against me and then give me up to the locals, claiming that I had taken him hostage?

"Chill," Lestran laughed seeing me hesitate. "I don't betray my friends."

A desk covered in papers and a holographic screen occupied the center of the office, so while my partner armed himself, I took a seat in the general's plush chair, causing it to wince beneath my armor's enormous weight, and commenced with some industrial espionage. Unable to understand the value of each separate paper, I photographed everything that got underway with my PDA, having first plugged my comm cable into the desk's data port. The office computer wasn't password protected, so I simply tasked my PDA with copying whatever it got its little hands on. Thank god I didn't have to worry about the device's memory—the player's PDA had seemingly limitless resources.

"Check out what I found," Lestran whispered to me loudly. His voice was so happy that I was forced to give up photographing the papers for a second. "This is an access key to a frigate!"

"And?"

"My escape plan had been to hide in the hold of a cargo ship or transport—one of the ones in the hangars below—but now, we can fly out of here on our own! With our own ship!"

"Do you know how to fly it?"

"Why sure! I've done the Training Sector eight times already, trying to get in with the pirates!"

"How many crew does a frigate need?" I again restrained myself from asking why Lestran was so eager to join the baddies. As far as I understood it, he had decided for himself that I was motivated by the same purpose and therefore could trust me.

"That's the beauty of it! The two of us will be enough!"

"There's one problem though—I never took the classes…"

"You know your colors, don't you? You can check out how to do it right in real life later. Oh boy!" my partner exclaimed once more upon opening a wardrobe.

"What now?"

"Oh—no big deal…Just, here—catch!" A symbolical bag of money came flying in my direction—the developers of Galactogon, it seems, had decided to implement the transfer of money between players in a manner that was universally recognizable. Being utterly symbolic, the bag could contain anywhere from one credit to several billion. The symbol here mattered more than the size.

Acquired credits: 15,339 GC.

"That's exactly half, I swear," added Lestran. "When you're done with the data, change your clothes." My partner indicated another wardrobe: "There are some pretty good class-C clothes in here—with high resistance stats. Plus several medkits, grab them too. I'm gonna check out that safe, for the time being."

Acknowledging my partner with a wave of my hand, I turned my attention to my PDA's display, which had projected a strange notification: *"General, you requested information that has been classified as 'Secret.' Please enter your access code…"*

It seems that my PDA had already copied everything that there was in the office computer and had begun to send its little tentacles further out, where, of course, it encountered some protection. Knowing that to go on would be probably pointless, I nevertheless ran a search on the data I already had for the string "Code"…Who knows those developers were thinking…

"Access Code Accepted. You have gained access to the KRIEG Project…"

The KRIEG Project? The same one that the mysterious stranger had mentioned in solitary? To my immense surprise (and grave failure on the part of the general), the access code was

---

recorded in a plaintext file with the very descriptive name "Access Code." The file contained only one line, which once entered in the password prompt, allowed me to peek where I shouldn't have. I say "shouldn't have" because literally a moment later, the following notification appeared on the screen: *"Unauthorized data transfer detected. Download progress: 77%. Access to Project KRIEG has been limited. General, please remain in your seat— you will shortly be contacted for verification..."*

"Lestran, we've got a problem!" I instantly apprised my partner. "It looks like we need to get out of here!"

"General Trank!" A holographic head of some Qualian appeared about three feet above the desk and began yelling with a voice full of authority. "On what grounds...WHO ARE YOU?"

Counting my blessings for not having removed my armor, which kept my face a mystery to the screaming head, I slammed my fist down on the comm's holo-crystal, cutting the transmission. I ain't scared of you, hollerin' head...

"You're right, time to boogie," Lestran agreed, throwing two blasters over his shoulder. "I'm not getting anywhere with this safe anyway—don't have the skills for it...Are you going to change or not?"

"Sure," I said and, not wishing to make my friend suspicious with my hesitation to grab some more loot, approached the indicated wardrobe and opened its doors. To my further satisfaction with the mechanics in Galactogon, I didn't have to remove my armor to change the clothes underneath. It's not that I distrusted Lestran, but...

"What do you think?" smirked Lestran, once I literally froze in my tracks before the wardrobe. Under the clothes and the medkits (which quickly took up residence in my inventory), the wardrobe also contained one item which, having read its description, caused me to swear in surprise:

Journeyman's Satchel with Anti-Grav. Weight: 1. Item class: D-44. Decreases weight of items in satchel by 200.

"There were only two of them. I took one for myself. Nice little item, eh?"

The item was more than nice. Considering that things in Galactogon have their own size and weight, having an extra two hundred units of carrying capacity is simply a godsend to a starting player. Along with the money I'd accumulated, I was beginning to loathe the idea of deleting my current character. Pirates, after all, could be a swell crowd to run with. As soon as the opportunity presented itself, I would have to read a bit about the game's shadow guilds.

"Stan, my man, gather all the information you can find about pirates in Galactogon and copy it to a separate file. I'm interested in both locals as well as human pirates," I ordered, popping momentarily out of the somatic interface. I was unwilling to leave this question for later. If we ever did manage to get off this planet, I wanted to know everything there was to know about piracy in Galactogon.

"Alright, let's scram," Lestran offered, approaching the

door and pushing a bookcase onto it. The door was hung to open inward, so unless our pursuers decided to use their weapons, it would take them a long time to break into their boss's office.

"Let's go," I agreed, but then, feeling suddenly mischievous, I inquired: "Where'd you say the safe was?"

For a player dressed in marine armor, breaking a safe out of the wall was a question of several seconds. Several strange cables ran from the safe to the wall. These I cut with my built in knife. If that was the alarm, then it wouldn't do us much harm, and if that was a dead switch that destroyed anything inside the safe…Well…we could simply consider ourselves unlucky. Putting the safe in my bag, which could easily accommodate this new weight due to its newly upgraded carrying capacity, I set off after Lestran.

"Here we are," my partner whispered, peeking through a slit in the hangar's door panel. "There're three engineers in the hangar repairing something. Shall we wait until they leave?"

"We don't have time to wait. Pretty soon the general will return to his office and find the door blocked. Even a local can do that math. You took several manipulators, didn't you? Those are quite powerful against defenseless creatures. I don't suggest we use the blasters—might damage the ships."

"In that case, you get those two on the right and I'll take that one on the left. I'm going in!"

The procedure for restraining the careless technicians was in no way different from the earlier one involving the instructors and the guards—lift them up high and let them down (not lightly). Repeat as necessary. To my immense surprise, there was no one else in the cavernous hanger. Either there was a personnel shortage here, or everyone had taken off to help track down some renegade player—me, that is.

"Check these beauties out," Lestran uttered lovingly after he had dealt with his engineer and gotten a chance to look around the hangar. It contained nine ships—two frigates, five interceptors, a harvester and a transport. It became more and more evident to me why gamers loved Galactogon so much—up close, the vessels were quite impressive. Still not knowing which frigate would be ours—the green one or the blue one—I simply marveled at the stately might of each ship. Each line and curve was exactly where it needed to be. Two giant beam cannons in the nose cowling and two more in the fairings of the forward fuselage made the frigate seem like a formidable weapon. Each frigate was about three hundred feet long, much larger than the smallish interceptors and the harvester. Only the pot-bellied transport approached it in its dimensions; however, even for an inveterate landlubber like me, it was evident that you couldn't get far in a tub like that.

"The blue one is ours, I'll tell you what to do!"

We couldn't help but grab four repair bots along our way to the ship. Since repair was Lestran's main occupation, he was fully capable of not only controlling these strange, arachnoid creatures, but could also fix my armor with their help. Over the past hour, I had gotten so used to my suit, that I didn't even notice it anymore. That which had initially struck me as incredibly

---

inconvenient (for example, the HUD) was gradually beginning to seem ideal to me. Maybe I should become a marine after all?

The entrance to the ship was right behind the forward bulkhead. With a trembling hand, Lestran put the access key to the door, which instantly opened with a slight hiss of steam.

"Look at that! Alright, Surgeon—let's figure out whose ship this is now rather than later. The system is asking me about it—which one of us should I register as its owner?"

"Me," I replied without a second thought. "One of us can't fly it. You said so yourself, so we'll play together. But if it weren't for me, you'd still be doing the Training Sector over and over again. That's number one. Number two is that since we're heading to meet up with some pirates, the ship owner has to be the one whom they're interested in. Otherwise they'll just attack us, take the ship and then tell us to get lost. I already received a notification that Galactogon's shadow guilds are curious about me. Have you gotten one?" I turned to Lestran, eloquently tipping my head to one side.

"Well then the robots are mine!" Lestran burbled petulantly. "And we split the loot 50-50!"

"That works for me."

"What a greedy pig you are," my partner said, still unwilling to calm down. He did something on the panel before him and I received a pretty welcome notification:

You have unlocked the "Captain" Achievement. You are now the owner of a spaceship.

You have acquired a space frigate. Weight: 250,000. Item class: D-77. For a detailed description of the frigate, please consult the ship's manual.

You are the first player to own this frigate and have the right to change its name. The current name is Dratistan.

Uh, excuse me, but no! I have very little desire to go flying around in something called the *Dratistan*.

"Couldn't think of anything more clever?" quipped Lestran, when the ship's name changed. "Sit here. I'll explain to you what sequence you need to press the buttons in. I'll sit beside you and plot our course. Do you even have a slight idea of where we need to go?"

"I do. First into space and then to some backwater planet without resources. We'll leave the ship there, then pop out of the game and check out the instructions. I won't take a single step further until I know how to fly. By the way, how are you on time?"

"I'm fine. I've got a month at least." Lestran pointed at a dark-red, almost maroon, button and continued, "Check it out, first we need to start the reactor and after that..."

I listened eagerly to Lestran's introductory lecture on piloting a space frigate. Of course, I could absorb the entire process this very night by finding some emulators, but at the moment we needed to take off and fly away, having broken through the planetary defense ring—and that, as my partner pointed out, was a problem in and of itself. Especially, he underscored, for a ship with a name like ours.

START THE GAME

Listening attentively and writing down the sequence of commands, I smiled to myself: Today would see the maiden voyage of *The Space Cucumber*. My Stan would be happy to hear the news…

CHAPTER THREE

FLIGHT

'm starting the engines," Lestran narrated his conjurations over the control panel. In principle, one person was enough to fly a space frigate, but you had to choose either between flying the thing or manning the shields and guns. The control mechanics did not allow for both to be done at the same time.

"Frigate *Dratistan*, please explain your engine start," a voice instantly demanded over the intercom.

"We are conducting a test fire of the engines and reactor," Lestran replied, signaling me to stay quiet. "They've been acting up lately and we haven't been able to figure out why. I mean, we already took the hyperdrive apart and changed the power cells— nothing helps."

"The facility is currently on high alert. Please cease all

---

testing procedures on the frigate."

"Guys, guys, what are you talking about? If I don't find the problem, General Trank will eat me bones and all! He personally ordered us to get the frigate working like new!"

"I don't know anything about that," the voice replied less confidently. "Shut down your engines immediately!"

"Understood. As you wish. Please state your name and rank so I can pass it on the general. You know yourself what happens when his orders aren't followed—so I'd like an official prohibition against further repairs. Please give me your name and I will happily shut off these damn engines!"

"Alright, alright. I'm sending over a marine squad to protect you while you run your tests." It seemed that the general had such a reputation on this base that arguing with him was dangerous to one's wellbeing. "Signing off!"

"And now our future is in your hands, Surgeon. We'll need to destroy that marine squad quickly. You'll only get one shot off—after that it'll be a melee."

"No there won't." I jumped up from my seat and ran to the ship's exit. "Follow me!"

The bodies of the three engineers we taught to fly had not vanished (according to the forums, if you take a local's equipment, his body will vanish after a minute, but if you leave the equipment, his body will vanish only after 24 hours—a convenient feature when you're in the midst of a large battle). Running up to the bodies, I began to strip one of its clothes. After that, I shoved it under the ship and heaped some tools on it—hoping against hope that it would vanish before the marines arrived.

"If they start shooting, we won't get off the planet," I told Lestran when he caught up with me. "You have experience as an engineer, even if remotely. It's time to use what they taught you. Put this on—you're going to pretend to be a Qualian worker."

"Not a bad idea but where do you want me to get the gray skin and third eye?" sneered my partner, nevertheless stripping the second corpse. Using the manipulator I pulled the third worker closer to us, undressed him and also concealed him under some instruments—if we were going to risk it, I was going all in.

"Hey—anyone alive in there?" No sooner had I managed to hide the body than the squad leader's voice echoed in the hangar. Lestran needed only a few moments to put on the engineer's robe and pull the hood over his head. I, meanwhile, thanked Galactogon's mechanic of allowing me to change clothes without removing my armor for the nth time.

"Over here!" I yelled, waving at the three marines that had popped up into the air. These guys were so good at controlling their suits that I even started to feel a little shame about my own clumsiness. I could fly too theoretically speaking, but in actual fact... "Since we're not allowed to be inside the frigate, we decided to test out this faulty armor. What a heap of junk...How do you boys even move in them?"

My irritation seemed so natural that, gently landing on the floor, the marines merely smirked.

"And who asked you to squeeze into it?" asked the squad leader. He was wearing a newer-generation suit, which had some kind of weapon that didn't look like a blaster mounted on its right shoulder. The other two troopers were wearing the same suit as I was, with the slight difference that theirs were still in one piece.

"Just my natural propensity to do dumb stuff and wanting to prove to myself that I could. Something's jammed in it though—it's not letting me get out. Now I'll have to ask the senior engineer to help me take it off...Hey, listen, fellas—do you know any special commands for this thing? It just wouldn't do to make an engineer work in marine armor!"

"Sorry, bud," the squad leader was in such a good mood that he even clapped me on the shoulder, "we've got nothing like that. You'll have to hold on—the only way is to cut you out. We've seen this kind of thing with that model—sometimes the release latch gets stuck. By the way, where'd you get that thing anyway?"

"Recruit training," I went on spinning my tall tale. "Someone trusted those bunglers with a real suit and they managed to break it half to death! I got it running with some elbow grease and good old Qualian knowhow and then decided to test it out myself...Darn those newbs! I have another question, by the way: What's going on in the Training Sector? Why are you boys running around, keeping us from testing engines? As far as I recall, and I've been here—well, I can't even remember how long I've been here—as far as I recall, nothing like this has ever happened before!"

"One of the recruits went Section 8. He managed to get his hands on a manipulator and wiped out several scores of civilians. Our assignment is to neutralize the psycho."

"Well, you better check this one right away!" I pointed at Lestran, who gave such a start at my words that his hood slipped off his head. It was too late to hide his face, so my partner proudly raised his head and looked defiantly first at the lieutenant and then at me. There was so much determination in his eyes that I even felt happy to have such a partner—even now, he wasn't about to betray me.

"Recruit Lestran," said the lieutenant, having checked his PDA. "According to our data, he is recorded as missing—all the other recruits have been found."

"What do you mean 'missing'? I've been sweating those frigate engines with this engineer since this morning, trying to find the problem, and you guys have him as missing? How is he going to get his experience points?"

Once again, I sounded so genuinely baffled that the marine became stumped himself.

"Okay, I will make a note that Recruit Lestran has been located...You said he's been here since this morning?"

"Ten o'clock to be precise. Or, wait, no," I cut myself off, pretended to check my PDA, cursed the armor for getting in my way and muttered something along the lines of "how do you people live in these things." Finally, I clarified: "Ten-o'-three, in the a.m."

"I'll log it. Okay. We're going to take a spin around the hangar to make sure that our renegade isn't hiding here somewhere. After that, you two can go on with your engine tests."

"Before we get back into the ship, have one of your guys

check him from head to toe," I proposed. "I'd rather not feel like there's an orbital station about to come down on me."

"Sure, no problem. Alright boys, let's go," ordered the lieutenant and the three of them flew up into the air.

"Maybe you should be an actor?" Lestran whispered, stepping up beside me. I really didn't want to leave until the bodies of the real engineers had vanished—who knows what kind of questions the marines would start asking if they stumbled upon them. By my estimations, there were only a few seconds until...

"What's that noise?" one of the marines asked, banking elegantly over us, once the clatter of falling tools resounded across the entire hangar—the bodies had finally vanished.

"I'm learning how to walk!" I muttered irately in reply and took an exaggerated step forward, teetering to keep my balance. "It's not enough that this junk heap is malfunctioning—these damn servos will end up breaking my leg in half!"

To be honest, I was risking a bit too much by speaking so informally. However, my brief acquaintance with Galactogon had taught me that the locals were capable of anything, so the best thing was to stick to the matter at hand. An engineer stuck in a suit of armor, in my opinion, would have been more than merely irritated with everyone around him—he would also seem like he'd happily tear in half the guy that brought him the faulty equipment to begin with. I could only hope I wasn't overplaying it.

"We've checked the hangar. No sign of the escaped recruit!" reported the lieutenant, returning to us. "You may go on with your tests—the ship is clear!"

"You boys coming with us?" I asked just in case.

"No, we will continue our search. Good luck with your repairs—and getting out of that suit!"

"How long did you prepare for that?" Lestran asked shocked when we turned back to the frigate. "To lie so well and react to the situation without showing your nerves...When you called me a recruit, I almost soiled my pants! I was ready to kill you then, but you it turns out had it all thought out."

I didn't say anything but just kept walking to the frigate— at first unsteadily, while the marines were still in the hangar, and then quickly, turning on my thrusters, flying into the ship and landing into my seat, relieved. A shiver coursed through my body and a fit of nervous laughter overtook me, almost forcing me to the floor—I'd never had to bluff so hard, even in Runlustia.

Forcing myself to calm down, I explained to Lestran the reason for my laughter—had the lieutenant asked my name, I would've been a goner. Had the lieutenant asked for my supervisor's name, I would've been a goner. Had the lieutenant asked anything at all, I would've been a goner...However, the grizzled warrior had only seen a reasonable guy dressed in the same suit as his soldiers, which naturally led him to feel some sympathy towards me. This was precisely what I had tried to bet on, making a show of my clumsiness. Improbable, but it worked!

"Frigate *Dratistan*, you are cleared for launch through door number two," said the by now familiar voice when we got back into our seats. Instantly, a giant door in the ceiling above the ship began to slide open.

START THE GAME

"Roger that," Lestran said happily, getting ready to do his magic over the control panel.

I, however, felt like pushing out luck some more. Understanding perfectly well that I was risking everything that we had achieved up until that moment, I pressed the call button and said into the open channel, "I have a question—who's the wise guy who decided to disarm the frigate? For optimal testing conditions, we need a full loadout, including torpedoes and a full cargo hold. We're as light as a feather right now and feathers don't do well in combat! I'm not prepared to sign off on our tests under these conditions!"

Lestran had showed me how to work the shields and armaments, and I had been shocked to discover that our frigate was as toothless as a babe—the beam cannons had no energy cells, the torpedoes had been unloaded, the hold was empty. I should have probably kept my mouth shut, but...

"Pursuant to Directive 7742.33, all space vessels stored in the hangar must..." the voice began surprised, but I went on risking it. It's not like anyone was closing the hangar door, after all...

"We submitted a request for comprehensive tests! With a complete battle loadout! Please get in touch with General Trank—he will confirm that I personally asked for his signature! Goddamn it, how much more crap can you put us through! If you don't immediately load the frigate's holds with raq, return the energy cells and torpedoes—you'll have to repair this frigate yourselves! I'm sick of this! I tell you, my entire division will quit and go to

Shylak XIV—they need good engineers over there! Then, you can explain everything to the general yourself. The lieutenant already told us about the renegade recruit—but what do we have to do with that? We've already been checked over so thoroughly, that..."

"Raq?" There was so much astonishment in the dispatcher's voice that I even smiled. If this were real life, I basically would have just asked him to fill the ship's cargo holds with gold.

"Obviously," I answered without hesitating. From what I had read in solitary, raq was one of the heaviest and at the same time most valuable resources in the game. "We need to check the ship at maximum capacity. If I could stuff a neutron star in here, I'd do it without a second thought!"

"I don't see your request anywhere," the voice replied, faltering.

"Excuse me, who am I speaking to?"

"Junior Comms Center Dispatcher Gartil."

"Ah, I see...Pass me up to someone a bit more senior then, Junior Dispatcher Gartil."

"I am unable to do that, sir." (Oh look—I had been knighted!) "All our manpower has been channeled into finding the AWOL recruit..."

"How long have you been working here?" Ignoring Lestran's imprecations to end the conversation and get off this planet as soon as possible, I put a finger to my helmet, indicating that I wanted to be left alone.

"One month already, sir!"

"I see...Okay sonny, forgive me but I have no choice. I'm terminating the testing procedure."

"Please wait!" A hint of determination appeared in Gartil's voice. "I'll find that request later—I'm ordering a full load out now! Sir?"

"Roger that! Thank you, Gartil. If everything works out for us, I'll buy you a drink! And I'll make sure to recommend you to the general. He likes decisive and confident individuals! And I can see that you are quite the individual!"

"Thank you, sir! Please forgive me but there is another problem!"

"Another problem?" I tensed up. Was my story about to fall apart at the seams?

"The warehouse only has enough raq to fill half of your ship's holds. I have a solution, though—we can load your holds with two prototypes. According to my data, our scientists have been using the adjacent hangar to develop some kind of new engine. They've paused their work at the moment. The mass and dimensions of the prototypes are perfect for filling the frigate's holds to maximum capacity!"

"Load them up!" I said, realizing that I had been holding my breath and finally releasing it. "I can see I wasn't wrong about you, Gartil!"

"I'm doing my best, sir! I've relayed your orders to the deck personnel. The cargo will be delivered to you in five minutes. Best of luck with your tests. May I help you with anything else?"

"You can make sure that the orbital stations don't zap us by accident. Over and out!"

Having disconnected, I leaned back in my chair, which seemed to utterly ignore my immense weight, and closed my eyes wearily. To my great surprise, my hands were shaking so bad that I felt like I had just spent a week drinking, while my pulse was going as fast as a machine gun. If everything worked out now, the Qualian Empire would be off limits to me forever. Personally, I would never forget something like this, much less forgive it...

"Loading has commenced...sir," said Lestran, admiration seeping into his tone.

"Make sure they don't slip us anything we don't want," I asked my partner without opening my eyes. "Meanwhile, I'll read about how to manage the frigate's shields..."

"We're taking off," Lestran announced about seven minutes later. Our ship trembled slightly, leaving the flight deck. "Engaging stabilizers," added my partner, putting an end to the tremors. If I understood it correctly, these stabilizers had to be turned on either before or simultaneously with lift-off. I didn't tell this to my pilot though, as he was just then trying to guide us through the hangar door. Control comes with experience and anyway, Lestran was an engineer, not a pilot. I'd get a hang of flying once I got a chance to read about it some more. Then you would see me zooming all around Galactogon hither and thither. Let him do the flying for now...

"We're leaving the atmosphere. I'm plotting our jump," my partner went on describing his actions. On my screen, however, an alert popped up, notifying me that we were being targeted by an orbital station. "Hyperdrive initializing, thirty seconds until we jump..."

"Frigate *Dratistan*, this is General Trank! Return to base immediately or I shall order your destruction."

The voice was so menacing that I got chills all along my body. It looked like poor Gartil was already in trouble ...

"Twenty seconds," Lestran whispered, letting me take control of the situation.

"This is the captain of *The Space Cucumber*! I am officially announcing the rechristening of this spaceship as well as the ship's transfer to my command. I am also expressing my categorical opposition to the practice of feeding Training Sector recruits organic food in the mess hall! Pursuant to the Emperor's directive, recruits must be fed not only organic food but also some sort of vegetable, preferably corn. Considering that this imperial edict has been grossly violated by the facility's administration, I will be forced to apprise the Emperor of noncompliance on the part of the facility's Executive."

"Whose noncompliance? What are you even talking about? Identify yourself immediately, or I will order your termination!"

"Five seconds." Lestran's face expressed the smile of a man who believed in the impossible.

"My name is Surgeon...Pirate Surgeon!"

"Fire on my..." began the general. I never heard the end of his sentence, for the stars became lines, leaving hundreds of

---

parsecs between us and the Training Sector.

Your rapport with the Qualian Empire has decreased. Current Rapport: -100,000.

You have unlocked the "Qualian Pariah" Achievement. You have reached the limit for negative rapport with this Empire. From now on, all enemies of the Qualian Empire will be neutrally disposed towards you—and all close allies of the Empire will try to destroy you.

The shadow guilds of Galactogon wish to meet with you. The rendezvous point is Planet Qirlats in Confederation space. Your contact person is Hilvar.

"The shadow guilds are curious about me!" squeaked Lestran, who it seems also received some kind of notification.

"Where are we going, ya great curiosity?" I asked my excited partner.

"Haven't the slightest idea! I picked the first coordinates I saw and sent the ship there. We're coming out of hyperspace in a minute—then, we'll see where we are."

"I received a notification that some people want to have a chat with us. But I'm not about to head off to a meeting with strangers unprepared. It's eight in the evening at the moment. We'll pop out of hyperspace, find the closest planet, land on it and take a break. We can reconvene tomorrow at nine, you down?"

"No need to ask, sir! I'll be here on deck waiting for you at 8 a.m.!" replied my partner, unconsciously switching to a deferential tone.

"In that case, I'll need your help. I will leave my armor onboard. It needs to be repaired. You're an engineer, aren't you? You can use this as a chance to gain some experience with your robots…Will you do it?"

"Sir, you are insulting me. You'll barely get a chance to blink your eyes, before everything will be brought to a better state than it ever was! Here we go, leaving hyperspace now…"

The star-lines contracted back to points, the hum of the hyperdrive fell quiet, and *The Space Cucumber* froze in infinity…

"Surgeon, are you okay, sir?" Lestran became worried after a few minutes. I had never yet been in deep space and so far from planets, stars, people…My mind understood very well that I was only in a game and that everything around me was merely the play of my imagination and modern technology, yet my heart still trembled in reverence. Before my eyes lay the blackness of infinity, a testament to the fact that a person is no more than dust mote in an enormous universe—it was an unforgettable sensation…

"Are there any planets in the vicinity?" I asked my partner, trying to speak in my normal voice. I didn't wish to show Lestran the awe Galactogon just made me experience—a few hours would go by and I would become acclimated to these surroundings. Until that time, I preferred to maintain my composure.

"Scanning now…There are two star systems within ten minutes' flight from us. One is planet-less, while the other has a gas giant and several small asteroids. Judging by the description, the Altan Alliance battled the Voldan Alliance here. Human players were involved in that battle, so all the planets have been stripped of resources entirely. We are in a dead sector..."

"An excellent place to lie low for a bit. No better, in fact. Head for the system with the asteroids. By the way, can anyone find us?"

"Unlikely. The Qualians, even if they give chase, only know our vector. They have no idea how long we were in hyperspace. I know this is just a game, but even in a game there must be some logic. Look—what do you think of that planet?" Lestran pointed at a humongous boulder that we were slowly approaching.

"It'll do. Work your piloting magic and set us down. We'll meet tomorrow as agreed—at nine..."

The cocoon's cover slid aside, after which the built-in seat lifted my poor body practically vertically, easing my egress. A convenient thing, these modern game cocoons. Only a few years ago, the player would have to get out of this coffin on his own. It looked like a dead man had suddenly gotten a craving for someone's blood. Despite the life support system, one week in the cocoon had a significant impact on coordination, so the first five-ten minutes, the player resembled a zombie more than a human. Considering that he had to clamber out of a giant box, we used to call capsules just that—coffins...

"Welcome back, Master," Stan instantly chirped. "I have

gathered the data about Galactogon you requested and transferred it to your PDA. The information about piracy in the game has also been collected and..."

"Stan, fill me a bath and make dinner," I said, interrupting the smart home's report, "and put together a report about recent events in the Training Sector that I just fled from. I need to know the reactions of the Qualians and the other players...In general, get me everything you can find about that. Also, I need a frigate emulator—that's top priority."

"Alex, what's up! Where'd you go? Want to go somewhere and chill for a bit? It'd be nice to catch up, find out what you're up to, what waters you're swimming in...Anyway, come on out of your man cave and give me a call..."

"Stan, when did this message arrive?" I asked the smart home. The bath hit me so hard that I almost fell asleep in it and decided to go through my voicemail to keep awake. I had spent the last four days in Galactogon and could easily have missed some visitor knocking on my door. Starting with the phone calls, I instantly came across Alonso's message...

"Two days ago," reported the program. "Per your preferences, all incoming calls are being redirected to voicemail. The only exceptions are emergency services and law enforcement; however, no such parties have called during the given reporting period."

If our society continues to develop at the same pace as

today, there will come a day when machines will fully replace us in all vital activities. Already, a lowly piece of software designed to monitor my comfort inside my house has begun to make excuses for itself, pushing all the blame on my shoulders. When the day comes when it also starts bringing home girls behind my back, we'll be able to confidently say that humanity is done for.

"Place this caller on the whitelist and call him back for me. Let's do it over video too."

"As you wish—Alonso is on the…"

"Alexis, you have lost your damn mind!" roared Alonso, shielding the screen with his body. "No big deal—I'm here eating dinner with my lovely wife and suddenly there you are shaking your bits and pieces in our face! You could at least cover yourself a little, you damn nudist!"

"At least it's clear now why he hasn't found himself a girlfriend yet," added Alonso's wife, setting my teeth on edge. Despite the fact that this woman was the love of my best friend's life, I just couldn't ever maintain friendly relations with her. For some unknown-to-me reason, over the five years of knowing each other, Lucille had never been able to stomach me and made sure to point this out every chance she got. Like now, for example. "Hey! I have a few girlfriends with flexible standards. I can introduce you…"

"I'll call you back!" Alonso blurted and ended the call. Despite all my gaming knowhow, all I could think of was to cover my lower stomach with my hands and mentally curse out Stan for only putting salt in the bath and not some soap for foam. And yet, why the heck would I think it's a good idea to call Alonso from the bath? What an overgrown ninny I am.

"Really, you are a piece of work!" Alonso called me back about twenty minutes later and instantly went on the offensive. "Why would you give Lucy such nice ammo for the future? Anyway, where've you been?"

"I found some work related to Galactogon. So I had to spend some time in there. I called you as soon as I got the chance. And in general, stop yelling at me! I accept your offer by the way and would be happy to go hang out with you somewhere. How about tomorrow?"

"I can't tomorrow," Alonso said dejectedly. "I started playing Galactogon too and I need to get through that damn Training Sector as quickly as possible. How much more do you have?"

"Ten game days," I suppressed my desire to tell him about my recent triumph and merely offered him my remaining time after solitary. Until the moment when I would meet Alonso in Galactogon and we would both agree to a partnership, our friendship would have to remain outside of the game.

"Huh! I've been playing for a month already and managed only ten days. What are you, living there?"

"Well, that's why I haven't be around for so long. By the way, why'd you suddenly decide to get into Galactogon? What happened to looking for work?"

"That's exactly what it is—I'm working there. You know that Lucy has been buzzing around Galactogon for three years already. She got an account as soon as she went on maternity leave. Now my little bunny is the family breadwinner and I'm just a mooch. So she offered me to join her guild."

"She has her own guild?" I asked surprised. I knew that Lucille played, but her being a guild leader was news to me.

"Yup. A guild with two space cruisers, four frigates, a dozen fighters and three harvesters. I kept wondering where all the money was going. Turns out she's been pumping it into the game on the sly. Not all of it of course, but a pretty nice chunk all the same. You want me to talk to her? Maybe she'll take you on as well? She may think of you whatever she likes, but she can't argue against your gaming experience."

"Sounds enticing. What empire is she part of?"

"We're with the Vraxis. Boy those bugs are ugly..."

"Damn! I am with the Pyrrhenians and I don't have very good rapport with Altan," I went on dissimulating to protect my Surgeon. There really was no way for me to get into that alliance already, but I didn't want to explain why. A friend is a friend, but a billion pounds is better.

"Altan?" Sergei frowned, not understanding what I was talking about.

"One alliance consists of four empires," I explained. "Did you read the lore?"

"Nope." My friend's face broke into a pleasant smile. "You're the game scholar—that stuff doesn't interest me. My job is to get out of the Training Sector and join my bunny. So I can't hang out tomorrow—I've got a repair exam. Let's set a date closer to when we graduate. Just don't disappear on me, okay?"

"Agreed! In that case, I'll see you. I really need to get some sleep. I have a flight exam tomorrow as well."

Alonso disconnected. Wistfully, I thought about how I had just lost one of my companions. My giant friend—the size of a bullock—would never go against his wife's wishes. He was crazy in love with her, so a path to piracy was out of the question for him. Just like my path to him...It followed that we would be playing on opposite sides of the barricades. And the natural logic to these kinds of situations had it that we'd meet face to face during some battle. The important thing was for us to keep our hostilities in-game...The last thing I needed was for that situation to spill over into the real world.

Pirates...pirates are squires of the knife and blade, gentlemen of fortune, cosmic marauders who dedicate their lives to pillage and plunder. To my great surprise, the symbol of pirate membership in Galactogon was the familiar Jolly Roger. It wasn't hard to fashion the flag, but only the leader of the pirates could assign it to your ship, and the leader was a certain local called only "the Corsican," whose base of operations was Silmaar, the pirate capital sequestered somewhere on one of the planets of the Confederacy. Very few players had had the pleasure of meeting this persona. There was little information about what race the Corsican belonged to and the little there was, was contradictory— he was either Qualian, Precian or Pyrrhenian. At any rate, as the forums had it, to become a pirate, one would first have to attract the attention of the shadow guilds. That was the only way to get a meeting with the Corsican.

There were quite a number of player pirates too. More accurately, there were only several dozen "official" pirates, but an uncountable amount of your basic mortals who had banded in groups and attacked anything that moved. These miscreants didn't interest me at all. There were no locals among them, which automatically ruled out finding out more about where the planet with the check was located. That left only the Corsican and his Brotherhood of the Jolly Roger.

Of the select few players who had received the official status of pirate, the most famous was a girl named Marina—or, as everyone referred to her, "Kiddo." She was the captain of the A-class cruiser *Alexandria*. Her intermittent raids brought lucre to her raiders, along with good old fashioned fun, bad imperial rapport and a modicum of respect from other players. There were many who wanted to find their way into Kiddo's service.

"Master," said Stan, interrupting my study of the history of pirates in Galactogon. "Dan Cormak, the head of the Black Lightning guild, wishes to meet with you."

"Bring him up." I glanced over myself in the mirror just in case, still smarting from my encounter with Lucille. It wouldn't do to bare myself before the beard.

"What's up! I'll get straight to the point: I want to purchase those engines you misappropriated from the Training Sector!" Dan came right out with it. Only now did I begin to really believe that he was the head of one of the best Qualian guilds. He had a sharp, shrewd look about him, and this was supplemented by an aura of almost palpable authority, a stern voice and no beard at all.

"I don't know what you're talking about," I replied, stonewalling. Were it not for my four years' in the Emperor's Court, I would have probably folded. But the psychologists who had worked on developing the NPCs in Runlustia had earned their pay. As a result, I had experience with intelligent guys with an intimidating amount of charisma.

"Five hundred thousand credits, guild membership, and we'll level that frigate you stole up to A-class for you," Dan continued to ply his line, as if he hadn't heard me at all.

"I feel like we're speaking two different languages here." I wasn't about to surrender. "Let me apprise you of recent developments in my life: At the moment, I am in the Training Sector. I just passed a repair exam today. Now—what frigate? What engines? What the heck are you going on about, Dan?"

"So you're trying to tell me that you didn't steal a frigate and flee the Training Sector with Listakt?...err, Lekstat that is...hmm...no, that's not it. Oh, what's his name—Lestlim!"

I kept looking at Dan's projection stupefied, while mentally, I marked him as a dangerous foe. I had come across his kind before too—the beard's (okay, ex-beard's) current trick with the name was quite an ugly little maneuver. Were I to prompt him with the correct name—it would become impossible to play dumb, for in that case, Dan wouldn't have been the one who knew my partner's name. Well, well!

"I'm sorry—if that's all you wanted to tell me, I'm going to hang up now. I'd love to get an A-class ship and five hundred thousand credits, but I have nothing to offer you for it, certainly not some kind of engines."

"Very well," said Dan, somewhat stunned by my not having fallen for his ruse. "When you're done with training, get in touch with me...Can you tell me again what your comm number is in-game?"

"I never told it to you to begin with," I smiled. "And I'm not about to start today. You screwed me out of fifty grand—the guide you gave me is posted on the forum. It's my own fault of course, but you took advantage of me, so I've decided to have nothing to do with your clan from now on. Best of luck to you, Dan Cormack! End call..."

Okay now. Considering that the head of the fourth-ranked guild knows about the stolen ship, those prototypes that that Junior Assistant to the Senior Advisor to the Deputy Dispatcher gave us, must be quite valuable. I'll need to take a closer look at them tomorrow...I've talked to Alonso and read about the pirates, what else should I do? Oh! The most important thing—how to fly a frigate!

"Stan, my man, start up that frigate emulator and make me a whole gallon of coffee," I ordered, after which I got into the game capsule, put on my VR helmet and entered the emulator. It was going to be a long night tonight...

START THE GAME

"Master, your request has been processed. Would you like me to display it on screen or would you like breakfast first?" Stan's pushy and meticulous voice extracted me from my pleasant dreams. Last night—more accurately, this morning—I had stayed up till three polishing my frigate flying skills as well as my mastery of the marine armor. Only once I understood that my brain couldn't bear anymore and was about to rebel if I didn't immediately go to bed, did I order Stan to wake me at eight and find any and all information about our flight from the Qualian forums. Dan Cormack had contacted me a little too quickly for comfort, demanding the return of the engines. Something wasn't right here.

"Make some coffee," I mumbled, my eyes still closed. "Tell me what you dug up."

"Last night, the Qualian Emperor issued a call to action to all imperial subjects. A certain player named 'Surgeon' had stolen a next generation engine prototype. Whoever managed to recover the engines would receive a reward. The reward itself wasn't publicized, but it was hinted that it would be a substantial one. The search for Surgeon has commenced not just in the game— the Qualians have publicized your escape vector—but in reality as well. Guild leaders are offering up to ten thousand credits for any information about Surgeon—or fifty thousand for the recovery of the engines. The prices vary. The pirates have washed their hands of this incident. All of the pirate sites, both in-game and in real life, assert that Surgeon is not one of their number and that they 'condemn the deeds and behavior of this mad player.' Please forgive me, Master—that is a direct quote and not my personal opinion. May I digress briefly from the report?"

"Alright," I asked, intrigued. The news had brought me wide awake. If such a tempest had broken inside the game, then Lestran and I had really taken something very valuable. The most important thing was to make sure that he didn't leak the information—I had to get back into the game immediately.

"You activated panic mode. Over the past seven hours I have logged twelve attempts to break into your mail account, of which three were successful. The hackers were interested only in your contact information. The digital money that we left as a honeypot was not touched."

"Thanks," I offered the machine, understanding perfectly well that my gratitude was misplaced…It was simply a habit that I had formed in Runlustia: Thank everyone you can and maybe someone will give you a mission. "Bring on the coffee."

The fact that people were interested in a player who had decided to find nonstandard ways of getting through the Training Sector worried me. You didn't have to be a tremendous genius to figure out that what happened with the Qualians yesterday…It had been dumb of me to show myself to Cormack. You could never identify a player by his account alone, but once you had seen him…Although generally a lazy bunch, once a lot of money was involved, gamers were capable of putting in some extra effort.

"Did you read what they're saying about us?" Lestran

asked excitedly, as soon as I signed back into the game. As promised, my companion had entered the game much earlier and had already fully repaired my Qualian marine armor. "Did you get a handle on piloting?"

"I think so, but I'll need practice," I answered, letting the system dress me. "Listen, let's get something straight. Being on bad terms with the Qualians is one thing, but being on bad terms with other players is something else entirely. I read that you and I stole some terribly powerful prototypes, that the Emperor wants them back, that the players will start looking for us not just in Galactogon but in real life too. Consequently, either we go on together and keep our mouths shut about what we have—or we divvy up the loot right this moment and go our separate ways."

"Hah! What's a game for if not being on bad terms with everyone? I'm with you, sir, and I've got no interest in talking to anyone about anything!"

"In that case, tell me: Why pirates? What do you need them for?"

"I..." Lestran faltered but finally took a deep breath and spilled it: "I want to join the crew of *Alexandria*!"

"And?" I didn't fully understand Lestran, who was looking at me now almost defiantly. It felt like he was some captured separatist who had just told his captors that it was he who had blown up that bridge.

"Marina, the ship's captain, demands anyone who joins her crew to sever ties with any groups they belong to."

"Okay, so go ahead and join her—what do you need me

for in that case?"

"Because she won't just take anyone! Only veteran players. I know that she doesn't have enough good engineers, so I decided to focus on that occupation—but I'll have to leave you, sir. And in any case, she'll ask you how I performed as part of your team, so..."

"Hold on. You want to tell me that you restarted this game several times all over again only because you wanted to get into someone's crew?" I asked baffled.

"It's not just any crew. They're some of the best players in Galactogon! Have you even read about her?"

"Only that she is the deputy-head of the Brotherhood of the Jolly Roger—which, actually, I'd like to get into too. So we're heading the same way, you and I—for now, at least. Did you take a look at those engines we stole?"

"I..." Lestran became abashed. "I basically only logged out to take a look at the forums and...I didn't have anything else to do—the bots got the suit working on their own, so I..."

"You installed them on the frigate," I figured.

"Uh-huh. Pretty simple...Also, if anyone gets us, the cargo will get dumped, but if the engines are equipped then they'll be resurrected along with us..."

"Got it...Did you manage to check your work?"

"Well, no. We decided that you'd be the pilot. Plus, if I'd turned them on, someone could've picked up the heat signatures. I noticed some suspicious ships pass through this system. Who knows, maybe they were looking for us, or maybe they had some business here…"

"Did they see us?" I tensed a little.

"Sir, you are insulting me. We're stiller than water here, lower than grass…"

"What'd you do with the old engines?"

"Put them in the holds for now, but they're not good for anything. Just your ordinary D-77 frigate engines. We won't even find a buyer for them. I left them strictly just in case—as backups for the prototypes. Those aren't tested after all, so who knows what'll happen with them. Plus, we got extra room in the holds now. The old engines turned out smaller than the prototypes."

"Okay. What class are the prototypes?"

"B-30. At first I was afraid that they would be class-A or even legendary, in which case there'd be no way I could put them on the ship, but it worked out."

"Do you know how to work the weapons and shields?"

"Of course! Before I decided to reset my character, I was a gunner in the Qualian Navy, so I'm familiar with all the buttons I have to press…Oh crap! Surgeon, a Qualian scout just jumped into the system. There's a bit too much traffic here for my liking—it's not a popular system normally…"

Just in case, I opened my PDA to see what he was talking about. A scout is a smallish vessel that's pretty maneuverable and can be piloted by one player. For optimal operation, however, it requires a crew of three: one pilot, one gunner and one shields operator. As far as armament goes, a standard scout does not have torpedoes—only two beam cannons in its nose and a turret in its tail. Naturally, the stock loadout could be upgraded with a pair of torpedo nacelles, but a vessel of this type did not rely on direct engagement, preferring maneuverability and speed. As a result, among lone-wolves, scouts were second in popularity only to interceptors. However, whereas interceptors were limited in their operational radius—they could not fly too far from their base—scouts were free to prowl Galactogon's expanses at will.

"Welp," I decided, "let's take her out and see what this scout wants—and what *The Space Cucumber* can do. Let's dance, boys!"

CHAPTER FOUR

THE FIRST BATTLE AND ITS AFTERMATH

"Shields are up. We're ready for battle," said Lestran as soon as I finished the preflight check. That took me about ten minutes, during which the scout managed to traverse half the solar system. Annoyed at my own carelessness (why didn't I just sign in earlier and bind the launch procedure to one button?), I gritted my teeth and hoped that the scout had not travelled too far. I really wanted to test *The Space Cucumber* in battle and the scout made for a perfect practice target. The emulator had taught me how to fly but no emulator could prepare you for combat with real players. That kind of experience only came through real battles. The only silver lining I saw was that the scout was at most a D-class and therefore wasn't likely to be equipped with active sensors. In other words, the scout hadn't seen us sitting on our planetoid.

"Let's go," I said nervously and lifted the frigate from the planetoid's surface. As I piloted, I barked orders at myself for the sake of practice: "Bearing 200, thrust at 50%."

"They've seen us," Lestran instantly announced. Indeed, the scout was turning sharply in our direction. According to the forums, the Qualian Emperor had made no mention of *The Space Cucumber* being armed, so everyone basically reckoned us easy prey that, beyond simply being destroyed, could also be boarded and captured. Judging by her actions, the scout had a crew of three—two of whom were about to try to get on board my ship. Well, well…

"Jerks aboard frigate *The Space Cucumber*," said a mocking voice over the ship's comm, "my terms are as follows: Surrender your ship, return the engines and restart the game with new characters. Neither you, Surgeon, nor you, Lestran, have any more business in Galactogon!"

"Greetings to you too, three derps in a scout," I replied, no less mockingly, "I hope you have something fun to do with the time until your next respawn. Our fun will be blasting you to pieces!"

"Yeah? Best of luck with that. Ey, Dora—light 'em up…"

Thrust 100%, bearing 22, roll to portside…As I had assumed, an emulator was one thing and real players who knew how to fly were something else entirely. The idea was supposed to be that we approach one another until our weapons are in range and then trade shots head to head. The scout, however, released two torpedoes at us and then darted sharply upwards. Of course, in space upwards and downwards don't really make sense, so more precisely, the scout turned perpendicular to us, baiting us with his bilge a little too obviously...

"Oh! I'm going to let him have it in his belly!" Lestran chortled, seeing our enemy's maneuver.

"Hold your fire!" I commanded, sensing a trap. My meager experience with flying a ship—all ten minutes of it—was screaming that this was not something one should do. It followed that this was some kind of ruse. "Work on the incoming torpedoes, without using the cannons. That's an order!"

"How am I supposed to knock them out without shooting them?" Lestran asked surprised. "They'll smash our shields to pieces."

"In that case, we'll perform a tactical retreat," I decided, turning the ship sharply around. According to the manual, a torpedo's effective range was 0.1 parsecs, so all we had to do was run for the other end of the solar system."

"Where ya going there guy?" the scout came over the intercom again, as soon as I had turned the frigate and begun to flee the torpedoes. Having engines of their own, the missiles instantly adjusted their trajectory, but their engines were no match for *The Space Cucumber*'s.

"I'm going to a part of the solar system that doesn't stink as much as this one," I said. "I've heard that end there's a pleasant-smelling place."

"Why'd you do that, Surgeon?" asked Lestran. "We

could've destroyed the torpedoes, after all."

"I want to see what *The Space Cucumber* is capable of," I said honestly. "How she behaves during acceleration, how well she maneuvers. For instance, we haven't even pushed these new engines to twenty percent yet. Why not try it out? We should use the chance we have now, before someone a bit scarier shows up and we have more pressing problems to deal with."

"You're waiting for someone scarier?"

"Of course! Surely that scout's already sent our coordinates to his people and there's a frigate just like ours on its way here. I doubt this guild would have a cruiser—but a frigate surely. It took us thirty minutes to get here. Let's play tag with the scout for ten minutes and get down to business after that."

The scout could not have more than four torpedoes on board, two of which were already somewhere out there. I wasn't too worried about the beam cannons. To breach our shields, they would have to shoot at us point blank for several minutes, which obviously I'd never allow. Two more torpedoes, however, did make me nervous, so I went on playing tag. Better safe than sorry, if you ask me.

"Running's no good," smirked the scout, briskly adjusting his course and heading to cut us off.

Bearing 120, thrust at 45%—I adjusted *The Space Cucumber*'s trajectory relative to the chasing torpedoes and scout, leaving them further behind us. If Runlustia had no flying in it, I'd probably be in trouble now—it was very difficult to orient oneself in a three dimensional space. Even two hours in the emulator—during which the system had prompted me with what I needed to press and when, as well as what to look for and what could be ignored—was not enough to get a hang of piloting. Only practice could do that—and a lot of practice at that.

"Okay, I'm a bit puzzled," Lestran spoke up again. "According to the mechanics, our beam cannons are powered by the ship's reactor, meaning we don't have to worry about ammo or anything ...If I were in the scout, I'd already be wondering why we're running instead of trying to knock down their shields."

"Agreed," I replied after a slight pause during which I checked my PDA. Beam cannons would keep on shooting as long as there was power for them, and we had tons of power to spare. "Use the tail turret."

"Roger...though, it's pointless at the moment. We can't knock down those torpedoes—they have their own shields—and shooting at the scout from this range...I'm not that confident in my abilities. Anyway, the tail turret consumes power like no other. I only brought this stuff up so you'd know."

"Then we'll just continue on our way," I reasoned, yawing even further to port and throttling up to 60% thrust. Hmm...This girl was pretty spry—both the scout and the torpedoes quickly fell far behind us.

"And how long are you planning on running scared?" came the mocking voice. "You know, I'm getting tired of this. My dinner's going cold back in real life!"

"Multiple bandits to portside, starboard and straight ahead! They're all around us!" yelled Lestran, seeing what I saw:

Five more scouts jumped out of the depths of space, surrounding us—two high and low on both flanks, and one more ahead of us. No matter what vector we'd take now, at least two scouts could move to intercept us. What could I say? These boys really had played this one well.

"Maybe you're done wasting our time now?" asked the same voice. The torpedoes launched earlier were far behind. The monitor was showing that they had reached the limits of their range so I didn't have to worry about them any longer. But the newcomers were a pressing problem as it was.

"Any ideas?" I asked Lestran, trying to calculate some way out of this mess. Six versus one—not deadly odds, but I still didn't have enough piloting skills to be sure of surviving, much less winning this one. Lestran had no ideas either. "In that case, we'll have to improvise. Here we go!"

The sharp turn made my head spin for a second—the ship's artificial gravity responded perfectly, while the gaming capsule translated the inertia to our frail bodies.

"Hold on!" I warned my companion by rote habit, worked out in Runlustia where you really could fall off a griffon if you didn't hold on. "Once we're within 200 clicks, launch a torpedo and be ready to deflect the two that he still has."

"Roger. I'll let him have it right in his mug!" Lestran answered joyously, feeling the heat of battle.

At 80% thrust, we were simply flattened into our seats. I don't know how Lestran felt about it, but even in my armor, which soaked up the majority of the inertia, I felt extremely

---

uncomfortable. Note for the future—all pilots should be made to wear this sort of gear. For some reason, I hadn't come across this mentioned anywhere, as if it was just assumed by default.

"The hell are you doing, ya jerk?!" the first scout's voice suddenly sounded surprised. The scouts above and below us began to move to help him, but were catastrophically behind—catastrophically for the first scout, that is…

"Fire!" I yelled as soon as the distance between us and the scout reached zero.

"Fox Three away! It's locked on!" Lestran yelped happily, managing his duties despite having to work two stations. "Torpedo inbound, portside. I'll try to deflect it with the shields."

"You're one dead newb…" came over the speakers right before a notification popped up before me:

You have unlocked the "Destroyer Rank I" Achievement. Experience required to level all your vessels has been decreased by 1%.

New level reached: Frigate The Space Cucumber (Class-D) is now Level 78. Durability and power restored by 30%.

"Grab anything you can," I ordered, making another sharp bank and stopping *The Space Cucumber* in the spot where our torpedo had smashed into the scout. Our scanners were now showing wreckage in its place, and that's exactly what I wanted. "You have ten seconds!"

"A repair kit! Got it!" my partner instantly replied. "Allows us to repair 5% of the ship's paintjob. Shall we get out of here?"

"Why?" I smirked. "The game's only beginning...We'll continue in the same vein!"

Bearing 90, thrust to 75% and yaw to portside—which, as the flight instructors advised, allowed you to dodge the majority of beam shots without having to use your shields—and we were already flying headlong into the next scout, approaching us from the right.

"He's belly-flopping again!" This scout jerked up her nose and showed us her bilge, almost begging us to send a torpedo straight into it. A strange maneuver considering that his allies were approaching us from all sides. "Should I fire?"

"No!" I replied again in the negative. Instead, I made another bank, turning the frigate 180 degrees.

"Take it easy!" groaned Lestran when I jacked the engines to 85% power. "You're not transporting potatoes over here!"

"Fire!" I yelled, nearing our pursuers. It seemed that the pilot of the scout behind us had not expected a seemingly ordinary frigate to be so agile and so was late with his belly-flopping maneuver. No sooner had he begun to pitch his nose than there were a mere 200 clicks between us (a click being Galactogon's standard unit of distance). Whatever the point of their fancy maneuver, these guys were already too late.

"Roger that! Fox Three! It's a hit! Crap! Two more torpedoes—incoming from portside. Our shields won't deflect them!"

START THE GAME

"We're leaving." Turning *The Space Cucumber* 90 degrees, I headed away from our pursuers. There was no time to pick up the loot from the second downed scout—there were three ships already within breathing distance from us. Maybe a little latter...Thrust to 70%, bearing 140...

"Shields to stern. Four torpedoes inbound aft—two are fizzling though." Lestran narrated the information scrolling across his screen. "Surgeon! Look!"

My HUD began to pulsate, but I had already spied our next quarry with my own eyes—the scout that had shown us her bilge earlier hadn't managed to adjust in time and had fallen behind the pack. Three ships were chased us as fast as they could and the one that fell behind was trying to intercept us, having launched a torpedo as a screen. She was the next one on the menu then...Even if the belly-flopping was a trap, which I didn't doubt for a second, I wanted to see what the purpose of that strange maneuver was.

Bearing 90, thrust to 80% and off we went!

"I'm hammering the torpedo's shields." I didn't have to explain anything to Lestran—he already understood what I wanted him to do. "Got it! No new torpedoes...He's diving up again! Should we wait?"

"Let him have it all the way," I advised. "I want to know what all the belly-flopping is about!"

An explosion blossomed straight ahead of us and instantly vanished in the vacuum of space—the torpedo that Lestran had hit hadn't lived a long time.

"I've got a lock!" my partner informed me. "Fox Three is away. Contact in five...four...three...two...what in the hell?!"

Indeed, that was the right question and I had to make a note to myself to check out how I could equip *The Space Cucumber* with that thing. As our torpedo neared its target, a hatch slipped open in the scout's bilge and some kind of strange device popped out—and somehow captured our torpedo. The giant missile, equipped with its own shields and engine, enabling it to dodge its target's beam weapons, was suddenly locked down by some kind of force field, which jammed all its functions—even our sensors lost track of the torpedo, as if it had detonated. This was no good. I wasn't about to hang around and keep feeding these scouts with extra munitions.

Thrust 95%, yaw to portside, bearing 90 and *The Space Cucumber* began to zoom away from her pursuers with all her virtual sails. I had no desire to stay and finish them off. I wasn't that experienced yet and it would have been dumb to risk all that raq in our cargo holds. We needed to escape this system before someone even scarier showed up.

"Enough fighting," I explained my maneuver to my partner. "We need to offload the raq and find a homeworld before we start taking risks. Therefore...Oh boy! Lestran, battle stations!"

This last exclamation was intended more for myself, since my partner was already boosting the shields to maximum.

"You said that they wouldn't have a cruiser! Just look at that thing!"

"I was wrong! We have no time to turn—we'll head right

into her! As soon as we get closer, launch the torpedoes! All shields forward! I'm going full throttle!"

My panic was understandable—a leviathan had surfaced from the depths of space to pay us a visit. The cruiser *Dauntless Warrior* was a D-class vessel like *The Space Cucumber* and yet by all indications, she surpassed us exponentially in everything except perhaps speed and maneuverability. It looked like it would be better to just dump the raq and run than to try and fight this humongous, terrifying and deadly vessel—which, appearing not far from us, opened fire without any preliminaries or discussions.

I wondered how many interceptors were in there. According to the manual, giants of her size could carry up to 120 interceptors, 10 harvesters, plus scouts and transports—oh, and about 500 marines to top it all off. I really doubted that this guild could have mobilized so many players (even to avenge the scouts we'd downed) on such short notice, so it was safe to assume that *Dauntless* was operating at half capacity. Or, more likely, a skeleton crew of fifteen players, the minimal amount required to fly her. So we still had a chance to get through, but the last thing I wanted was to tangle with any interceptors at the moment.

"They're going to burn through our shields!" Lestran almost whimpered, watching his screen.

"It'll be okay. We have some powerful engines in this baby. They'll get us through," I replied, trying to thread our ship between the fatal beams of *Dauntless*'s ten nose cannons.

My plan was as simple as it got—fly at full speed right under the hull of the enemy cruiser, launch all our remaining torpedoes (for fun) and then get the heck out of this stupid system—first using our regular engines and after—when we got a minute of peace—by jumping to hyperspace. By the time that giant tub turned herself around and picked up steam again, our trail would have long gone cold.

"Ten torpedoes heading right for us! Damn, I don't have time to both hang the shields and do point defense!"

"Don't worry—if we make it out of here, we'll find us a gunner. Heck, we'll get two! Hang on—we're passing under her hull…"

"No-no-no! Not under her hull!" Lestran screamed wildly, forcing me to reflexively yank the frigate aside.

"Full shields to starboard!" I yelled, realizing that I had just served us up on a plate. The cruiser, however, didn't rush to take advantage of this chance to burn down our starboard. Instead, her bilge flickered, unleashing a larger version of the flea catcher we'd seen earlier. This time, though, we were the flea. Interceptors began to file out of the cruiser along with the device, but this wasn't important anymore: We had already been captured by the flea catcher's force field.

"Frigate *The Space Cucumber*! This is the captain of *Dauntless Warrior* speaking. If you surrender peacefully, we are prepared to allow you to keep ten percent of whatever's in your cargo holds. You have one minute to make your decision. I know that you have no self-destruct mechanism on your ship and I will not allow you to jump to hyperspace. If you do not comply, I will take everything and send you back to your Planetary Spirit. The minute starts now."

"What if we just let him have it with all the torpedoes we have?" I asked my taciturn partner.

"Won't work," Lestran shook his head. "That force field has locked down our systems, including the torpedoes. Even if I took manual control and tried shooting the beam cannons at them, it'd take us two hours to drill through their shields…Damn it! Wasn't it obvious that if their scouts had those capabilities, then the cruiser would have it by default?"

"Alright, alright, don't grumble. Better let's think about how we can get out of this…"

"Surgeon, sir, pardon me, but there simply isn't a way! They've got us right by the scruff…"

"Time's up! What did you decide? Resist our boarding party and die, or surrender your vessel and keep 10% of your cargo."

I could understand the cruiser's captain: To board and capture *The Space Cucumber*, his marines would have to breach her hull, make their way inside, kill us and only then take the ship. Why spend money on repairs, if you could just take her through bargaining? They didn't care one bit about us, after all—only those engine prototypes.

"Alright," I decided. "No point in losing 10% of the cargo, so we…"

"Attention all vessels! Attention all vessels!" A woman's voice burst from the ship's comm, cutting me off. "This is the captain of the cruiser *Alexandria*. I am declaring this system a no-fire zone. If one of you scoundrels shoots, I'll open fire from all batteries. I hope everyone understands that this is no bluff!"

"Kiddo!" exclaimed Lestran almost reverently, hearing the voice of Galactogon's top pirate. An A-class cruiser had popped into our solar system.

"Captain of *Dauntless Warrior*, release...err...release *The Space Cucumber* immediately." Marina's voice came over the intercom again.

"Are you prepared to fight the Cyanide Guild?" responded the captain who had captured us. His tone, however, was not as assured as it had been a minute earlier.

"Is that a declaration of war, Nadeep?"

"No, Marina—we don't want to fight, but we also need that frigate. We deserve a reward for her capture!"

"This ship is mine and I advise you to come to grips with that fact," the girl replied coolly. The two were discussing our fates as if we were some piece of furniture that needed to be arranged in the proper corner. "I need to scan her computer banks."

"So all you're interested in is data?" Nadeep seized the chance of getting his prey after all. "Not the ship herself?"

"What am I going to do with that tub? A D-class frigate with no upgrades—she's an ordinary fleet ship. I don't collect trash. Once I see that there's nothing of interest on the ship, you can have her."

"Along with her contents?"

"Only if she's not stuffed with raq," smirked the girl.

"If they have even a kilo of raq on board," Nadeep's voice

became jovial with relief, "I formally promise to pay those poor fools the official market rate for it and let them keep it to boot! I'm feeling gracious today!"

As his laughter was now echoed by Marina, I could no longer contain myself and asked, "What's the current market rate for raq?"

"Fifty GCs per kilo," replied Nadeep and addressed Marina: "Tell your guys to get ready to latch onto *The Space Cucumber*. I'll be releasing her in thirty seconds."

"Okay. If I don't find anything interesting, you can have her…"

"Guys, guys, before you start plundering my vessel, I'd like to figure out this raq deal," I spoke up again. "My total cargo capacity, as far as I know, is one hundred tons. Half of that—so fifty tons—is pure, unadulterated raq. Now what did you say it costs again?"

The silence over the ether was music to my ears.

"You have fifty tons of raq on board?" Marina inquired carefully.

"Why do you think the Qualians are after us? For the prototypes? Hah! They want their raq back!"

"So you do have the prototypes after all?"

"I do."

"Forgive me, dear Nadeep, but I'll be taking *The Space Cucumber* after all. By the way, who am I speaking to?"

"This is Surgeon," I introduced myself.

"Very well. Surgeon—I will make sure that the Cyanide

Guild will pay you the money they promised. Did you hear that, Nadeep?"

"Who do you think I am to believe any random person I meet? Marina, he's trying to play us off against each other like two kids! How would a ship from the Training Sector have raq on board? Much less fifty tons of it?"

"That's not hard to check," Marina replied. "Surgeon, open you hatch for my interceptor to dock. My officer will check out your claim. Nadeep, you can send one of your own too."

"Of course…"

Two-and-a-half million credits popped into my character's account about ten minutes after the high commission visited my ship. Nadeep showed up in person to get a look at the bastard (that is, me), but I didn't take off my suit of armor, while Lestran prudently hid himself in the cabin. We didn't feel like showing up on anyone's radar too much.

"So how'd you guys get away anyway?" asked Lisp, Kiddo's representative. Marina had sent over such a scrawny player that I was even a little worried about him and wanted to give him something to eat. He looked like one burst of wind would carry him off if he didn't take something heavy with him when he went out.

"That's classified," I shook my head. "Until I've processed it and checked it to my satisfaction, I won't be revealing it to anyone."

"I understand," Lisp nodded approvingly and returned to

his examination of our engines. "Right...Uh-huh...Interesting. Marina, can you hear me? The ship's computer's got nothing—I checked. But these prototypes are really something. My recommendation is we take them and level them up to A-class as soon as possible. Judging by their growth curve, they should make *Alexandria* 35% faster...Yeah, that is a nice little boost...What should I tell these two? Hmm...Are you sure? No, Marina, of course I'm not arguing...Alright, that's what I'll do then."

Lisp screwed up his face, as if he was about to tell us some unpleasant news.

"Alright, here's what's gonna happen," he blurted out. "We're taking your ship and everything on it. You'll be dropped off on the nearest inhabited planet. You have plenty of money now, so I think you'll be okay. Basically, sirs, you need to get off our ship now. Come on, I'll take you to *Alexandria*."

Nice and simple. Fifty tons of raq and the prototypes had piqued the pirates' interest in my *The Space Cucumber*—so now they were kicking us out like some meddlesome kittens. And if you don't like it, that's your problem. I scanned Lisp's armor. It was A-class and equipped with some extra boosters. I understood that messing with him would be a waste of time. He'd smash me to pieces without a second thought. And, after all, I still had no idea where I'd respawn—perhaps, it'd be in the same exact Training Sector we just escaped from so heroically...I really didn't want to find out, so I gritted my teeth and followed Lisp to the shuttle which brought us to *Alexandria*. I could at least be thankful that they hadn't zapped us from the get-go.

"Make yourself comfortable in the guest quarters. We'll reach the Rost System in four hours. That's where you get off. And don't worry—the system is in Confederate space, so you won't be in danger of those Qualian freaks showing up," said Lisp, jumping out of the shuttle and seemingly losing all further interest in us.

Realizing that I wouldn't get much support from Lestran who was already all puppy eyes looking around the ship of his dreams (even though the insides of this cruiser were no different than those of any other), I called Lisp back: "Why freaks? They seem like the most humanoid race out of all the ones in Galactogon..."

"Why freaks? Why, because they're freaks—that's why!" It seemed like this was a sore topic for Lisp. He stopped, turned around and even took a few steps back to us. "When we decided to cross Cyanide, we were thinking that your ship would contain some kind of information that would help us in our struggle against the Qualians. But of course y'all had not a damn thing beside those engines! In the end, all we got for our trouble was beef with a new guild...Eh! What am I wasting my breath on you for!" Lisp cursed, turned and continued on his way.

So they were looking for classified data? And they weren't after just the ship? They had assumed that the ship's computer would hold something that would help them against the Qualians!

"Hold on!" I yelled in his wake. "The ship couldn't have had what you were looking for! What idiot would copy his entire PDA to the ships' computers?"

START THE GAME

"His PDA?" Lisp stopped dead in his tracks and craned back to look at me.

"Hi! Hello! Pleasure to meet you. I think we should chat," I said, starting to feel more in my element. "I'm a reasonable man—commerce is my game."

"On what grounds...WHO ARE YOU?" The nice thing that distinguished Galactogon from other MMOs (Runlustia included) was that you could go back to any moment in the game you'd played and play it back. Moreover, the logging system allowed playback in multiple formats—written, audio and even video. Using this last feature, I projected the events in General Trank's office onto the screen that Marina provided me with. The legendary captain turned out to be a normal girl of average size. She had no distinguishing features—a normal appearance, a normal uniform, a normal voice. Everything about her seemed so average and ordinary that I began wondering how this 5'0" girl with piercing gray eyes had become such a legend among gamers. Though, perhaps those eyes of hers did suggest an answer: Their gaze was so direct that I felt like they were about to jump out and, using little adroit paws, dig into my brain and start rummaging around there for the information they wanted.

"As you see from the video, my PDA contains 77% of the data I tried to download from the Qualians. And, I should mention, parts of this data are classified 'Top Secret.' If I'm not mistaken, this is exactly what you are looking for and the main reason for why the Qualian Emperor declared us enemies of the empire."

"Are the shadow guilds interested in you?" Marina spoke up for the first time. Once again—her voice was as normal as that of millions of women...The more I learned about *Alexandria*'s captain, the more curious I was becoming about how she got where she was.

"Sure, 'interested' is a fair way to put it. I am supposed to meet some guy named Hilvar on the planet Qirlats."

"Oh really..." Marina hummed pensively—and signed out of the game. Lisp and Anton (her executive officer) followed suit. We were left alone with several normal players—perhaps just to make sure that we didn't start pressing random buttons. Although, what buttons are there to press in the guest quarters anyway?

"What do you want in exchange for your information?" The officer corps of *Alexandria* took about thirty minutes to discuss the current situation. During that time, I managed to sign out myself, have a cup of tea and wash up. I also gave Stan a good talking to for providing with me such a crappy emulator, which had featured not a single scenario involving that force field trap thingy.

"Not much," I instantly replied. "You give me my ship back, prototype engines and all. As well as all the raq in its cargo holds. I'll find a way to dispose of that myself. Next, you help us meet Hilvar, and you introduce us to the Corsican. Lestran and I wish to become members of the Jolly Roger Brotherhood. Oh and also, I'd like to have my frigate leveled up from D-78 to C-99."

START THE GAME

"Why not just take *Alexandria* while you're at it?" Anton grumbled, but I ignored his outburst. It was clear that in this company, Marina was the one making the decisions and she had listened to my demands without batting an eyelid. And if she was so impassive, then I could afford to be a bit more brazen.

"*Alexandria* would be too much for me, but I wouldn't say no to four decent players from your database. I'd like to fill my crew and, anyway, you need to develop your potential crew members. But that's just a preference I have—I'll leave it entirely up to you. Coming back to my demands, I have one more. Among the data that I stole from the Training Sector, there's something about a project codenamed KRIEG. I need to relay this information to a certain Precian named Rrgord. I'd like your help finding him and reaching him. As perhaps you understand, my rapport with the Altan Alliance aren't great at the moment..."

"There aren't any off-planet missions in the Training Sector," Marina interrupted me, finally showing some kind of response to my demands.

"There's no raq there either, or a frigate filled with it, or the possibility of dumping a bunch of data and getting off the planet with it. I agree with you—none of this exists or is possible, and yet here I am sitting in front of you. I guess I'm just a phantom..."

"What else?"

"I'd like us to make an alliance..."

"An alliance?" Marina interrupted, surprised. "Pirates don't have allies."

"That's the problem. I have no assurances (and you can't give me any ones I'll accept) that as soon as we get back into our frigate you won't blast us to spacedust. I don't want to fight you. I want to fight with you."

"You have engines that I need for my ship," Marina shrugged. "Once they've been leveled to class-A, they'll provide 35% more power than we have at the moment. Giving them up is off the table. It's too much."

"If it's off the table, what can you give me instead?" I backpedaled, perfectly understanding the captain of *Alexandria*. "How about engines that aren't quite as powerful but still better than the cheap crap that was there by default."

"If we level your frigate to C-class, we'll be able to give you the engines that are currently on *Alexandria*. They're advanced modifications of A-class proton thrusters. They'll let you jump to hyperspace in forty seconds. They're a little weaker than the prototypes on your *The Space Cucumber*, as you call it. Will you be happy with that exchange?"

"Completely," I agreed with the girl.

"Then we move on to the raq. I can't let you go with fifty tons of raq—I'll be laughed out of the game if people find out. I will take 60% of the raq and in exchange provide you with A-class marine armors. And you can consider me onboard with your crew request—you're right, we do need to train our reserves and there's no room on *Alexandria*. We can see how they handle themselves."

Commerce really is my game. Very much so. But for

START THE GAME

Marina, it was more than a game—commerce was just that, commerce. The more I learned about this girl, the more I realized that in Runlustia I would have carried her in my arms, marching happily under her banner. Leaders like her were worth their weight in gold.

"I'll introduce you to Hilvar no problem—he's an ordinary local-intermediary. But meeting the Corsican will present difficulties. Before he agrees to meet with you, you'll have to prove your mettle as a pirate. Hilvar will add to your status in that regard. By the way, why are you interested in the Corsican?"

"A personal mission that has nothing to do with piracy at all. I am looking for a certain bit of information, but you're right: It's better to have positive rapport by the time I do discover it. Hilvar will suffice…What about that Precians then?"

"Well, when it comes to project KRIEG, you've piqued my interest and I'd like to know how you received that assignment. Specifically, I don't want you to tell me how it happened—I want to see how it happened. That's my only condition."

"What can I say…" I had to make up my mind quickly, so I weighed the pros and cons and finally projected the episode in question onto the screen. I was in Galactogon for a specific reason, after all, and this reason had nothing at all to do with the missions I got along the way. I needed to find that planet.

"There's no solitary in the Training Sector," Marina said, sounding less sure already. "How did you get there?"

"Forgive me, Marina, but I was hoping to sell that information. We still haven't decided the issue of allying ourselves—or at least declaring neutrality and non-aggression—and you're already trying to pry this info from me. Keep in mind that I paid for it myself. Maybe I paid for the wrong guide that made no mention of solitary, but I spent real money all the same and not a small amount of it."

"You could have bought information about the tournament," Marina instantly replied. "It's frequently sold to starting players, but solitary...Hang on, we need to talk this over..."

Once again, the three players signed out of the game, leaving us alone with the help.

"Surgeon, why didn't you mention that mission to me?" Lestran instantly inquired.

"Because you and I never had time to talk at any length," I responded. "Remember? First we had to flee, then we were resting and after that came the battle. I simply didn't have time to tell you. It's not like I asked you to leave the room to keep this secret from you now. You're my partner and I want you to know everything that..."

"Oh-oh-oh! Thank you!"

My partner's face flushed with such a sincere smile that I couldn't keep myself from asking, "Listen, maybe it's a dumb and rude question, but...how old are you anyway?"

"Fifteen," blushed Lestran. "I—I graduated three years earlier than my grade. You could say that I'm using you for your recommendation. I still have a year before I go to university. They don't take squirts like me. So I bought myself a Galactogon capsule."

"Got it. So you decided to become a pirate to prove that you can be as bad as your friends?"

"Well…" It seemed like Lestran couldn't blush any further, and yet he did, turning almost purple.

"Okay, I agree!" At this point, Marina returned with her officers. "We will introduce you to Hilvar, help you complete some of his assignments and then you'll earn pirate status. Then we'll be able to enter into an alliance. But my condition stands—I want to know how you found your way into solitary. And I want to know now."

Shrugging my shoulders, I went back to the first moments of my time in the game and projected them onto the screen. If they wanted to see, let them.

"When are you guys online?" I asked my new crew. Like we agreed, Marina had provided me with some players who needed extra training, and thereby filled out *The Space Cucumber*: two gunners named Haggis and Tristan, a shields operator named Wally, a marine named Miloš, Lestran the engineer and me—the captain. The crew of *The Space Cucumber* at your service.

"Twelve hours a day," the newcomers replied practically in unison. I don't know what the girl had told them, but they were behaving as if their future pirate careers hinged on my every word. I had no doubts that at least one of the newcomers would report everything that happened aboard *The Space Cucumber* to the necessary parties, but I took a philosophical view of this fact: If I know ahead of time, I'd nothing to lose. I could safely reckon the four to be planted agents, while Lestran was a deserter, regardless of his age. That would be peace of mind enough for me.

"Excellent. Repairs to our ship will be complete in about an hour. Who has any suggestions for upgrades?"

"Is there enough money?" Haggis said offhand. "We can replace two of the beamers with electromagnetic cannons. That'll let us deal with shields a little better. But luxuries like that don't come cheap. We can also install a flycatcher…"

"A what?"

"A lockdown generator. A device that'll let us capture torpedoes and small enemy ships. It's a nice little gizmo when you're fighting one-on-one, but it costs as much as…Well, it's only a matter of money, really. Finding a use for it won't be a problem."

"Well then we'll see how much you flycatcher and the EM cannons cost once we get to Qirlats. Miloš, do you have an armor suit?"

"Class-A, Level 2. There's an armorer aboard *Alexandria* who can hammer out suits nonstop. Marina gives them out to anyone she deems worthy."

Making a mental note that the marine on my crew was a special one, I turned to the player who was to manage the shields station.

"What do you say, Wally? What do we need to change to

make our game go better?"

"You want me to be honest?" smirked Wally. "Or do you want me to tell you what you want to hear?"

"Let's do honesty. What's the point of listening to idle praises? I can sing them myself."

"Speaking honestly, this isn't a ship. It's more of a newb-level tub. The only thing worth anything here were the engines. But those are gone now too. Sure, we've got upgraded A-class engines on the frigate now, and that's more than enough—but all you have to do is recall what it was like flying with the B-class prototypes. I had time to look at the video of how you did, so…The ship's reactor requires only one thing—we need to take it and scrap it. The outboard sensors need to be modified—any interceptor can knock them out and then we'll be dead in the water. The ship computers were fatally out of date last year already. They need to be updated as well…I won't even say anything about the backup feed circuit and the electrical system in general. We need to deal with those first of all. The reactor needs a second shielded circuit, which simply isn't there at the moment…Damn—there's an ungodly amount of work here! My estimate is that the cost of the upgrades will come in at around eight hundred grand, no less."

"Is that including Haggis's suggested armaments, or just what you need?" I asked discouraged. When I stole the frigate I had no idea that it was so insufficient. I was even surprised that we had managed to knock out those two scouts.

"No, that's just what I'd need. Don't know much about

cannons, but I'd guess that they'd come in at three hundred as well."

"Five-twenty," Haggis butted in, "and that's without the flycatcher and with Marina putting in a good word for us. The locals want crazy prices for A-class equipment."

"And so," I summarized, "in order for you to stop thinking of *The Space Cucumber* as a tub, we need to spend 1.3 million GCs on upgrades?"

"Well…" Lestran spoke up. "Since everyone's getting presents here, I'd like to add that I need a new repair bay. More precisely, I need one in general. The ship doesn't have one at the moment. We're at C-class with 6 free slots for various toys. We can spare one for repairs. Then we'll be able to survive a direct torpedo hit, for example. How much it costs though, I have no idea."

"I looked at the torpedoes," Tristan threw in his word. It looked like the whole crew were out for blood. "We might as well launch them all at the closest star and walk away happy that it has more fuel to stoke its fires. Currently, we're equipped with low quality, underpowered and easily destroyed dummies. I'm amazed that you managed to kill those scouts with them. If we change the auto-loading system and the torpedoes, we'll be able to increase our firepower by two or three times and increase our torpedo capacity to forty without having to reconfigure the ship."

"In that case, along with the EM cannons, I'd upgrade the tail turret too," Haggis spoke up again. "Since, honestly, we'll find ourselves running away pretty often."

START THE GAME

The only player who was perfectly happy with my ship was Miloš, since the marine armor and blasters were entirely his own. Typically, a frigate carries a space marine for only one reason—to board an enemy vessel, so all of Miloš's equipment was entirely his own.

Having put together the list of my crew's needs, I raised my eyebrows in astonishment. The estimate that the boys had given me, including cost of labor, amounted to two million credits. After taking her 60% cut of the raq, Marina had bought the other 40% that I had, paying me the market rate for this resource. As a result, I had the money on hand, but when it came to spending it on ship upgrades…Galactogon really was a dreadful drain on the family budget.

"Alright, it's decided. We're getting the upgrades," I concluded, barely believing the words coming out of my own mouth. "In a few hours we'll be landing on Qirlats. We'll take a day's break. Everyone fixes everything that he deems necessary, while staying within the budget." I assigned each crew member a limit on what he could spend. "We'll reconvene exactly 24 hours after landfall and take off to see what we've made of *The Space Cucumber*. We'll have to work hard to get that money back…"

CHAPTER FIVE

MEETING HILVAR AND THE FIRST MISSIONS

In actual fact, everything turned out much better than any of us had imagined. In the process of leveling out frigate to C-class, Marina did something no *Galactogon* player had ever done before—she became our patron of sorts.

"Surgeon, the Captain wants a word with you." About an hour after our crew meeting, one of *Alexandria*'s crew approached me. "Come with me, I'll take you to her."

Instead being taken to the captain's deck as I had expected, I was brought to the cruiser's repair hangar where the repairs to *The Space Cucumber* were underway. Marina was standing several steps from frigate, which glimmered and distorted in the force field surrounding it. She was carefully listening to her engineer who was explaining something to her animatedly.

"I've never heard of a player escaping from the Training Sector before," said the captain of *Alexandria* without even looking at me, "so I will consider you to be the first. I was quite pleased that you didn't act like some princess and start bargaining for every byte of the data. And since the contents of your PDA are invaluable, I've decided to make you a present. Here it is!"

The force field vanished, relinquishing *The Space Cucumber* to my sight.

"Please forgive me, but a frigate outfitted with its stock equipment is a very sorry thing indeed. When I mentioned that I wasn't into collecting garbage, I wasn't equivocating one bit. Your *The Space Cucumber* was just a heap of scrap, but now…Obviously she has plenty of room for improvement—but that's your problem now. If we're going to be allies, I'd prefer not to lose you to the first bandit that comes along."

While Marina was explaining the reasons for her patronage, I plugged my PDA into the onboard computer and tried my best to contain my excitement: a class-A reactor; two class-A EM cannons in the bow and one more in the stern; a brand new torpedo autoloader, including the torpedoes themselves; an upgraded computer; an upgraded life support system; an upgraded…

I got the impression that not a single piece of the old *The Space Cucumber* remained on board this ship—except for her name of course. Even the hull had been worked on—Marina's engineers had mounted absorbers along its length, allowing us to take a hit from a beam weapon in the event that an EM cannon had knocked out our shields.

"This is must have cost so..." I stuttered, trying to skirt any talk of money. But Marina read my mind.

"According to my people, the upgrades cost us seven million. A brand new frigate costs about seventeen. Don't make that face. Besides the cost of labor to upgrade this stuff, I didn't spend a single credit. A pirate with a big ship is a lucrative occupation, especially when it comes to collecting various metal scrap...though, that's not true. I had to spend money on increasing her class and leveling her—but that was a reasonable expenditure, given the info you gave us. While we were at it, we managed to offload some of our cargo. I don't keep frigates in my service but I just can't bring myself to throw away or sell even useless equipment. I think, we can say we're even now, you and I."

"We sure are," I muttered, abashed. "I'm not even sure that I'll be able to avoid being in your debt now..."

"Anything's possible," Marina smiled. "And consider changing her name. Ship names aren't supposed include definite articles, you know. Alright, enjoy her, I'm off..."

"Wait," I stopped the girl and, as if deciding to show all my cards, added, "that wasn't everything that we stole from the Training Sector."

"Not everything?"

"Nope. There's another thing." Opening my inventory, I produced the safe I tore from the general's office and placed in my journeyman's satchel. "With all due respect, I don't like being in anyone's debt."

"Lisp, I need you down here at the frigate ASAP!" Marina instantly barked into her comm unit, transfixed by the safe. "Where'd you get it," she asked, barely managing her emotions.

"The general's office. I'll tell you right off the bat—I have no idea what's in it. Could even be a bomb. So…"

"D'you call me, Cap?" Lisp appeared beside us.

"Yes. Your next assignment is right there." The girl nodded at the safe. "Put on some class-A protection and get to work. I don't want the ship damaged."

"Five seconds," said Lisp, squatting down by the safe. "Huh! Where'd you find this antique?"

"Antique?" I echoed surprised.

"Uh-huh. Safes with mechanical locks were released in *Galactogon* only during the first few years. After that, they switched to electronic locks…Cap, we'll need a bit more than five minutes here. I'd even venture to ask for an hour."

"Do what you have to," Marina nodded in confirmation. "Surgeon, you'll have to forgive me, but you and your crew will have to remain on board my ship for a little while longer. I want to know what's inside the safe."

We ended up having to wait six hours.

As soon as the door fell off (there were no booby traps thankfully), Marina invited me to be the first to see what was inside the opened safe. I was its lawful owner, after all. Inside, I saw five sheets of paper covered with a crooked Qualian scribble.

It was the first time I'd seen handwriting in a game—even in *Runlustia*, a medieval game, the Emperor's edicts were printed with special typewriters. In the futuristic world of *Galactogon*, on the other hand, finding a handwritten text was like finding a trespassing mammoth in the jungles of the Amazon.

I passed the sheet to Marina, who became absorbed in reading it, while all I could do was sigh plaintively—having no knowledge of Qualian, the document may as well have been Chinese to me.

"Anton, I need you in the repair hangar ASAP," the girl said into her comm. It took Marina about five minutes to read one of the sheets, shake her head in puzzlement, reread it again, curse, read it a third time and call her XO.

"What do you think?" she asked the player when he appeared.

"That's impossible..." muttered Anton, having read the text. "It's simply not possible!"

"I'm of the same mind. Surgeon, could you tell us please how you got this safe?"

Shrugging my shoulders, I selected another part of my logs, approached the closest screen and began to transmit my ransacking of General Trank's office. Based on how things were going, Marina should have just asked me for all of my logs dating back to the beginning of my time in *Galactogon*.

"Hmm," said Anton as soon as the video ended, "looks like greed's no sin after all."

"You can say that again. Lisp!" Marina turned to her

engineer, who was fiddling with some equipment beside my ship. "I'm convening an emergency officers meeting! You have thirty minutes."

"This is all very wonderful," I said, placing the other four sheets of the general's scribbles back in my inventory. Unlike items that were equipped on a player, it was impossible to take something from his personal inventory without his permission. *Galactogon*'s developers had made this tiny concession to the preservation of property rights. "Only, we still haven't determined how much these papers are worth."

"You can't be..." the girl began but instantly cut herself off, thinking better of it. "Okay, what do you want?"

"At the moment, I do not want anything. My ship, I can see, has been upgraded. I've got money too. I guess all I need is information. A leg up in the piracy business. I'd like to know how to best build my career in piracy: whom to target, whom to befriend and whom to avoid. Which clans or guilds are trustworthy and approachable and which ones will try to kill a pirate on sight. You're not the only one who needs information, you see."

"Why are you in *Galactogon*?" Marina suddenly asked.

"Not for the fun of it—believe me. I have a certain private purpose and the more highly-placed the locals I interact with, the closer I'll be to it. Is it a deal?"

"Deal," the girl agreed. "You'll get the info you want."

"Marina?" Anton asked with surprise.

"I've made my decision! Surgeon reminded me of the time when...Never mind, forget it. It's in the past! Everyone start getting ready. We're going to Qirlats."

If flying through deep space could evoke a feeling of unlimited freedom, then landing on a planet offered nothing but a couple of gray hairs. Like all cruisers, *Alexandria* was not designed for planetary descents, so my crew and I made the landing in *The Space Cucumber*. Initially, I had a few moments to marvel at the beauty of the fully urbanized planet beneath us, which appeared to be basically one enormous city. The more we descended, however, the more I had to focus on controlling our craft.

The air traffic controller's banter was a particularly nice detail:

"Come in *The Space Cucumber*, bearing 10, berth 336, we'll bring you in...Change of plans, *The Space Cucumber*. set bearing to 27, berth 8225...*The Space Cucumber*, your approach has been altered again, set bearing to 443, berth 2201, we'll bring you in..."

Marina and her shuttle plummeted off far below us, whereas I (as a newcomer to the planet) had to dart endlessly from one side of the planet to the other, relying on ATC's instructions and the landing guide beam that my ship was following. Interceptors, frigates, shuttles and scouts whizzed all around us. I felt like we had found our way into a great swarm and the slightest mistake would lead to *The Space Cucumber*'s destruction. I'd never wish such a landing on anyone.

"Purpose of your stay on Qirlats?" No sooner had we

---

settled in our berth than three locals approached our ship. Introducing themselves as customs agents, they scanned the ship from her nose to her tail in search of any contraband. Once they had determined that we were clean, the customs agents began to ask us questions.

"A meeting with Hilvar," I replied. Marina had told me right away that on this planet everything that a player did was scrupulously recorded and thus affected his Rapport with the authorities. Accordingly, she advised that we conduct ourselves as honestly as possible. Although Qirlats enjoyed the status of a neutral state that was a member of the Confederation, in actual fact, this was one of the resupply bases for *Galactogon*'s pirates—both the official and the unaffiliated ones. The important thing was not to bring in any contraband and to pay your customs duties.

"The berthing fee is one thousand credits a day. Your minimum stay must be two days. The invoice has been sent to your PDA," said one of the customs agents, after which we left the ship and emerged into the city.

"Where'd they put you?" Marina asked, as soon as I called her comm.

"Berth 2201."

"Stay there. We'll come for you in a second."

As the forums helpfully informed me, until the time when my Rapport with the planet's locals reached 100, the Qirlatsi authorities would treat me accordingly—I could expect peripheral public berths, constant jerking around during landing and customs inspections. Such were the rules throughout all the planets of the Confederacy. Those who wished to get away from the main in-game empires, just have to live with it. However, once you completed a hundred or so missions, the situation would change drastically and you would begin to feel loved and wanted. Just like in the real world.

"Allow me to express my veneration for the great captain," said a blue-skinned Precian pirate, all but prostrating himself on the floor before us. Marina had brought us to a small and inconspicuous building that resembled a barn but was actually the center of the planet's administration. The unofficial one, that is. Passing through the main entrance, we found ourselves in an enormous space without any barriers. Dim light chined through the few dirty windows, barely illuminating the floor and having no effect whatsoever on the gloom beneath the ceiling. "What brings the right hand of the Corsican to our planet?"

"I need to see Hilvar," said the girl, completely ignoring the Precian rolling around at her feet. She was looking somewhere ceilingward, as if that was where the local boss was.

"What does the Corsican wish with Hilvar?" inquired a creaky voice. The gloom at the ceiling began to roil with something. My suit's motion sensors outlined a barrel-shaped silhouette of a torso. Then my infrared sensors kicked in and I made out the five foot tall body of a Precian. He held a piece of

---

fried meat that resembled a chicken leg in one hand and was aiming a blaster at us with his other hand. Despite the fact that it would take a minute for a C-class blaster to penetrate an A-class suit of marine armor—a length of time sufficient for us to kill everything in a hundred yard radius—finding oneself facing the business end of a blaster did not feel like a warm welcome.

"Relax, Hilvar," smirked Marina. "I am here only as a go-between. Geez, by the time anyone even gets to you, they'll have thought better of being a pirate three hundred times. My job is to introduce you to Surgeon and his people. After that, I'll wash my hands of this whole thing. There is nothing of interest to me on this planet."

Having said that, Marina turned to me and added, "Once you become a pirate, I will be happy to welcome you on board my ship as an independent attaché. Our plans for an alliance between our ships remain standing. You'll get the information you requested tomorrow—it only needs to be collated into one file. How about that document from the safe, then?"

"Here," I got the sheets from my inventory and handed them to the captain of *Alexandria*. I had made sure to make copies of them earlier. "Don't forget about that Precian."

"My people are looking for him already," replied Marina, placing the papers in her inventory. "Give me your comm number. Once I get the information, I'll call you. And don't hesitate to call me if you stumble on something interesting. Do you know what I mean?"

"It's hard not to," I smiled as she entered my number into

her PDA. I made a mental note of adding my crew's comm numbers too. For some reason I hadn't thought of that. These things had been much simpler in *Runlustia*.

"In that case, best of luck to you!" Marina and her three bodyguards turned around and left us alone with Hilvar who had been patiently waiting for the players to finish their conversation. Convenient thing that—and one that's implemented in all games: You never see NPCs whine about how we're wasting their time and how they have better things to do than to stand around while we jabber on. I wish real life were like that.

"So it is you who wishes to see Hilvar?" the Precian addressed me. "With Marina's help, I see you've skipped all the preliminaries. Now here you are. What do you want?"

"I want to become a mighty pirate," I replied, not discouraged that Hilvar wasn't exactly welcoming me with open arms. "I escaped the Training Sector, stealing a frigate in the process, and then got into a battle with some scouts who gave chase to us. That's how I met Marina. She helped me get here, skipping, as you pointed out, all the typical barriers."

"So you want to be a pirate?" creaked Hilvar, pensively scratching his jaw. "I heard of your escape, yup, heard of it I did. But of course, destroying a couple scouts with a frigate is no great feat. Escaping the Sector, sure—that makes you interesting enough for me to give you audience. But scouts…downing a few scouts is nothing to brag about around here."

"How many then do I need to kill to attract your interest?" I asked, understanding what the Precian was getting at.

START THE GAME

"Two cruisers, or ten frigates, or thirty scouts." Hilvar rubbed his hands murderously. "Doesn't matter which Alliance they belong to—only the killcount matters. Even other pirates are fair game. Once you can prove your mettle, we can talk about the other things, yes we can. My assistant will take you to the Spirit—I can see that you still haven't chosen a homeplanet. As a sign of good will, I will pay for your binding procedure—for a future pirate brethren, so to say…Gamadan!" the Precian yelled into the depths of the building. "Take Surgeon to the Spirit!"

The first Anorxian I'd ever seen emerged from the depths of the building: a robot that floated lightly in the air despite his great weight. How this creature managed to move horizontally remained a great mystery, since he did not seem to be equipped with engines or propellers or any other similar methods of conveyance. I made a note to read more about this wondrous race.

"Please follow me," Gamadan said in a metallic voice, flitting freely among me and my crew. "The Spirit of Qirlats resides in the neighboring building."

"Is there really no other way?" I managed to ask Hilvar before he rose too high to hear me. "Is the spirit of space piracy really just destroying ships? Doesn't *Galactogon* have hidden treasures, unplumbed mysteries or at least pirate hunters to kill? Does the whole point of piracy really come down to destroying ordinary ships?"

Hilvar froze in his ascent. Having hung in the air for about ten seconds, he slowly turned around to face us, without descending however.

"Treasures?" he almost hissed, turning into one giant lump of anger. What had I said to elicit such a reaction? "Unplumbed mysteries? You think that just because you've wheedled an audience with me, you've grabbed a god by his beard? You are no one—you have no name! I hereby double the required killcount for your ship. Now you have to destroy twice as many ships as before."

"I'll destroy five times as many ships as you originally assigned," I said, drawing a gasp from my crew, "but you'll give me an extra mission. I don't care what it entails—treasures, mysteries, pirate hunters—as long as it falls into the spirit of our brotherhood."

"YOU ARE NO BROTHER TO US!" roared Hilvar and instantly appeared right before me, his blaster pointed at my head.

"I'm no sister to you either!" I replied, drawing my own blaster in the blink of an eye and pointing it at Hilvar. The space around us began to roil—columns rose upward bearing formidable cannons, robots appeared from nowhere, taking aim at us. A force field flashed to life around Hilvar, separating him from his enemies—but, since my blaster was flush with his forehead, I found myself inside of it as well. A pretty uncommon NPC, this one. I'd never have thought that a simple conversation could have turned into such a crisis. I didn't doubt for a second that I was doing the right thing—the logic of the conversation had brought me to this point, not my personal ambitions, so I knew that I was acting within the rules of the scenario. I wish I knew what those rules were though. "If you're not willing to treat me like a brother, I propose you think of me as a distant relative from Brazil, where there are many three-headed monkeys!"

"Where is this planet Brazil?" asked Hilvar, frowning and momentarily forgetting his anger. "And what is a monkey?"

"Forget it. Look, Hilvar—I just don't understand why you're so irate," I said, without lowering my blaster from the Precian's face. "I'm sure that you have nothing to gain from me destroying a bunch of the alliances' ships. That's too simple. I'd like a bigger challenge. But your reaction surprises me. Let's start again—my name is Surgeon and I want to become a mighty pirate. Will you help me or not? Here, I'm putting my blaster away."

Carefully, without any extra movements, I moved my weapon away from Hilvar, noting in the process that my crew was already strewn about the floor, overpowered by some energy net against which even Marina's A-class armor could do no good.

"Ten cruisers or fifty frigates or 150 scouts," the Precian said calmly, accepting my offer of a fivefold increase in the killcount and lowering his blaster as well. "That is the mandatory requirement for receiving a pirate's patent. As soon as you get it, you may go meet your Corsican."

"He's not mine and I have nothing to do with him," I parried. It seemed that there was some kind of trouble between Hilvar and the Pirate King. Our appearance in Marina's company had spoiled Hilvar's attitude to us somehow. I wondered whether the girl had known about this or not. "I met Marina in space, helped her and she helped me in exchange—to meet you, that is. I don't know who the Corsican is or how I'm supposedly related to him. I doubt very much that he's even ever heard of me."

"He's not lying, boss," came Gamadan's metallic voice. "In any case, he believes what he says."

"So you aren't one of the Corsican's men?" asked Hilvar, narrowing his eyes incredulously. "What about your people there?"

"I'm not willing to vouch for them right this moment," I replied, shrugging. "Marina gave me four of them and I haven't checked their backgrounds. The fifth one, Lestran, is someone I trust completely. But you'll deal with me, not with them." I bent down to the Precian and whispered, "My crew doesn't have to know anything about the business between you and me."

"You mean—if there will be any business between you and me," Hilvar whispered back and moved aside. "I need time to consider your proposal, Surgeon. I won't change the killcount requirement. You'll get your pirate's patent only after you've provided evidence of having destroyed the required number of enemy ships. As for additional missions, I do have a small task for you. If you manage it, we'll talk further. I need you to go to the planet Daphark and locate a local named Tryd. Give him this envelope and do the missions that he gives you. After that, come back to me and we'll discuss any further business we may have. Go on—you need to bind yourself to the Planetary Spirit. Release his men!"

START THE GAME

Your Rapport with Hilvar has improved. Current Rapport: 3.

The two bettors, the president and the mogul, had claimed that only a few locals knew where the planet with the check was located. For some reason, I had decided that the Corsican would be one of them. However, the current situation suggested that the pirates had some bad blood between them. Maybe I would meet the Pirate King in some distant future, but Hilvar could help me here and now. My opinion, therefore, was that I needed to exploit this relationship to its utmost.

Unlike the Qirlats' shadow administration, the abode of its Planetary Spirit corresponded to its status. The whiskered sentries alone, armed with pike, suggested plenty. Wearing steel, A-class cuirasses, they were holding a fairly whimsical variation on a blaster, disguised as a pike, in their hands. Each of the sentries was also surrounded by a personal force field, which offered slightly better protection than mere armor. Meanwhile, the proud and independent looks on their faces spoke to their happiness with their work. Even locals, after all, were capable of affecting negative emotions. Nothing of the kind, however, was to be seen on the sentries' faces.

"State the purpose of your visit," one of the sentries said in a deep voice, obstructing my way with his pike's spearhead.

"They come to bind themselves to this planet," replied Gamadan for me. "We wish to bring these six adventurers to the Spirit. Hilvar has offered to pay their fees."

"You may pass," the pikes moved aside, granting us passage.

"You must go on by yourselves now," Gamadan said. "Only newcomers are allowed to see the Spirit."

The procedure of binding ourselves to our new homeworld turned out to be both interesting and boring. We entered a large auditorium, about thirty yards in diameter, most of which was occupied by a hovering and transparent sphere about ten yards in diameter. A thin thread or tentacle coiled out towards each player. As soon as it touched him, a message appeared asking whether we wished Qirlats to become our new homeworld. I pushed the "Accept" button and received the following notification:

You have unlocked the "Homeworld Sweet Homeworld" Achievement. Future binding fees decreased by 5%.

From here on out, Qirlats would be my home...

"Ten cruisers?" exclaimed Lestran as soon as we returned to our ship. I had to hand it to my crew: While the negotiations were underway and after, during our binding, no one had said a single thing about what had happened. Now, however, left on our own, the people began to revolt. The first, unsurprisingly, was Lestran: "Maybe we should just reset right now?"

"Considering what *The Space Cucumber* has become, I see nothing impossible in getting that killcount," said Wally. "But I do have one issue—I won't fight Marina. If that Hilvar turns out to be an enemy of the Corsican and consequently, of Marina, then I'll have to pass right now."

"Me too."

"And me!"

All four of my hired guns had their say. Then Wally spoke up again: "I understand that you see us all as Kiddo's men, but we'd be better off discussing what our plans are while we're still ashore."

"That's fair," I nodded. "I suggest the following: Until tomorrow, we'll say that you are all still *The Space Cucumber*'s crew. Later today I'll discuss the situation with Marina. If she has no objections to some of us having positive Rapport with Hilvar and perhaps negative ones with the Corsican, then you all stay. Otherwise, you can return to her. Forcing anyone against their will is the last thing I want. Furthermore, I still want you to look over the ship to see what other improvements can be made, considering her current condition. My proposed budget for upgrades remains the same."

"Surgeon, let's decide on a schedule then," Haggis spoke up. "What time do we sign in, what time do we sign out, how many times a week, what our days off are and what our salaries will be? I don't want to play this thing 24/7, 365. We need time to rest too—especially since many of us have families."

"Salary?" I asked astonished, hearing a word I'd never expected a gamer to utter (or, rather, a word that was rare for a gamer wishing to prove himself). "Guys, I have no money to pay you with. You can have any loot we get from piracy…but a salary? Why do you want a salary all of a sudden?"

"Because, if things don't work out, there won't even be any loot," Miloš replied. "You call all the shots, but we're the ones that have to do the grunt work. In my last guild I got twenty thousand GCs a month, which were taken out of my loot. In a good month, no one even saw my salary. But if the captain went off into reality, I'd be sure to get some kind of compensation. It's only fair that way."

"So twenty thousand credits a month will be enough for everyone?" I looked at my crew, waiting for a response. In theory, there was some sense to what Miloš was saying, and I actually wholly agreed with it. But the amount astonished me—a mere twenty thousand. That's a pittance for a *Galactogon* player. The planetary binding alone would have cost us thirty grand each if Hilvar hadn't covered it. It wasn't super profitable to change one's homeworld.

"Sure," Tristan, who had stayed quiet until now, nodded his assent. "Twenty is a standard salary for a soldier. It doesn't make sense to pay more. Or less. What about the work schedule?"

"Five days a week. From 9 a.m. to 6 p.m., with a break for lunch. If we need to linger in-game to finish something, then you'll get one-and-a-half times your share of loot. We'll try to resolve any issues during working hours. Mondays and Tuesdays will be our days off, since that's when the least number of players are online anyway."

START THE GAME

"That'll do," decided Wally. "I'm down. Figure out the Corsican thing with Marina and then we can get on with some cosmic buccaneering."

"We'll meet tomorrow at ten then." As soon as all five of the players agreed to the schedule and we signed some preliminary contracts, stipulating the chief terms of their employment, I leaned back wearily in my chair and pushed the "Sign Out" button. Before that, I had spoken with Marina and received her assurances that our Rapport with various locals wouldn't affect her and the Corsican in the least—so we could work with Hilvar as much as our hearts desired. The important thing to keep in mind, she said, was to make sure that the head of the Jolly Roger didn't see me as an enemy. In that case, any alliance between *The Space Cucumber* and *Alexandria* would become impossible. While she was at it, Marina also asked me to send her the video of our negotiations, since Hilvar's negative attitude toward her boss struck her as extremely surprising. I had to say no, however, because if Hilvar found out, then all my efforts would have been in vain. I thought I'd sounded convincing enough, though I could feel Marina's displeasure over the comm.

"Greetings Master," Stan offered his standard greeting as soon as the cocoon's lid slid aside. "Shower, mail, dinner?" added my smart home, reciting his standard script.

"All of the above," I slipped out of the cocoon, stretching wearily. "I need you to find me everything there is about an NPC named Hilvar. I want to know all there is to know about him. What'd you find out about Rrgord?"

"Unfortunately, there is no information about this individual. My analysis of other search requests on the forums yields a probability of 80% that this NPC has been added recently to the game as part of some new mission sequence. He seems to be some kind of secret agent who goes by several names."

"Got it. What's going on out here? Any news of note? Read me the newsfeed."

"Protests and civil disobedience stemming from the termination of *RunIustia* have seen the game's former players express their unhappiness with its termination. *Galactogon*'s stock has grown by 10% and continues to maintain a steady growth. The authorities are investigating the death of one of *Galactogon*'s best players, after he flew his flyer into the Mayor's office. The day after tomorrow, the band Meathook is scheduled to play a concert in…"

"More about the previous story," I interrupted Stan's report, wondering why a *Galactogon* player would suddenly die IRL.

"According to law enforcement sources, John Levin, the head of the Zarathustra Guild, crashed his flyer into the Mayor's office. Considering that this gamer was one of the first flyer pilots and had been involved in developing flyer training software (some of which you yourself have used), the circumstances of his death have raised suspicions. The Gard-Series flyer, which Mr. Levin had been piloting, was equipped with an active collision avoidance system, making even willful collisions impossible. The former leader of Zarathustra managed to do so nonetheless. One circumstance stands out: According to law enforcement, Mr. Levin had recently relinquished his position as guild leader to his deputy and made an entirely new character in *Galactogon*, returning to the Training Sector to start from nothing. All of the Rapport he had accumulated was wiped clean. Investigators believe that the cause of Mr. Levin's death was a dispute involving the deputy's unwillingness to return his position to Mr. Levin. The investigation is currently still ongoing with…"

"That's enough," I said, succumbing to gloomy thoughts. John Levin—a gamer of immense experience and enviable connections with the powerful of this world—had suddenly decided to start *Galactogon* from scratch. You don't make a choice like that because you're in a bad mood or just had some stupid argument with someone. Obviously, John had a reason that he could not say no to…like one billion pounds sterling! That had to be it. John had been one of the twelve sent into *Galactogon* by the betting Masters. My chances of getting that check had just grown by a twelfth…Damn! What was I thinking about? Someone had killed John! I had flown a Gard flyer enough to know that even if you wanted to ram the thing into a wall, its configuration would stop you. All aspects of the flyer's safety mechanisms had been considered thoroughly.

So he had been murdered. Now I needed to know the reason—was this really an internal squabble within Zarathustra or a deliberate assassination of one of the gamers in search of the check.

"Stan, search request: I need any information you can find

about *Galactogon* players who have reset their characters in the past month. If all twelve started simultaneously, then their previous characters would've been deleted that same day. Any public sources, forums, social media and anything else you come across. I need lists of people."

"Understood. Will there be any further instructions?"

"Yes. Find me two former *Draanmir* players, IRL names: Constantine and Eunice. Both started playing *Galactogon* the same time I did. You can find their pics on my phone. What's the status of panic mode?"

"Panic mode is still in effect. There have been three attacks over the past 24 hours, two decoy VMs have been breached and ransacked. After gaining access to the system, one of the attackers made some poor choices, seemingly having decided that the system was entirely his; this gave me time to trace the attack vector back to its origin. This yielded a residential address belonging to a Dan Cormack, the guild leader of the Black Lightning, as you are already aware. Will there be any further instructions? I advise you to lodge a formal complaint with law enforcement, while requesting to remain anonymous."

"Agreed," I replied after a little thought. If any Qualian scum (even if one born here IRL) had decided to break into my system, he deserved to have his fingers broken. I didn't like doing that kind of thing myself, but I was acquainted with several wonderful fellas who would jump at the chance to dig around some hacker's system. Best of luck to you, Dan Cormack.

Stan had finished his biography of Hilvar by this time, so I began to study it.

He was a local of the Pyrrhenian race. The first stop for any player wishing to become a pirate in *Galactogon*. Even if the player never made it into the Jolly Roger, he'd still have to deal with Hilvar. Planet of residence: Qirlats. Missions types: messenger, ship destroyer and local abduction. Upon reaching a Rapport of 20, Hilvar would send the player to the headquarters of the Jolly Roger where—I didn't need to know that yet. What else was there about Hilvar? One of the cofounders (along with the Corsican) of the official pirate guild of *Galactogon*, the Brotherhood of the Jolly Roger. Left his leadership role several years before the game's beginning to become the first obstacle that players who wish to join the shadow guilds of *Galactogon* encounter. It fell to Hilvar to determine who would become a pirate and who wouldn't. The Corsican's former right-hand man.

Ho-hum…

The bad blood between Hilvar and the Corsican was turning out to be a river. There was no other way to explain his visceral reaction to seeing Marina. Moreover, it was safe to assume that Marina had grasped this perfectly. It would have been dangerous to underestimate the intelligence of *Alexandria*'s captain. Consequently, the Corsican was well aware of Hilvar's dislike of him and yet allowed him to maintain his position as first recruiter. Why?

"Stan-my-man, I've got another assignment for you." Realizing that I needed to know more, I turned to my chief researcher. "Dig up anything, even if it's gossip, about the relationship between Hilvar and the Corsican. And dig around in *Galactogon* lore. Maybe there'll be something worthwhile in there."

"Understood," reported my smart home. "Your criminal complaint has been submitted to the proper authorities and you have been issued a case number. I have preliminary search results concerning players who began their characters the same day you did. Currently this list includes 382 people from every part of the globe. Shall I filter these results for our country?"

"No, I'll need all of them," I replied, understanding perfectly well that the betting Masters could have found players from anywhere. "Could you tell me please about the search algorithm?"

"Forum posts referring to a newly created character, personal websites, public requests to tech support."

"Am I on the list?"

"No, I have been unable to find any mention of you."

"Cancel that search then. There's no sense in looking for competitors that way. Just to make sure—is John Levin on the list?"

"No, this player was not identified during my analysis."

"Got it...Prioritize collecting information about piracy and finding Eunice and Constantine. Limit that search to our country. They had no accents. Anyway, get to it...Wait!" A thought had suddenly come to me. "Replay my vidcall with Cormack."

"...I'm guessing you sent your requests not just to us, but

START THE GAME

to all the other Qualian guilds as well—so you may be sure that
Sergei Smolyanov is already well aware of your vidphone number
and email. That bit of info is free by the way. If he weren't such a
jerk—and from an enemy empire besides—I would absolutely be
on board with his whole secrecy thing. A hundred thousand
dollars is a very big sum, after all..."

"Stan, get me a bio of Sergei Smolyanov as soon as you
can: who he is, where he's from, where he's going and why.
That's highest priority. Everything else is secondary. I need that
done by tomorrow morning."

That night, however, sleep took a long time coming. The
panic mode ringing in my head demanded some kind of action,
but nothing reasonable would come to mind. I knew too little and
couldn't discount the possibility that I was simply being paranoid.
What did we have?

First. Twelve players were hired to find the check. All
twelve were distributed throughout the different empires of the
game. My first challenge then was to figure out what empire John
Levin had been assigned to. If he had been sent to the Qualians
as well, then my fears would be baseless.

Second. I had been told that a certain Sergei Smolyanov
was prepared to offer $100,000 for information about new players.
And so we put our thinking caps on and began to think: About four
hundred players started the game the same day I did. So then,
what, was I supposed to assume that Sergei was the lunatic son

of some billionaire, willing to spend an ungodly amount of money on *that* harebrained scheme..? Utter baloney. There's only one possible conclusion—Cormack was my only enemy and no one else. Why tell me all that, after all? To find a way into my network? Possibly...I needed to keep thinking and wait to see what Stan would come up with in the morning.

Third. Let's assume that my fears were founded and someone was tracking down the contestants. And why would this be only limited to the players? After all, the betting Masters found me easily enough. A billion pounds was a large enough amount of money to have an effect on people, including those who may have been close to the two bettors. It followed that my address, appearance, electronic identity and basically all the information there was about me or the other eleven contestants was in the hands of the betting masters, and one or both of them could easily have passed it on to some ringer that they were paying to eliminate us. Say, half the prize in exchange for the ringer eliminating the contestants of his protégé. But golly! What was I even going on about? If I was correct, then I was a potential corpse standing in the way of someone's fortune. The only thing that could save me was my premature exit from the Training Sector, which would have given me a head start of, say, two-three weeks. But no more. As soon as the ringer left the Sector—let's take the worst case scenario in which the player has no money but no limit on playing time either—the elimination process would begin. I needed to move as soon as possible, even if temporarily.

Fourth. We, the players, were not allowed to make

alliances in game, but no one said anything about real life. I needed to find Eunice and Constantine, tell them about my suspicions and offer to work together. Correction—let's assume the worst case, in which one of those two was the traitor. In that case, I could meet with them only after I had moved—and only virtually—and with a scrambler. What a prize this check was turning out to be.

Fifth...

"Good morning, Master," the alarm clock in the person of Stan woke me at eight in the morning. Since I hadn't finished my fifth point, I decided to consider it moot. "Breakfast is served. You've received a notification concerning the criminal complaint you filed. Dan Cormack has been arrested. Aside from the unlawful access of your virtual space, he is also being charged under several statutes that can not be disclosed due to the ongoing-status of the investigation. The authorities thank you for your vigilance and request your credentials in order to furnish you your reward. How do you wish to respond?"

"Send them over," I replied without a second thought. As a law-abiding citizen it was extremely advantageous for me to receive a reward from the police. Future employers and sponsors would take notice of the authorities' official recognition of me. If I did manage to find the check (something I couldn't even let myself believe was possible at the moment), it would be good to cover any financial bases involving the powers that were. Stuffing myself with another sandwich, I cooed: "Stanley, what'd you find out about Smolyanov?"

"Unfortunately there was no mention of this person in any public sources," Stan reported with notes of sadness in his voice. "My analysis suggests an 80% probability that Mr. Cormack invented this person to earn your trust. Further analysis of the data stolen from your network reveals a focus on uncovering bank account numbers. It seems that..."

Finishing my breakfast, I grinned at my own paranoia. One half-stupid hacker (even if he was a guild leader) had been enough to cause me all kinds of nightmares. I needed to take things easier and relax a little.

"Hello everyone!" I said upon entering *Galactogon*. "What's new with our dear *Space Cucumber*?"

"I've come up with a slight improvement to our defenses," Wally reported, "but implementing it at the moment is pointless. It's not like we're going to take on a Legendary anyway. They've done such a number on *The Space Cucumber* that...Heck, they even pinned on a self destruct button."

"That's nice and all, but there are a few presents here that aren't welcome in the least." Haggis pointed at his screen, bringing everyone back down from cloud nine. "Take a look there, Wally. This is up your alley."

"Hmm..." puzzled the shields operator peering at the screen.

"What is it?" I couldn't help but ask.

"A bypass to a device that's been installed between the fire control system and the shielding generators. They've planted a bug on us. If its owner wanted to, they could take over our weapons systems and leave us toothless. And that goes for both the blasters and the torpedoes."

"First thing I thought to look for," Haggis explained. "I heard once that Marina managed to capture some enemy ships without firing a single shot. And the ships in question had only recently been upgraded. In fact they were fresh out of the drydocks...I guess Kiddo has people working in the shipyards of other clans. It takes some fancy equipment to install one of these bugs."

"Alright guys, I'm delaying our departure by another 24 hours," I instantly made up my mind. "I need a full sweep of the ship for any insects that don't appear on the ship's schematics. I'd rather avoid any surprises. One request—we're only looking for them. We're not trying to remove them. At the moment, we only need to know how many of them are onboard."

There were four bugs altogether: one on the fire control system, the second on the nav computer (presumably to track everywhere we went), the third on the self-destruct mechanism, and a fourth which logged everything going on in the ship as it flew. While the ship was landed, the bug turned itself off, so it was very difficult to find it without knowing what to look for. We found it nonetheless.

"We can block them with our shields," Wally suggested when we started discussing what to do with these Grecian presents. "They'll go on functioning as normal, but as soon as someone connects to them from outside, the shields will block them.

"Won't work," Haggis shook his head. "They could run a check on the bugs by, for instance, sending a test command once a day. The shields will block the incoming connection and whoever put the bugs there will know that they've been compromised."

"I don't see what all the hoopla is about. Just remove them and that's all she wrote!" Miloš said, bewildered.

"Marina didn't put them there for no reason," I shook my head. "In her view, all of you are future candidates for her crew. She needs to be able to monitor how you act…"

"Then we should place jammers next to them wired to the captain's controls," Tristan spoke up. "Let them steer *The Space Cucumber* all they want. As soon as things get dire, we'll jam them and reclaim control. For both us and Marina, that'll be a onetime occurrence, so we'll have to wait for the right moment when everyone will least expect it. And we have to keep in mind that while we're flying, there can be no talk of the bugs or our knowledge of them. What do you say?"

Everyone agreed with Tristan's proposal. Wally installed jammers around the bugs and rewired them straight to the reactor, bypassing any communications equipment, after which I requested permission for departure from ATC.

Newly-refitted, *The Space Cucumber* set out on her first official voyage.

CHAPTER SIX

THE TRIAL OF THE SPACE CUCUMBER

T he rest of that day, as well as the next, turned into one big training exercise.

We zoomed from one end of the Qirlats System to the other. For target practice, we obtained permission to destroy a lifeless asteroid and generally spent that day-and-a-half becoming comfortable with operating the various systems aboard *The Space Cucumber*.

No one wanted to set out on a maiden voyage into zero security space in a new ship, so we landed a harvester on the asteroid. Miloš began shuttling back and forth between the ship and the asteroid, practicing fire support, resource extraction and harvester disassembly, after which we would extract both the marine and the mining equipment from the asteroid while shooting at a theoretical enemy.

We launched torpedoes and caught them again using our flycatcher and, after the asteroid had been destroyed, started maneuvering between its debris, testing my piloting skills and Wally's shield management.

Tristan and Haggis blasted their cannons in different directions, aiming at targets that only they could see, and only Lestran sat quietly at his station, periodically pushing some buttons to send the repair bots to the parts of our hull that had suffered collisions with the asteroid's heavier fragments.

Marina finally sent over the piracy guide I had requested late that afternoon. It covered everything from important locals and their whereabouts, to safe havens, important players and their guilds. Studying the guide, I kept shaking my head in perplexity. Were those four little sheets from the safe really worth so much information? In her message, the girl had asked me to keep the guide's contents private because it had been gathered by her people over the course of several years, breaking not a few rules in the process. There were however no other constraints on disseminating the information, say to private parties. I got the impression that Marina trusted me as a potential ally, but I had to instantly reject this idea since I wasn't in the habit of believing in fairy tales when real money was at stake. It followed that the guide had been composited and edited in a manner that, even falling in the wrong hands, would somehow help the captain of *Alexandria*. However, even this edited information was much more detailed than everything that Stan had been able to come up

---

with. Gamers posting to forums weren't very fond of discussing their buccaneering exploits in any detail.

There was another question that troubled me during our testing of *The Space Cucumber*. Had we really found all our stowaway insects? There was no way I could be 100% sure that those four bugs were all that had been slipped onto our frigate during her refit. I decided to snag Lestran during the crew's days off and go with him to some neutral planet where we could have some neutral party sweep the ship. Stan had already identified four such technical bases, which would not instantly attack us due to our pirate affiliation. I decided to deal with this issue as soon as possible. It also made sense to run background checks on the four players flying with me. As one of my closest companions was fond of saying, "Believing people is okay—just make sure you shoot first and ask questions later." I really hoped it wouldn't come to that.

"Warning: Active hyperspace scan detected," *The Space Cucumber's* onboard computer reported in a robotic voice, catching us unawares. We had been in hyperspace for thirty minutes and had traveled halfway to the planet Daphark, where Hilvar had sent me with a message to a local named Tryd. No one had expected any surprises. You couldn't change your course in hyperspace. *Galactogon* offered no way of braking externally and *The Space Cucumber* had no jammers to block hyperspace scanners. All we could do was sit and watch the monitors which instantly reported our imminent capture and extraction from our hyperspace jump. *The Space Cucumber* was yanked into deep space about halfway between Qirlats and Daphark.

Hyperspace scanners and the disruptor beams required to yank a ship out of hyperspace could only be installed on a cruiser. Further, to pull off such a trick, you'd have to position specialized tracking beacons along the trajectory of the hyperjump. If you calculated the velocity of your target, you could capture it and yank it into a point of space of your choosing—for example, right in front of an entire armada. The type of vessel yanked out in this manner didn't matter one bit. It could be a lowly harvester or a Grand Arbiter—the mechanics governing its ejection from hyperspace worked flawlessly every time. The only limitation was that you could only trap other players' ships; the locals could travel without any problems, paying no attention to this aspect of the game.

One of the main sources of guild income in *Galactogon* was control over the hyperspace lanes between planets. With two or three cruisers in its fleet, a guild could comfortably announce a toll for the hyperlanes it controlled. It would hardly occur to their victims to try to fight, and the guilds yanked basically every vessel that passed through the lanes under their control. Of course all such tollgates had been identified long ago and the tolls themselves were well known. Players could save time by paying the toll ahead of time at the point of departure and thereby receiving an EZ Pass—a beacon which would send special signals in response to hyperscans. But again, all this was the case for well-known and well-traveled hyperlanes. Every once in a while the guilds would go to war over control of these routes, but

---

such conflicts generally took place in alliance space. I had no idea why someone would erect a hyperspace trap between Qirlats and Daphrak—two Confederate backwaters. As far as I knew, there weren't so many players who passed this way, so there was no way that maintaining such a trap would even pay for itself.

But the fact remained— *The Space Cucumber* began to decelerate and emerge from hyperspace.

"Shields are up!" said Wally as soon as the hyperdrive disengaged. "Four torpedoes straight ahead. We're being targeted with EM cannons. They want to knock out our shields!"

"I've got a lock on the three closest torpedoes," Tristan instantly added. "I'm taking them out in five, four, three…"

"Multiple bandits stern-side," Haggis reported. "Four torpedoes…"

"Two cruisers straight ahead," Wally managed to add before I could react to the situation. Practice all you want in simulators and training missions, until you're used to real battles, you'll find yourself constantly one step behind.

"Arm the flycatcher Tristan. Haggis, you take the rest of the torpedoes. Wally—don't let them hit us. Here we go!"

"That's *Dauntless Warrior*!" yelled Lestran, parsing the torrent of data scrolling down his screen. "Seven cruisers, thirty-two frigates and a hundred interceptors! It looks like the entire Cyanide fleet is here!"

I threw *The Space Cucumber* into a sharp ascent, showing *Dauntless Warrior* our bilge. It was the standard maneuver to capture torpedoes, but, no sooner had I reached my desired heading than yet another cruiser materialized in front of us and launched a spread of torpedoes. They really had us by the tail now...

"Tristan, launch torpedoes straight ahead. Take them out!" I ordered, making my decision instantly. Any adjustment to our trajectory would force *The Space Cucumber* to lose inertia, becoming a sitting duck for her enemies. I didn't know about *Galactogon*, but in *Runlustia*, players who were on giant elephants felt themselves fully secure and tended to lose their vigilance and reflexes—which fact I had exploited more than once. This was no different. Common sense had it that, seeing another cruiser dead ahead of me, I should have banked sharply, avoiding a direct engagement. The cruiser's flycatcher alone guaranteed her victory. I was sure that they'd want to capture us. There was no way they wouldn't. Considering that a swarm of frigates and interceptors roiled above and to the sides of the cruiser, there would be no point in trying to break through there— the alluring emptiness under her bilge however...An inexperienced player would definitely try to pass beneath her, falling right for the flycatcher and making my enemy only happier.

"Just not under the bilge!" yelled Lestran, reading my move and deciding that I had gone utterly nuts.

"Three torpedoes down, one got through," Tristan reported, ignoring everyone around him and focusing on his job. "We don't have time to shoot it down."

"Deflecting won't work either," Wally added. "Get ready— we're about to take a hit."

START THE GAME

"Lestran—emergency repairs! Direct hit incoming…"

The Space Cucumber shuddered, the screens shut off for a moment—but then came back on.

"Hull Durability is down to 20%. Power is 40% below nominal. The hull's beam absorbers have been wiped out. Our portside has been crumpled…I need ten minutes to repair half of the lost Durability."

"Gunners, on the count of three launch torpedoes at that cruiser's bay doors. Get ready! One…two…," I ordered, ignoring Lestran's report. We had survived a direct hit from a torpedo and continued on our course. There were no further missiles ahead of us, but I could see perfectly well how the cruiser's bilge opened, releasing its flycatcher. It began to head toward us. The distance between *The Space Cucumber* and the cruiser grew smaller and smaller. Giving my enemy another second, I yelled, "Three!"

"We've been captured!" Wally said almost instantly, while all of the frigate's instrument panels went dark. Having taken control of our ship, the cruiser's captain wasted no time and simply cut off all of *The Space Cucumber*'s onboard systems, turning us into a giant hunk of metal.

"Thirty seconds until the torpedoes hit," added Wally. "Us, that is. The ones that were coming up from behind…"

"Hey! My screen's come back on," Lestran said puzzled, as I squeezed whatever juice *The Space Cucumber*'s engines still had in them. The acceleration pressed us into our chairs, but I managed to note my two gunners launch one more torpedo apiece. A pretty little window popped up before me, reminding me that all of this was no more than a game:

"A Pirate I Was Meant To Be" Mission Progress: 1 of 10 cruisers destroyed.

You have unlocked the "It's Not How Big It Is—It's How You Use It" Achievement. You have destroyed a vessel larger than yours. Damage done to all ship types increased by 10%.

You have earned a new title: "Improbable." Your ship has reached a new class! Current class: B-1. Two additional slots unlocked. Durability and Energy have been restored by 100%.

"Whoa—B-class?!" Miloš whistled from his observer's seat. As a marine, he couldn't do anything to help us so his job was simply to enjoy the show.

"Marina's people leveled us up to C-99, so everything's as it should be," I said what everyone already knew and pressed the rejuvenated *Space Cucumber* to its max. The experience we gained for destroying the cruiser was distributed across all our equipment, but the ship itself received the biggest chunk of XP.

"We won't get very far," Haggis pointed out about a minute later, turning away from his tail turret. Fully repaired and conjoined with the aft EM cannon, the tail turret presented a compelling argument to the interceptors chasing us from keeping up their efforts. "The cruisers are turning to give chase. We've got two good engines of course, but we can't compete with ten of the same type...As soon as they get some steam, we'll be done for. They won't offer us a second opportunity to shoot at their cruisers.

They'll knock us down from behind…"

"It's too bad they're all D-class," muttered Wally. "If they were at least C-class, it wouldn't feel so bad, but D…"

For a little while we were silent flying away from the armada, and only Haggis giggled spitefully, knocking yet another interceptor down to half its Durability. Without resorting to torpedoes, it was too hard to kill them, but damaging them enough to force them back to their cruiser was a task that my gunner managed perfectly well.

"They're gaining," said Wally, pointing at six bleeps on his screen. Even if they were still far away, the steady rate at which they were closing the distance…"ETA seven minutes. They won't let us bounce to hyper, so…Maybe we should self destruct? We'll come back as C-class, basically like we started…If they grab us with a flycatcher, the self-destruct will stop working too."

"Asteroid belt dead ahead," said Lestran. "We can go through it and gain several minutes. The cruisers won't go straight through. The rocks are too big. We can slip through though. Even if we die, good luck finding our wreckage."

All of a sudden a crazy idea entered my mind and began to scream: "Try me!" Giving in to its pernicious influence, I inquired, "Guys, what do we need to go into hyper again? I know it's a dumb question, but I'd like to know for certain. I've got this idea."

"To jump to hyperspace we need the destination coordinates," began Wally. I had already noticed that he was very familiar with *Galactogon*'s technical details and was therefore a valuable hire. The main thing I had to keep in mind was that he was ultimately working for Marina. "And it'd be nice if those coordinates weren't in fact the center of some star. Also, we'd need forty seconds of inaction while the hyperdrive initialized for the jump. Aside from that, the ship can't be painted by a disrupter beam and…Well, that's it. Those are the three main requirements; everything else is secondary."

"How many of those can we do at the give moment?"

"Just the coordinates. We have several star systems straight ahead of us. We won't even have to alter our heading. As for the rest, we don't have a free second, let alone forty, and they'll instantly hit us with their disrupter beams as soon as we try to initialize anyway."

"How long until we reach the asteroid belt?"

"About two minutes," Wally sounded doubtful. "Are you really considering going through it, Surgeon?"

"No," I shook my head, causing my shields operator to lower his shoulders in relief. "We won't fly through the belt. We're going to hide ourselves in it…"

"WHAT?!" All four players' exclamation was so simultaneous that I couldn't help but crack up. Only Miloš, relaxing in his chair, laughed with me. What else could you expect from a marine?

"We'll be pulverized instantly!" Wally spoke up, as soon as I had adjusted our bearing. "Our shields aren't powerful enough to withstand an asteroid impact and our beam cannons won't destroy them. And using torpedoes will do nothing but clear the way for the guys chasing us. What's the point of flying through?"

"Lestran, what's the size of that belt?" I asked my partner, ignoring Wally.

"About one AU wide and one AU deep. I can't get a length reading, so I'd say at least one hundred AUs in either direction...Listen Surgeon, I have to say I agree with Wally—this is madness."

"You're the one who brought up suicide," I grinned. "It's too late to take your words back." I took a look at my crews' closed helmets and couldn't help but explain: "Look, I'm not going to try to fly through it! I don't think I'm an ace or anything to try to pilot the ship by reflex alone. My plan is to fly into the belt and hide among the asteroids. If they can't see us, they can't use their disrupter beams on us. We'll land on an asteroid and kill the engines while we initialize the hyperjump. Maybe we'll have to take the asteroid with us, but the important thing is to skedaddle. You see what I'm saying?"

"The reactor might not handle it," Wally replied after some thought, "if we tow the boulder with us. And we can't kill the thrusters while inside the belt either—we'll need to be able to dodge the asteroid...Damn! I would turn and take at least one frigate or several interceptors with us, but I have to say that your idea is doable...crazy but doable...I'll try to get the most out of the shields. That'll buy us some time."

"In that case, battlestations! We're going to pay a visit to the wandering rocks!"

"Hey jerk, where you think you're going?" the ship's comm suddenly came to life for the first time since the ambush. Nadeep, the captain of *Dauntless Warrior*, had decided to pay us a personal visit.

"We're taking a field trip!" I parried, braking the ship. Entering an asteroid belt at full power would have been pure suicide. "Someone told me that they're giving out donuts straight ahead, so I've decided to check it out! I'd love some donuts about now."

"You think we don't know how to flush you out of there? I'll blast that damned belt to pieces!"

"Go ahead and blast it. I don't have any plans for it anyway. Alright, no offense but I've got to go—more pressing matters to attend to."

"I'll..." Nadeep managed to begin before I cut the transmission. It would only be a distraction.

Lowering my speed to the minimal setting and thereby allowing six giant cruisers—as well as their attendant swarm of interceptors and frigates—to almost catch up with us, I took a deep breath and plunged *The Space Cucumber* into the asteroid belt. Tristan was blasting salvoes from the tail turret ceaselessly. Wally was deftly hanging and re-hanging the shields that the interceptors kept knocking down and simultaneously deflecting the smaller debris. Haggis was firing torpedo after torpedo at the asteroids we had passed to create a cloud of shrapnel four our enemies. Lestran was darting about like a singed cat, fixing different parts of the hull and complaining that he had already lost

---

three of his repair bots. Miloš was giggling nervously in his seat and I was trying my best to avoid the larger boulders. *The Space Cucumber* was moving slowly but making progress into the asteroid belt all the same, finding her path through the chaos all around.

"Durability's down to 70%," moaned Lestran. "I don't have time to fix everything! Try to be more careful, Surgeon!"

"If we keep going straight," added Wally, "we won't find the room to wait while the hyperdrive engages. Cyanide's calculated our trajectory. They're blasting their way with torpedoes into the heart of the belt. Those cruisers have plenty of them…We need to adjust our course to fly parallel to the belt."

"A Pirate I Was Meant To Be" Mission Progress: 11 of 150 interceptors destroyed.

"I have a feeling that they won't just let us waltz out of here," smirked Tristan, sending another interceptor to meet its maker. Unlike in open space, it had become hard for the interceptors to get a safe distance away from *The Space Cucumber* and Tristan therefore now had time to finish off the little spacecraft.

"Two beam cannons down. We're down to one!" Miloš reported happily a minute later. He was the only one who managed to keep track of the readouts on his screen. As soon as I adjusted our heading, everyone had to work harder. Even Haggis, who began to hammer the interceptors from the side cannons and torpedo launchers. I had it worst of all though—I was constantly letting boulders through to us, causing the hull to creak under the strain of the impacts. Lestran was cursing up a storm but repairing my errors all the same. Tristan started singing some kind of pirate ditty, as if he was some buccaneer running from the Royal Navy. Wally was muttering something incomprehensible to himself...The atmosphere in *The Space Cucumber* was a tense one indeed.

"We've lost our beam cannons!" Milos said after a minute.

"Torpedoes are done too," smirked Haggis.

"But we don't have any pursuers either," Tristan added sadly. "I have no one to shoot at anymore. I think we lost them, for a bit at least."

"Hull Durability is down to 15%, our reactor is down to 22%," Wally reported. "We won't get much further."

"Then let's land," I decided, choosing the most promising looking boulder, "for example, right there!"

A humongous asteroid was turning lazily not far from *The Space Cucumber*. It was large enough to hide an entire cruiser. Huge craters formed by impacts with other asteroids, fissures, caves—it would have been difficult to find a more ideal place to secrete ourselves.

"Come on then—surprise us," grinned Miloš when I did a flyby of this tiny planetoid, unwilling to let any pursuers see where we had decided to land.

"Durability down to 5%. Reactor's in the red at 12%," Wally reported wearily once we had alighted on the asteroid. I should admit that I had plunked us down pretty hard. The asteroid was spinning ceaselessly, so after deciding on a landing spot in the shadow of an enormous mountain, I had tried my best to match its rotation and lost track of my surroundings—which instantly made themselves known with a powerful asteroid strike to our hull, finishing off what remained of our portside engine. We would need a full-fledged overhaul station to repair our ship now, and we still needed to get there somehow. Slamming down heavily onto the asteroid and stirring up a cloud of dust in the process, *The Space Cucumber* got lucky for the first time during the battle. The scout drone which Wally launched at the last possible moment revealed that we had fallen several dozen yards into a fissure and caused a landslide along the way, which covered us entirely with debris. Basically, *The Space Cucumber* had now dropped off the Cyanide Guild's radar.

"...hell are you, you dweeb?" While Lestran and Wally busied themselves with emergency repairs (attempting to jump to hyperspace with 5% hull Durability was a very bad idea) I turned on the comm and instantly heard my friend Nadeep. "Anyone see their wreckage?" he asked his subordinates on the open channel.

"The only wreckage is from the ships we lost. Most likely they landed on an asteroid and went dark," came the reply from one of the players, making me want to give him a pat on the back for his guesswork. "We can destroy every asteroid along their last known trajectory. They couldn't have gotten far."

"D'you hear that Surgeon? I know that you can hear me! We're going to smoke you out, you son of a dweeb! You might as well blow yourself up now."

As soon as I found a moment, I called Marina. The nice thing about comms in *Galactogon*, compared to the ones IRL, was that even if the person you were calling was in another part of the universe, your conversation still took place in real time with no delays. In that sense, the in-game physics were very different from the real world.

"I'm listening," Marina answered.

"Hey, this is Surgeon. You got a minute?"

"Not really but what's up? What's going on?"

"Well, here's the situation..." I painted the girl a picture of our battle with the Cyanide Guild after they had ambushed us in hyperspace.

"Okay...what do you want from me? You got yourself into this mess—now dig yourself out. If things come down to it, blow yourself up. We put a button on your ship."

"Eh, don't worry. I'll figure that out myself just fine. I want you to consider something else though: How would Nadeep know that we were going to Daphark? Even assuming that Hilvar sends every player that comes to him to that planet, how would Nadeep even know that we had gone to Qirlats? I definitely didn't tell anyone about that. And when you were capturing *The Space Cucumber*, you hadn't yet been ready to ally with me. Do you understand now why I'm calling you? I'm not complaining—I'm trying to warn you."

"Are you sure that none of your..." Marina began and instantly cut herself off. She had been the one who had supplied me with my crew after all. "Thanks for the heads up, Surgeon…If you're right, I'll owe you one. Where are you now?"

"Asteroid belt in the Ramtil system, but we don't need help. We'll figure it out ourselves. We'll just make some repairs and then be on our merry way. Just make sure to take care of your moles."

I hung up and leaned back in my chair. There was nothing else for me to do. The Cyanide Guild could only have plucked us out of hyperspace if they knew ahead of time that we were jumping between planet A and planet B. There was absolutely no way that Cyanide controlled that hyperlane normally. Consequently, this had to be a deliberately planned revenge for the money they'd lost. Moreover, Nadeep had clearly known that we were flying a wholly retrofitted frigate. Otherwise, he would've only brought his own cruiser. I wasn't even sure what would have happened in that case. A stock D-class cruiser was comparable in strength to an upgraded C-class frigate. But when the cruiser brings an armada as backup…

"They've begun to destroy the larger asteroids," said Miloš, watching the feed from the scouting drone. "I'd guess that they'll get to the one we're on in ten minutes."

"Lestran, what do you have?"

"We can try to get out of here in about two minutes. I can get the hull back up to 12%, but we simply don't have enough repair materials to fix anything else."

"Wally?"

"I need a couple minutes as well. I'm diverting power to

the remaining engine. I think that'll let us limp out of here. I'm just not so sure that we'll be able to tow the asteroid with us. If that was possible, everyone would be doing it already."

"Who knows what we'll actually tow with us. Maybe it won't be the entire asteroid and just some part of it. Or maybe we won't take any of it at all. Of course, maybe we won't go anywhere at all either. Until we try it, we won't know. But I can tell you one thing—I don't much feel like blowing myself up. A class-B ship is quite a thing."

"I'm done!" Lestran reported. "Repairs are complete. Durability is at 11%. It's slowly degrading due to the debris that's pressing down on us."

"In that case, let's get underway," I said, seeing that Wally was ready as well. "Initializing hyperjump procedure…"

"Alright then. So that's why no one ever tries to jump right from a planet's surface," I muttered as soon as we reentered realspace and saw what had become of us. The jump to Daphark had taken no less than an hour, but there had been no way to tell whether the asteroid had come with us or not.

The good news was that the asteroid, as such, had not in fact come with us. The bad news was that *The Space Cucumber* was now encased in a giant layer of rock about a hundred feet thick, which had effectively turned our ship into an enormous and smooth, boulder. We only managed to establish the thickness of this epic structure after Miloš busted through the external hatch and then used his blaster to drill into the rock.

"We don't have a hull anymore," smirked Wally, checking the ship's status. "Or, more precisely, our hull is now a giant boulder that's fused with the ship. The engines won't work, the sensors won't work and we have no idea where we are now. I propose we exercise the self-destruct option."

"What's with you and blowing ourselves up?" I grumbled. "Are we near Daphark or not?"

"We should be, but there's no way to tell now. The changes in the ship's mass could have affected the jump. An hour in hyperspace is enough to toss us into literally any point of *Galactogon*. The only thing we can say for sure is that we're not inside a star. Otherwise, Miloš would have been incinerated instantly."

"Alright, since there's no other way out," I replied after some thought, "we'll reconvene tomorrow at ten and try to jump to Daphark in short hops instead of one long one. I want to thank all of you for today's battle. It was sweet." Having said that, I activated the self-destruct procedure and took a deep breath. I really didn't want *The Space Cucumber* to go back to class-C.

A second later, I took another breath and repeated the self-destruct procedure.

After another ten seconds, I wasn't taking breaths anymore, but simply hammering the self-destruct button sequence.

"Something's not working," Miloš pointed out emphatically

and then broke out in a fit of laughter. "We don't have the power in the core left to activate the detonation. What an 'epic fail,' as the ancients used to say."

To say that I was surprised would have been an understatement. Finding oneself immured in a giant stone sarcophagus without a single exit, is quite a thing even for a computer game.

"Hey Marina, this is Surgeon again. Got a minute?" I instantly called the girl. If we couldn't destroy ourselves from within, then we had to destroy ourselves from without.

"Only if you make it quick. How's the battle?"

"That's what I'm calling you about. We managed to jump into hyperspace from an asteroid and..."

"Say that again—you did what?" Marina interrupted. It sounded to me like she could barely contain her laughter. "Wait, wait, I'm going to put you on speakerphone...Alright, Surgeon, all the officers are here. Could you repeat what you just said?"

"I can see now that I probably shouldn't've done that, huh? By the way, partner, it's not very nice of you to mock me like this. I've been in *Galactogon* like two months and haven't yet had time to learn all the nuances. But since you want me to repeat it, I will. We jumped into hyperspace while still on the surface of an asteroid."

There was some tentative laughter despite what I'd said, but Marina instantly cut off the speakerphone.

"Sorry," she said calmly, "it's just that any captain knows not to jump into hyperspace while even close to any kind of mass, much less on the surface of a planetoid. I lost a ship like that myself many years ago, so...How thick is whatever you're encased in?"

"One hundred feet of solid rock."

"Do you have enough power to blow yourself up?"

"No. I don't have anything at all at the moment—neither energy nor any idea of where we are, nor any means of returning back to..."

"That's precisely your biggest problem. You guys could be anywhere at the moment. Even in a different galaxy. The developers had some fun when they wrote the code for jumping with an unaccounted-for mass. Basically, you've been carried to some unknown reaches of *Galactogon*. And that'll happen every time. I tried it out several times by stuffing extra powercells and a nav comp into a scout. After the jump, we cut a way out through the rock and found ourselves on the map. And each time we'd be in an utter backwater. So if you want to know where you are at the moment, then finding your ship will be basically impossible."

"Is there really no solution?" I asked sadly.

"Sorry, no. There isn't. In your situation, I recommend you stuff your inventory with anything of value or importance, point the blaster at your head and pull the trigger with your toe. You can't save your ship anymore, so at least save a part of your equipment. Read the forums. They do a good job of describing a jump from a planetary surface and its consequences. Later!"

Marina disconnected, leaving me in utter shock. I didn't even want to think that she was saying the truth, so I turned to my crew and issued new orders.

"Guys, we have a small problem. We'll meet again tomorrow at ten, as usual. Until then, I'd like you to study the question of jumping into hyperspace from some planetary surface as much as you can. Tomorrow we'll decide how we're gonna get out of here…"

I waited to sign out until my crew had departed, leaving *The Space Cucumber* last like a true captain.

"Greetings, Master," Stan began to run through his customary script as soon as the cocoon's lid slid aside. "Shower, mail, dinner?"

"Cancel everything," I replied, getting comfortable at my work desk. "I need everything you can find about hyperjumps."

"A jump through hyperspace is one of the most complicated processes in Galactogon, technically as well as mathematically. The jump initialization takes 60 seconds (this time may be decreased to 40 by equipping the ship with a more powerful navigation computer or engines), during which the onboard navigation computer calculates the jump vector, its duration and the point of egress.

The calculation takes into account only the dimensions of the vessel; however, it is worth pointing out that in actual fact, the hyperdrive sends the space around the ship into hyperspace as well. The dimensions of the total actual space sent to hyperspace depends on the power of the vessel's hyperdrive and may vary from between an offset of three feet for scouts, up to an offset of

---

one hundred feet for cruisers. An imperative condition for performing a successful hyperjump is that the ship remain utterly uninfluenced by any outside force for the duration of the hyperdrive's initialization. This includes beam attacks, collisions with other vessels' hulls, close proximity to a foreign mass, and solar flares. The vessel should also not be painted by a space disrupter beam...The larger the difference between the real mass sent to hyperspace and the mass as calculated by the navigation computer, the larger will be the deviation at the point of egress."

Stan supplied me this excerpt from the official game manual, pointing out that this information was included in the mandatory training course for ship captains. I never imagined that my smart home would start giving me lip too. The above text was followed by real examples provided by other players—and here I was forced to really sink my head in despair: Everyone claimed in unison that the only way out was to abandon their ship. The cruisers fared worst of all—even a marine in a suit of armor couldn't drill through one hundred feet of rock. I made a note to order Miloš to start trying to drill through first thing tomorrow anyway though. Despite the fact that 99.9% of all the posts on this topic ended with the scuttling of the ship and starting all over again, I found several mentions of a way out of this impasse. First it was necessary to break out to the surface of the ship. After that all the crew members could gather in one place wearing suits of armor, and setting their suits' thrusters to full, slingshot the ship at the closest star. This process could take a while—distances in

Galactogon were in no way small—but doing so would force your ship to be respawned. There were no other plausible options—only miracles like someone stumbling on our ship in the middle of nowhere. Every player said the same thing—jumping into hyperspace from a planetary surface was just not done. Where had they all been earlier?

"Master, you have an incoming call from one of the members of your whitelist. Will you take it?"

The panic mode, which I had never canceled, allowed only a few people to get in touch with me—more precisely just one: Alonso, my companion from my time in *Runlustia*.

"Excellent! I see that you're not bathing today?" he greeted me sarcastically. "What are you getting into?"

"I just got out of *Galactogon*. Was going to go jog for a bit. Why? Got a better idea?"

"Do you even need to ask? You owe me our wake in honor of *Runlustia*! It's been a month already! You thought I forgot? While Lucy is battling it out in *Galactogon*, I propose we meet up and have a drink."

"Deal. What about you? Haven't seen you IRL much lately. Doesn't seem like you."

"Eh, I'm exhausted with all this studying I have to do—you know how much I hated being a monkey in *Runlustia*. All I do in *Galactogon* is study, study and study some more. I only have a week left in the Training Sector, but I just can't keep 'playing' at the moment. I need some downtime. How about yourself?"

"Well...Let's meet up at the bar and I'll tell you..."

START THE GAME

"Get out of here!" Alonso exclaimed after I told him my story with the pirates. Ordering another pint, he leaned forward to prop his head up on the bar and looked me up and down with half-sober eyes. "So you are the Surgeon?"

"Yah, but again—not a word to anyone about that. I'd rather not run into Cyanide IRL."

"If all you say is true, I'd start looking for you myself. Dang! To get out of the Training Sector without even completing it! To destroy a cruiser of a guild and get away in one piece! I am just quivering with jealousy here! I still have to sweat it out in the Sector, like I told you. And then Lucy has another three weeks as well."

"Lucille is in the Training Sector?" I asked surprised. "I thought you said that she was the head of a guild or something."

"You can't say a word about that to anyone either!" Alonso placed a finger to his lips conspiratorially. "She deleted her character a month ago and handed off her guild to her deputy. It's only temporary of course, but now she's an ordinary player like you or I...Although, I guess you're doing better than just ordinary."

"Why would a guild leader reset her character?" I asked sounding puzzled and trying not to betray the adrenaline that had suddenly flooded me. Had Lucille too been brought into the bet?

"Well, you see, Alexis...I can't tell that to anyone, even you. Lucille will kill me if she finds out. She only spends seven hours in the game a day and always comes out unhappy and

---

angry—so, forgive me, I can't tell you about that."

"Not even a thing, Alonso," I reassured my friend, clapping him on the shoulder. "I understand perfectly. As I recall it, you're playing with the Vraxis?"

"Uh-huh and boy am I sick of those chitinous mugs! You know, it was much more pleasant to look at elf girls than these bugs…Want to have another drink? Remember how we set off the Black Death?"

Taking him up on his offer, I called over the bartender and ordered another round of beer. I wanted to show Alonso that I was still on the same wavelength as he. Meanwhile, a single thought occupied my mind—I had found one of the remaining ten players who were looking for the billion pounds with me. I had to find the other nine…

"Master, I have prepared the information you requested," Stan woke me early the next morning. My head felt like a hundred church bells had suddenly decided to play compositions of their own creation and which were in no way in harmony with one other. I was scared to even imagine what was going on inside my mouth, and here was Stan with his "information you requested"…Lemme sleep, you robot!

"What you got?" I managed, forcing my tongue to move.

"I have identified the two players pictured on your phone. Would you like to see their personal information?"

"Come on then."

"Constantine Gauranga, age 29. Resided at…"

"What do you mean by 'resided?' Why the past tense?" I

interrupted Stan. Even through the fog of my hangover, the sentence set off alarm bells.

"Mr. Gauranga passed away in an accident eight days ago," replied Stan, taking my hangover right off. Constantine was dead?!

"What about Eunice?"

"Eunice Dormouse, age 30. Current place of residence unknown. Has lived here in this city for the past nine months. I found information about her contacts and her phone number on the web. I'd like to point out that it seems she too has turned engaged panic mode. I found her phone number only by parsing old logs in the game *Draanmir*. All newer data, from the past two years, were either deleted or are outdated. Neither her email, nor her phone, nor website is currently active. Would you like to contact Eunice?"

"Not at the moment," I shook my head, pushing away the encroaching weakness. "Give me something to help with my hangover and prepare the capsule. I need to get back into *Galactogon*. Although, wait—send her a message that I want to talk to her. You can add that at least two of the twelve are already dead."

"Your message has been sent. The capsule and the anti-hangover shot have been prepared. Do you wish to eat your breakfast?"

Even thinking of that turned me inside out, so I said no and dove back into *Galactogon*, freeing my mind from the morning's hangover.

CHAPTER SEVEN

AN UNEXPECTED ENCOUNTER

That's it. That's the last of them," said Miloš, hauling out the last powercell from the harvester.

Our attempt to wire the harvester's power supply into the contour running to *The Space Cucumber*'s self destruct mechanism had failed miserably, wiping out basically half of the Elo we had on board. Elo was the universal fuel in *Galactogon*, so we decided to move on to plan B, which consisted of drilling a hole in our stone egg.

Like ancient lizards awoken by some cataclysm, we began to whittle away at the ossified egg—but it turned out that making a small opening was one thing and carving a full-sized passage through which we could get out to open space was something else entirely—not exactly the proper task for a simple combat blaster. Miloš melted away the rock piece by piece, while we ferried the melted piles to the cargo holds.

Once the blaster's powercell was finished, we wired it into the harvester's powercells, but even those were eventually all but exhausted.

"How much more do we have to go?"

"About three feet. We should have enough juice, but...Personally, I'm not sure what we'll do afterwards. My armor has 15% power left and I assume that you guys have not much more than that. We'll be able to change the ship's orbit only once—after that, we're icicles. What do you think, Surgeon? Maybe we should shoot ourselves before it's too late?"

"And admit that we've wasted four hours for nothing?" I smirked. "Sorry, but no way. Let's get to the outside and then see what our chances are. Maybe we're only several days' journey from some star and already falling towards it as it is. We'll always have the chance to respawn. I don't feel like losing the ship in such a dumb way."

"Didn't Marina promise you a new frigate?" Wally spoke up. But I interrupted him right away.

"What do we need an F-class tub for? What are we going to do with it? With *The Space Cucumber*, we defeated a cruiser. All we'll be doing in an F-class frigate is running from Cyanide from one system to the next. If there's a chance of saving the frigate, we need to take it. If not, we'll think about something else..."

That morning Marina had called me to ask how things

were going and suggested that we abandon *The Space Cucumber*, taking with us anything of value we could carry. The captain of *Alexandria* promised to give me and my crew a new frigate. It would have to be F-class, albeit with whatever upgrades she found on hand. I promised to consider her offer as soon as we'd reach a dead end in our attempts to salvage *The Space Cucumber*. Then, we got to work, toiling to get through the rock and, now, when there were only a few feet left until the end, my crew turned out to be utterly demoralized. We needed a single goal that could unite us, but at the moment I couldn't see it. Everything was just too bad.

Our emergence into open space wasn't even greeted as a victory—by that point, Miloš's blaster had been fully discharged, so we had to use Wally's, then Lestran's. We finally broke through with Tristan's rifle. By the end of it, Haggis and I were the only remaining armed players on *The Space Cucumber*. At least our weapons had leveled up to class-D...and a full D at that...

The bungled hyperjump had brought us to the center of some uncharted solar system. All my PDA could do was whine pitifully, finding no nav beacons. Scans of the sky map also revealed nothing about what part of *Galactogon* we were in. I would have to get Stan on this job. If anyone could figure out where we were, he would. The only thing we could say at the moment was that we were lost...like, really lost.

"Flying to that star would take days upon days," Wally appraised the situation as soon as we had all emerged from the ship. "If we point her at that star and expend all the fuel our suits

---

have left to accelerate her, then—give me a second—then considering the star's mass, *The Space Cucumber* will fall into the sun in seven months. That's under ideal conditions, mind."

"Guys," Lestran suddenly exclaimed from the other side of the frigate, "take a look at this!"

We floated over to the engineer who was pointing at a direction away from the sun and saw a small spot, set apart from the surrounding stars by its blue-green hue.

"*Planet with vegetation*," my PDA happily reported. "*Belongs to the category of planets which have an indigenous flora and fauna. Probability of finding Raq: 0%. Probability of finding Elo: 74%. Probability of finding...*"

The PDA went on reporting a ton of information about the planet, without, however, providing its name or location in the game's universe. It was a typical planet with vegetation somewhere on the periphery of *Galactogon*. There were millions of such planets.

"Hmm..." Wally said expressively, evidently calculating something. "Hmm..."

"How informative," Tristan replied sarcastically. "Well, don't leave us in the dark—pun intended. What'd you come up with?"

"My preliminary calculations suggest that that planet is moving toward us and will pass literally clicks from us. If we adjust the frigate's trajectory to intercept its orbit...I have no idea how we'll land the ship without engines, but heck, this part isn't rocket science: We should be smashed into a pancake. What do you say?"

"Which way do we adjust?" I instantly made up my mind. If there was a way to save *The Space Cucumber*, I was all for it.

"We have two hours until contact, so let's all push from this side." Wally instantly flew over to the far side of the rock cocoon, pressed up against it and opened his suit's throttle to maximum. "What're you all standing around for? We might not get another chance!"

With two percent power remaining, each player began to push *The Space Cucumber*. And once the power ran out, we headed back into the ship. If the frigate was doomed, it was preferable to be inside of it and respawn all together. Otherwise, we would have to spend a long time looking for our belongings at the "graveyard"—the place where players' ships respawned.

"Ten minutes until reentry," said Wally, checking his PDA.

"Listen, how do you know all this stuff anyway?" I asked unable to contain my curiosity any longer. "Whatever crap happens to us, you seem to have either a plan or a tool to deal with it."

"I want to become a navigator," Wally smirked mysteriously. Our suits' power went down to basically zero, so we took off our helmets in case we needed to shoot ourselves in the head with blasters.

"And?" I didn't understand such a mysterious admission.

"The captain of the ship is the one who makes the decisions about how and where the ship goes," Lestran explained for Wally. "All ships—with the exception of cruisers—combine the role of captain and navigator into one player. But a navigator on a cruiser is an indispensable position. After all, it's he who pilots this giant vessel through space. Marina has utterly insane requirements for her navigators. I once read how…"

"I am currently fifth in line for the position," said Wally proudly, as if admitting that he was some superman. Judging by the reactions from Lestran and the gunners, this wasn't too far from the truth.

"Let me see!" Tristan exclaimed, as if he had heard some wondrous news.

Wally pressed several buttons on his PDA and a hologram appeared of a fiery number five. The sacred significance of this presentation remained a mystery to me.

"Well then!" Haggis cursed and patted the shields operator on his shoulder. "You'll be our protégé in case of anything. Fifth navigator…I can't believe it. How is it that Marina let you go?"

"Seven minutes till contact," replied Wally, smirking, and as he did so, *The Space Cucumber* began to shake from side to side. "We're entering the atmosphere. I suggest that anyone who doesn't want to go prematurely buckle up snug…"

Our crash onto the surface was so violent that I was almost ejected out of my captain's chair. For a second I lost consciousness and naïvely decided that this was it—the respawning sequence in *Galactogon*. My body felt broken and stars played across my eyes. I planned on appearing on Qirlats and resuming my travels in the frigate, but…*The Space*

Cucumber was not in agreement with this kind of continuation:

Hull Durability is now 1%. The ship requires a complete overhaul to fly again.
All life support systems have shut down.

A hundred feet worth of rock skin had cushioned our entry into the planet's atmosphere. As we plummeted to the surface, the rock layer took the brunt of the impact, distributing the damage evenly across the ship's volume. Everything took damage from the fall, even our suits, but the worst news was that *The Space Cucumber* had remained in one piece—our rock cocoon had saved us from respawning. As soon as my vision cleared, I realized that neither Lestran nor Tristan were with us. It seemed that they had failed to buckle in securely enough and had as a result been smashed and smeared against the transparent cabin windshield. On the floor, I saw several spare parts for armor and an empty engineer's blaster, suggesting that our two departed friends had been on board until the end.

"It didn't work," Wally sounded disappointed as he stretched his neck. "Now we'll definitely have to abandon the frigate—I have no idea how to destroy it. Maybe we can chip away at the remaining 1% with a pickax?"

"Yeah of course, but..." I began but cut myself off. I didn't want to abandon *The Space Cucumber*. I didn't want to abandon her very badly! I hadn't stolen her and improved her to lose her like this over nothing.

START THE GAME

"I think my armor's out of power," Miloš fretted. "You guys can figure out what our next move will be. I'm going to get some rest. Surgeon, you can still move, can't you? Send me back to Qirlats. I got nothing else to do here..."

"Me neither," added the second gunner. "Shall we meet up again tomorrow at nine and decide what to do next?"

I didn't say anything and simply raised the blaster, pulling the trigger twice. Since the players had already taken off their helmets, it wasn't too difficult to send them to respawn. Literally ten minutes later—the length of time it takes to respawn in *Galactogon*—they would appear back on Qirlats.

"Wally?"

"I guess I should get some rest too. How are you holding up?"

"I don't even know...I just don't want to lose the ship in such a stupid way. Such a childish mistake..."

Raising my blaster a third time, I left myself alone on *The Space Cucumber*.

My marine armor beeped mournfully, reminding me that its batteries were almost empty. I had to make a decision. I could either shoot myself with my blaster and go respawn with everyone else, or I could leave the suit in the ship and go look for some way of destroying *The Space Cucumber*. A countdown timer appeared, showing that I had all of thirty seconds to make up my mind. If I couldn't come to a decision during this time, the suit would become my little tomb and I wouldn't get another chance to respawn for about a week—when I would finally starve to death.

This particular form of suicide was always an option in *Galactogon* too...

As a great man once said, "Alea iacta est." My suit of armor beeped one last time and fell silent. Fresh air drifted in from the hole we had drilled through *The Space Cucumber*'s hull, so I was alright wearing my regular clothes. It's funny but players tend to wander around *Galactogon* without their armor suits, wearing them only when they're on board their ships—I, however, had grown so comfortable with that hunk of steel that, now, I felt naked. The repair materials that had been left behind by my crew were enough to repair my blaster, ensuring that it wouldn't randomly explode in my hands when I tried to use it. However, its ammo did not increase as a result. The blaster had about twenty more shots in it before it turned into a shoddy metal club, so I would have to be very careful with when I'd choose to use it.

The only good news was that, according to my PDA, there was a great likelihood of finding Elo deposits on this planet. The distinguishing feature of this resource was that you didn't have to actually refine it to stuff it into your energy cells: It was enough to simply place your powercells on the Elo and in several minutes, they'd be ready to go. Though, even here the developers had included several limitations. You could only use this method to recharge the powercells of one fully-assembled item. If you simply put an empty powercell against a lode of Elo, the cell would remain empty. Plus, you could only charge items using these Elo lodes—Elo already stored in a powercell, for example, didn't have such properties. Finally, the most unpleasant limitation for any guild that came across such an invaluable lode was that the lode would deplete, growing smaller in proportion to the energy that had been transferred from it. You couldn't use one lode of Elo forever—sooner or later it would run dry.

I had no plans for enriching myself, but if I could find an Elo deposit, I could drag my armor over there to recharge it, then use it to cut a hole in *The Space Cucumber*'s hull and remove the harvester. Then I could use the harvester to activate the Elo lode, charge *The Space Cucumber*'s reactor and finally activate the self-destruct mechanism. Now I began having regrets that I had so quickly dispatched my crew back to Qirlats. A few extra hands could have really come in, well, handy. Although, again—surviving on an unexplored planet without marine armor...

"Wally, it's Surgeon. I'm going to tinker with *The Space Cucumber* for a few days. I'm hoping to find some Elo. If nothing works out, I'll pop back to Qirlats. Gather the other guys tomorrow morning. I'll get in touch with Marina and ask her to sponsor us with that frigate she mentioned. We can't say no to such an offer. Until I show up, I'm making you captain. Good?"

"Good—only don't disappear for too long. What do you want us to do?"

"Head to Daphark—just not directly—and find Tryd. Try to do any assignments he gives you. The only thing I ask is—if he wants you to destroy something, find any excuse you can to avoid doing it. We can't afford to risk losing another ship."

"Roger! I'll get in touch with you again tomorrow at ten so that you can confirm me taking over to the others. Just in case."

"What do you think—where's the best place to look for Elo?"

"Can't help you there. That stuff could be anywhere. There aren't any restrictions about that. Read the forums. There are probably surface deposits of the stuff which I haven't heard about. I'm a navigator, after all, not a miner."

"Alright, call if anything. Over and out."

With a bitter glance at my petrified marine armor, I retrieved both of my manipulators from my inventory and crisscrossed them behind my back like a ninja. A blaster is a blast and all, but it was nice to have a tried and true instrument handy. Then, taking the blaster as well, I began to slowly make my way through the rock corridor—despite our fairly soft landing, *The Space Cucumber* had not deigned to roll onto her side.

You have discovered the planet Karlaton. Please assign this planet a second name.

You have unlocked the "Discoverer I" Achievement. A share of the resources discovered on this planet belongs to you. Current resource share: 5%.

The notification, appearing as soon as I stepped out onto the ship's hull, forced me to freeze, dive back into my rock egg and sign out into reality. I wouldn't take step one on a newly-discovered planet without knowing everything there was to know about this topic. What if, as the discoverer, I get to make any wish I wanted? Like, say, a complete overhaul of my beloved ship. Until

START THE GAME

I knew otherwise, Karlaton would remain off limits to me.

"Greetings Master," Stan cranked his music box.

"I need everything there is to know about newly discovered planets. Bonuses, advantages, facts, gossip and just a basic rundown about that game mechanic. You have two hours, so drop everything and get to work. Wait, no—make me dinner first. I'm hungry."

"As you wish," Stan instantly replied. "Eunice has responded to your message, do you wish to see her reply?"

"Sure."

Stan swiveled one of his screens toward me and projected several lines of text onto it:

"Alexis, my regards! Good news! In actual fact, five of the twelve are dead—not two, as you thought. One of us is very deliberately and systematically killing his competitors and I have no reason to think that you aren't the killer. In two months I will be out of the Training Sector. We can talk then. But only in-game. I'm not about to talk or meet anyone IRL. As soon as I get out of the Sector, I'll send you my comm's ID. If you're innocent, my advice to you is change your place of residence. There are too many people who know Alexis Panzer, Runlustia's famed Paladin."

"Stan, where'd the message come from?" I instantly asked.

"The message came through an encrypted channel. I cannot determine its sender's coordinates. If you wish to initiate an official trace, please provide your approval for the filing of form 582U-EZ. Only upon receiving official permission from the authorities..."

"Cancel that. There's no point doing that now." I didn't feel like getting in touch with the police and explaining myself.

"In that case, allow me to remind you that in two days you have scheduled a meeting with law enforcement officials, during which you will receive an award."

"I remember. Whatcha got about the space exploration?"

"Projecting to screen now." Stan replied. "I will be appending further data as it is compiled and systematized."

As Eunice's letter gave way to excerpts from *Galactogon*'s manual and forum posts on the topic I'd requested, no matter how hard I stared at the words, they refused to arrange themselves into logically coherent sentences—Eunice's message still rang in my head: *"Five of the twelve are dead."* If Lucille—our disagreements be damned—was also part of this thing...

"Stan, bring up the contract for the billion pound check wager. I need the organizer's contact info. I'd like to talk to them."

"You have reached Thompson." The male voice answering my call was saturated with bureaucratic undertones. Though he had only said four words, that had been enough for me to understand much about this person. I'd seen plenty of his kind before during my time in *Runlustia*.

"Good day, my name is Alexis Panzer. I am one of the participants in the check wager. Your contact information is in the contract, so..."

"Alexis!" the man interrupted me. "It's very nice to hear from you. If I am not mistaken you are playing under the handle 'Surgeon' and you are with the Qualian Empire, no?"

"That's correct. How shall I refer to you?"

"You may call me Dmitry. How may I be of service?"

"Dmitry, I received news today that five of the twelve gamers brought on to your wager have died. This leads me to fear for my life. I am calling you because I would like to hear your official statement on this issue."

"True, we are aware of this issue and are currently trying to resolve it by any means necessary," the supervisor of the project informed me. "We have assigned a bodyguard to each project member. We are keeping a close eye on all the neighborhoods where our members live, so you have nothing to be worried about. We have everything under control."

"Thank you for that explanation," I mumbled, utterly unconvinced by Dmitry's confident and cheerful voice. Any time they tell you everything's under control—it's time to panic.

"Alexis, I don't wish to come across tactless, but how did you learn about the participants' deaths?"

"From the web and my own inference," I replied. As silly as it seemed, I wasn't about to betray Eunice. Aside from making it impossible to figure out what the conversation was about, an encrypted channel also prevented any record of a conversation ever having taken place. "One of the dead was in my trio. I identified him by looking for his physical appearance in public news outlets. The others I got more or less by accident. Until our conversation, I had no assurance that they were also participants. Now I can see that my reasoning did not betray me."

"Thank you for the explanation. I assure you that we are doing everything in our power to ensure that you face no obstacles in your performance of the duties you have undertaken. May I help you with anything else?"

"No, thank you. You have reassured me," I told Dmitry and hung up. I would bet the head on my shoulders that now was the time to be really worried.

"Send Eunice the following message: *'You are right, trust no one. Get out of the Sector, then we'll talk.'* Next—I need you to find an apartment and devise a plan to move us there secretly. The one condition is that no one can know that I am moving at all. Understood?"

"Understood. Searching for a fitting residence now. Please forgive me, when you said the word 'us' were you speaking of yourself in the plural or did you have someone else in mind?"

"Us. I need access to your resources through a secure line. You yourself will stay here and remotely interface with the system in the new house. That's an important condition."

"Understood. Master, I have completed processing the data about discovering new planets. Do you wish to see the results now?"

"Sure. Let's see what you got..."

"A Planet discovered by a player has two official names—

START THE GAME

---

one that was assigned to it by the developers and another that the discovering player gets to assign it...A player who discovers a planet receives X% (depending on rank) of all resources extracted from this planet...Additionally, the discovering player receives a +10% bonus to the probability of discovering a unique item..."

This was pretty boilerplate stuff that, aside from suggesting that I could win the lottery, told me nothing of value. The forums too bore no mention of any first wishes. It was as if *Galactogon* players had never even heard of such a thing. In my beloved *Runlustia*, when a player discovered some new land or area, he received several nice rewards, including a wish of his choice...Here, on the other hand...As for the unique item (I just couldn't pass this detail by without checking it out further), in *Galactogon* this could be anything and everything—from an energy sprite to an entire solar system. The important part was that this item would be singular in the game, having no analogue whatsoever. Considering that, like with all items in *Galactogon*, this item too could be taken at will by anyone who cared enough, its use to me was about zero. I didn't exactly wish to become a collector of rarities. And yet that +10% was immense, since the base stat to begin with was 0.001%.

Thus, the only boon from my discovery of this planet was the money I could get from selling the naming rights. There were plenty of self-absorbed donkeys and suchlike narcissists in *Galactogon* and they would jump at the chance to name a planet after themselves. And, it should be said, of these, the male

---

contingent far outnumbered the female one. Stan even showed me an official blog dedicated to the purchase and sale of secondary planet names. The prices started at ten thousand dollars for a planet on the periphery of the known galaxy and went all the way up to tens of millions for planets closer to the center. The only requirement was precise coordinates of the unnamed planet's solar system—that is, a luxury I could not afford at the moment. If I knew those, I could have convinced Marina to send me at least one of her scouts. A pair of torpedoes was all *The Space Cucumber* needed...

Before climbing back into the game capsule, I spent some time staring at the wall in meditation: As fraught as my relations were with Lucille, I had to let her know that five others had already been killed. I realized that Alonso would get it right in the nuts, but better he get it from a wife who's alive than hold me responsible later for staying silent.

I decided to let Lucy know as soon as I finished moving to the new apartment Stan was still looking for. Only after that— better safe than sorry.

Please assign this planet a second name.

The first thing I saw upon resigning into *Galactogon* and stepping out of the ship was a dialog box asking me to enter a new name. Considering my salary, ten thousand dollars wouldn't mean much, so I selected the input box (you had to enter the name by hand) and christened my planet.

START THE GAME

Name accepted! Planet Blood Island welcomes its discoverer!

I didn't feel like thinking about it and simply named the planet according to the pattern I'd already adopted. If I ever got out of here, the name would remain a fitting memorial to *The Space Cucumber*'s untimely shipwreck. Otherwise...well...any captain would be proud to make even such a minor contribution to the memory of his first ship.

Blood Island turned out to be a very green planet. Huge green ferns rose against a vista of mountains, their thick trunks camouflaged by a chaos of smaller trees, bushes and grasses. My PDA deemed the various avian species darting about as "mostly harmless." It felt like I had a discovered an evergreen Eden. The only interruption in this flowering spectacle was the enormous crater caused by *The Space Cucumber*'s crash landing: a hundred or so yards of disrupted turf and broken saplings. I was sure that after a few months, the frigate would be entirely buried by Blood Island's vegetation.

I gathered any food there was to find on board and had to smile to myself—considering that a player in *Galactogon* could go hungry for no more than two days, I would definitely have to depart Blood Island in a week. We had not bought any supplies on our way out of Qirlats, as most players only ate when they were planetside anyway. As a result, *The Space Cucumber* only contained the three daily rations that had been there when Lestran and I first boosted it from the Training Sector. If I skipped a day, I could stretch this food to last a week. After that, I'd either find myself on Qirlats from starvation or...or I'd find myself on Qirlats with my ship. Obviously, I preferred the second option.

I found a cable in Lestran's repair bay and used it to shimmy down from the hull. It's not like the Elo would come to me, so I'd have to take a look around the planet. If I had my marine armor, I would've kicked in my thrusters and circumnavigated Blood Island in a few days, but...Well, that was yet another "if" too much.

"What up Surgeon?" Wally called me that evening. "Marina sent us the frigate as promised. Since you're not around, I took on the role of captain and registered the new ship under my name. You don't mind, do you?"

"Of course not. It's looking like I'll be here for at least a week," I mumbled, wearily leaning against the trunk of the nearest tree. "What's up with you guys otherwise?"

"We made it to Daphark today and found Tryd. His missions for us consisted of destroying several F-class orbital stations, delivering a couple messages and ferrying some Qualian. Pretty basic stuff on the whole. It's more work for the ship than for our crew. According to the forums, Tryd's gonna make us run around for several weeks, so you have plenty of time."

"Don't worry, I'll be back soon," I smiled and joked around with Wally for a few minutes before turning off my comm and looking wearily at the dark jungle around me. I had managed to traverse about twenty clicks in the direction of the mountains on the horizon. The jungle was an impassable mass of latticed trees and branches, vines, grasses, bushes and other large plants. Thick green snakes coiled in the branches of the canopy. I was getting the impression that all this life teeming on this planet had been made for me alone—as nowhere along my way had I encountered so much as a single trail. Even in the best conditions, it would have been impossible to traverse this morass if it weren't for my two fully-charged manipulators. I put away my blaster in the first few minutes of my journey, since shooting at the plants would have been pointless. The manipulators, on the other hand, lived up to their name. Branches, grass, vines, snakes—all of it went flying out of my way. That which refused to fly, crawled. When the first snake, irritated by my rude treatment of its tail, attacked me, I almost met my Planetary Spirit. I managed to react to its lunge in the nick of time, however, stopping its hissing maw several yards from my face. The manipulator did its job well, pacifying the serpent. After the snake's skull finished its exchange with the nearest tree trunk, I received a notification that my weapon's experience bar had grown by several points. Searching the dead snake, I found "Venomous Saliva," which could be used in the forging of armor. What else was there to do but smile contently and open hunting season in earnest? I instituted a mini-genocide of snakes, birds, monkeys and anything else that got underfoot. (At one point it even occurred to me how nice it was that there was no PETA on this planet.) I was pretty sure that Blood Island had never witnessed such an extinction event. The thing that perplexed me the most, though, was that all the animals

I encountered seemed to live up in the trees. It was as if this newly discovered world had never gotten around to evolving land-based animals.

Or so I thought…

After my chat with Wally, I was about to pop out to reality when I heard a fierce roar come from the jungle before me. It sounded like a trumpet's call—as though some unknown creature was calling me to battle. The roar came again just as fiercely and insistently. Although, I thought, maybe I simply hold myself in too high a regard and that call has nothing to do with me at all. Perhaps these were just the mating calls of the local macaques and all that was going on was two males were squaring up to fight over a female…

As I advanced towards the sound, the trees ended abruptly and I found myself in a small clearing, no more than fifty yards across. Looking closer I realized that the clearing was artificial—the bushes and grass had been carefully flattened or uprooted. On the opposite side of the clearing from me stood the source of all this belligerent ruckus—a humongous, nine-foot-tall creature that bore a close resemblance to the common rhinoceros.

"What's up? Wanna chat?" I said, putting my manipulators away and retrieving my blaster. My two clubs would be useless against such a monster and there were no boulders I could pick up and throw at it.

"Grrr!" replied the creature and, fixing me with its three eyes (the third being on its forehead), charged in my direction.

START THE GAME

Judging by the speed it accumulated, the beast was not much disposed to idle chatter. Too bad for him…

"They never want to talk," I muttered, taking aim and pulling the trigger. Even if my blaster wasn't as powerful as Miloš's, it would be more than enough to…

Melt in my hands?

The beast charging in my direction turned out to have the very pleasant name "Cryptosaur" and the very pleasant characteristic called "active resistance," which instantly incinerated my blaster as if it were some plastic toy. Puzzled, I stared at my hands, then up at the three-eyed cow with a horn on its nose that was still closing in on me. I had the presence of mind to jump back only thanks to the reflexes I had accumulated in *Runlustia*. Jumping to the sides wouldn't have helped—the beast would have caught me anyway. In jumping backwards I wanted to mitigate the damage I knew I would take. It seemed to have worked…

The beast struck me with such force that I flew about thirty feet backwards. If I had remained standing in place, then instead of its forehead I would've met its horn. After a short flight through the brush, my back encountered a giant tree trunk, which I slid down along, getting tangled in the vines and bushes the length of the way. My breath had been knocked out of me. It was painful to even move, much less attempt to untangle myself and flee from the monster. If it weren't for the clothes I'd pilfered from the Training Sector, I would've been waiting ten minutes to respawn in Qirlats. Without breaking its stride, the cryptosaur busted through the bushes and rushed past me, dodging the collision with the tree at my back. I heard the cracking of branches and the rhino came barreling past me in a different direction, seemingly calculating a path for a final killing blow.

"*Kaldaran daragost!*" a mighty, somewhat croaking voice drowned out the tramp of the cryptosaur, which was busy turning around for the coup de grace. "*Rekvasta narguler!*"

Hadn't I already told myself to learn the in-game languages? This wasn't *Runlustia* where you could buy a mission in any store—*Galactogon* was much closer to reality in that sense. You had to do some studying here if you wanted to understand anyone besides other players—and quite pointless studying by the way, since none of these language existed in real life.

Doing my best to remember the spoken phrase, so I could run it past Stan later that night, I worked on catching my breath and tensely awaited the appearance of this new representative of the local fauna. The hit I had taken from the cryptosaur had been a pretty bad one.

"Surgeon, *kardane delrogast?*" Even though I expected the newcomer to appear from the direction of the clearing, where I had heard the initial shout, the stranger appeared right above my head. Flabbergasted, I found myself looking at a three-foot-tall butterfly, which the developers had deigned to give four arms, a pretty unremarkable human face, two giant horns where the antennae should have been and, well, sentience. If it weren't for its bright blue, pupil-less eyes, this creature could easily be taken for a person who could see what my name was like anyone else in the game.

"I don't understand," I shook my head, answering Warlock—a member of the Uldan species. I had always paid close attention to images when studying the various Galactogonian guides, yet I had never seen either any Uldans or butterflies among the game's species. This just meant that Stan would have more work to do tonight.

"*Kardane delrogast?*" Warlock repeated, evidently not understanding me either. The undergrowth behind the giant butterfly crackled as the cryptosaur returned for another visit. Taking a seat on the ground just like a trained dog, it froze, waiting for the Uldan's next command.

"I don't understand," I insisted once more. Assuming that locals in *Galactogon* behaved as they did in other games, I couldn't pop out IRL to find out what I was being told. If I did, I'd lose contact with this Uldan and then get smashed to pieces by the unfettered cryptosaur upon my return. "I only speak English. I don't know any other languages."

"*Dernast shradnalar,*" Warlock shook his head sadly, flicked his wings and swooped up into the air. "Zartas!" he commanded, pointing at me—at which, the cryptosaur charged. The last thing I remembered was the melancholy expression on the face of that giant butterfly.

Dang! I'd lost *The Space Cucumber*.

"Greetings, Master..."

"Stan, hack the *Galactogon* servers if you have to, but I need this text translated," I said, sending Stan a recording of my last ten minutes in *Galactogon*. After a moment's thought, I also sent over the star map I had photographed in the vicinity of Blood Island. "After you translate the text, I need to know anything you can find about this mysterious butterfly named Warlock, the overgrown rhino that killed me and a full analysis of the star map. Download any maps you can find and analyze every possible viewing angle. I have to know where that planet is located."

In ten minutes, my character would respawn on Qirlats, so I was planning on signing into the game one more time and leaving the respawn area. After death, the player reappeared in the abode of the Planetary Spirit and it was considered bad form to remain there for a long time. There weren't any fines or anything—it just wasn't done. A weird custom, of course, but whatever: You don't get to make up the rules when you're still a newbie. Tomorrow morning I would call Wally and spend some time simply grinding for positive Rapport with the pirates. Unfortunately, it'd be much harder now to fulfill the mission Hilvar had given me.

"Understood. Processing now. Master, while you were absent, I found several new places of residence matching your search criteria. One of them is located in this city. Two more are in the suburbs and one is in the capital. I would like to point out that most landlords require personal information from their renters, therefore…"

"Let me see the two in the suburbs," I interrupted Stan's droning. I really needed to do something about his tone. The more he worked for me, the more he sounded like a nagging wife—"this wasn't right and that wasn't right" etc. I'd trained him too well.

"Alonso! What's going on?" I called my friend as soon as the apartment issue was settled. The place that Stan found turned out to be so fitting that I had literally nothing to object to. The new place featured a direct and encrypted line to my current house, properly installed alarm systems and a location that was quite a distance from the city center yet still on a busy street in a nice neighborhood. Considering that the house it was in also had an underground passage to a neighboring lot, I could safely assume that it had been designed by some paranoiac. Though, to be fair, I learned about the alarm system and the underground passage only after signing a rental agreement and an NDA with the owner, who insisted on seeing his future tenant in person. It seemed that he liked something about my face because he signed the contract almost instantly—having first haggled about the price a bit. In my view, one hundred thousand a month for a house was too much, considering that my salary was five hundred thousand, but all he would give up was a measly ten thousand. The landlord dug his heels in and was about to say no completely, so I had to give in. If it had to be ninety, then let it be ninety. My safety and peace of mind was worth more anyway. After I sent him the master codes, Stan set up a connection to the new house, scanned its systems and disappointed me with the news that my new residence did not come with a game capsule. This begged the question of what to do next—move the capsule I had, or buy a new one. The second option won out, despite the exorbitant price for that hunk of steel—another fifty thousand dollars. If there were specially trained agents monitoring my house, then all my attempts to keep my move secret would come to naught as soon as the movers showed up. I needed to approach this problem creatively.

"What's up!" Alonso replied enthusiastically from his end of the line.

"Listen, I have this thing...Lucy, hey, don't leave!" I managed to call out, seeing Alonso's wife in the background of the vidphone screen. "I have some business to discuss with you."

"You want to ask me to keep mum about your little friend?" said this gentle and wonderful specimen of womanhood, making me second-guess what I was about to do. Should I warn this bitch? Nah—she could go to hell.

"So what'd you want, Alexis?" asked Alonso, casting his wife a stern look. It took me another second to come to my senses and understand that he wasn't guilty of anything at all and if something were to happen to his wife, then we'd both regret it. Together.

"Alright, here's the situation—just hear me out and don't interrupt me..."

"...So I'm about to move, even if it's only for half a year or so. Better safe than sorry...You understand. I called because I wanted to warn you. What you do with this information is up to you guys of course."

"Thank you!" said Lucy and for the first time in the three years I'd known her, I saw her other side. She was no longer some rambunctious cutie that had come to dislike me for whatever reason (most likely because Alonso constantly blathered

---

on about our adventures together). No, she was now serious and composed—as a guild leader should be. "What Empire are you in?"

"Qualian," Alonso answered for me, giving me a guilty look. It would have been silly of me to be angry with him. Whatever friendship tied us together, family was more important and so if there was a potential threat to his spouse, it had to be intercepted as soon as possible. But goddamn it all! Why had I told him about my escape?! "He's already out though. Only took him two weeks to get out of the Training Sector…"

"So you're Surgeon," the girl concluded without asking any further questions. "As you already know, I'm a Precian. I won't tell you my name. If everything you said is true, then I can't trust anyone—even the messenger. I can promise one thing. I won't harm you purposefully, at least until I find that planet. Once that happens, I won't let anyone get close to it—including you. And again—thank you. You've convinced me: I won't tell anyone about you…"

"The gaming capsule has been ordered. It shall arrive and be installed tomorrow at 9 a.m. Master, how do you intend on moving to your new home? Allow me to suggest several options…" As soon as my conversation with Alonso and Lucille had ended, my smart home reminded me of its existence. No, I've got to say again—Stan had really changed recently.

"Let's see it," I waved my hand and got comfy. I had done my duty and it was time to look out for myself.

"Do you know how to drive at least?" smirked the technician who had come out in response to my complaint about a (supposedly) faulty game capsule. I would have never imagined that there would be a service in our world that specialized in secretly moving those who believed themselves under surveillance. All it took was four grand and I'd be secretly whisked away from under the noses of the agents watching me—even if they knew that such an operation was underway.

The first thing the plan called for was hanging a bug jammer on me (even though the technician would sweep me first anyway)—just in case one would be planted as soon as I went outside. Afterward, we were to exchange clothes and then I was supposed to leave my house, get into an ordinary-looking truck (not a flyer) and drive to my safehouse where I would switch with another person sitting in the back, and crawl through a secret hatch in the truck's floor into the tunnel to my new place...Listening to the logistics of this operation all I could do was shake my head, unable to comprehend why all these things existed in our computerized world. I pointed this out to the technician, objecting that as soon as I'd leave my new house, I'd show up on video surveillance and then they'd identify me and notify the relevant authorities. Yet the secret moving service surprised me even here—the technician explained that I wouldn't have any need to leave my place for at least a month. Meanwhile, they would plant a person wearing a mask of my face in my old house and it would be him who'd go out periodically to get some fresh air, letting himself be seen by any surveilling parties and

START THE GAME

---

letting them know that I was at home as per usual. Pure craziness!

Satisfied at last with my new home and having made certain that my new network gateway would still go through my old home's server, I wired over the money. The nameless technician waited long enough to see the funds appear in the company account—and handed me his uniform. The move had begun...

CHAPTER EIGHT

CREW SELECTION

Unlike my old, Spartan house, where I sought to maximize free space, the new place smacked of antiquity. It featured massive, plush furniture (dusted hourly by a robo-maid), a very authentic fireplace with a rocking chair before it, and carpeting that my feet sank pleasantly into. Thus, in addition to the already ample array of technical gadgets and amenities, I found that my new expensive and luxurious house was fully furnished.

"Stan, did you find anything about the *Galactogon* butterfly?" Having brushed my teeth and washed my face, I resumed terrorizing my irreplaceable assistant. I could hardly imagine what I would do without him.

"Master, the data analysis is still incomplete," Stan answered in a culpable tone through the new home's smart home. "My analysis of official sources yielded nothing. I am currently parsing the forums…"

START THE GAME

"Are you trying to tell me that there is no official mention of this creature?" I asked surprised.

"Without having analyzed a sufficient number of sources and having no access to…"

"Stan—get to the point!"

"I am unable to find any of the requested information for both the first and second search requests," said Stan, seemingly deciding to admit his helplessness. "Whereas establishing the search vector for finding Blood Island is a matter of time, I am simply unable to find any information about this strange creature or its race in any public sources. The word 'Uldan' does not show up anywhere, just like the word 'cryptosaur.' No such animal is listed in *Galactogon*'s bestiary. It is as though you managed to land in an entirely different game…"

"How about the translation of Warlock's speech?" I changed the subject, seeing that my virtual friend was at a total loss.

"This request is likewise impossible to complete. Only five unique words were pronounced, yielding no logical meaning. A contextual analysis suggests that, in this language, one and the same word can carry two utterly contradictory meanings. Much like the word 'cleave' in English. I am very sorry, Master, I do not have the resources to complete this request either."

"So all that you can help me with is finding the planet's coordinates?" I clarified.

"Not the coordinates, but the vector, following which one may encounter a star map similar to the one in the photo. I will be unable to say, however, exactly how far along that vector the planet's solar system will lie."

"What's the approximate time to completion for that task?"

"About three to four weeks. At the moment, a portion of my resources is dedicated to monitoring the new house. Accordingly, this estimate may grow by another week. Do you wish me to accelerate my work on this task?"

"No need," I shook my head, even though Stan couldn't see me. "Yank me out of the game as soon as the new game capsule is delivered."

Giving the universal game capsule (which came with my new home by default) a skeptical look, I shook my head, sighed deeply and crawled into it. I wasn't used to using generic consumer crap. It seemed, like I would have to do something about this too...

You have died. Do you wish to resurrect on Blood Island (current planet), or shall you ask your Planetary Spirit to resurrect you back on your homeworld (Qirlats)?

Seeing this notification appear before me, I simply couldn't contain a squeal of joy. During my preparations, I had read everything there was about how ships and their captains respawned—but I had never gotten around to reading about marines fighting on planets. I had figured that this information wouldn't be necessary. It was too bad for me—players who died on some planet were given a choice: respawn on that same planet or return "home." And until you made that decision, you couldn't actually enter the game. Sometimes in life, it's a pleasure to find out you've been wrong all along. I wasn't about to lose *The Space Cucumber*, after all! Plus I was now pretty curious about this Warlock. Who was he? And why did he have a pet rhinoceros with three eyes? I wouldn't have minded having one of those too…

You have chosen to resurrect on Blood Island. Entering game in 5…4…

The game respawned me on Blood Island several feet away from my ship. Overnight, the jungle had not yet managed to cover the path I had made through its green majesty, so I had no trouble heading back in Warlock's direction. Using one of the three remaining powercells, I got out a manipulator and headed off to find a big boulder. If the cryptosaur had active resistance, then my manipulators would fizzle out as soon as I try to use them. Luckily, I'd already had to deal with this problem before. The manipulator had enough charges for a week of continuous use, so I didn't have to be too thrifty with it now. That poor rhino. Hunting season had come. The important thing was to find a nice heavy rock.

"Grrr!" the beastly roar of the cryptosaur was music to my ears. Another blow from my six foot pebble sent the animal flying, knocking it off its feet and slamming it against a tree. Waves of iridescence coursed along the rhino's body, as if the animal was trying to adjust its active resistance; however, there wasn't much it could do against a rock coming at it at speed—this was elementary physics at its most vivid.

I came upon the animal in the same clearing where it had sent me to my first resurrection. I got the impression that the rhino was like a guard dog for some nearby home. Warlock was nowhere to be seen, so I climbed up a tree, heaved up the rock I found with my manipulator and sent it flying onto the overgrown monster. The startled beast's legs splayed out in different directions and it collapsed heavily onto its belly—casting about its head in search of the assailant. Lifting the boulder again and thereby drawing the rhino's attention to it, I moved it a few yards aside and then instantly launched it into the animal again. Mass and acceleration did their job—the cryptosaur couldn't dodge in time and merely oinked when the rock knocked it off its spot and stamped it into a tree. The only bad thing was that the rhino finally spied me. I understood that I'd been found out.

And so we began to dance.

I lost count of how many times I wanted to pat myself on the back for having climbed up a tree. Over and over again, the cryptosaur slammed into the huge tree trunk, trying either to break it or to clamber up to me—which, given its dimensions, would have been quite a sight. This wondrous beast couldn't jump, so I calmly and evenly accelerated the rock and cast it into the teeming animal mass, time after time forcing from it gasp after gasp. The strange thing was that the life bar hadn't appeared, as if it didn't exist at all—and yet with each blow, the cryptosaur's movements grew slower and slower. Considering that this was a game and a monster of this type wouldn't weary easily, I could safely say that I was beginning to win.

"Surgeon! Stop!" After ten minutes of this exercise, the cryptosaur stopped in its tracks and collapsed in a motionless heap at the foot of the tree. I got no experience for the kill, which meant only one thing—the beast was still alive. Raising the boulder into the air once again, I got ready to drop it straight onto the rhino's head—when I was stopped by Warlock's exclamation. The Uldan butterfly had alighted on my branch.

"So you do speak English after all?" I asked sarcastically, lowering the boulder to the ground beside the cryptosaur just in case.

"I do not know what 'English' is, but my *glardirant* identified your speech as a very impoverished variety of a language spoken by an experimental race of creatures called 'Qualians.' When I realized that you had returned to this planet, I had to go visit the *shalrandan* so that I could learn to communicate with you. The cryptosaur was supposed to slow you down…Why have you come here to Karlaton?"

If a local wishes to start a conversation, it's pretty dumb to ignore him. Since the butterfly turned out to be so garrulous, who knows, maybe he could help me salvage *The Space Cucumber*. Therefore, I made myself comfortable on my branch and began to relate how we got into our last battle, how we jumped to hyperspace, how we found the planet and how I sent my team on furlough, remaining here to save my vessel. It wouldn't have made sense to keep all this secret from this bit of AI…

"Your rock shell won't allow your ship to leave the planet," said Warlock, flitting about *The Space Cucumber*. "Even if you fill her with Elo, the self-destruct won't do anything. The rock layer will preserve the hull and, consequently, the ship as a whole. To bring her back to order, you'll need to get her back up to space and then hit her with one of your torpedoes. There's no other way to save this ancient frigate."

"She's not so ancient," I replied defensively, looking askance at the cryptosaur. When I told the local humanoid my whole story, he decided that he wished to look at a modern spaceship with his own eyes—as if he hadn't heard *The Space Cucumber* come crashing down onto the planet to begin with. What a bunch of weirdos were the locals here. The cryptosaur came with us, barely walking on its short legs—it looked like I had worked it over rather well and now it kept casting glances at me, so that at least one of its three eyes was constantly upon me, as if plotting some kind of revenge.

"She's not ancient in terms of when she was made. She is ancient in terms of when she was designed," Warlock explained. "We stopped building such ships many millennia ago, deciding that they were too faulty."

"Millenia? How old are you anyway?"

"At the moment, I am 122,342 years old," came Warlock's

astonishing reply. "I was left here as a planetary protector and therefore did not participate in the galactic war. Maybe that's why I'm talking to you right now, instead of floating out there somewhere."

"Why did you call the Qualians an experiment?"

"Because they were created artificially. We were looking for a way to fight the Vraxis and experimenting with the different races. Qualians and Precians are our children—created to protect the planets. We granted reason and knowledge to our creations but, as we see now, the experiment was a failure. Over the 70,000 years since the death of my race, our creations have devolved significantly. Technologically as well as linguistically. Am I correct in assuming that you are looking for something?"

"I don't even know what to ask," I droned. "If the difference between what you and I know is too great, then it won't make sense to ask even for a bit of wisdom, since no one living would understand you. I'll try another approach—tell me, is there a bank check for a billion pounds on this planet?"

"No," Warlock shook his head. "The item you are looking for is not here."

"WHAT?! You know what I'm talking about?"

"Uldans always held their prophets in high esteem. I was once foretold that a searcher would come to me and ask me about a check. Then, I would have to tell him: 'He who finds freedom will show you the way, but first you must show him that you are worthy.' This is the phrase that has kept me from going to my rest—after all, our prophets were never wrong. Now my mission is complete. I can calmly return to the ether. Goodbye my child..."

"Wait!" I yelled, seeing Warlock begin to melt into the air as if he was a player signing out into reality. Stan would dissect Warlock's message and provide his best guesses for what it might mean, but at the moment I was after something else too. "How do I get off this planet?"

"Send yourself to resurrection and lose the ship," replied Warlock, coming back into focus a little. "You have learned how to speak to the Planetary Spirits, so you may die bravely and find yourself reborn on your homeworld. You do not have the resources to save your frigate."

"You don't say," I smirked. "If you give me this planet's coordinates, then I'll be able to call..."

"Seventy thousand years have passed—in the course of which many stars, civilizations and empires have been born and died. Do you really think our coordinate grids will match? Don't keep me here, Surgeon. I have grown weary."

"Listen, I understand that you can't wait to get to the ether and all that, but you already waited a hundred thousand years, so you can wait another hour. You said that I can get my ship to space and destroy it there. Is there something I can use on this planet to do that?"

"No," the butterfly shook his head again. "This planet has no such devices that will allow you to launch that mountain of stone into space. However..."

"However?" I looked inquisitively at Warlock, who'd fallen

silent.

"There is a ship on this planet that you could use. If you recharge your frigate with Elo and then turn on your onboard computer—then, I believe my ship's AI will be able to connect to your frigate and synchronize the data, including the navigations network. Then you'll be able to find out the coordinates of this planet and call your friends to come help you."

"Well why didn't you say anything earlier?" I asked surprised. "What do I need to do to get this ship?"

"You must pass a test," Warlock brought me back to reality. "You passed the first one already—the marine has recognized you as his leader. Now you have to convince the rest of the crew."

"Sorry—I must have missed something," I said, flabbergasted. "What marine are you talking about?"

"Why this one," the butterfly replied and pointed at the cryptosaur. "The ship that you are interested in requires a crew of four, and each crew member must be on board for the ship to fly. You became the captain and you've managed to convince the marine that you are a worthy leader. That leaves the gunner and the engineer. If you want my ship, you'll have to convince them…"

"The rhino is a marine?" I blurted out.

"He is not a rhino. He is a cryptosaur," Warlock corrected me. "A cutting-edge combat droid—the last of a series built by our scientists. Typically, he wouldn't even notice a physical attack, since his defensive systems are top notch, but the designers did not account for a boulder pounding him for several minutes.

Taken by surprise, his systems suffered a temporary fault. He's better now and sees you as a leader who is capable of making extraordinary decisions. If you manage to get the ship, in this cryptosaur you will have a unique warrior. And I should point out that his armor is much better than the marine armor on board your ship at the moment. You can't even compare the two—they're like day and night."

I didn't need an Uldan fortune teller to tell me that I had received a mission—and one that I would never mention to anyone. Otherwise, even today, hundreds of cruisers would show up over this planet and start pouring fire all over the place. Even though I'd be happy to return to the main part of the galaxy, it wouldn't be a good idea to pass up on a ship whose owner referred to my *Space Cucumber* as a tub. And considering that I also had the opportunity to pick up three robots along the way too...

"Where should I look for them? And, listen, you don't have any food by any chance, do you? I won't be able to hang around here for long otherwise..."

The jungle of Blood Island sped past me as rapidly as trees flashing past a bullet train. Even though the cryptosaur was looking out for my safety, this only meant avoiding collisions with the larger flora. He seemed to consider everything else to be a minor and insignificant obstacle and bulldozed his way directly

---

through it. What I liked most about the marine was that in addition to his main role, he was also a high-speed heavy tank. I had had some doubts when Warlock told me where I could find the gunner and suggested I ride the rhino to get there faster. I figured my chances of remaining on the back of this monster were not great—I've never been much for cowboys and whatnot. However, after the cryptosaur finished his transformation—restructuring his upper back to create a seat and then generating a force field canopy around it—I could not say no to taking a ride in such a machine. I would be very sorry indeed to part with this epic beast—a marine-tank would come in handy on any planet that required a space-borne assault.

According to Warlock the gunner was in the neighboring forest. I never understood how you could delimit the boundaries of different forests in one giant jungle, but my tank seemed to understand perfectly well where he was and where he was going.

Eventually the cryptosaur slowed down and began to make circles, trampling a clearing in the morass of vines and vegetation. Once he had made it, he raised his head and bellowed a piercing roar. In response came a no less savage scream, letting me know that the gunner too was some kind of zoomorphic robot. When I had asked Warlock what he looked like, the butterfly simply shrugged his shoulders and asserted philosophically that I'd know him when I saw him. I've got nothing against riddles and multipart missions, but I've had the habit of preparing for my missions meticulously since my time in *Runlustia* and, at the moment, everything was coming down to chance—

which was beginning to irritate me.

With surprising grace, the cryptosaur deposited me gingerly on the ground and stepped aside. I shook my head in astonishment—it had all happened too quickly: First I was sitting on his neck and then suddenly I was standing on the ground and, though but a moment elapsed between these two events, my consciousness could not catch up to it. There was no way in hell that I could pass up a chance to have this rhino on my team!

The scream came from the forest again, reminding me why I had been brought here. I took out my manipulator and dragged the nearest boulder toward me. This one was a crumb compared to the one I had used to pacify the marine, but I simply hadn't bothered to load extra inventory onto the cryptosaur, assuming that there would be enough rocks on site. It turned out now that that had been a poor assumption to make.

The scream sounded a third time. The bushes on the other side of the clearing parted and the gunner came walking toward us.

"So that's who you are," I let slip once I saw what I was dealing with. The gunner was a gigantic, four-armed orangutan, bearing the no-less grand in-game title of "Strabosaur." If it weren't for his extra pair of arms, his seven foot tall stature and the pair of holstered blasters which the strabosaur wore like a cowboy, I would have had great difficulty telling this creature apart from the primates I'd seen in the zoo: He had the same orange fur, pronounced lips and general bodily proportions. It seemed that whoever designed this creature hadn't seen the need in thinking about it too much—why put in too much effort designing a one-off mission?

"Oooh-ooh-aah!" yelled the strabosaur, stopping at the edge of the jungle. Bending his knees and spreading his arms, the orangutan bore such a resemblance to a cowboy preparing to draw his revolvers that I couldn't help but crack up. What was the deal here anyway? Was I supposed to duel this distant cousin (far removed) of mine in order to convince him to join my crew? Alright! Sounds awesome! Especially since I didn't have anything aside from a manipulator.

The cryptosaur stood to the side and as soon as I adopted the proper posture, mirroring the orangutan, began to pound on the trunk of an uprooted tree.

Boom! Boom! Boom! Pause.

Boom! Boom! Pause.

Boom! Shoot!

To be honest, I was completely unprepared for such lovely entertainment. No need to do your homework—reading forums and whatnot—simply show up, see the monkey, shoot the monkey. I realized that I didn't stand much of a chance against four blasters, so as soon as the cryptosaur gave the signal (I never figured out why he decided to be our second to begin with), I took a giant leap to the side and rolled toward the jungle. I knew I'd be no match for the strabosaur in open terrain.

Knowing that I was in a game in which the locals would react to my improvisation, I varied my speed as I rolled along the ground, trying my best to keep the trees that the rhino had felled between me and the orangutan. The singed wood chips and pieces of plant matter that burst all around me from the gunner's fire reassured me that I had chosen the correct strategy. Even more reassuring was that I was still alive a whole ten seconds after the duel had begun. The important thing now was to keep moving and do so at a varying pace—otherwise the dumb program would be able to predict my motion and send me to my Planetary Spirit. Considering how long it took us to get to this clearing, I'd have a time of it walking here on foot again.

"Oooh-ooh-aah!" Ooh-ooh-ooh!" came the disappointed chatter as soon as I dived into the jungle. I went on rolling, ignoring the orangutan's complaint, until I reached a large tree. In a second I shimmied up it, realizing even as I did so that it would offer no cover against a blaster. But at least I wouldn't be found here instantly.

"Grrraaa!" bellowed the marine who, like the orangutan, seemed displeased with my turning tail. It seems that he had really wanted to see an epic firefight and my tactical retreat had foiled his expectations. Excuse me, but no! Since I wasn't given any time to consider the situation before the duel started, no one was going to make me budge an inch until I'd finished thinking everything through...at my leisure.

Carefully parting the branches between the clearing and myself, I appraised the situation one more time. The cryptosaur, who had begun digging the earth with his horn, was clearly not my ally—judging by his unhappy growling, he was unhappy with me. Until I managed to deal with the gunner, the marine was not to rely on. It was too bad.

The orangutan was still standing in his initial place, looking in my direction. Shivers ran down my spine. For a second, I thought that the gunner could see me. I forced myself to remain still and after a moment, the gunner's gaze dulled: From that distance it was hard to tell, but I definitely felt that my current position was no longer under the strabosaur's close scrutiny.

And so! What paths to victory were there, considering that all I had was a manipulator? Right away, the tried and true move suggested itself. I could find a boulder and fling it at the primate. However, several obstacles stood in the way of this plan. I'd have to get up close to the strabosaur, reveal myself by raising the rock and then manage to manipulate the rock while being shot at from four blasters. If I had had my marine armor on, I'd at least risk this maneuver, but…The gunner was right at the tree line. If I could sneak up behind him and…

As if he'd read my mind, the orangutan took several steps forward and froze right in the center of the ninety-foot-wide clearing. The only upside to the current situation was that he stopped looking in my direction and instead seemed to expand his angle of observation. The AI had calculated my maximum speed in stealth mode and begun to monitor the probable directions I could attack from. I guess the strabosaur's defense-AI wasn't as primitive as I'd thought.

After five minutes of watching the gunner, I came up with a new, crueler plan. First, I assumed the worst: that this robot too has active resistance, which would melt my manipulator as soon as I'd point it at my target. I understand that this sounds a little daft, since the mission has us shooting each other, but given my history with these things, it just made sense to play it safe. In that case, I couldn't point my manipulator at the orangutan—doing so would destroy the device. However! The blasters that this beastly ancestor of mine was holding had no such defense—unless of course some utter psycho designed said ancestor and his weapons. Accordingly, if I used the manipulator on the weapon then…Well, it was worth a shot.

I discarded the idea of pelting the orangutan with rocks after the first attempt. Having waited until the orangutan turned 90 degrees away from me, I lifted a tree trunk that was lying beside him and was just about to fling it at the gunner's back—and I mean "was just about to"—because no sooner had the trunk moved than the strabosaur turned, drew all four blasters and reduced this once-proud tree to a few wisps of ash floating to the ground. I froze, afraid to move and only after a minute—once the gunner's attention had faded—did I retake my seat on the branch. So much for that idea.

I decided to go with my other plan. Having waited until the strabosaur had almost turned his back to me, I aimed my manipulators at the top two blasters, locked on and, sighing sadly, yanked the blasters in opposite directions. The idea was to keep the orangutan guessing about where I was, since he still had the bottom pair of blasters and arms—which is precisely what this orange gorilla used.

I hadn't managed to yank the blasters away from him—

the strabosaur grabbed onto them like a drowned man clutches at a straw, and all I managed to do was to splay his upper set of arms akimbo. I was immediately happy with myself for not waiting to attack when the ape had turned its back to me completely. The gunner had reckoned accurately that if his arms were being splayed in opposite directions then either I must have been in front of him or behind him. Bending his bottom pair of arms in an entirely unnatural manner—so that the top pair was pointing in one direction while the bottom pair was pointing perpendicularly—the orangutan began to pour fire into the jungle from all four blasters. The cryptosaur darted away from his companion, unwilling to fall victim to friendly fire, and seeing this, I decided to change my course of action. If the primate was unwilling to release his weapons, then, I wondered, how would he feel about flying with them?

The manipulators' effective range was only ninety feet or so, so I got to my feet (the noise from the burning and falling trees was so great that no one could hear my movements anymore anyway) and began to lift the blasters I'd captured higher and higher.

"Oooh-ooh-aah!" At first the strabosaur failed to notice that his feet had left the ground and went on shooting. However, as soon as I lifted him thirty feet up, he began to howl plaintively. Even though this was just a game, I was sweating bullets and my arms were all pins and needles, but I began to spread the weapons in different directions, using my thumb to increase the manipulators' range. When a message appeared telling me that the range had reached its maximum, I stopped pressing the button and simply sat back and enjoyed the sight. One manipulator could not have lifted such a monster. But working together, the two manipulators managed the task admirably, dragging the orangutan to an unimaginable height of sixty or so feet. Considering that there weren't any trees around the strabosaur which he could've latched onto or used to break his fall, the drop now facing my gunner was quite formidable.

"Oooh-ooh-aah!" Hints of fear surfaced in the strabosaur's scream and, abruptly, the blasters in his paws ceased firing.

"Meet the crew" Mission Progress: 2 of 3 crew members recruited.

The notification that popped up was so unexpected that I almost dropped my gunner to his death. Two of three! That left the engineer—and I already had a decent plan for how I could recruit him: Lift him fifteen yards in the air and wait until he recognizes his glorious leader. Oh, how naïve I was...

It seems that the orangutan had been designed alongside the rhino, because the two merged seamlessly. My tank grew in size. Two blasters appeared beside the horn, suggesting that the strabosaur hadn't vanished but merely become integrated in the machine, after which all three of us dashed off back to the initial clearing.

"The gunner," Warlock shook his head respectfully, as if he had doubted my ability to handle his mission. "That leaves the engineer who also performs the shields operator's role. You will have to travel beneath the earth, so leave the marine and the gunner here. They won't help you in the subterranean world."

"I need to go underground?" I asked surprised, since this dashed my plans for pacifying the engineer-shields operator.

"That is correct. The engineer is a creature who dislikes sunlight very much and prefers to spend all his time under the soil around here. No one else hangs out in his tunnels, so you won't confuse him with anyone. The entrance to the engineer's kingdom is right behind you. Until we meet again!"

"What?" I managed to yell before the earth under my feet dropped down, dragging me with it. Once again I had been thrown into the thick of another mission without a chance to prepare myself. How much more of this could I take? It took one glance around to understand that nothing good would come of this. I was in the middle of a round chiseled tunnel that was about five feet wide. Its rough-hewn walls suggested that this passageway had been created by artificial means, while the dimensions spoke to those of the engineer who had made it. I quickly recognized whom I was up against—I'd often run into giant worms in *Runlustia*, who'd gnaw similar passageways for themselves. If the width of this monster was five feet, then I was scared to even imagine what his length would be—simple math yielded more than 30 feet, at a ratio of 1:10. (I think that's the minimal ratio of a worm's width to his length under normal growing conditions, but I could be wrong.) In any case, I wouldn't be able to lift a creature that large with my manipulators.

"Warlock!" I shouted up into the opening overhead, which

was so perfectly round it could have been a specially made elevator to shuttle players up and down.

"I'm listening!" The butterfly's head popped up against the circle of sky.

"Ask the gunner to give me one of his blasters."

"You won't need it!" the ancient assured me, after which the opening closed, leaving me alone in the dark.

Realizing that there was no point in just standing there, I spread my arms and, touching the walls for the sake of balance, began to make my way along the passage. To compensate for the sudden loss of sight, I opened all the in-game windows I had available to me—showing me my current status, inventory, buffs and various other statistics. This didn't make the corridor any lighter, but it became a lot easier to move forward—my brain now understood that rather than going blind, someone had simply turned out the lights.

After five minutes of careful progress along the tunnel, I saw a flickering light far ahead of me, resembling weak candlelight. Instantly closing all the game windows, I hurried onward as quickly as I dared. I didn't even consider the possibility of the light being some kind of trap—like the kind used by deep sea fish—since I had not encountered a single branching passage during my walk and could only move forward anyway. If, that is, forward was even a concept in that dark place.

The light grew brighter with each step, gradually growing into the white light at the end of the tunnel. Figuring that an ambush could be waiting ahead, I slowed down as I approached the exit, crept up to the end of the passage and peeked beyond it. My eyes had already adjusted to the light, but I still had to doubt their accuracy for the first several seconds, for the passage had led me to an enormous well-lit cavern, in the center of which stood a huge and working factory. Yes, that's right: a factory! Droids flitted here and there. Sparks flashed as one thing was transported past another. Long smokestacks dumped black smoke, as if the factory was powered not by Elo but by heating oil or even coal. And in the center of this industrial conflagration, lying upon the flat roof of the factory and pulling levers and yelling at the robots, was the slizosaur.

Like the strabosaur, the slizosaur had four arms. Like the cryptosaur, the slizosaur had three eyes. But that was the end of his similarities with the crew of the ship of the ancients. The slizosaur was a giant serpent, and his body was covered in an intricate ornament that constantly mutated in shape and color like a kaleidoscope. The head of this creature was no different than that of any other snake, except for the third eye. Also, the mouth kept opening and closing, as if the snake was saying something instead of hissing as snakes typically do. Only then did I notice that I couldn't hear a single sound from the bustling factory or the screams of its chief executive. Looking closer, I realized that there was a barely glimmering layer at the exit to the catacombs. It took me a minute to find the source of this force field and check its attributes: "Universal Noise Dampener." The device managed its job perfectly well, cutting off any sounds from passing beyond the limit of its glimmering field, while simultaneously filling my mind

---

with cognitive dissonance—I had the feeling that I had gone deaf. Devoting another minute to look over the tunnel's exit for an alarm system and not finding it, I carefully stepped through the portal.

And instantly the noise crashed down on me.

The sound was so intense that I really did lose my hearing for a moment. I kept my eyes on the snake which went on issuing orders (except, now, I really couldn't hear these). I moved forward, hoping that my hearing would finally adapt to the surroundings and begin to discern the various sounds, instead of the uniform metallic crashing that was coming through at the moment. Passing about sixty feet, I took cover behind a smallish pile of rocks, which were strewn all over the place in the cave, and took a moment to assess the situation. I couldn't check the snake's attributes or abilities, so I had absolutely no idea how I could possible defeat it. The ceiling was about 150 feet above me, but even two manipulators wouldn't be able to lift that monster and the cave seemed to have no boulders to throw at the engineer…Even the pile of rocks that I had taken cover behind, consisted of pebbles that couldn't possibly be used to take care of a five-foot-wide snake.

Half an hour of sitting behind the pile didn't yield anything. It was true that I began to distinguish different sounds in that noisy chaos and even discern the snake's speech. No one was paying attention to me, but the task at hand of recruiting the engineer had not advanced one iota. The engineer went on sitting on the roof of the factory, engrossed by his levers and ignoring the surrounding world. Sighing bitterly because I understood that I would have to do something I hated—take an unnecessary risk, that is—I crawled out from behind the pile of rocks and strolled over towards the factory.

"Greetings!" I called out, stopping two yards from the snake's gigantic tail. I had been allowed to calmly approach the factory, walk around it, find the ladder to the roof, clamber up it and walk up to the control station. It was like no one cared a bit what I was up to here. Taking a closer look at the engineer, I barely suppressed a gasp of astonishment—the engineer was about thirty feet long. This begged the following, quite reasonable question: Exactly what kind of vessel was this ship of the ancients that could be crewed by four intelligent beings of absolutely enormous proportions? And how would they all fit on deck?

"I got no time for this!" the snake replied in Qualian and without the hint of a hiss. "Come back in twelve years. I should be done with this project then."

"I don't have twelve years!" I shouted back, shocked. "I need your help!"

"Everyone needs my help!" parried the serpent, without even turning to look at me and still manipulating his levers. "Warlock gave me an assignment—and told me to send everyone his way. As soon as he says the word, I'll deal with your problem. But for now get out of the way—I'm about to get to the most intricate part of the operation."

The levers began to shift and click faster. All four hands of the engineer flashed with a great speed—at some point he even brought his tail to bear—and he seemed to completely forget about my being there. I was really beginning to dislike this state of affairs. What was this whole "go do this but we can't tell you what" thing? A catch-22 mission? Or just a bug in the scripting? The butterfly knew damn well that the engineer wouldn't cause me any trouble—otherwise he would've let me have a blaster. At the same time, this was a computer game—there had to be a way to do the mission. By definition! The snake claims that Warlock ordered it to listen only to Warlock's orders. But the same butterfly sent me here to convince the engineer to join me, knowing very well his previous orders. A contradiction? In general, yes it was— and one that would be impossible to resolve without the ancient captain being there…

"Cease ignoring me this instant!" I ordered, as soon as the chill of realization had run down my spine. "As the ship's captain, I order you to end your work on this project! From this moment on, you are under my command. I rescind your previous captain's orders! Are there any questions?"

"No, captain, sir!" retorted the engineer, finally turning to face me and smiling contentedly. "The ship is ready for voyage. The bridge has been modified to fit your dimensions. Shall I deliver us to the surface?"

"Meet the crew" Mission Accomplished.

Despite the fact that there was no overall list of missions in *Galactogon*, the system would dutifully notify you if you completed one. Such was the current notification about the

---

completed mission—I had succeeded in gathering a crew for the ship of the ancients. All I had to figure out was how I could transfer the data from *The Space Cucumber* to the new ship in order to establish my coordinates.

CHAPTER NINE

THE SHIP OF THE ANCIENTS

Slizosaur, strabosaur and cryptosaur. This was no mere crew. This was the dream crew of any gamer—a huge, 30-foot-long snake, a four-armed orangutan and a 9-foot-tall rhinoceros.

The really surprising thing was that out of this entire zoo of prehistoric fossils (at least this was what their names suggested), only the snake knew how to speak. The orangutan-gunner and rhinoceros-marine only knew how to perform the orders they were given.

"Hmm...Honestly, I didn't think that you'd make it," Warlock admitted as soon as I appeared from below ground, riding the engineer. The snake hadn't dallied. As soon as I saw the mission accomplished notification, he bent down, inviting me to hop onto his back. His body transformed before my eyes. A comfortable-looking seat appeared and I realized that the snake, like the rhino, was an artificial creation. It's dumb of course to distinguish between real or artificial beings when it's all part of a game anyway, but if we were in reality, the slizosaur would have been a robot. An enormous, autonomous, artificially intelligent robot.

"In that case, before going to my rest, I'll give you control of the ship," Warlock went on and held out an oblong item that looked a bit like a pyramid with a small base. This six-inch-long object was also twisted along its central axis, a bit like a wrung towel, so I had no way of associating it with anything I'd ever seen before. Basically it was a strange twisted pyramid with buttons.

"This is the command key," Warlock explained when I looked up at him perplexed. "My fellow Uldans were a bit lazy and didn't feel like always having to go fetch their ships. So they fabricated a command key that let them control their ship remotely. Considering that all you need to do at the moment is transfer the frigate's data, take off from the planet and send out an SOS, there's no reason to explain all the functions of the key to you..."

"I have a different proposal," I interrupted the butterfly. "Why should I call for help, if I can just fly over to the frigate and blow it up? I wouldn't even need to copy her database. All you'd need to do is show me how to work the weapons. My *Space Cucumber* will automatically pop up in the graveyard and no one will ever find out about this planet. Why show anyone this troika?"

I nodded at the robots. "If someone finds out about them, this planet will become a very popular place for my ilk."

"There is a seed of reason in your words," Warlock said after considering my offer. "I like your idea, but in that case, I need to teach you how to pilot the ship during atmospheric flight. It's decided then! Look," the ancient bent down to me and began to show me various button combinations on the command key. "This is how you call the ship..."

The training lasted about ten minutes, during which Warlock showed me how I could call the ship, open her, initialize the engines, block access for others, unlock the crew stations...As it turned out, the three huge animals didn't actually enter the ship like the captain, but simply attached themselves to her hull: The marine took up residence in the bilge; the engineer coiled between the pressure hull and the outer hull, connecting to the reactor; and the gunner clambered up to the very top of the ship and merged with a special nacelle from which he could coordinate point defense and the rest of the weapons systems. This left the player, who remained inside the ship along with four free chairs which could be used as passenger seating. At least, this is how Warlock described the situation to me, without showing me the actual ship. When the time came for that, well...

Basically, my jaw hit the floor when I saw this miracle of ancient engineering.

Every vessel in *Galactogon* had a pretty standard layout consisting of the engines, a reactor section and a front compartment for the crew. In one way or another, this design was replicated for every ship, from the mighty cruiser to the lowly scout. The only difference was the presence or absence of certain external attachments—sensors, weapons and shields. All the ships were basically shaped like flat triangles, so I expected anything but a gigantic, perfectly round sphere with a metallic surface. There was neither a visible entrance, nor openings for weapons, nor portholes, nor sensors—this ancient artifact had nothing but a smooth and metallic outer shell. Having walked around the ship, I couldn't contain my smile—the sphere didn't even have engines. I had no idea how this thing was even supposed to fly. And yet I had just seen it come flying in over the mountains, so I just had to assume this capability on faith...It was becoming difficult to believe the game manual's claim that *Galactogon* employed realistic physics. This was downright impossible, after all!

"My ship," Warlock said proudly. "I showed you how to control it, how to enter it and how to fly it. I have nothing else to tell you, so I can calmly go to my eternal rest. Goodbye, Surgeon! I am happy that you allowed me to discharge my ancient duty..."

The butterfly's body began to melt and literally after a few moments, the ancient who had been standing beside me vanished, having melted into the air around us. The cryptosaur and strabosaur bellowed a mournful dirge, while the slizosaur bitterly remarked, "Goodbye, old captain. You have earned your rest."

Having paid its respects to Warlock, my crew froze awaiting my orders. They made no motion to go anywhere and made no move to take up their positions on the ship, so sighing with ease because I had finally found a moment of peace, I opened the main menu and signed out of the game. I had done enough for today and needed some rest. Additionally, I needed to figure out the text inscribed on the command key—I wanted to know what Warlock hadn't gotten around to telling me. I was sure that Stan would now be able to figure out this language...

Something told me that I could under no condition abandon this ancient ship!

"Master, we are at defcon 4!" Stan reported as soon as the cocoon's lid slid aside. This phrase was so unexpected that I even froze for a moment: My smart home typically welcomed me back with an entirely different greeting.

"Report!" I ordered, climbing out of the cocoon out to the floor.

"Two hours ago, a truck flyer lost control and crashed into your former house. Almost half the house has been destroyed. The damage is particularly severe in your bedroom and the room with your gaming capsule. The communications systems and my mainframe have not been affected. First responders discovered the remains of your substitute under a fallen wall and identified him as an unemployed citizen named Alex Lowell. The shipping company which owned the flyer has already contacted me, wishing to settle the incident with you. In any event, they will be held accountable for manslaughter. Law enforcement wants you to contact them as soon as possible. I have prepared a text for your interview with them. You may study it if you like. You were in

Galactogon during the event, as evidenced by the game's logs."

"Why didn't you let me know as soon as it happened?" I almost yelled in irritation. My home had been destroyed while I was playing with some robot animals?! "Dial the police this instant!"

"There was no immediate threat to your life, so per the protocol, I…"

"I said, call the police!" I barked, interrupting Stan. If I hadn't moved, then…It was frightening to imagine that I could have been in that cocoon and—and that would have been it! One less gamer looking for the check! Only an idiot could believe that a truck flyer had strayed from its course purely by accident. Those things fly high above the city and are subject to strict oversight. I was shaking with adrenaline. I had never encountered something like this. Nevertheless, my mind went considering this catastrophe. Someone with access to flyers and their configurations first killed a famous gamer and now made his way down the list to me. And the betting masters dared insist that they had everything under control! It was pointless to even call them—they couldn't tell me anything…

Lucille!

"Stan, put me in touch with Alonso this second!" I yelled, wishing to warn the girl. Even if she was the mastermind of the assassinations (which was impossible to check or prove), I couldn't not warn her. And yet, when the vidphone connected, I saw a police officer instead of my friend.

"Alexis Panzer?" the cop asked in a low, gruff voice.

"That is correct."

"This is Captain Simo, municipal police. Thank you for finding the time to contact us. Tell me, please, are you aware of the incident with you residence?"

"Yes, but I would like to know the details."

"We would too. If it's not too difficult, could you explain why you contracted the services of the 'Anon Movers' company?"

"I thought that this kind of information was confidential…"

"That is correct, but that was the case only until one of their employees died. At the moment, this company is very interested in cooperating with our investigation. Therefore, I will repeat the question, why did you contract the services of Anon Movers? Were you afraid for your life?"

"Captain, I will deal with this question myself." Suddenly the screen with the police officers split and an aging man appeared in the new half. He was also wearing a uniform, albeit one that seemed to outrank Captain Simo in seniority—as was corroborated by the captain's instantly deferential look.

"Yes sir," the captain retorted, confirming my guess and froze in expectation of his orders. I never imagined that the police were so strict in their discipline.

"At ease, captain," the old man said benignly, as though he'd expected exactly this response to his sudden appearance. "You may go. I am personally taking over this case."

The second half of the screen with the captain's visage vanished and for a short while, the old man and I studied each other in silence. I didn't know about him, but I had absolutely no idea how to conduct myself—judging by the captain's reaction, I was faced with some kind of top brass, and yet I felt no trepidation before him. In general, I had ceased to process everything that was going on as reality—instead, I felt like I was at an audience with the Emperor in *Runlustia*, waiting for him to address me first.

"So, you believe that someone is hunting the contestants?" the old man broke our silence without looking away, as though he was carefully monitoring my reaction. My heart skipped a beat when I realized how he had articulated his question…He hadn't said "hunting you" period, or asked "why did they attack you" period—no, he had specifically used the words "contestants"…This could only mean that the old man was in the know.

"According to my sources, five of the twelve are already dead," I cast my line. If I was wrong, I could still wriggle my way out and if not, then…

"There are six of you remaining," said the old man, his words hitting me like a ton of bricks. I managed to stay on my feet, but the realization that six of the twelve participants had already been killed turned my legs to rubber. This was not what I had in mind when I agreed to take part in the wager. "We are watching your every move and every breath. We are monitoring your communications in-game, and yet we still cannot figure out which of you six has done all this. The contest organizers are worried. They have engaged the best detectives—but everything has been in vain. We still don't know which of you has a helper and how his orders are issued to him. Did you think that you could absolve yourself of suspicion by arranging for a flyer to crash into your house?"

"Excuse me?" I asked baffled—and suddenly, it struck me: They were suspecting me too!

"We understood each other," the old man cut me off tersely. "Until the investigation is complete, I suggest you remain in the house you are in at the moment. You may consider this a house arrest. The court's decision in the matter will be delivered to you within the next few hours. You may order whatever you require through your smart home. Any contact with the outside world must take place either through me or my subordinate. Our contact information will be included in the court order. Are there any questions?"

"I know another participant—a woman. I have a request: Could you make sure she's resettled? I really wouldn't like for another out-of-control flyer to fall onto Lucille."

"All of the remaining contestants will be resettled today. So your request is too late. Is that all?"

"Yes," I nodded. "I have nothing to hide, so I give you permission to use my private data as you see fit. I understand that you will use it anyway, but for the sake of the record...Tell me, is Eunice, one of the three who were with me, still alive?"

As much as I wished to refrain from broaching this topic, Eunice and I had spent a night together and, as a true gentleman, I was compelled to take an interest in her wellbeing. She wasn't going to talk to me and she had deleted her vidphone account, so I could only find out through the old man how she was doing.

START THE GAME

What if she was one of the six victims?

"Please wait for the court order and continue your search for the prize planet. Thank you for giving us permission to use your private data. That makes things a bit easier for us…And, yes, she is still alive."

The screen blinked and then dissolved, leaving me deep in thought. So that's how it was!

We really were being targeted and eliminated—and the organizers of this "last man standing" contest had really taken an interest in the massive demise of their contestants. Considering their status, I had to assume that they had checked everyone and everything. And yet, the flyer that had come crashing down onto my house couldn't care a bit about that—as well as whoever had arranged for that to happen…

A few hours later, as promised, I received the court order decreeing my house arrest. The police took all the issues of settling the matter with the flyer's owners on themselves. I was assured that my childhood home would be completely repaired in a matter of weeks, settlement money quickly appeared in my account and it was already late at night when I could finally count on some peace from the day's happenings. I couldn't even think about signing back into *Galactogon* to temporarily forget the day's events. At three in the morning, Stan gave me a dose of sleeping pills and insisted I take them. According to him, I was beginning to show signs of prolonged, heightened blood pressure and would run the risk of a stroke if I went on this way. Only after I took the pills and sat down on my couch did I understand the magnitude of the shock I had experienced. Once my body relaxed, my psyche lost all control. I began crying like a little child whose favorite candy had been taken away—and was utterly incapable of stopping. My tears flowed like a river and all I could do was simply wipe them away and wait for the next batch, pressing my knees to my chest. It's embarrassing to admit, but the best paladin of *Runlustia*, the winner of tournaments and vanquisher of terrible monsters was sitting and bawling like a little child, having realized that he could have easily been in the place of the person who had replaced him. If Stan hadn't found me this house, then there would have only been five contestants left…

Jesus Christ!

I finally fell asleep late in the morning when the sunlight had already begun to stream through my shutters. At some point my eyes closed and when I opened them again, it was night out.

"Good evening, Master!" Stan's voice instantly greeted me. "Repair work on your house has already commenced. You have received $700,000 in damages from the trucking company. This amount is on top of the cost of the repairs. The insurance company has also paid out for your claim on the house in the amount of…"

Stan went on, explaining how the flyer that came crashing down on my house was actually a quite profitable incident—but I only began to shake all over again. It's not like something like that happens every day, after all.

"Get the capsule ready," I interrupted his report. "How is your search for the vector to Blood Island going?"

START THE GAME

"As I already told you, I do not have enough resources to perform this task in a timely manner," Stan instantly switched over to the topic at hand and began making excuses. "There is insufficient information to…"

"Alright, I'm changing the assignment," I said, getting to my feet. "The old one's not so important now…"

Having fled to *Galactogon*, I found my team in the same exact place where I'd left them a day and a half ago. The three animal-robots stood frozen like wax figures, patiently awaiting their commander's orders and making absolutely no move to deal with their own business. Unlike the players, who have their limits, this team was utterly perfect for my search of the planet with the check. A thought instantly flashed across my mind—why would I ever abandon this round ship and return to *The Space Cucumber*? Marina would probably be more than happy to buy my old frigate, since she had invested quite a bit of money into her anyway. And this sphere would be more than enough for me, even regardless of her level and speed. She had an advantage you couldn't argue with—she didn't need a human crew. For instance, what if I had decided to sign into the game at night and my human crew was nowhere to be found. Then I wouldn't be able to go anywhere or do anything. Thanks but no thanks: I didn't need such encumbrances during my search. It was quite enough that flyers were falling on my house.

I felt a twinge of regret for not sending Stan an image of the command key so that he could decipher the writing on it, but I pushed that back—now was not the time for self-reproaches. I needed to forget everything—the attempt on my life, the things I'd lost, the things I wanted. The important thing at present was the game and the search for the check. This was why I had logged in to *Galactogon* anyway—I had learned a long time ago to leave problems that concerned my life back in reality. The game was only there for the players. Fixing my error, I slipped out of somatic-immersion, made a copy of the command key and ordered Stan to decipher it ASAP. No point in letting him relax...

"Man your stations," I ordered my crew, activating the ship. The perfectly smooth sphere twitched as several passages opened in its surface—for me and my crew. Whereas my entrance looked like any other in a typical spaceship—like in *The Space Cucumber*, for instance—the entrances for the animals were quite amusing. For example, hand holds appeared for the orangutan, along which he instantly climbed up to the top of the shining ship and vanished in some kind of nacelle that wasn't visible from the ground. A giant hatch opened for the rhinoceros in the ship's bilge, revealing various machines and equipment within, and the giant machine trotted into its berth, with the hatch closing instantly behind it. The snake simply slithered up to the hull, drew up as high as it could and coiled itself around the ship. The last thing I expected was for the ship's surface to suddenly turn liquid, sending waves along her expanse, as most of the snake simply sank into the ship, leaving only its tail to protrude. A second later

---

the tail drew into the hull too and my command key flashed with a green light—the crew had taken up its positions. That left the captain—but no sooner had I taken a step toward the ship than my comm came alive with a shrill ringing. Someone with my number wanted to speak to me.

"Hey Surgeon!" came Lestran's happy voice as soon as I picked up the call. "We're already done for today and I stayed back 'cause I wanted to have a chat with you. How's your search for the Elo going?"

"Not very well, for now," I said just in case. Lestran was a nice kid and all, but…"I already found the lode and just have to figure out how to get all this stuff to work. I think that by tomorrow, *The Space Cucumber* will be in the ship graveyard ready for pick up."

"Wonderful! We really need a fifth player. Wally's an awesome dude and all, but it's not like I escaped the Training Sector with him. Plus, he's too careful—we never go after large ships and spend our time hunting minnows instead. It's boring! It'll take forever to become a pirate this way. Come back soon."

"I will, don't worry," I assured him and ended the call. The time had come to see what the ship of the ancients could do.

You have unlocked the "Star Wolf" Achievement. You are now the owner of a unique ship.

You have acquired an uncategorized ship. The closest analogous category is the cruiser. Weight: 650,000. Item class: B-44. For a detailed description of this vessel, please consult the

---

ship's manual.

You are the first player to own this ship and may change her name. There is no current name.

"*Warlock*," I replied without hesitation. The Uldan had helped me acquire this wonder and given me all the requisite rights and access, so it was only right to commemorate him by naming the ship in his memory. An uncategorized B-class ship was not simply an unheard of power—it was a danger to the game's balance. I could see that I was done playing for today, as the rest of the evening would have to be spent in studying the ship's manual as well as the ship itself.

And, while I was dealing with formalities, I knew it would be best to insure myself just in case. For, ignorance of the law was not a valid legal defense.

Dear Galactogon Admins,

During a mission, I obtained an uncategorized, B-class ship, which is a unique game item. I hereby request that you confirm that I obtained this vessel without infringing on the game's logic or rules, and that I am indeed the only owner of this game item.

Respectfully yours,
Surgeon

Even back in *Runlustia* I learned that if you didn't

understand something, it was better to ask. This game item could cost anywhere from one credit (if it couldn't fly) to tens of millions (if it really was ancient and unique). If the admins decided that all I could use it for was to lift off and destroy *The Space Cucumber*, it'd be pointless to argue with them, since that was exactly what I had been given the ship for. Everything else was up to me.

However! As I had not (in my view) broken a single rule or mechanic, I should be able to do with the ship whatever I liked—up to and including flying it back to the main game world. It would suck to suddenly show up in such a unique vessel in the middle of all the other players, who'd instantly decide they needed to have one too...

Crud! Really—I hadn't even considered that! From what I could gather, there were thousands of players in *Galactogon* looking for and collecting unique items—if not tens of thousands—so showing up in *Warlock* would be extremely stupid. The collectors would start such a hunt after me that I wouldn't even have time to look for my check—I'd be spending all my time running from the players coveting my ship.

What could I do? Sell it and go on traveling in *The Space Cucumber*?

Why—that was an option! Surely there'd be plenty players who'd open their purses for such a lovely sphere...

The question was whether I actually wanted to part with it.

Welcome to the Warlock ship manual. Select a topic you wish to study:

GALACTOGON BOOK ONE

As soon as I activated the manual, twenty or so topics popped up on my screen, running the gamut from guest accommodations to the research lab, which, it turned out, *Warlock* had too. I would need a lot of time to study everything in depth and therefore started with the very first topic—a general description of the ship. The important thing was to start— everything else would come later.

Dear Surgeon,

Thank you for contacting Galactogon *Tech Support. We hope that your time in* Galactogon *has been pleasurable—for our part, we...*

There was so much pointless boilerplate in the letter I received back that I was even surprised. It looked like the players had turned to the courts because of *Galactogon's* tech support so frequently—claiming that the associates weren't polite enough or in-depth enough and so on and so forth—that it felt like every sentence in the letter was born of some piece of litigation.

START THE GAME

Scanning the boilerplate and noticing that the letter even addressed neglect of pets while in-game, I finally reached the gist of this missive:

In response to you request (Ticket #730003) we hereby notify you that your use of the uncategorized ship does not infringe on any game regulations, and you have discovered her within a mission sequence involving the search for ancient and unique items. Thank you for your inquiry and please keep in mind that...

This was followed by another mile of text about how to properly exit a capsule, how to pay attention to the time you spent in-game, as well as how lucky we all were that there was such a wonderful game to begin with. It looked like the game's tech support was fond of telling fairy tales—so all I could do was say farewell to these fabulists and get back to my new ship.

Finally certain that *Warlock* belonged to me alone and that I was free to fly it wherever I wished, I went on with my study of the ship's manual.

And so!

This miracle of engineering was equipped with two graviton drives, which were paired with hyper-accelerators. I had no idea if such a combination was even physically possible, but the ancient shipbuilders had evidently decided that this was a good idea. Let's see how right they were. Due to the particulars of these engines, it didn't matter one bit where the ship's bow or stern were. Accordingly, the ship's maneuvering characteristics were very different from those taught in the Training Sector. Basically, if *Warlock* was equipped with an inertia dampening system—which would prevent the player inside from being smeared all over the cabin (the IDS wasn't equipped by default, but had a slot for it)—then the ship could jump in any direction at any moment in time. At any speed...Such a chaotic little ball would be able to dart all over the place, utterly befuddling both its enemies and their targeting systems.

The ship had three defensive systems—shields that were similar to that of *The Space Cucumber*, hull-mounted beam absorbers, and as I decided to call it, an anti-torpedo system. I didn't manage to figure out exactly how this last one worked—it seemed that I would need to keep reading about the finer points of defense—but the basic gist was that the shields operator (that is, the snake) could lock onto an inbound torpedo and capture it. The torpedo would freeze in place and turn into something like a mine—as soon as some ship approached it, it would explode. Moreover, along with being captured, the torpedo was also reconfigured to become a unique kind of trap—as soon as a flycatcher caught it, the torpedo would begin a self-destruct countdown of three minutes. This seemed calculated based on the length of time it generally took a ship to approach a captured torpedo and load it on board. The anti-torpedo system could only interdict and capture one torpedo per minute, so it wasn't exactly a gamebreaker, but if you could combine this with the ship's insane maneuverability...There were some pretty good possibilities here! Frigate-level ships, to say nothing of scouts and interceptors, were very frugal with torpedoes. Having only twelve torpedoes on board, no player would pass up the opportunity to pick up a free one floating in space. With this system, their ship was as good as dead, since a torpedo detonating inside a frigate would blow it to tiny pieces. Even a cruiser wouldn't find that too pleasant—if one did decide to capture one of those perilous things. Of course, one torpedo couldn't take out an entire cruiser—but the damage would be severe.

I couldn't help but smile when I reached the armaments section. Even though I was already on cloud nine, this aspect of my new ship took me even higher. First of all, the ship had six beam cannons distributed along its entire perimeter, which could rotate however the gunner wished. That is, the cannons were free to move along the hull, as though floating in water, and in so doing, seemed to break all laws of physics. This was simply impossible, after all...but here I go repeating myself.

Like the beam cannons, the ship also had four EM cannons to knock down enemy shields, as well as twenty-two A-class torpedoes and an autonomous torpedo manufactory that would create a new torpedo every five minutes.

Two independent reactors, a repair bay, a hangar for assault droids which already contained thirty-two fully-armed droids, a research lab, a cargo hold with several hundred units worth of capacity (unfortunately empty), an advanced onboard computer...When I finally realized what I had received, it became clear to me that this ship would have to be mine! I couldn't care

---

less how much money I'd get for it—there was no way I'd part with such a piece of equipment. Finding the self-destruct button and sighing with relief, I made a perhaps faulty but understandable decision: *Warlock* would become my new ship, while *The Space Cucumber* would be transferred to Lestran's command. I didn't want to sell the frigate, since I understood perfectly well that *Warlock* would become the prize for the entire gameworld and a temporary safe-ship in the form of the frigate would come in handy. Before anything else, however, I needed to transfer all the cartographic data from *The Space Cucumber* to *Warlock* and then respawn the frigate—it would come in handy again. While I was at it, I could charge my marine armor—I felt naked without it in this game. I couldn't understand how players could go around without wearing one.

Adjusting captain's chair and control panel to captain's ergonomics.

Activating the ship, I encountered my first surprise—the chair was adapted to fit its new owner. Considering its former Uldan owner had two huge wings on his back, the seat had been built in a manner that did not exactly allow me to kick back and enjoy my flight. At first I wrote this off as a trivial discomfort, since nothing could be perfect after all, but as soon as the ship came on, the captain's chair instantly began to transform to fit my, human, ergonomics. This was quite convenient. I'd have to try it again after I'd put on my armor.

START THE GAME

Several screens popped up before me, displaying the surroundings outside of *Warlock* at different scales, which included even a view of the current solar system. Then, as the ancient had told me, a control orb appeared. This was a miniature of the ship hanging in some kind of magnetic field. Along with the mini-ship, the projection also showed the surrounding environment, scaled to fit the ship's current speed. Considering the ship's ability to change her course instantly, this means of control was quite specific. There were neither levers nor buttons—just a simple projection which could be moved in space. An amazing device!

Carefully touching the projection, I lifted it above the planet and felt myself sink into my chair as the ship began to move. The map's scale instantly changed to accommodate *Warlock*'s current speed and I moved the projection in the direction of *The Space Cucumber*'s location. The testing phase had begun...

"Captain, the data transfer has been completed—recoding is underway," the slizosaur informed me after we stretched a long cable between *Warlock* and *The Space Cucumber*. It seemed that in deciding that energy could only be transferred through a cable, the developers had decided to accommodate reality at least in some way. I'd have had a good long laugh if I had been able to simply transmit the Elo's energy straight into the frigate through

---

ninety feet of rock. Thankfully, the devs spared me the laughing fit, making the recharge process of *The Space Cucumber* quite realistic.

Adapting my seat to the dimensions of my marine armor, I received the snake's report that all the data had been transferred from *The Space Cucumber*—with the exception of several spy modules that were sending the ship's coordinates somewhere into space. I guess we hadn't found all our stowaway insects after all!

...Establishing current location...

...Current location established...

...Nearest inhabited planet: Zamir, Pyrrhenian Empire (Voldan Alliance).

...Calculating optimal hyperspace route...

...Hyperspace route calculated—ETA: 30 minutes.

One of the screens displayed the known parts of *Galactogon* along with a distant point which indicated the location of Blood Island. My eyes almost popped out of my head once I realized how far my thoughtless hyperjump had taken us from the known systems. This may as well have been as far as anyone had ever gone from the chief, inhabited systems of *Galactogon*.

"Computer?" I said aloud, by habit more than anything else. Long, long ago, Stan had become if not my friend, then an invaluable component of my life, and I had become so used to communicating with him by voice that I automatically tried it here too. As I had already found out, for instance, *The Space*

START THE GAME

Cucumber's computer did not respond to such voice commands.

"Orders, Captain?" replied the space around me. My jaw dropped: the ship was "alive!"

"Give me a brief report on the ship's status," I decided to try a test phrase to get a sense of how developed the AI was. I had just finished looking over this same data several minutes ago and wanted to see what the ship would tell me about the same information.

"Taking into account that the information you just reviewed accounts for 90% of the ship's status report, I will add that the assault droids require Tiron to function at full power. The assault droids suffered cumulative damage of 47% after the last battle. Most units require a complete overhaul. Only four droids of the thirty-two on board are currently battle-ready. It is also preferable to refill the ship's Elo reserves. Current onboard energy reserves will last about a week under typical operating conditions. One hundred thousand years of standby have an effect even on a *Klamir*-type ship. All systems are currently nominal. There are no deviations, aside from the crew's status. Crew readiness is currently at 25%. The crew requires further training. It is not recommended to engage another ship in direct combat until the general level of crew readiness has reached 50% or higher. Planetary scan complete. Elo reserves have been identified. It is recommended to fully mine the identified Elo lode. Do you wish to dispatch the harvester to do so?"

"We have a harvester too?" I asked, riffling through the ship's attributes with astonishment. I could swear I had not seen it in the ship's manifest.

"The cryptosaur model attached to this ship as a marine and droid commander has the additional capability of mining certain resources. A harvester performs the closest analogue to this function in this galaxy; therefore, I took the liberty of substituting the semantic sense of the word. The cryptosaur can extract the Elo."

"I approve the extraction," I managed, and one of the screens flashed over to show the cryptosaur's first person view. The hull opened and the animal burst out as fast as it could in some direction known only to him. Although, that's not true—the onboard computer knew that too, but...Oh! By the way!

"Computer, what is the proper way to address you? Do you have a name, number, model or personal preference?"

"Negative," came the response. "The former captain did not use my voice functionality."

"In that case, I will refer to you as Braniac. It's just not nice to not have a name. What do you mean when you say the captain didn't use your voice function? Do you have some kind of telepathic link option or something?"

"No, the former captain used the command key. As a rule, the Uldans did not like to use voice commands."

"Got it. Tell me, do you have any information concerning the history of this race? Who are they? Where did they come from? Why did they disappear? What wars did they fight? Maybe you know where their secret bases could still be located?" I asked the last question out of sheer curiosity, knowing very well that—in this ship and crew—the *Galactogon* devs had already given me an utterly insane present. By the looks of things, nothing short of a cruiser could challenge a klamir (as Braniac referred to this ship type)—everything else would be sheer suicide. Even a flycatcher would do no good against her. I could tear up a frigate's shields and blast her apart with my beam cannons without having to resort to torpedoes. I couldn't understand why the designers had decided to introduce such an imba, game-breaking ship, but I was happy to be on my side of this issue. She was mine, after all. I could even risk taking on a cruiser—*Warlock*'s class was much higher than I had expected. I thought that B-class ships didn't just fall from the sky, but the game had proved me dead wrong.

"I have transferred all information about the Uldan race to your personal PDA," came Braniac's reply. "Including a description of their wars, history, origins and eventual demise. As for secret bases, unfortunately..." There followed a short pause, during which I shrugged my shoulders and smiled, thinking if no, then no. "According to my calculations, there is a probability that one of the Uldan bases survived. All the others were based on planets that no longer exist."

"One base?" I barely squelched an expletive. "Where are its coordinates?"

"Considering current imperial territorial and administrative divisions, the base is located on one of the three moons of Zalva, the capital of the Precian Empire. The Uldans built their bases deep underground, so, assuming that the moon is still in one piece, the base should still be there."

All my joy at hearing that there was an ancient stash after all evaporated as soon as Braniac told me where this stash was. From what I knew about the game, a solar system containing a capital planet was basically in the center of the empire and was therefore one of the best defended places in that empire as well. Those systems were swarming with Grand Arbiters—against which other ships were nothing but toys. Players could only go to such a system by receiving an invitation and considering my not-so-friendly relations with the Altan Alliance, of which the Precian Empire was a part, obtaining such an invitation was beyond impossible. It was too bad...

"The cryptosaur has found the Elo lode and has begun mining it," said Braniac, directing my attention to the appropriate screen which showed a huge clump of a blue mineral, surrounded by scorched earth—Elo irradiated and destroyed anything around it. The rhino didn't try to reinvent the wheel in extracting the resource and did what his kind normally do—ran at it at full speed. His horn struck the lode, knocking off a piece of the mineral, at which the rhino simply ate this fallen piece. After just ten minutes, the cryptosaur's capacity bar filled up and he turned to go back to the ship to unload.

"Ten hours left until the lode has been fully exhausted," Braniac commented on the mining progress. What a good name I'd given him! "Travel time is ten minutes. I recommend we approach the lode and shorten the harvester's trip length."

"Agreed," I nodded my head and gingerly touched the control orb. "Gunner, get ready to destroy the frigate as soon as we are at a sufficient distance from it. Engineer, tell the cryptosaur that we are headed toward him—tell him to wait for us by the lode."

"Consider it done, Cap," the snake instantly responded as I carefully lifted *Warlock* from the ground. The time had come to say goodbye to *The Space Cucumber*.

Frigate The Space Cucumber has been destroyed. Due to its destruction, all ship attributes have been decreased by one class. Current ship class: B.

"Lestran?" I called my partner as soon as *Warlock* alighted near the Elo lode. The rhino instantly got onboard and threw up everything that he had managed to mine by that point. A robotic arm emerged from the wall and loaded a heap of Elo into a container. Fun little operation this…

"Hey Surgeon!" the young man answered chipper as ever. He was still in the game.

"I have an assignment for you tomorrow. I need you to go to Qirlats and retrieve *The Space Cucumber* from the graveyard. Wally isn't around, so I'm giving you this assignment. Can you handle it?"

"No need to ask, sir! Hold on, what about you? You can't kill yourself?"

"No, it's not that. I'll show up a bit later. Return the frigate she gave us back to Marina and tell her thanks. Then, continue doing Hilvar's missions. Agreed?"

"Alright! Everything will be done to a T."

After I hung up, I spent a few minutes watching the cryptosaur mine the Elo lode, running to the ship and back, and finally signed out of the game. I had had enough adventures for today. The main testing of *Warlock* would come tomorrow. The important thing was for Stan to decipher that command key...

CHAPTER TEN

THE PATCH

"**G**ood morning, Master!" Stan chirped as soon as I opened my eyes.

My night had been a restless one. I kept having a nightmare in which I kept dying in different ways—either I'd get blown up, or crushed, or shot. And every time the murderer was a different person whom I'd never seen before: A man with sideburns, a tight white T-shirt and strange brass knuckles that resembled three long claws. A young girl in black skintight clothes that resembled latex, who moved so fluidly that the murder would begin to resemble a dance. A weird looking guy in green clothes with the emblem of a lantern on it...It was quite a night.

The only good thing was that the night had ended and the day during which I was to test out my new ship had finally come. If she was half as a good as her description made it seem, then I'd be sure to donate some money to the game's admins—presents like that deserved recognition.

GALACTOGON BOOK ONE

"What's new?" I asked Stan as I sat down to breakfast. My chief deputy found the wherewithal to provide me with everything I needed, even in this new, strange apartment—as though trying to soften my time in house arrest.

"Repair work on your old home is underway. All the debris was hauled away overnight. Today the contractor will begin to reframe the walls. You have received a message from the police, notifying you that your reward will be awarded to you upon your release from house arrest. *Galactogon*'s game servers are offline today due to a major update. I have finished deciphering the text on the command key…"

"Stop!" I interrupted Stan's report, despite the fact that the deciphered text was very important and was a priority matter for me. "What update? Why didn't I hear about this earlier?"

"Everyone has just found out," explained my smart home. "A global update has been rumored for a long time—to the point that most players have begun to ignore such rumors. The developers have maintained their silence until today. Basically, no one was ready for a patch of this magnitude. Also, I would like to point out that the information you initially requested about *Galactogon* asked for important game mechanics, the history of races, ship piloting, game economics and a search for coordinates based on several images. At no point did you ask about the probable future condition of the game or its forthcoming updates. As a result, I decided that this information was not pertinent and omitted it from my reports."

"Hmm…" I replied expressively to Stan's explanation and

shoveled the next load of pancakes into my mouth. An unannounced patch is a pretty curious thing. Many companies, even the one that ran *Runlustia*, used this tactic—after all, most of the testing was done not by the players but by QC programs. And yet, I found it strange that no one had leaked that this was going to happen. It's basically impossible to keep such information secret until the last moment—unless of course, *Galactogon's* IT security was impeccable. "Alright, put together an outline of the changelog and find me an exhaustive description of any changes to piloting mechanics. They have published something like that, haven't they?"

"Yes, the new information should be posted on the official site. Displaying it now." A projected screen popped up in front of me and began to fill with neat lines of text. My eyebrows rose higher and higher as each new sentence entered my gray matter. It was as if the new information was too much for my head and had inflated my brain up against my skull. I could see now why they had shut down *Galactogon* for an entire day—a typical patch could easily be applied within an hour, without the servers even going offline. But the game designers had cooked up a colossal adjustment to the game's mechanics, including the additions of entirely new pawns.

And so!

Galactogon now had several new types of vessels— among which there was still no mention of my new spherical klamir. Players now had access to the following ships, in ascending order of power: interceptor, scout, shuttle, transport, blocker, monitor, corvette, frigate, albenda and cruiser. The albenda—a monster housing fifty players—was basically no different from an un-upgraded cruiser. But the new updated cruiser…Well, I couldn't even imagine how anyone could take one on anymore. There was also the harvester, but players couldn't control it, so that tub was not included in the list.

Since the basic flight mechanics hadn't changed, this expansion to the game's fleet, was just about the only thing of interest to captains—and still it was but a drop in the bucket of what the developers were now introducing to *Galactogon*. The patch was directed above all at the engineering side of the game. Engineers now became incredibly useful, desirable and, well, basically indispensable to any ship. Thus this patch would be a godsend to any players who'd chosen this career, as they would now be the masters of repair and upgrades. They could tinker with the engines, weapons, armor, fuselage—if you wanted to improve anything, an engineer was what you needed. In addition to all that, they could now create individual robots—including gigantic robo-titans. It seemed like someone on the dev team had gotten tired of the marines lording it over all the planet-bound plebs and decided to buff another class for the sake of variety. All you had to do now was obtain one of these titans and learn how to control it—no amount of marines would be scary after that.

What I couldn't help but be happy about was a new macro-mechanic called the cosmic raid—once a week, a humongous asteroid would come flying at a random, Confederate planet. The players would have to all get together and destroy this boulder. On one's own, even with *Alexandria*, you couldn't deal with a monster like that—you wouldn't have the time and weapons. So uniting with other players was now mandatory. Naturally, this meant new missions and rewards, new opportunities for building Rapport and new factions, new planets, new trade routes, new mechanics, new, new, new...

Since most of *Galactogon*'s competitors had shut down, swelling the games userbase, the developers decided they had to make some concessions and simplified the game somewhat: At last, there would be a list of missions. Until now, it was up to the players to decide whether they had received an actual mission or not—and only a rare notification every once in a while would assure us poor bastards that we were indeed on the right path. The patch introduced a journal which would list the mission that a local had given to the player, as well as the current missions' progress. On one hand, I couldn't understand why they hadn't done that earlier—on the other, it was nice to see that someone was listening and thinking about the game's future.

According to the number that Stan displayed in his outline, there was about twenty-two new additions to the game, starting from the new ships and ending with new skins for the ships, so I didn't delve too closely into the whole list. And yet, all of this was eclipsed by the patch's main addition—for the first time in the game's history, a common foe had appeared! An aggressive race from another universe had launched an invasion of *Galactogon*—threatening all twelve empires at once. In order to provide the players with an incentive to participate in the defense of their galaxy, the invaders had by some miracle managed to kidnap a representative from each empire's ruling dynasty. Even the Anorxian Empire—an empire of robots ruled by a CPU—had one such weak link in its hierarchy. Twelve princes and princesses had gathered at a symposium for how to defend their universe—and that's where they were all kidnapped. It was a pretty story, but the point was simple—the designers wanted the players to drop everything and go save those hostages, committing themselves to war with this new enemy...

"Master, someone has come to see you," said Stan, tearing me away from my study of the manuals. I glanced at my watch and my eyebrows, already exhausted from all their recent jumping, tried to take off one more time. I had been sitting in front of my screen for six hours. There had been so much new information to read and process and it was so interesting that I hadn't even noticed the day go by.

"Am I allowed to receive guests?" I asked puzzled, understanding very well that Stan was not exactly the right person to ask.

"No, but the visitor has full law enforcement clearance. However, I am not authorized to open the door. You will have to do it yourself, Master. The visitor has provided you with the option of choosing."

"I'll open it," I replied, getting up. Taking into account that I was under close guard—and that Stan had not noticed anything out of the ordinary—there was no threat to me. My mind could benefit from going outside and talking to a living person, considering that I'd been locked away behind four walls like some criminal.

But I was mistaken in thinking so. No sooner had I opened the door and seen who had come to visit me than my good mood evaporated like a puddle of ether. It was too bad and I regretted it and couldn't do anything about it...

"Good day, Alexis," said my guest, the old man whom I had already had the pleasure of meeting by vidphone. And who, basically, was the reason for my confinement. "May I come in? We need to have a chat."

"Please do," I stepped aside, not comprehending at all why he'd even asked for permission. Given his rank, if this geezer had wanted to chat with me in person, he could've just as easily ordered me hogtied, placed in a flyer and brought to him. "Would you like some tea or coffee?"

"Water, if I may," replied my guest, taking a seat. Stan instantly cooked up a glass of water, while I took a seat across from the old man and began to nervously wait for him to start the conversation. Waiting I could do—my gaming career had taught me that well.

"I have two piece of news for you," the old man got to it, still without having officially introduced himself. Perhaps he had assumed that I would know his name. "The first is that we still have not managed to establish who is eliminating the contestants. The prize money is large enough to justify murdering all other competitors. According to the terms of the agreement, the search would still be on even if only one contestant remained.

Consequently, you are still one of our suspects and are prohibited to leave these premises. That's number one."

The old man fell silent, returning to his glass of water and giving me the chance to process this news, which, of course, wasn't really news to me at all. If I wasn't still under suspicion, then I wouldn't have been sitting in a cage like a hamster—so all I could do now was to stay sitting there and await the second piece of news. It wasn't likely that a person of this caliber would decide to visit me in person in order to tell me that I was still in time out.

"I like your composure," smiled the old man, scooting the glass aside. "No unnecessary emotions, no yelling, no demanding I respect your rights. You're not even interested in who I am—as if you already know."

"Yelling, as I understand it, would be pointless. You're still not going to release me. My rights have been limited by the court's decision—I've already received the judgment text. As for who you are…Why would I care? The only thing I wouldn't mind knowing is your name—since, it'd be nice to know how to address you. I don't imagine you'd like me to call you 'old man' or 'grandpa,'" I replied, holding my voice in check. I could not afford to let any implication or irony or some other emotion sneak into it—I had to simply assert facts at the moment. I didn't much feel like letting someone see that I was uncomfortable.

"Colonel Walters," smiled the guest. "You can call me by that name. Well, well. In that case, let's get to the second bit of news. Tell me, are you familiar with our government's children's policy?"

START THE GAME

"Excuse me, I didn't quite hear you right," I asked shocked, discarding my neutral demeanor. "What children?"

"Just, you know, children. Kids, tykes, toddlers. Smalls who scurry about and try to crawl into various nooks and crannies and make a big stink about eating their veggies. You know—children."

"I'm sorry but I can't say I know much about them," I replied, trying to regain my composure and squelch my emotions. What did kids and government policy have anything to do with anything?

"That's what I figured. In that case, if you indulge me, I'd like to read you a short lecture. As you are aware, in recent years the national birthrate has been plummeting in relation to the mortality rate. As a result, the government has taken a close interest in any and all pregnancies and even begun to take them under its oversight…"

Col. Walters went on detailing what I already knew, by and large. Following the mass automation of human labor by robots and machines, our planet experienced a demographic boom—the rapid economic growth spurring a growth in family size. It became normal for a family to have three or four children. However, this did not last for a long time—that is, it lasted until the invention of somatic immersion and video games that could exploit that technology. Despite the fact that the elites own and control these games (*Galactogon* is no exception), it was simply impossible to overlook the drastic drop in the birthrate. In a mere twenty years, the population's desire to have three or four children gave way to an utter refusal to have children whatsoever. I could say for myself that I simply couldn't even imagine living with a little monster who would dash around my home, make a mess all over the place, yank the cables out of my gaming capsule and demand I spend time with it.

In time, the government took notice of this negative trend and initiated programs to contravene it. There was nothing they could do about the games, but they did introduce enormous benefits for new parents and their children, effectively making the second and third child the family's breadwinners. Abortions were banned. Public awareness campaigns were launched. Maternity leave began to kick in in the first month of pregnancy and was fully paid for by the state. Basically, they created a machine that would use various incentives to combat populace's gradual migration into virtual reality—and currently, this machine was going at full steam. The only thing I didn't understand in all this was...

"That's all very well, but I still don't understand: What does any of this have to do with me?" I asked Col. Walters as soon as his lecture drew to a close. It was nice to learn new things and all, but it's also good to know what the point of learning it is. At the moment, I didn't understand.

"That's the second piece of news. You're going to be a father soon..."

WHAT?!

"What the hell are you talking about?" All my cool popped like a soap bubble, unleashing all my feelings. This was simply unacceptable! I couldn't care less who this geezer was—I wasn't about to sit around and watch him lie to my face just to see what kind of reaction he could get from me. After all, I could have been the murderer of six people! "You're losing your mind from all your suspicions. I haven't left my cocoon in about five years! You know, Colonel Walters, it was a pleasure speaking with you and listening to your lovely story about how the government cares about our children, but I think I'd like it if you were on your way now. I have a patched *Galactogon* waiting for me. As you yourself pointed out, the search goes on even if only one of the contestants remains. So basically, you're bugging me now."

"Here's the paternity test," smirked the geezer, producing some sheets from his briefcase and not even thinking of getting up from his chair. "According to these, a certain Alexis Panzer is the biological father of a child that is about to be born to a Eunice Dormouse. You are free to request an independent test (even a DNA one, if it so strikes you) whenever you like. Eunice is in her second month of pregnancy and the government will do anything it can to ensure that she gives birth to a healthy baby. Regardless of whether you recognize the child as your own or not, the fact remains that you, Mr. Panzer, are the father."

"Eunice?" My rage vanished in a flash, replaced by the lovely memory of our first meeting—the night's drinking that had led to something greater. Had I really done it?

"I can see that it's starting to come back to you," the old man smiled again. "One of the contestants is in the second month of pregnancy and that, in combination with the current situation, brings us to a dead end. Which is precisely why I'm here."

"I don't understand anything anymore," I muttered, reclining in my chair and staring at the wall. Eunice was pregnant? Pregnant from me? I was going to be a father?

"According to the contest's rules, the contestants are not allowed to cooperate with one another. However, under the law, a father is required to take part in the raising of his child, beginning with the moment of conception. On the face of it, this is a conflict of interests and the contest organizers don't know what to do."

"You didn't come here without having figured out a way out of this situation," I ventured despite my confusion. This was easily the last thing I had expected.

"It's true, I have certain ideas about what could be done," my guest assured me. "You two need to move in together and start a family."

"WHAT?!"

"Why the outburst?" Col. Walters jerked up his eyebrows, evidently reveling in the situation. "I see nothing bad in two young people, who will have a child in short order, forming a family—a building block of this great society. That is the only way that both of you will be able to continue your search for the check without infringing on any laws or contracts. Otherwise, both you and Eunice will be disqualified. No one is allowed to break the law, even the President."

"I'm not sure I understand. How are we supposed to avoid violating the contract where it clearly states that there can be no cooperation between the participants?"

START THE GAME

"That's precisely where the loophole lies. You will continue searching for the check as before—but instead of participating as Alexis Panzer, you will be participating as the Panzer Family. Eunice Dormouse will be officially suspended from the contest, since, according to the law, it is unlawful for her to work or perform any contractual obligations. However, Eunice Panzer, as a spouse, is allowed to help her husband in his own pursuit of the check. With that said, no one is even thinking of deleting her character or account configuration. She will still be a contestant, albeit under a different alias. There is no other way to ensure that both of you can continue in the contest. It's either form a family or we force you to terminate your contract. The choice is yours."

"Why only mine? There's also Eunice, who would never agree to something like that..."

"Like I said, the choice is yours and your alone. Are you willing to continue your search or shall I terminate your account configuration?"

"That's the second time I hear you mention the account configuration. Am I correct in assuming that we are being tracked?"

"Every step," the old man nodded. "I was just reading a report about how your coordinator was unhappy with your hasty decision to leave the planet you discovered without exploring it to its utmost."

"But..." I cut myself short, trying to let this obvious hint that there were still more goodies to be found pass by without unnecessary comment. If I started to argue, they could simply take them away. Instead, I chose to go with the typical phrase one resorts to in atypical situations. "How much time do I have to think this over?"

"About five minutes, no more," my guest replied, shrugging. "I can appreciate your current frame of mind, but you need to make this choice immediately—do you wish to go on with your search or is this where you get off? If you choose the former, then the Panzer family will continue the search. If you choose the latter, as soon as your home has been repaired, you will be returned to it. You will keep your current character and everything you've acquired so far, but you will be unable to get that check—even if you somehow find the planet that it's on. You can think about it and weigh the pros and cons, but you have to arrive at a decision before I leave here. Otherwise, a decision will be made for you, and that will be disqualification."

A family...

A vacuum... dishes... diapers... real manipulators... rows and tantrums arising from misplaced socks... nerve damage arising from constant nagging...

There was such a load of nonsense rushing through my mind that I was even taken aback with myself—did I really believe all this about having a family? Theoretically, I wasn't losing anything at all—after the contest was over, we could easily get a divorce. No one had prohibited us from doing so as long as I spent time with the child and took part in his upbringing. But the very fact that I was suddenly being forced to make a decision like this stressed me out—no one seemed to be taking our feelings into account. Neither mine, nor Eunice's. Well then the devil could take them and their damn contest to the deepest deeps! I could survive fine without all this crap!

"Thanks for the heads up," I said, getting up from my chair and letting my demeanor show that there was nothing further to discuss. "I will try to be a good father, but I must reject your offer. You don't make a decision to form a family on your own. If I'm going to do this, then I'd only do it after meeting with Eunice personally. If I only have five minutes, then I must wish the remaining contestants well. Thanks for stopping by!"

"No, thank you for not disenchanting an old man," said Col. Walters, also rising to his feet. "You will have the chance to talk it over with Eunice in two hours. I will have someone pick you up. If either of you had answered otherwise, you would have both been disqualified from the contest. This was precisely why I came to you in person. I wanted to personally witness your reaction. You can go get ready now. You have an important meeting ahead of you. I'll see myself out. Goodbye…"

"So this is where you live now, huh hubby?" Eunice asked, glancing around my apartment. "It's not much, but I see possibilities. Oh! That's a Darlik guard circuit, isn't it? Why haven't you turned it on yet?"

"Because I have absolutely no idea what a guard circuit

even is or why someone put it in here, I answered sincerely. "And we agreed—when we're alone together, we're partners—not spouses."

"Are you sure we're alone right now? I wouldn't express myself in such absolute terms if I were you."

Our rendezvous at the restaurant—which the cops drove me to—was pretty relaxed. We were sitting across from each other, not knowing what to say, until the girl came out with the key phrase: "I want to go on looking for that check." After that, it was like a dam breaking. We spent the next hour talking over everything that we could—yes, we'd get married, but there would be no family in actual fact—at least for now. And by "family," we meant sex. There had been more than enough of that when we first met two months ago. I would recognize the child as my own and take an active part in its upbringing. The doctors gave Eunice permission to stay in the game for another four months—as long as she remained under their close supervision. But there was an advantage here too—from here on out, Eunice would play in my game mode—that is, she would no longer have a limit on her playing time. Though, she couldn't pump money into the game either.

"That's no problem," Eunice assured me. "I already have a scout that I've pumped up to A-class and equipped with all the best equipment I could find. So I'm ready to go explore. The main thing for me right now is to get out of the Training Sector. I still have about fifty game days left in there."

After our meeting, the detectives whisked Eunice and me

to a very quick civil ceremony, issued us documents attesting our marriage and dropped us off back at my place, where some engineers were already installing the second gaming capsule. It really was very strange to see a stranger in my house, even if this was just a temporary state of affairs. But I was ready to make some sacrifices for that check. And anyway, as much as I didn't like it, the fact was that I'd have to have a relationship with Eunice for at least the next twelve years while the child grew up. So showing my dislike of the situation wouldn't do any good. I mean, I was still a kid myself...

"What kind of system do you have installed?"

"What do you mean?"

"Do you control your home yourself or do you use software?"

"Oh! You're talking about the smart home. I have a Daphne-2130 with expanded functionality. Stan's the name."

"Excuse me, Master," Stan butted in. "My system version was updated to Daphne-2135. You personally approved the upgrade."

"Master?" Eunice rolled her eyes. "I can see that humility might not be your strong suit."

"Yup," I nodded, barely keeping myself from cracking up. I liked to watch the way guests reacted to Stan calling me Master—that's the way people were after all...

"Stan, scan this address." Eunice scribbled a series of digits on a sheet of paper and held it up to one of the cameras. "You can find my Daphne—she's a 2135 too—at this address. I

---

need her here. Grant her full access and let her have 50% of the system resources."

"Do it, Stan," I told my assistant when no confirmation followed Eunice's command. "Give Eunice full access rights too. User category: family."

"Master, allotting 50% of system resources to another system will impair my communications bandwidth with this residence. I should also point out that certain modules do not support multiuser mode..."

"You can retain control of those," I quickly decided, but, upon seeing Eunice's eyes narrow, added, "although, on second thought, let's assign those as they come up. For now, go invite our new guest and make sure she's accommodated."

"Yes, Master," Stan said with such melancholy in his voice that for a second I forgot he was just a piece of software.

"Did you configure the interaction module yourself?" Euncie asked, taking a seat. "Your Daphne's pretty particular. I get the impression that you've rewritten her entirely to suit yourself. Or added something to her."

"There're some additions," I agreed. "But we can talk about that some other time. Stan orders my food for me. By the way, what's your Daphne's name? Does she even have one?"

"Now I know what you've added to yours," smiled Eunice. "My Daphne has no personality—she's just a smart home. Alright, let's talk about life some other time. I'm more interested in *Galactogon* at the moment—and finding that check. Are you out of the Training Sector yet? What empire are you with?"

"Master, I've performed your request," came Stan's detached voice, letting me know that my home had just become twice as smart. He sounded upset! "Are there any further instructions?"

"Put together a summary of my character's current progress and send it to the other Daphne," I said and turned back to Eunice. "It's a long story. I'd rather you just looked it all over. While he's getting that ready, tell me about what you've accomplished. Who are you? Where and when are you going to emerge?"

Eunice turned out to be a Precian marine. Having an enormous budget at her disposal, she bought herself a scout, since she planned to explore on her own, leveled it up to A-class, bought three marine armors, a huge armory of weapons, and a personal spacedock outside of R'shion, a backwater of the Precian Empire. Basically, as soon as she'd emerge from the Training Sector—currently she was planning on doing this in a month and a half—all of *Galactogon* would be open to her and all she'd have to do was get on with her search for the prize planet.

Right after the wedding ceremony, Eunice and I signed new contracts for the contest so that, from now on, if one of us was to find the check, the other would automatically receive an exact copy. In essence, we were no longer competitors, having become equal partners. This was why I ordered Stan to send her all the information there was about my character—there was no point at all in hiding anything from each other now.

"You know, Lex," said Eunice in a much warmer tone as

soon as she had familiarized with my game history, "I was wrong. Maybe you didn't realize it, but to be perfectly honest I thought you were an utter newb—even if you did manage to augment your Daphne with a personality matrix. But there's no newb on the planet that could do what this says you did. Can you show me how you managed to get all this? I'm asking only because I really don't feel like sitting in the nursery for another seven weeks. I only have four months left to play until I go on leave and I'd like to use them to their utmost."

"Stan, pull up the video logs from my game. Let's watch a movie…"

"BUT—I THOUGHT there's no solitary in the Training Sector..?

…

"What is a KRIEG?

…

"Get out of here! Did you really make a hyperjump from an asteroid?

…

"A klamir?!"

We spent the next three hours watching my exploits in *Galactogon*. Eunice's exclamations ran the gamut from initial mockery and dissatisfaction to surprise and even reverence towards the end. When the movie ended, there was a short silence during which we sat and considered what we had seen.

START THE GAME

Even I, having gone through all these events myself over the last two months, could hardly imagine that I had managed to acquire so much. A unique ship with ancient technology, three locals who were my crew and who were ready to go conquer *Galactogon* whenever—not just when they felt like it—a mysterious mission involving the KRIEG…I had so many things to do in *Galactogon* now, in addition to my search for the prize planet, that I simply had no idea of when I could even get around to doing all of them. Just the planet with the secret Uldan base would involve god-only-knew how much effort—and I still had to figure out how to even get to it. I found it unlikely that the Precians would simply let me waltz into their capital system and go digging around one of the moons in their sky. Heck, they wouldn't let me anywhere near the system at all…

"I can't possibly do all this," Eunice said wistfully. "Even if I start over from scratch and get into solitary, I'll still have to spend a month sitting in it. It's easier to finish my training and come out as a recruit. One way or another it's still two months. Damn!"

"Unless of course I come and break you out," I laughed, suggesting the first thing that popped into my mind. Considering that Training Sectors were guarded by Grand Arbiters, the most powerful ships in *Galactogon*, this was a completely insane idea. No ship could even come close to the planet where the recruits were being trained.

"Break me out?" Euncie looked at me pensively, after which her eyes glazed over—the girl sank deep in thought. "A jailbreak…"

"Listen, that was a joke," I backpedaled. "There's no way to get a player out of a Training Sector. No one's even come close."

"No one's ever come close to stealing a frigate full of Raq and flying it out either. Nope, no one's even come close...As for attacking the Training Sector—I saw in the movie that you have a pretty good relationship with Kiddo, right?"

"Let's say I do," I agreed. "We're kind of like partners."

"She is the only player who's managed to attack the Qualian Training Sector and gotten away with it. That raid happened a year ago. The players still remember it with reverence. It was the only time that some players managed to knock out a Grand Arbiter. Of course, *Alexandria* was destroyed in the process, but Marina proved that nothing was impossible."

"I'm not about to risk *Warlock*," I instantly bristled. "She doesn't have a cruiser's firepower. A Grand Arbiter wouldn't even notice me."

"That's the point though. There's no need to get into a fight," smirked Eunice. "While you were sitting in solitary and getting your klamir, I found out quite a bit about what other players do in this game. Marina started that battle herself. She wanted to see if a Grand Arbiter really couldn't be destroyed—but before that she did everything she wanted to in the Training Sector. She landed on the planet, placed a planet destroyer—that's a type of bomb—and flew away in peace. She only got into the battle once she was almost out of the system. I only have four more months, Lex. If we don't manage to find the prize planet in that time, you'll have to keep looking on your own. I'll have to drop out. Help me escape."

"Listen Eunice, this is pure madness…" I began to refuse, but fell quiet, encountering the girl's pleading eyes. In the end, this was just a game and even if *Warlock* got destroyed, she would come back—all I'd have to do first was bind her to a homeworld. After all was said and done, if I decided to pass on this exploit…why, I simply wouldn't forgive myself later: I had had the chance to do something heroic and instead I took the safe route? Wasn't I paladin finally?

"Alright, get me all the info you can about your Sector— the planet's name, where it is, where I can land on it, where the extraction point should be, what the system defenses are. I need to know everything there is, so I can react properly to any changing circumstances. As soon as *Galactogon* comes back on line, I'll speak with Marina. I'll try to find out from her how she managed to land on the planet. Without any further information at the moment, I suggest we plan on breaking you out in a week— that will give us time and ensure that we don't relax too much."

"Okay," the girl's eyes lit up with the promise of work. Even though we were both adults, our habit of earning our living through games showed itself—we were both ready to set off on this adventure like it was nothing. After all, any adventure could bring profit. "Tell me, where's the bathroom around here?"

"Straight down the hall and on the right. My bedroom's on the second floor, but I typically sleep in the living room. You can have all of the first floor. There're two bedrooms here, pick whichever. There's a kitchen here, but I don't use it. That's what Stan is for. I've basically put him in charge of all everyday issues. If you have any questions, let me know. I'm off to bed. We've got a hard day ahead of us tomorrow..."

"Master, Eunice wishes you to come down to her," came Stan's voice as soon as I got under my sheets. Aside from having no front door, the second floor wasn't much different from the first. The same exact two bedrooms, living room, kitchen, bathroom. Maybe I could call the technicians and have them move my capsule up here? I'd run into the girl less that way. Any way you spun it, she was very pretty and sooner or later I'd start to hit on her. Did I need that? "She says that she can't go to sleep in a strange new house—without first hearing a bedtime story. Forgive my lack of tact, but Eunice has another request—she wishes me to warn you that it's not proper to read bedtime stories without having first showered."

Two hours later, I discovered that I would go on living on the first floor after all...

CHAPTER ELEVEN

WARLOCK'S FIRST BATTLE

Welcome to the updated Galactogon! You may find the changelog in the updates section of the official knowledge base.

The following modification has been made to the "Star Wolf" Achievement: Your ship's stats have increased by 10%.

A vast tome of notifications rushed past my eyes, telling me about the new additions to the game. However, I ignored everything concerning the new patch. I already knew all this and was much more interested in two things: how my crew was doing and the missions list. Over my almost two months in the game, I had come across some mystifying situations which could have been interpreted to have been missions. So the first thing I did was examine the UI for the new button with an icon of a scroll, clicked it and got down to reading.

"A Pirate I Was Meant To Be – Part 1": Destroy 150 interceptors (11 of 150 destroyed), or 125 scouts (0 of 125 destroyed), or 100 shuttles (0 of 100 destroyed), or 75 monitors (0 of 75 destroyed), or 50 frigates (0 of 50 destroyed), or 20 albendas (0 of 20 destroyed), or 10 cruisers (1 of 10 destroyed).
Mission Reward: "A Pirate I Was Meant To Be – Part 2."
Failure Penalty: None.

My progress in this first mission upset me a lot. As I understood it, Wally and the crew had already sent several ships to their graveyards and made some progress—which, however, had not counted for me. That was no good…It was nice that the list had grown somewhat with several extra ships, but I would still have to catch up with my boys.

"Treasure Hunter": Find your way to the secret Uldan base located on a moon of the planet Zalva.
Mission Reward: Unknown.
Failure Penalty: None.
Mission Key: Klamir Warlock.
This mission is available only to owners of a klamir.

The second mission upset me as well. Of course if I ever did find my way to the ancients' secret base, I'd pillage it until there was nothing left, taking anything I could. But I had basically

---

no chance of getting onto a moon of the Precian capital.

As I understood it, imperial core systems were off-limits to players without an invitation. And even if I did somehow obtain one of those, I'd be allowed to travel through the system only under armed escort—something I didn't want to deal with at all. I wasn't about to split my loot with the Precians. It looked like this mission would remain as chaff in my journal until the end of my gaming career.

"The KRIEG": Tell the Precian Rrgord that the Qualians have completed the KRIEG, as well as how you discovered this information.

Mission Reward: Unknown.

Failure Penalty: Unknown.

This mission may not be delegated to another player.

I had to read this description several times before I sighed deeply and painfully. This mission, which I had assumed would bring me an ample reward, basically turned out to be a trivial sidequest. I couldn't complete it on my own, as I had to work on finding that check and I couldn't sell it to someone else either. By the look of it, Rrgord would have to remain in the dark about the KRIEG, since I wouldn't go looking for him on purpose.

"Engineer, give me a planetary status report," I said, taking the captain's seat and noticing that the marine-rhino-harvester had finished mining the Elo lode. I was about to go back to the main game world, but I decided to listen to the old man's advice and check out Blood Island some more. Eunice and I had agreed that she would spend the day finding out the name of the planet she was undergoing training on—and, if possible, its coordinates. I still had to make several calls on my comm, but I'd get to that in due time. First—the planet's status.

"Blood Island is capable of sustaining life. Its particularities are that it has no active Planetary Spirit. As far as resources go, scanners reveal only three Elo lodes, of which we have already exhausted the largest one. Blood Island's landmass consists of two continents that comprise 60% of the planetary surface..."

"Hang on," I interrupted the report. "What do you mean there's no active Planetary Spirit? Does it not exist at all, do I have to buy it somewhere, or does it simply need to be activated?"

"The Spirit may be activated," replied the snake. "In that case, in the event of destruction, you will be resurrected on Blood Island. To activate the Spirit, you must give me the command to activate it and bind you to it. The process will take thirty minutes."

"Do it!" I ordered my engineer, barely suppressing a squeal of joy. The calculations suggested that the distance between Blood Island and the explored part of *Galactogon* was about an hour's flight in hyperspace—with the option of popping out into reality during the jump. As a result, if *Warlock* was destroyed, there'd be no danger to me. Having a backup spaceport that was unaffiliated with an empire or the Confederacy was a pretty nice advantage. For example, I could sell it to Marina, the captain of *Alexandria*. A pirate who had made enemies with most of *Galactogon* would jump at such an opportunity.

By the way!

The ship's hull rippled as the snake left its station and plunged straight down into the planetary surface—however, I didn't have time for pretty effects. I had only half an hour to resolve a whole host of issues. I figured I'd start with the most pressing one.

"Marina, how are you? This is Surgeon."

"I can't really talk right now. I'll ask Anton to get in touch with you," the girl replied. I didn't know whether she was telling the truth or this was some kind of ritual in which I'd have to go through the help to earn the right to an audience—and I didn't much care. If I could only talk to Anton, then Anton it would be. But before disconnecting, I managed to blurt out:

"Reason I'm calling is a planet I've found that's an hour's flight from the populated systems. I just activated its Planetary Spirit. I'll wait for your call."

Wally was next on my list. I had to touch base with him about the mission progress. Judging by the mission description, my human crew's wanton destruction of locals was in no way furthering my own mission progress. Last time I'd checked there had been eleven destroyed interceptors and so it remained now. This was no way to build Rapport with Hilvar.

However, I never got a chance to discuss this with Wally because my comm suddenly lit up and began squealing madly, informing me that someone wished to talk to me.

"I'm listening," I said, surprised by the call. Only a few players knew my number in the game—and I had just spoken with about half of them.

"Surgeon, this is Marina," came the voice of *Alexandria*'s captain. "What's up with that planet?"

It turned out—or at least Marina claimed so—that she had been in a meeting when I had called. Due to the recent patch, a portion of the Confederate planets had declared war on the pirates. According to the administrations who had remained loyal, the new common enemy required a unified front and therefore splitting up forces to make sure the pirates didn't cause trouble would be a drain on resources. As a result, a majority of Confederate space had decided to refuse to harbor the Brotherhood of the Jolly Roger any longer, and many pirates, Marina included, had begun looking for a new place of residence. Marina didn't mention how she felt about my unexpected offer—though it was dead obvious that she now suspected that I had a mole in her crew. Coincidences like this were simply impossible. And I wasn't going to waste my breath convincing her otherwise.

I told her honestly how I found the planet, how I named it in commemoration of my first ship and how I activated the Planetary Spirit. I didn't give her the exact coordinates, however. The time had come to make a deal.

"What do you want?" Marina asked straight out as soon as I was done. "I gave your crew a ship. We're partners. You have plenty of money. Seeing as how you haven't yet mentioned the coordinates, you want something from me. Get on with it."

START THE GAME

"I need to break a player out of a Training Sector," I replied. "And I need to do it in the next week or so. I need to know how you managed to land on a hostile planet without drawing aggro from the planetary defenses."

"Are you offering me the planet in exchange for simple info?" I could hear unvarnished sarcasm in the pirate's voice. "Or are you going to want my help too—as my ally and all? I'm not big on sending my cruiser to the graveyard again."

"All I want is information. I'll deal with the Grand Arbiters myself. I just want to grab the player and get out. You don't happen to know what'll happen if an unbound player dies above the Training Sector? Where will he respawn? The ship's homeworld—since he doesn't have a homeworld of his own—or back in the Sector? Seems like an interesting question," I added already for my own benefit. When I had begun planning Eunice's escape, I quickly encountered this befuddling question—what would happen if she died and ended up back on the training planet? If so, our efforts would all be in vain.

"We don't know that at the moment," Marina's XO, Anton spoke up on the comm. "No one's died on the Training Sector yet. At least until we saw your little adventure there. Not everyone manages to acquire a manipulator."

"Sorry, forgot to mention—you're on speakerphone," explained Marina. "The entire officer corps of *Alexandria* can hear you at the moment."

"What's up all," I said, still considering Eunice's escape plan. "So what about that info—will you share it? And I mean share it—since I'll give you the planet's coordinates either way. I got nothing to hide from my allies."

"We'll consider your offer and get back to you around lunch. You're going to be in *Galactogon* all day, right?"

"Yup. I'm planning on staying late. Listen, Marina, it's a dumb question but since we're already talking, have you found out anything about that Rrgord guy? What's up with that mysterious Precian?"

"Erm..." a pregnant silence filled the ether. "Did you read the changelog at all or what?"

"Obvi," I said surprised. "But what does the new patch have to do with a Precian I was told to find long before the patch? The devs wouldn't mess with continuity like that."

"Right...Tell me, what is the main change in the new patch?"

"Marina, I am flattered that you want to try your Socrates on me, but let's do this a little more directly, okay? Just tell me straight out—did you find out who Rrgord is or not? I won't figure out your hints either way."

"He's the Precian prince who's been kidnapped by the invading Zatrathi. He is being held captive with the other eleven figureheads of the ruling dynasties. Rrgord, or 'The Libertine,' as he is called—he is the only Precian who has an enormous frigate that's controlled by only one being—is the heir apparent for the Precian throne. According to the lore, Rrgord grew up far away from the game's main events and was carefully protected. Few knew anything about him—so it's all the more surprising that you managed to stumble across a local that mentioned him. There are no other Precians named Rrgord."

The Libertine...

I felt an immense sense of relief when Marina told me all this—I had been wrong after all. Warlock hadn't been talking about Hilvar—the freedom loving pirate, no! He had meant Rrgord, the heir of the Precian Empire, who'd been kidnapped by the Zatrathi. Thus, the only local who could surely tell me where to look for the prize planet had become the focus of the entire game. Rescuing him on my own was out of the question, and joining with other players to fight the Zatrathi...Well, it wouldn't be long before they'd requisition my *Warlock* for the sake of saving the universe or whatever.

I sent Marina the coordinates to Blood Island and signed out of the game. I didn't feel like talking to Wally anymore. I needed to get Eunice to sign out so I could discuss the new developments with her. Did it even make sense to extract her from the Sector, now that it was impossible to free Rrgord?

"Stan, pull Eunice out of *Galactogon*, will you?" I said as soon as I'd emerged from my capsule. The house that we'd found ourselves locked in had been designed for only one gaming capsule, so the cables from the new one were now strewn all over the floor. The technicians had tried to bind them together of course and hide them as best they could, but still it wouldn't be too unlikely of an accident if I snagged one with my foot and yanked it out.

"That's unfortunate," said Eunice when I told her the

news. "Although…On the one hand, it sucks, but on the other, we know for sure now who could help us find the prize planet. We just need to figure out how to get past the Zatrathi. Have you tested the ship already?"

"No. I spoke with Marina. She promised to send me some info about how she managed to land in the Training Sector. After that, I figured I should talk to you first. Did you find out your planet's coordinates?"

"Not yet. I got the name, though. I'm on Vozban in a system called Gantanil-3. The planetary defenses seem pretty standard—two Grand Arbiters and six orbital stations. I haven't gotten around to reading up about the system garrison, but I'd guess that it is quite significant. I can't even imagine how Marina managed to pull it off."

"We'll know this evening. Sorry that I yanked you out of the game—it was silly of me. I don't know what came over me, but I really started thinking that it'd be better to hold on to what I already have and put the search on the backburner."

"Eh, I feel you. A unique ship with a unique crew is not the kind of thing one commits recklessly," Eunice offered supportively. "So if you decide to stash your sphere somewhere and go on fighting in your frigate, I'll understand."

"Uh-huh. Considering that *Warlock* is better than *The Space Cucumber* across the board—twice as good in some areas—then…Alright, I'm going to go back and test the sphere out. This evening it should be clearer whether we should still plan to break you out. I recommend you get back to your training.

START THE GAME

Personal experience suggests that being untrained is not much fun in *Galactogon*. Stan! Get the capsule ready..."

"The Planetary Spirit has been activated," my engineer reported as soon as I returned to the game. All I had left to do was shake my head in astonishment and look at my watch—it hadn't felt like thirty minutes had already gone by. How time flies! "Blood Island is now the homeworld for *Warlock* and its entire crew."

"In that case, man your stations! We're taking off!" I ordered and wriggled into my marine armor. The time had come to see what *Warlock* was capable of.

For the next half hour I dashed back and forth across the solar system, trying to understand the principles behind piloting the klamir. Even with its upgraded engines *The Space Cucumber* was no match for *Warlock* in speed. By my calculations, a class-B klamir could fly one-and-a-half times faster than an A-class frigate. The orangutan was blasting asteroids left and right, showing off his accuracy and reaction time. The engineer/shields operator put on a master class in shield placement, deflecting the asteroid fragments away from the ship. For my part, I threaded the ship between the scattering rocks and focused on getting a handle on its avionics. Only the marine had it easy, snoring peacefully in his berth in the bilge. What I liked most about the locals was how unfinicky they were—they were told to test the ship and that's what they did, speaking up only to help me out when I had made some mistake. There was no whining to the effect of "I need to get back IRL" or "Let's go blast someone already" or "What the hell are we doing anyway? Let's start some trouble and figure it out later." More and more I didn't feel like parting with this new setup.

"Surgeon, this is Marina," the captain of *Alexandria* called me up about an hour later. "Accept the transmission request I just sent you—it's got a link to a video that shows how we managed to land on that Training Sector. Thanks for the planet. One of my guys checked out what you told us. We'll be arriving in-system pretty soon. Tell me, that round ship that's bouncing around the system like a ping-pong ball—is that you?"

"Yup. I'm trying out my new toy."

"Partner...I need to know—what, how and where'd you get her?"

"She's a klamir. Got her on Blood Island by an act of god. There's no other. Marina, I know that this might sound wrong, but this ship is off-limits to you. At least for the next three months. I need her for my own personal business. I'd be happy to show you what she can do as well as how I came by her, but your engineers are not allowed on board. Or any marines, for that matter. Sorry."

"You do understand that if you show up in that ball in the populated part of *Galactogon*, the whole fraternity of antiquarians will come after you in short order?"

"I understand that very well. But I don't have much of a choice at the moment. I'll say it again—I need three months. No one will steal my *Warlock* until then. As soon as I'm done with my business, we can have a talk about studying the orb. There are many curious things here."

"I hear you. In that case, you owe me a link to a video

about how you managed to get your hands on that ship. Best of luck to you, partner. I know as well as anyone what it means to have a personal goal that you have to give your all to achieve. If you need my help, call. I'll send you Anton's and Lisp's numbers as well. Over and out."

"What are your orders?" Braniac asked. "Shall we continue testing the ship? Over the last hour and a half, crew readiness has reached 32%. Our probability of defeating a similarly-equipped opponent currently stands at 20%."

"In that case, set course to the Glastir system," I decided, choosing a Confederate system on the periphery of *Galactogon*'s populated space. I didn't want to jump right into the thick of it. First I wanted to see how *Warlock* would handle a battle with neutral ships. If I had all day, I had better use it to its utmost.

"ETA is one hour and ten minutes," Braniac instantly replied. "Commence hyperjump?"

"Do it," I said and the stars around us instantly stretched into thin, white lines. Braniac did not need to enter anything into the system, as he himself was the system. The more time I spent with this ship, the more I liked it. But it was important not to get too used to it—I could easily become over-reliant on it.

"Braniac, pull up the video from my PDA," I issued another command, after downloading Marina's video from the link she'd sent me. It was time to find out how this girl had managed to land in the Training Sector...

"Ten minutes until we emerge from hyperspace," Braniac warned me just in case, tearing me away from my contemplation of the video I had watched. Despite the fact that the video itself was only ten minutes long, quite a lot of things had been crammed into it. If I had to summarize Marina's "masterpiece," I'd paint the following picture:

1. Capture an imperial service vessel. And I mean capture—not destroy—the plan requires a senior imperial official to succeed.

2. Hack the onboard computer until the captain engages the self-destruct procedure. Here, Marina managed to keep the ship in one piece by bribing several locals and instructing them in what they needed to do. It was the locals on board the captured ship who prevented the captain from self-destructing and granted Marina access to the ship's computer.

3. In this manner, you obtain landing codes reserved exclusively for the Very Important Local on the captured vessel. It's worth pointing out that you have to keep this VIL alive, since as soon as he dies, the codes become inactive—a particularity of the game that's worth keeping in mind.

4. Using the codes, you gain access to the Training Sector's defense system and thereupon transmit an official SOS, announcing that your own ship is about to

---

perform an emergency landing. The strange thing is that the same trick wouldn't work on trade planets or on any planet where the emperor is present. You can only do this kind of thing on the Training Sector and several other key imperial planets. I was grateful that Marina mentioned this fact, since I was already considering using the same technique to get onto my Precian moon.

5. The planetary defense forces then contact your ship and begin asking what's happened to her and why she doesn't match the VIL's customary ship. One of the biggest disadvantages to hacking the VIL's ship's computer is that doing so bricks the vessel. Completely. It can't be transported to a repair-dock, it can't be destroyed, it can't be touched whatsoever. But all you have to do is explain that due to a battle with some enemies of the empire, the ship's parameters have changed and that all that's keeping her together now is spit and good old imperial knowhow. Marina pulled this trick twice and it worked both times.

6. After that, you land in the Training Sector. Here, Marina messed up—she tried to land on the planet in her cruiser, instead of the shuttle she normally used. The cruiser was not designed for this kind of thing and plummeted to the planet like the hunk of metal it was— never reaching the landing spot she had chosen beside the barracks that housed the recruits. The second time,

Marina used a frigate and peacefully descended to the Sector, emerging to meet the senior officer in charge of the Sector. She told him that the VIL was on his deathbed and so could not descend to the planet himself. Then she asked for emergency medical assistance. This triggers an assistance request, giving the players five minutes to do whatever it is they came to do, return to the ship and make their run out of the system. This was the point where Marina turned and attacked the Grand Arbiter, realizing perfectly well that she was committing suicide. The girl just couldn't believe that it was impossible to destroy that ship. She didn't send me the battle itself—just its last moments showing the Grand Arbiter breaking apart and a notification appearing that her ship had leveled up—right after which, her ship was destroyed too.

At that point the video ended. And this was precisely what I spent the rest of my hyperjump contemplating. None of this would work for me if I didn't first find a Pyrrhenian VIL of my own. The captain would destroy the ship long before the rhino would make it to the flight deck. Plus, it'd be necessary to keep the cryptosaur's dimension in mind—it was unlikely the ship would have the space to allow him to move around freely. That left the assault droids. I had 32 of those bad boys in my hangar, but only three or four were battle-ready. The rest would need to be repaired and I had no time for that.

START THE GAME

So, in the end, I was at a loss about what to do next…

"Leaving hyperspace in four, three, two, one," Braniac said, paying no attention to my contemplative state. "We have reached the Glastir System. The nearest planet is…WARNING! THREAT DETECTED! HOSTILES INCOMING!"

"Shields are up," the snake instantly responded, pulling me out of my shocked state and forcing me to evaluate the situation. As soon as I did that, I had to curse through my teeth—I had managed to plunk us down square in the midst of the Zatrathi fleet. The entire solar system was swarming with the fragments of some developers' hallucinations—which by some error had become the Zatrathi ships. There had been no description of these new spacecraft in the changelog and now that I saw them firsthand I began to wonder what drugs the game artists had been on when they cooked up this stuff. Each one resembled a huge formless blob which bristled with dozens of sharp-tipped and crooked appendages—more reminiscent of stalactites or stalagmites than parts of a ship. Everything was jagged, corroded, huge, lacking any symmetry and yet somehow still flying. Even my modest knowledge of physics told me that this kind of design should not have been capable of spaceflight at all. But I guess the designers had been unconcerned by this.

Warlock's main screen was helpfully informing me that the klamir was being locked onto by hundreds of enemy ships. The only good news was that the composition of the invaders' fleet was pretty ordinary—they had the same old cruisers, scouts, frigates etc…just spiky and scary-looking.

"Braniac, jump us to any part of *Galactogon*—just get us away from here," I ordered, taking over the ship's controls. I didn't much want to become a hero who'd smashed himself headfirst against this enormous armada. As a rule, such heroes tend to acquire their status posthumously.

"I am unable to perform your orders," Braniac instantly responded. "It is currently impossible to jump to hyperspace from the Glastir system. Judging by the disruption field that's blocking our egress, the source is the fleet's flagship—identified as an orbital station. My recommendation..."

"Seven torpedoes inbound. Contact in twenty seconds," the snake drowned out Braniac's voice. "The gunner can destroy five. One will be captured. That leaves one which must be evaded, while he reloads. What are your orders, Captain? Shall we give battle?"

"Battle stations!" I decided, realizing that it was too late to listen to Braniac's advice. All that was left was either to die and respawn or to try our best to get out of there in one piece. And if I preferred the latter option, I needed to get on with it.

"Contact in ten seconds..."

Carefully, I placed my hand on *Warlock*'s projection and moved it. This was instantly followed by the feeling of intense acceleration, which, partially absorbed by my armor, still forced me to struggle from making any sudden movements. We began to travel away from the torpedoes' trajectories—rendered on my screen as inbound red lines.

"Fire at will!" I ordered a moment later, realizing that the torpedoes had already adjusted their course but the orangutan hadn't moved a finger to knock them out. Here then were the first disadvantages to having a crew of locals—I would have to constantly tell them what needed to be done. Any human player would already be pouring fire in every direction—orders or not.

"Two cruisers off starboard, three above, 22 interceptors are currently flanking us to cut off a retreat," Braniac began chirping in my ear, even though my eyes could see all this just as well. To my surprise the angular ships turned out to be extremely fast and agile. Even though *Warlock* was flying at full power, the enemy was catching up on either side of us in a pincer maneuver. And not just interceptors or something—the huge cruisers were doing it too! In my view, the developers had gone too far. There was no way any player could run away from a battle with an enemy this fast.

"Thirty torpedoes inbound from port, thirty from starboard, forty coming from above, fifty from below and twenty-two straight ahead," the snake cheered me up after twenty seconds of this race between the turtle (me) and the hare (the Zatrathi). "Contact in twenty seconds…No interceptions possible…"

I looked at the space around us helplessly, completely unable to see a way out that did not involve having to respawn and lose a ship class. The invaders' fleet was closing around me like a giant set of jaws. Beams flashed against our shields, threatening to blast them apart, and to top it all off, the inbound torpedoes had formed a noose around us that would tighten in the next few seconds and turn *Warlock* into space dust and some floating loot. I'd lose a hundred levels and a ton of money on repairs, and my crew would probably lose some experience not even having fired a shot. We'd lose the twenty-two torpedoes we still had over nothing! Damn it all!

"Shields operator, do what you have to but we need to survive a direct hit from several torpedoes," I ordered, changing our course with the control orb. What was the point of running if we'd be destroyed either way? We had to give battle and knock out at least one enemy. Even if it was only an interceptor.

"Roger," the snake replied, without bothering to ask what it was I wanted it to do. This crew didn't question orders.

"Gunner, I need you to clear a path," I went on issuing commands, pointing *Warlock* in the direction of the biggest Zatrathi ship—the very same orbital station that kept us from slipping out of this place. "As soon as you get the chance, fire at will at the closest enemy ships. Make sure to save at least ten torpedoes."

"It will be impossible to clear a passage completely," said the snake—hanging another shield on our hull. The reactor had begun to whine—our Elo levels were approaching zero. A warning appeared, indicating that our beam absorbers were being overloaded—the snake had moved the shields from that side of the ship—and yet none of this mattered very much: We continued to fly *Warlock* at the enemy station at full steam. Basically, I only had one way out—ram the orbital station while setting off all the torpedoes I had on board my ship. Every other option would lead to defeat.

START THE GAME

"A Pirate I Was Meant To Be" Mission Progress: 12 of 150 interceptors destroyed.

You have received the "First Defender" title. You are the first player to destroy a Zatrathi ship in Galactogon. Contact any empire to receive a unique reward from the Emperor himself.

The notification almost knocked all my adrenaline out of me—Zatrathi ships counted towards my pirate mission and now I had a way to get into the central Precian system where the Uldans' secret base was located. It was no matter that the gunner had spent three torpedoes on destroying that interceptor. The fact itself was important—the Zatrathi could be destroyed despite the speed of their ships.

"Contact!" Braniac moaned as the ship shook. "Damage report: 54% of the bow-mounted beam absorbers have been destroyed. The graviton engines can no longer redirect thrust to the bow. Slizosaur Functionality is down to 22%. Ship thrust is down to 44%. Contact with inbound torpedoes in 20 seconds.

Braniac's report offered no good news, but we had broken through the noose of torpedoes, at the cost of half the ships' Durability. *Warlock* was instantly hit by dozens of beams from the circling interceptors and frigates, but at the moment I had one immense advantage—the enemy station's immense size prevented the Zatrathi vessels from maneuvering close to us, whereas *Warlock* could keep on bouncing in any direction it felt like—well, any direction, if you discounted the one that the torpedoes were coming from.

"Gunner, aim for the big ship," I ordered again and rotated the ship to show our enemies the already damaged side. I needed one side to remain undamaged and twenty seconds wasn't enough for the interceptors to breach the hull, as damaged as it already was. "All shields forward. We're going to ram them!"

"Seventy-two torpedoes inbound. Contact in 47 seconds," the snake said just in case. "Torpedoes are away. Damage report: The beam absorbers have been breached. The portside engine has been incapacitated. The research laboratory has been incapacitated…The torpedoes have reached their target. The enemy vessel has taken 35% damage. Warning collision imminent! Please take evasive maneuvers immedia…"

If before I'd thought that the torpedoes had really shaken us, I was very wrong. The ten torpedoes that I had held onto, managed to tear through the Zatrathi station's hull and rip off one of its appendages. Without giving it much thought, I pointed *Warlock* at the opening that had appeared. I was planning on flying into the center of the station and detonating my ship—perhaps even finishing off the enemy flagship—but the klamir turned out to be a surprisingly tough ship. The collision sent me and my chair flying into the instrument panel. Stars danced across my eyes—a very realistic touch—but it only took several seconds for me to again begin parsing Braniac's voice as I slowly came to.

"Damage report: Hull Durability is down to 16%. The beam absorbers are gone. Crew Functionality is down to 18%. Ship thrust is down to 4%. To continue flying, this ship requires an external overhaul, requiring seven tons of Raq. We are also

---

critically low on Elo. The current energy reserves are 13%. Unauthorized access attempt detected—and blocked. I have identified an open access port to the enemy ship's network."

"Hack it!" I replied, getting up. "How's the marine?"

"The cryptosaur is currently incapable of undertaking assault operations."

"What about the droids?" I asked just in case, still unsure whether I needed to activate the self-destruct or wait longer. The fact that we had survived our ramming attack and now had the chance to dig around in the Zatrathi internal systems, suggested that I needed to continue leveraging what little success I had had. Any downloaded data could easily be sold for a good profit. The main thing was to prevent boarding and capture.

"Four droids are ready to perform both assault and security functions," Braniac replied. "Shall I activate them?"

"Do it and send them here," I replied. "What's the status of our beam cannons?"

"They are incapacitated and require a full overhaul," Braniac came out with more bad news like a broken record. "The current status of the strabosaur does not allow him to use his personal weapons."

"Hang on, what happened to the torpedoes that were coming at us?" I remembered a bit late. Seventy missiles couldn't just vanish without trace.

"There is no more information about them—our external sensors have been destroyed. There is no visual contact. I have obtained access to the internal network of the enemy ship—what are your instructions?"

"Dump any and all data you can get your axons on. I'm interested in everything: from ship specifications to base locations to operational documents concerning the invasion."

"Roger that. I have obtained read-only access to the station's neural backbone. I have established *Warlock*'s location. Warning! There are currently 43 enemy assault squads heading in our direction. ETA of the first squad is three minutes. This squad consists of ten warriors. Downloading data now."

"Where are they going to come from?" I asked, smirking. It would have been silly to assume that the developers would allow my data dump to go unnoticed. Obviously, every available force on board the station would make its way toward us. Most likely, the inbound assault squads only included the security forces in our immediate vicinity. The station itself probably had much more soldiers than that.

"The last remaining passage leading to us is located about a hundred feet away," replied Braniac, displaying a projection of *Warlock* on the remaining screen. Hmm...My perfectly round ship had turned into a dirty, tattered, cracked cube with several holes that seemed to run all the way through it. *Warlock* had smashed up several decks of the station and come to a stop basically in the center of a large amphitheater. It was difficult to say why the station had such a facility, but the fact remained—a part of my ship was located in the arena, a part of it had knocked down the walls and crushed several rows of seats— while the opening that we had come hurtling through had already been sealed with some kind of force field. Braniac illuminated a smallish passage that the first ten Zatrathi—no doubt equipped with active-defense-equipped armor—would have to use to reach us. On the one hand, I had no chances of surviving against such a mob and it was perhaps better to blow up my ship before it was too late. On the other hand, the progress bar for the data transfer was moving quickly enough to give me pause for thought. Information was money and I simply could not pass it by without a fight. I'd have to make the best of what I had.

"Send the droids outside," I ordered, retrieving my two manipulators. Practice had shown that a manipulator was a very effective weapon in close quarters—as long as you had enough debris around you to throw around. In this case, there was only one possible approach and it was littered with junk. Plus, the droids had their own defensive systems, both passive and active. It was time to make a stand.

"I have located the station's cargo holds," Braniac went on reporting into my earpiece as I emerged from my ship...although, "emerge" is probably too strong a word. In actual fact, I had to squeeze between some wreckage and a crumpled door that refused to do what a door is made to do. Four droids—which resembled steel human skeletons fitted with servos, mini-reactors and blasters—crawled out of *Warlock* behind me and took up positions around the entrance to the amphitheater. These four would take the brunt of the first assault until I joined the fight.

"What's in the cargo holds?" I asked, more automatically than anything else, as I was more occupied with activating my manipulator and lifting a large piece of the hull wreckage around me.

"Forty-two tons of Raq, 32 tons of Elo, 22 tons of Trion, 13 tons of Shlir," Braniac ran down the list, forcing me to clench my fists helplessly. Forty-two tons of Raq was a jackpot that came along once in a lifetime, but I had absolutely no chances of getting it. I could now really appreciate the old proverb: "Honey is sweet but the bee stings."

"Continue downloading the data." I decided to change the topic, dropping the piece of hull wreckage to the ground. There was still a minute left before the first assault wave would arrive and I needed to conserve my manipulator's power—I had completely forgotten that I needed to recharge them and they were down to 50%. That would be enough to kill a couple Zatrathis of course...Oh! By the way! I still had no idea what those guys looked like! There had been no images in the changelog, I had been unable to see inside the interceptors during the battle, and Braniac had not offered any images of the assault teams on their way toward us. I wondered who, in the minds of the developers, could create these strange, angular, porcupine ships?

Just as Braniac had predicted—I received an answer to my question precisely one minute later.

CHAPTER TWELVE

THE ZATRATHI ORBITAL STATION

Accoding to the map that Braniac sent me, the only approach to the amphitheater where we had crash landed was through a doorway around which my four droids had now arrayed themselves. Beyond the doorway lay a thirty-foot-long corridor, making our current defensive position ideal. Anyone wishing to expel us from the orbital station would have to first charge into a barrage of four A-class assault blasters which were impervious to active resistance. However, I could not wield one myself as all the blasters were attached to the droids.

"Target identified." A notification from one of the droids popped up before me. "Awaiting orders to engage."

"Fire at will!" I ordered, overcoming my desire to approach the portal and peek into the corridor. I was very curious what the

---

Zatrathi looked like, but there was also see a steady stream of fire coming from the other end of the hallway, trying to knock out my droids. I was now engaged in my first serious shootout in *Galactogon* and could not help but notice that my warriors' blaster fire was blue, while that of our assailants was red. Did this convenient color-coding happen only when engaging locals or would the same thing happen in PvP duels too? It was very helpful to telling what was going on in the battle.

Droid #18 has leveled up. Current level: A-14.
Droid #29 Functionality is down to 2%.

A sudden silence descended on the amphitheater. The torrent of red blaster fire from the corridor dried up and my remaining droids lowered their weapons. The first assault had been turned away, though not without losses: The melted skeleton of Droid #29 lay on the ground.

"The next squad shall arrive in five minutes," Braniac told me some good news as soon as I realized that my four droids had just fought off ten Zatrathi. Ten for one really was a nice trade, considering that I could still repair the downed droid too. I wondered whether the droids would keep their current health or return healed when my ship respawned.

"How is the data transfer going?" I asked and then added, "What are you transferring anyway?"

"At the moment I am downloading the menu from the station's mess hall," came the shocking reply. "The channel

---

bandwidth and the incessant countermeasures are constraining my access to the network. However, I have already obtained a detailed plan of our station sector, as well as a detailed inventory of the items in the station's warehouse. I have also downloaded the crew quarters' cleaning schedule. The repair manifest is next in the download queue. Unfortunately, as I have previously mentioned, the channel's bandwidth does not allow me to download at a faster rate."

"Goddamn it!" Dropping my hands, I couldn't contain myself. Instead of blowing up the ship and selling operative information concerning the Zatrathi deployment, I was downloading some kind of garbage! The mess hall menu! But no, I already had much more valuable information—the crew quarters' cleaning schedule! I couldn't even imagine how I had survived without it until now.

Realizing that I had no further business on this station, I decided that I would at least get a look at the Zatrathi. Ten of them should be lying around the hallway right this moment and…

WAIT!

The loot!

How could I have forgotten that the dead Zatrathi should have dropped loot?

"Braniac, can any of the droids that are back at the ship move?"

"Two droids are still in satisfactory condition."

"Order one to carry the remains of 29 back to the ship and order the other to come escort me to the dead Zatrathi."

I didn't want to abandon my melted warrior. A new droid was expensive and an engineer could make the repairs, assuming he had the knowhow and the materials.

"Ten squads shall arrive simultaneously in three minutes," Braniac warned me when I entered the hallway. The three functioning droids had already entrenched themselves next to the doorway, taking up positions for the coming battle, so I decided against disturbing them. Instead, I had one of the damaged droids that needed repairs follow me, hobbling on one damaged leg and with his arm hanging limply at one side. Despite his current condition, this brave soldier managed to calmly carry twice the weight I could fit in my Journeyman's Satchel. I didn't want to leave the loot in the corridor. Before blowing up my ship, I'd first stuff my inventory with anything I could, making myself immobile, and only then meet my Planetary Spirit. I wouldn't leave my enemies a single crumb!

I did not get a chance to see what the Zatrathi looked like—there was nothing on the floor but ten small, virtual crates which represented the loot fallen from our vanquished foes. The bodies of *Galactogon*'s invaders had already dissolved, so I still had no idea what kind of creatures these were. Considering that ten squads would come visit us in three minutes—a hundred soldiers in total—I figured I'd get a good look anyway.

"The next assault wave will arrive in two minutes," said pedantic Braniac, bringing me back down to earth yet again. I hurried to open the remaining crates. As soon as I touched a shimmering, spinning crate, it would burst, dropping items onto the floor around it:

A blaster, some Raq and a metal token...A piece of armor, some Raq, an Elo powercell and a metal token...A powercell, a powercell, some Raq and a metal token...Some Raq, some more Raq, a piece of armor and a metal token...

"Let's go!" I commanded the limping droid as soon as the last pieces of Raq were in my inventory. To my surprise the droid had not come in handy. All of the loot had fit snugly in my inventory—and yet it had also given rise to a good number of questions.

I became the happy owner of an odd-looking assault blaster, three pieces of soft armor, fifteen pieces of Raq, ten powecells and ten metallic tokens which were almost exact copies of a sheriff's star-badge from the Wild West. I knew what to do with the energy—two powercells went straight to recharging my manipulators and another three to recharging my marine armor—but the Raq remained a mystery...as well as why the storm troops had it to begin with. The correct thing to do was to use the Raq to repair *Warlock*, but if I was going to blow up the ship anyway, then she'd come back fully repaired, regardless of what I'd do to her now. And this meant that I'd be wasting the valuable Raq for nothing. Then again, if I left it in my cargo hold, it would be left behind as loot at the site of the ship's destruction. So, again, I'd be wasting it. The only right thing to do was to leave the Raq in my inventory, hoping that we wouldn't get any more loot—my Journeyman's Satchel could only hold about 40 units of Raq total. Such a shame.

"The assault wave will arrive in thirty seconds. We have acquired fifteen units of Raq," said Braniac, showing that he could count too. "I recommend we use this to increase the Functionality of the slizosaur by 0.1%."

"Braniac, if we die and respawn, what will happen to the crew Functionality?"

"It will drop down to 10% plus whatever improvements we have made. In the case of the slizosaur, the engineer's Functionality will be at 10.1% upon respawning on Blood Island. The enemy has arrived..."

"Target acquired," one of the assault droids informed me yet again. "Awaiting orders to engage."

"Fire at will!" I ordered, grabbed the blaster I had looted and approached the doorway—three droids against a hundred Zatrathi was not a fair fight. "Braniac, as soon as I die, I want you to detonate *Warlock*."

"Roger!" replied the ship's computer, allowing me to turn my complete attention to the red torrent of blaster fire punctuated by rare bursts of blue.

Damage blocked...
Damage blocked...
Damage blocked...

Despite my trying my best to keep as close to the floor as possible—and generally trying to stay out of the fray—the barrage of fire from the hallway was so intense that it was simply impossible to avoid taking hits. The good thing was that, at the moment, my marine armor was soaking up all the damage and burning through its energy reserves in the process. Judging by the energy bar, I could hold out for another five minutes. As soon as the power ran out, I'd be doomed. But for now, my A-class marine armor afforded me the opportunity to get a close long look at the Zatrathi.

Mmm…yeah…

Several dozen metallic and whitish creatures which looked more like lumps of slime than sentient beings crawled slowly but surely along the corridor, holding in their numerous appendages blasters and energy shields which they used to block my droids' blaster fire. The Zatrathi did not seem to have legs, so it looked like they were sliding along the floor. It became apparent now why they had taken so long to get to our crash site—they simply couldn't move any faster.

All of this flashed through my mind in the first fractions of a second, without impairing me from pulling the trigger and adding my one blue blaster bolt to my droids' outbound three. Fire—block—fire—block—fire—block—the Zatrathi closest to me didn't raise his shield in time and, for a little while at least, the corridor had one enemy fewer and a shiny new loot crate.

You have gained XP…

You have received a unique title: "Semper Fidelis!"

You were the first player in Galactogon to destroy a Zatrathi in close combat.

Contact any empire to receive a unique reward from the

Emperor himself.

Another goodie in the bank—but I paid it no attention, at least for now. The discovery that my C-class trophy weapon was more effective than a Qualian assault blaster (which I hadn't even brought with me) was much more important. Either the Zatrathi weapon was simply better, or the difference in class made itself known (after all, I had been working with D-class instead of C-class), or the update had adjusted the output damage—but now it really seemed to me like I had a formidable weapon in my hands. One that offered me the chance to survive and even get out of this mess—as long as my armor held out...

Gained XP...
Gained XP...

"Cover me!" I yelled at the last remaining, firing droid as soon as my armor's power meter began to blink critically red yet again. Despite the fact that the system had guaranteed me five minutes of calm battle, a notification popped up just three minutes later asking me to insert another powercell or have my defense fall to zero. Then, I had to insert another cell and after that another and another...So by the tenth minute of battle, I had not a single powercell left and yet my armor and blaster demanded more Elo still. My droid had been blasted to pieces three minute earlier, leaving one last droid sitting not far from me but refusing to leave cover since his blaster had run out of power and I had no

---

powercells to give him. There was no way to get back to the ship either—if the Zatrathi had anything it was Elo, which meant their barrage kept up unslaked.

Understanding that the slugs would keep coming—the first hundred had already been joined by the rest of the 320—and that the only thing between me and this army was the hallway which could accommodate no more than thirty at a time, I decided to counterattack. What difference did it make under what circumstanced I'd meet my Planetary Spirit—on the floor or heroically blowing up among my enemies? The latter would be more fun anyway.

By now the corridor was full of shimmering loot crates, through which the slugs kept coming without taking any notice. If I risked it and opened myself to enemy fire, maybe my armor would hold out long enough for me to reach the nearest crate, open it and instantly use one of the powercells. I had no doubts that there'd be one in there—the first ten had all contained at least one. The only question was whether my armor would suffice and whether I'd have enough energy in my blaster to destroy the crawling Zatrathi. Either way, I'd never know if I didn't give it a shot.

"Kill the bastards!" I yelled more for my benefit than anyone else's and jumped to my feet to the covering fire of my last droid.

"Get some! Get some! Get some!" I yelled as I ran forward, sending blaster bolt after blaster bolt down the corridor. There were so many slugs ahead of me that I had no trouble

_____

hitting something, even if some of my shots were blocked.

Your Zatrathi Assault Blaster has reached a new class. Current class: B-1. All blaster parameters have increased by 20%. Durability and Energy have been fully restored.

Damage blocked...

Only that second notification could bring me to my senses and force me to take two more quick steps and dive to the ground, leaving less of myself for the Zatrathi in the rear to shoot at. A class-B blaster! This was no mere weapon—this was a...a...Well, I didn't even have the words to describe my joy. Yet the damage notification forced me to return my senses and look around myself. A loot crate lay right in front of me. My armor's energy meter was no longer simply blinking red—it had already gone dim several times, immobilizing me, so I reached as far as I could to the loot crate and pursed my lips in anticipation. Would it be there or not? Would I get lucky or not?

You have received the following items: Raq, Raq, powercell, metal token.

Got it! I couldn't contain a yelp of joy when the armor's energy meter went from dark-red to yellow. Twenty-five percent energy and three additional minutes of life. It may as well have been an eternity!

"Hold your positions!" I ordered my droids after picking up another ten crates of loot. Another 12 units of Raq, nine powercells and tokens, as well as two flexible pieces of armor allowed me to feel relatively safe. As long as I had the energy, my armor wouldn't be punctured...and it was already at A-89, which meant that Legendary was not too far off! Legendary Marine Armor! That would be a thing to see!

"What now, oh Space Invaders? Shall we have ourselves a proper war?"

Getting comfortable on the floor, I began to carefully aim and fire bolt after bolt down the corridor, periodically swapping the powercells in my blaster. If I got out of this slaughter alive, I'd need to make Marina some kind of present for giving me this marine suit—without it I would've been dead meat long ago...

"I am observing massive movement in the enemy sectors," came Braniac's voice as soon as I splattered the last slug from this mortal coil. I didn't know how the resurrection thing worked for them, but at the moment they had definitely departed this world. My blaster had gained several levels and my armor's XP bar was at the halfway mark, while the suit itself was in tatters—its Durability was just above 10%—but I had achieved my main objective: All the Zatrathi had been destroyed. I had sent 430 assailants to their well earned rest! Who'd dare refuse me the title of great warrior after such a feat?

"What movement are you talking about?" I replied, getting up. Even though this was just a game, no one said I couldn't feel mentally drained. With all due respect to myself, I would not be able to handle another battle like that.

"Enemy forces have begun massing on the borders of our

sector. Their speed is several times greater than that of the forces you destroyed, which suggests that these are Zatrathi marines. Assuming their current speed remains the same, fresh enemy assault squads will be here in fifteen minutes."

Damn it all again! It was like I'd just battled an army of janitors who, armed with brooms and dustpans, had wanted to kick us out of their station. No wonder they couldn't take out my armor. Now, however, the real assault troops had landed on the station and were rapidly approaching my position.

"How many of them are there?"

"According to preliminary data—twelve thousand. Their numbers continue to grow however. Unfortunately, I have no access to other sectors of the station and cannot provide accurate information about enemy forces."

"Got it...Alright, let's gather all the loot and put it in my inventory," I nodded at the four droids, calling them over. Wistfully, I looked at the four hundred shimmering crates of loot strewn all over each other and muttered, "Too bad we won't be able to get it all. Fifteen minutes is just not enough...Braniac, is there any way to delay the incoming horde? Even by ten minutes or so?"

"Analyzing data now...Affirmative—We have the option of blocking a corridor that serves as a bottleneck about 500 yards from here."

"Set up a remote uplink and throw the map up on my HUD," I yelled. Then, I unloaded all the Raq from my inventory and gave it to my droids. Who knew what I'd encounter in this station. Maybe the extra room in my inventory would come in

---

handy. Opening several other loot crates, I picked up all the powercells and then sprinted along the dotted red guideline that Braniac had projected on my armor's HUD. I needed to win at least half an hour in order to harvest all the loot, return to *Warlock* and pack everything in my bag before blowing myself up. Hopefully, this game would allow me to overload my inventory at the cost of mobility.

"What do I do now?" I shouted into my comm two minutes later and snapped in yet another powercell—running at top speed made the armor consume energy faster than powering its shields. I was facing yet another rounded corridor that resembled a cylinder built into the station. Its five-foot diameter forced even little old me to bend down in order to enter it. I could see nothing that could stop the enemy's assault squads. It was just an ordinary thirty-foot-long hallway.

"According to the station layout, this hallway connects two independent areas of our sector. If you blow it up, the enemy will be forced to repair it. This should afford you enough time to gather the loot."

"I don't have any explosives!" I bristled realizing that Braniac had just wasted five minutes of my looting time. If I couldn't do anything with the corridor (shooting at the wall had done nothing), then there had been absolutely no reason for me to come here.

"Analyzing data...Forty yards in the direction of our ship, there is a passage to some service quarters. According to the downloaded data, that area serves as storage for exterior panels used in station repair. Considering that you have two manipulators..."

I didn't listen any further and took off in the direction of this next waypoint. Braniac lived up to his name—if the corridor couldn't be destroyed, it could be obstructed! The Zatrathi marines would have some fun removing several rows of panels which would likely have beam absorption properties! I just hoped I had enough time!

"What's the code?" I bellowed, stopping in front of an inconspicuous, wide door— which turned out to be locked.

"I do not have this information," Braniac replied. "Analyzing data..."

To hell with the analysis! I pointed my blaster at the door and pulled the trigger as far as it would go—I had absolutely no time to sit there guessing the right code when I had a universal skeleton key right there in my hands!

"Enemy marine units will arrive in thirty seconds," Braniac informed me as I placed yet another panel into the corridor. The humongous, heavy and unwieldy slabs filled the entire corridor—I had made sure to tessellate them in order to make it more difficult to remove the obstruction. Basically, I had erected a pyramid of panels that had created a barricade fifteen feet deep.

"*Delrang gardan!*" came a terrible shout from the other end of the hallway. I caught a glimpse of a Zatrathi through the panels I had piled together. This was the Zatrathi marine. He wore a kind of brown marine armor which was outfitted with all kinds of knobs and appendages. His dark visor obscured his face and his limbs had multiple segments and joints. He looked quite imposing in short and I was sure that I was facing real warriors now. Their sharp, quick movements, their disciplined chatter, and the several attempts they made to shoot me through the obstacle I had erected—all suggested that these brown Zatrathi were quite different from their sluggish brethren. I wasn't sure anymore that I could've held out against these guys—class-A marine armor or not.

"Braniac, can you monitor the progress that the Zatrathi make in clearing my barricade?" Pushing my throttle all the way forward I flew back to the loot crates. "Can you estimate how long they'll be occupied with it?"

"I have begun tracking their progress. There is no preliminary estimate, however. Initiating scan of our sector. Warning! I have identified twenty life forms in *Warlock*'s current sector."

"Where?" I asked, slowing my pace. If twenty marines had managed to get through, my chances of surviving would plummet drastically. Oh but look! I was already thinking about survival, as opposed to gathering some loot. By the way, damn it, the loot…

"Opposite side of the sector, right beyond the station warehouse. The life forms are not doing anything. They are standing in place. Tracking them now."

The station warehouse!

What a crazy day this was becoming!

"Braniac, will my team be able to reach the warehouse on its own?" I asked, still running as fast as I could.

"Negative. In order to exercise the mobility function, overall Functionality must be at 15%. The current Functionality level of every crew member is 12%."

"How much Raq do I need to raise the Functionality by three percent?" I managed to yell as I zoomed into the hallway with the loot from the slugs.

"Fifteen units of Raq lead to a 0.1% increase in Functionality," came the instant reply. "Extrapolating from the previous loot yield of fifteen units of Raq per ten enemies killed, we can assume that there are 645 units of Raq among the loot in the hallway. This will lead to a 4.3% increase in Functionality. This would allow us to send the cryptosaur to transport Raq from the station's warehouse back to the ship."

One unit of Raq, if I remembered correctly, weighed about 5lbs. Consequently, 645 units would weigh in at about 1.5 tons...If we recalled that I managed to sell fifty tons of the stuff for several million...I began to see that maintaining my crew and repairing it after battle would cost me an arm and two legs! The only alternatives would be either to level them up from zero or dump a bunch of money into them...

"Let's do it," I decided, realizing that there was no time to waste. It was time to reap the loot harvest that my droids and I had sowed. "Get the ship ready to accept the droids with the Raq. They're going to feed the cryptosaur..."

START THE GAME

✴

Opening and organizing the enormous number of loot crates took me about an hour. By that time, as Braniac informed me, the Zatrathi marines had managed to burn through a mere two feet of the hallway that I had barricaded. I guess they had no manipulators with them. On the other hand, they did have an unlimited supply of powercells, which meant that I could expect them in the next eight hours or so.

I had no idea what I was supposed to do with 430 metal tokens. Most likely, I could trade them in for some kind of reward, so I wasn't about to throw them away. Anyway, the tokens didn't weigh anything and took up no space. Overall, the loot I received for my first battle included 22 blasters, about 100 pieces of flexible armor (which I had no idea how to use) and a mountain of powercells. I fed all my Raq to the rhino, who began to slowly move his legs.

"Braniac, plot a path for me to the warehouse," I ordered as soon as the last powercell had been hauled up to *Warlock*. Even if they destroyed us and all our cargo would drop in place, the Zatrathi would at least be grateful that I hadn't strewn their powercells all over their station.

While the computer calculated the route, my marine came crawling out of the ship, panting so heavily his sides were heaving. He had none of that former spryness with which he'd chased me around Blood Island. At the moment he seemed more like a mule who'd spent the past week sleeping and who'd suddenly been yoked and forced to haul hay. All he lacked were bags under his eyes.

"Follow me," I ordered, making my way along the path that Braniac had plotted for me. "Braniac, what's the distance to the objective?"

"Following the hallways, the objective is one mile away. Enemy progress through the barricade currently stands at three feet..."

Realizing that the Zatrathi marines would soon pick up some steam—after all, the obstruction I'd built was only about fifteen feet thick—I again engaged my acceleration and began sprinting. If I could at least save the rhino, respawning would be much more fun.

"Increase your Functionality to 50%," I waved at the rhino as soon as the door to the warehouse buckled under my blaster's fire. To my surprise, the cryptosaur hadn't fallen behind me, despite the fact that we had covered one mile in a mere four minutes—not a bad speed even for athletes.

The rhino sniffed the air like a real animal and took off at a gallop, weaving between the shelves of goods. I heard the clatter of falling metal, after which Braniac began to count: "Cryptosaur Functionality increased by 0.1%. Cryptosaur Functionality increased by 0.1%. Cryptosaur..."

"Stop it, Braniac. Where are those twenty life forms you mentioned?" I interrupted the computer and decided to take a look at the creatures that Braniac had mentioned earlier. "Don't forget to transport whatever's valuable in the warehouse back to the

---

ship. The gunner and the engineer can get to the cargo on their own, once the marine brings back enough Raq to get them moving."

Braniac plotted a new guide line to the life forms and I began moving in that direction. I had nothing to do in the warehouse myself and exploring the Zatrathi station was the sacred duty of any true player in this situation. I could sell the video log of my exploration for millions later on—the main thing was to drive a hard bargain.

"Braniac, the route you gave me ends in a dead end!" After about ten minutes of walking down a drab, slightly-undulating corridor, the route I had been following disappeared into a blank wall. Just in case, I made sure that I was looking at a real wall and not some hologram and even shot it a few times with my blaster to see if I could break through it. That having failed, I got in touch with the ship's computer. He was the one who'd brought me here, so perhaps he could explain where I was supposed to go now.

"There are no walls along this route," Braniac answered flatly. "Please continue moving forward."

"What do you mean there aren't any walls? What am I looking at then?"

"You are currently located in the middle of an empty hallway," Braniac continued without taking any interest in what I was saying. "According to the map I downloaded, the only walls in your vicinity are along the sides of the hallway. Please continue moving forward."

"There is no forward, Braniac. Reroute me around this hallway." Not wishing to argue with a simulation of a simulation, I decided to go around.

"Here is the new route," Braniac replied a second later and the virtual line on my screen updated. "I wish to remark that this is route is inefficient due to…"

"What's going on with the Raq in the warehouse?" I interrupted the pedant.

"Currently the slizosaur—the engineer and shields operator—is in the warehouse increasing his Functionality to 50% as you ordered. The strabosaur—the gunner—is currently at 13%. In three minutes he will depart for the warehouse. Please note that the enemy has burned through six feet of the obstructed passageway. The speed of their progress has grown."

"As soon as the slizosaur reaches 50%, tell him to start making repairs to the ship," I issued further orders. It didn't make sense to ferry the Raq to my own cargo holds because the enemy would get it all back when we hit the self-destruct anyway. But using it on repairs—that was a minus both to me and my foe. To me because the respawned ship would come back fully repaired anyway (albeit a class lower)—and to the Zatrathi because it would waste their reserves. If we couldn't take the stuff, we'd burn it…

"Understood."

"Stop! Before that, get the engineer to repair all the droids! Only after that, let him work on the ship." I even stopped in my tracks when the idea came to me. This was a great opportunity to use our access to all this wealth! It was unforgivable to have two living and two half-living droids out of a complement of thirty—especially since respawning wouldn't restore them.

"Orders updated," Braniac replied—and as he did so, I ran into another wall.

"Give me a third route!" I ordered, examining the wall closely. It was no different from all the others—except like the earlier one, it was positioned right across the hallway, preventing me from approaching the twenty life forms. This only made me want to see them all the more. No one's going to put in walls like this in a game for no reason.

"There are no other possible routes. These are the only two hallways that lead to the area in question."

"Braniac, it's time to earn your name!" I retorted, really getting into this hunt now. "If we can't get there directly, there must be some kind of vents or secret passages or something! Stop downloading the menu from the local restaurant and find me a way to get in there!"

"If you continue straight..." The computer continued to bumble pedantically, refusing to acknowledge the wall in front of me.

"I'm not going to go straight. I don't want to! I want to crawl around basements, sewage pipes and so on. Get on with it! Find a way."

"The requested information cannot be found..."

"Where does the door to my left lead?" Realizing that it

was pointless to expect a miracle from Braniac, I decided to do the planning myself. Looking around, I chose one of the numerous doors around me and decided to try my luck there. Maybe it'd work?

"A small 9x9-foot room. There is no description. This room has no further passages to other rooms."

Employing the station skeleton key (my blaster), I found myself in a small bedroom. A soft bed, a chair, a table, a latrine behind a separator—the rooms' furnishings simply screamed that a humanoid lived here. Not some slug or some brown four-armed marine, no—everything about the room and in the room suggested that the only creature that could use it walked upright on two legs. How many creatures in the game resembled humanoids? Out of the twelve empires, only six could brag about their resemblance to the human race. There were the players too of course, but I wasn't counting them.

Unless of course, this was a prison cell for a player!

Pointing my blaster in the direction I ultimately wanted to go, I pulled the trigger. I already understood that a B-class blaster was too weak for the hallways walls, but what would happen if I aimed it at this room's wall? It could handle doors fine, after all!

"You have passed into a neighboring room, having bypassed the standard system of hallways," Braniac reported, once I'd crawled through the small hole. The blaster hadn't done the job at first—but I noticed that the wall wasn't absorbing the energy bolts. Instead, it had begun melting, spitting molten pieces all over the place. I kept on and used two powercells worth of ammo to create a passage large enough to accommodate my armor and allow me to squeeze into the neighboring cell. Instead of a bed, this room had a perch near the ceiling—which suggested that this cell had been built with a Pyrrhenian in mind. They were the only ones who like to fly and roost up near the ceiling. Hilvar was one such example. So it followed that the Zatrathi stations had accommodations for each imperial race? An interesting factoid, if one that I wasn't sure was very valuable. I guess it didn't do me any harm to know.

"You have passed into a neighboring room, having bypassed the standard system of hallways," Braniac reported again, once I'd repeated the operation on the next wall. "Droid repairs complete. Thirty assault droids are now ready for battle. Crew Functionality is now at 50%. Ship repairs have commenced. Estimated time until completion—3 hours, 22 minutes."

"How much of the barricade do the Zatrathi have left?" I inquired, wishing to get a handle on how much time I had.

"The enemy has advanced nine feet. At the current rate of progress, the hallways will be breached in three hours and 45 minutes."

"Keep those repairs going!" I ordered, blasting the door to the third room. In the previous room, the door had led right into the wall that had blocked my passage in the hallway. But now...

"Braniac, update my route to those life forms," I shouted happily when I emerged into the hallway on the other side of the barrier. I'd made it! Who were these twenty that the Zatrathi had tucked them away like this? And, by the way—what if they were dangerous?

One hundred yards later, the corridor brought me to a large hall that was quite similar to the one that *Warlock* had crash landed in. The only difference was that this amphitheater was in one piece and divided in two parts with force fields. The twenty life forms that Braniac had identified were all behind the force field.

"*Derang avarta!*" came a terrible roar and a Zatrathi in brown armor approached the field from the other side. It only took me several moments to understand that he couldn't walk or shoot through the field, so I calmly entered the amphitheater arena and came to a halt several steps from the marine. The attachments on his armor, which I had first seen through the barricade I had made, were additional weapons—something resembling rocket launchers. Four arms with two elbow joints apiece, two legs, a disproportional torso and a head that was too large—with two slits for eyes. The appearance of the Zatrathi left something to be desired.

"Hello everyone!" I said in a business tone, looking past the marine to the others in the amphitheater. Hmm...One gray Qualian, one blue Precian, a flying Vraxsis, a Pyrrhenian, an Anorxian, a female Delvian (and a quite attractive one at that)...As I understood it, the group here consisted of one member from each of *Galactogon's* twelve empires—and they were all guarded by three slugs, three marines and two strange, dark blobs that bore more resemblance to fog than "life forms."

Twelve representatives of the twelve empires of *Galactogon*...

START THE GAME

"Who are you, soldier?" asked the gray Qualian—speaking the only in-game language my character understood.

"I'm Surgeon, a mighty pirate," I replied honestly. "I'm just looking around for some sweet loot to pillage and plunder—don't mind me."

"A pirate?" the Qualian asked surprised and barked something to the others.

"*Krandal gartava!*" the Zatrathi marine yelled threateningly. No one paid him any attention—all twelve prisoners approached the edge of the force field and began to examine me. The strange thing was that as they approached, the bombastic warrior stepped aside as if not wishing to draw further attention to himself.

"How did a pirate manage to find his way onto the Zatrathi flagship station?" the Delvian girl asked in a pleasant voice, turning flirtatiously with her puffy tail. The little fox had such a heavy accent that I barely understood her—and yet I couldn't help but notice that she knew Qualian.

"I was just passing by when I came across this place. So I figured I'd stop in and have a look around for some filthy lucre to misappropriate," I continued, suddenly realizing that I was standing before the twelve princesses and princes of the new global scenario. These were the very sentients that every empire and player in the game was currently looking for. An enormous reward awaited the person who could rescue them. And of course, Rrgord—the Precian prince who would know where my prize planet was—had to be among them!

"And do you often like to go wandering about these parts?" the girl went on inquiring.

"It happens," I shrugged and turned serious. "People, tell me, what would happen if I destroyed all of you now? Would you return to your respective homeworlds?"

"No." The fox shook her head sadly. "The enemy has unbound us from our homeworlds and made us truly mortal. If you destroy us, we will die for good. You wanted to save us by destroying us?"

"I was thinking about it," I confessed, suddenly realizing that I couldn't blow up *Warlock*. Even if I brought these aristocrats to my ship (which, by the way, I had no idea how to do), then if the Zatrathi blew us up, the princes and princesses would die too. I wondered whether the game devs had thought this through very well. You couldn't always predict everything. And the probability that the Zatrathi station would undergo an attack was pretty small. I also understood now why they hadn't tried to get at me from space—the Zatrathi were afraid of destroying their station! They needed these prisoners too!

Boy—what a dilemma this was!

"Has the station been cleared already?" the Qualian asked.

"No, this sector is blocked off. But the barricade will be breached in a few hours and a whole mob of these brown dudes," I nodded in the Zatrathi's direction, "will come surging to pay us a visit. I rammed the station wanting to do the most damage I could, but my ship survived and now..."

"How far is it?" the Qualian cut me off.

"About a mile and a half from here…"

"Nothing will happen to the station itself, but this sector will become uninhabitable," the prince said pensively. "The shockwave from your self-destruction won't dissipate over two miles and the blast will reach this hall through the corridors. Will this force field hold it?"

The Qualian said exactly what I was thinking—I couldn't blow up *Warlock* at the moment. In that case, I only had one way out—and one that I had already tried in this game…But I really didn't want to go through that again!

"I'd like to speak with Rrgord, but I don't speak Precian. Will you help?" I asked the Qualian, still contemplating what would happen if I self-destructed anyway. So I'd kill all this nobility…Well, things happen. This was a game, after all. Would the game logic blame me for their deaths? Would all the empires turn against me? What if the Confederacy joined them too? And the most important part—what would happen if I didn't discover where the planet with the check was?

"Have we met?" the Qualian translated Rrgord's speech for me.

"No, but I have some information for you—the KRIEG has been built!" I said, figuring that the Precian wasn't going to just tell me about the prize planet for no reason and therefore needed to be buttered up—for example, with news of the KRIEG's completion.

Instead of translating my words, the Qualian prince froze

in horror—his three eyes grew as large as dinner plates.

"KRIEG *slarata*?" Rrgord asked me directly frowning and turned to the Qualian who was still looking at me in shock. "KRIEG *slarata*?"

"*Delvar* KRIEG, *delron narapist!*" said the fox girl, also turning to the Qualian. Why, they all understood each other perfectly well here! And here I was feeling like I'd just sat down in Chinese 101. It was very pretty and all, but I had no idea what was being said.

"KRIEG *delvar*!" whispered Rrgord and jumping up to the Qualian who had just come to his senses, grabbed him by the scruff and hurled him into the force field. This was followed by a tremendous crackling noise, a shout from the Zatrathi guards, the screams of the princes and princesses, and the appearance of a global notification that everyone in the game would see:

Mourn, oh Qualians! Your prince has died a final death!

All trade deals with the Qualian Empire are suspended during the mourning period (30 days). All items belonging to Qualian players require 50% more XP to level up during the mourning period (30 days). All players incur -1000 Rapport with the Qualian Empire!

CHAPTER THIRTEEN

ESCAPE

Damage taken. Current health: 97%...
Damage taken. Current health: 94%...

As soon as the Qualian prince touched the force field, he became a small heap of ash and the field itself vanished.

A pause descended on the place—which the three Zatrathi marines used to their advantage. I was instantly hit with a barrage from their blasters.

What astonished me most of all was that my super-duper pumped up armor couldn't handle all of the damage and began to let some of it through to my character. This was highly unpleasant.

"*Slizaar!*" yelled Rrgord, stepping in between me and one of the Zatrathi warriors.

"Run, brother!" The fox girl translated, screening me from the other warrior. "They've put personal mines on us, so we can't leave the station! Get away from here!"

The third Zatrathi continued to shoot me, since none of the remaining aristocrats wished to risk their lives on my account, but the two warriors that Rrgord and the Delvian had blocked held their fire. Instead, they dashed toward me, producing some kind of shimmering clubs from their belts. This was followed by a new notification:

Damage taken. Current health: 91%...

"Save me Braniac!" I yelled, realizing that this notification had popped up against the floor—on which I was already lying face down, while the three Zatrathi continued to attack me. The armor was again insufficient to block all the damage and slowly but surely I was heading to meet my Planetary Spirit.

"Support is on its way," the computer instantly replied. "ETA is three minutes."

"That's too long!" I yelled in a panic when the next notification informed me that my health had fallen to 70%. I tried to get rid of the extra weight by squirming back and forth, but they were holding me so tightly that my armor suit refused to move an inch. "Tell them to hurry as fast as they can!"

"Activating 'Turbo' skill. Support will arrive in fifteen, fourteen, thirteen…one. Support has arrived. Your order has been fulfilled."

Damage taken. Current health: 22%...

START THE GAME

For the first time in the game I felt my head spin. Something raised me from the floor and threw me clear across the entire amphitheater, slamming me into the opposing wall with tremendous force. Several notifications popped up, but the blow had been so realistic that I completely lost sense of what was up and what was down. All I could see was a shimmering mass of something or other tearing around the hall knocking over the remaining eleven princes and princesses and slamming the Zatrathi guards into the walls.

"Cryptosaur Functionality is down to 10%," said Braniac, bringing me back to consciousness. "It is advised to send a squad of droids to transport the cryptosaur back to the station's cargo holds in order to replenish him with Raq."

"Is there any left?" I asked, through my teeth, getting up. My marine armor was on its last legs, with a Durability of 5%. I finally saw the rhinoceros, lying on his side with one of the Zatrathi's legs twitching beneath him. A second later the leg vanished, leaving a virtual loot crate shimmering in its stead. My marine was barely breathing. His tongue, burning with a red flame, had tumbled out of his mouth. All three eyes had rolled up. It was like the animal was on its deathbed, so—concerned with my crew member's life—I issued another command: "Braniac, send the droids over immediately!"

"Droids have been dispatched. ETA is seven minutes. To answer your earlier question: Per your earlier orders, all crew members have been restored to 50% Functionality, all droids have been fully repaired and ship repairs are almost complete.

The Raq levels in the station's warehouse are currently at 80%."

"As soon as the cryptosaur can walk again, tell him to start transporting the Raq to *Warlock*'s holds." I finally committed to the one course of action I'd been most hesitant about. "And get the droids on that too. I want the ship fully loaded in forty minutes."

"Understood," replied Braniac.

"Pirate, is that animal with you?" asked the Delvian girl, looking apprehensively at the fallen rhino. "Is he dangerous?"

"That's the marine from my ship. He's not dangerous," I replied, approaching the nearest loot crate. The other eight crates shimmered as alluringly as a new computer shimmers to an inveterate gamer. I had already seen the loot that the slugs dropped—now I wanted to see what the Zatrathi marines and the still-nameless fogs had dropped.

"Your marine moved as fast as lightning," the Delvian went on nagging me, while I popped open some loot: Raq, Raq, a token. The first crate, it seemed, belonged to a slug, since I had already seen such loot before. "That's impossible!"

"Well, there he is, helplessly wallowing on the floor. It begs the choice: Does the captain save himself or save his crew," I replied approaching the next crate. But in general the Delvian had a point—covering two miles in fifteen, okay, let's say twenty seconds if I count my conversation with Braniac, is a pretty unreal speed. The rhino must have travelled at a speed of about—let's see, 1.5 miles in fifteen seconds, convert that to an hour, that's...that's 360 miles per hour! No way! That's faster than a

---

flyer's top speed! Although, wait! He could've been at the warehouse! From there to the amphitheater was only 500 yards, so the marine's speed was closer to 70 mph...Also very fast—but at least I wasn't dealing with a total monster.

"Braniac," I ordered the computer, "assemble all the information you can find about my crew's capabilities. Sort it by skills and make sure to include any limitations that follow the use of such skills. I mean limitations like this cooldown paralysis that follows the triggering of the 'Turbo' skill."

"Understood. It will take three days to prepare a complete report for each member of the crew."

"Why so long?" I asked surprised.

"This task necessitates the processing of a large volume of data. I will have to commit 30% of my resources to preparing such a report."

"Is he dead?" the Delvian interrupted my conversation with Braniac and carefully approached the rhinoceros. Opening another crate I received more Raq, a powercell and a token. Eh! Again a slug! Or maybe this was the typical loot for all the enemies? That would be too bad. By the way, I'd need to remember to avoid fighting the Zatrathi marines one on one— they'd crush me without even noticing me.

"He's fine—relax! Better, tell me what you meant by 'They've implanted personal mines on us and we can't leave the station'? Nothing is keeping us from getting out of here at the moment."

"We cannot leave this amphitheater," the fox-girl

explained sadly. "Each one of us has been assigned an area on this ship. If we leave its boundaries, we will explode. My area, for instance, skirts right next to your marine. That's why the others can't approach him. You saw yourself what happened with the Qualian—it wasn't the force field that destroyed him. The personal mine did that."

Raq, a vial of black powder, a token—but this time a black one instead of a metallic one like the slugs had dropped. Hmm...It looked like this item could be used to build Rapport with some kind of faction, for example, soldiers in general or something like that. I saw no further use for it at the moment.

"You have two hours and ten minutes before the barricade is breached," my virtual pedant reminded me, giving me a new idea.

"Braniac, send over the engineer. I need his help. Tell him to bring his tools. There's some work for him here."

The Delvian placed her hand on the overheated cryptosaur, the way clerics would heal their allies in *Runlustia.* No miracle followed, however—the rhino continued to lie in a heap as before.

"He's hot," the fox-girl yanked away her hand. "Are you sure he's okay?"

"Sure I'm sure," I told her again. "Tell me, since we have several minutes, what is the KRIEG?"

"KRIEG *slarata*?" Rrgord repeated behind us, frowning. He was standing several feet away.

"I'm even more interested if every time I say that word,

---

the Precian highness there reacts the way he does," I pointed at Rrgord who'd narrowed his eyes in rage. No, there was definitely something sinister and curious about this word and now I wanted to know what it was all about.

"Where did you hear that word?" the fox found a way of asking me without indulging in unnecessary screaming or angry speeches in alien tongues.

The need of building some kind of Rapport with the Precian forced me to relate how my life in *Galactogon* had begun and communicate the gist of my conversation—or rather knocked exchange—in solitary. I needed to start pressuring the Precian into telling me about the prize planet, so I embellished as much as I felt comfortable.

"That's how I found out about Rrgord and the KRIEG," I finished my tale, noting that the droids had arrived, carefully lifted the cryptosaur onto some kind of hover-gurney (I had no idea we even had one of those) and departed back to the warehouse to revive the rhino.

"Braniac, have everyone bring their Functionality up to 100%," I ordered, realizing that since there were so many resources still at the warehouse, it'd be stupid to leave them to the Zatrathi.

The fox girl began translating my story to Rrgord, so I went back to opening the loot crates.

Raq, Raq, a powercell, a token—another slug by the looks of it and hopefully the last. The last two crates were slug crates too. I was long overdue for some primo loot.

Raq, a powercell, a vial of black powder, a black token—this was loot from the second fog.

Raq, a Zatrathi Combat blaster, a universal armor enhancer, a gold token—finally the loot from one of the three Zatrathi warriors. I whistled a little when I compared this combat blaster with my assault blaster—across all its attributes, including damage, magazine size, durability, and firing rate, the C-class Zatrathi Combat Blaster was about twice as good as my B-class Zatrathi Assault Blaster. If I had had this gun when I was facing the slugs, all I'd have needed was 400 shots to solve the problem of the crawling Zatrathi. And of course now it was clear why my armor couldn't handle the Zatrathi warriors as well as it could the slugs. If it hadn't been for the cryptosaur, I'd be back on Blood Island already.

Raq, a powercell, a universal armor enhancer, a golden token—the other two loot crates had the same contents, minus the blaster. No big deal—it's not like I'd be looking to sell them.

"Rrgord says that you deserve a reward. However, he is not currently in the position to give it to you," the Delvian translated the Precian prince's speech. "So you should contact his father. Rrgord will transfer the access key to the Precian capital system to your PDA. Do you accept his gift?"

Mission Unlocked: "The Imperial Gift."

Description: You have been given a unique opportunity to meet the Precian Emperor and receive a reward from him personally. Do you wish to accept this mission?

START THE GAME

I would be thrilled! The developers had even included a prompt allowing you to accept or decline a mission in this patch! This was an incredibly convenient feature. It was never pleasant when some shopkeeper would beg you to bring him one hundred million pig's tails. Before, you'd have to sit there and wonder: Did I get a mission or not? But now the players could decide for themselves what they were going to do in this game. Of course, the description did not explain what would happen if the player accepted or declined, but this was still a huge step forward. Before you knew it, they may even go so far as to turn *Galactogon* into an ordinary game, instead of some weird guessing contest.

"I accept the prince's gift," I replied, pressing the virtual button and dismissing the notification about my receiving the access key. "But I still didn't get an answer to my question: What's the KRIEG?"

"It is neither the right time nor the right place to explain this," said the fox girl. "Go now. You must save yourself and tell the rest of the galaxy about us."

"Not so fast," I smiled, seeing my engineer come crawling in. A gasp of astonishment came from the princes and princesses and they all clumped together from terror—it's not every day you see a 30-foot-long snake. I was forced to reassure everyone:

"This is another one of my crew members. Don't be afraid."

"Why?" the snake wondered, looking back at me. "Let them be afraid! I am a scary and terrible serpent. I will eat everyone and all that jazz! What'd you call me for anyway?"

"I need to get all these sentients out of here," I pointed at the noble crowd. "But they claim that they've been booby-trapped with some kind of personal mines. Can you figure it out? We can't leave them to the Zatrathi."

"Mines, you say?" the snake said pensively. His tail shot out in the direction of the hostages, wound itself around the Delvian and carried her back. The fox girl seemed convinced that she was about to be eaten alive.

"Curious," said the snake, carefully examining the girl's body. "Very curious...Oh! I see!" exclaimed the snake and carefully set the girl back on the floor. "The princess knows about..."

"She knows and there's no need to talk about it!" the fox girl cut off the engineer, obviously hiding something. "What about the mine?"

"Nothing. That is, I can't do anything about it. It's connected to the central onboard computer, so you can't just hack it on the spot. Does anyone have access to the station computer?"

"You know yourself that we don't, slizo-dude," I said.

"I'm a dudette, but that's beside the point. In that case, I won't be able to take off the mine. Or, to be more precise, I can take off the mine but doing so will decapitate the hostage. Will that work?"

"Zatrathi progress through the barricade has accelerated," Braniac advised me. "The barricade will be breached in one hour and ten minutes."

"Back to the ship!" I ordered and then turned to the Delvian: "Sorry, princess. We won't be able to rescue you this time. I have one more question for Rrgord, before I leave you. Please translate this for me: 'Where can I find the planet with the check?'"

"With the what?" the Delvian translated the puzzled Precian's response. "He doesn't know what you're talking about. Neither do I, actually."

"I have reason to believe that Rrgord knows the coordinates of a planet I am looking for. It would be a new, unexplored planet that he maybe came across while traveling around *Galactogon*."

"Prince Rrgord discovered seven planets and doesn't know which one you're interested in. Besides, he doesn't have all their coordinates memorized. They are in his ship's computer and his ship is back on his home planet. Ask his father. He will give you access to the ship and you can look up the info yourself. Rrgord will send you the access key now..."

As soon as I saw a notification telling me that I had received an access key to the prince's ship, I asked the Delvian, "May I do something for you? Maybe you want to pass along a letter, some message, or an item? I'll be telling all of *Galactogon* about you guys and I'll be sure to mention that we'll first have to capture the station and destroy the computer before coming to save you. But all that will take some time. I figured that maybe you..."

"You need to go to my home planet—here's the system

access key—and find Alviaan. Tell him that I...that we...tell him that 'we made it!' He'll understand what I mean."

Mission Unlocked: "The Stork and the Fox."
Description: Notify Alviaan, First Councilor of the Delvian Emperor, that the princess and he have "made it."

The Delvian froze and I could see even through her furry face that she was blushing. I had never seen such a strange mission description and had to read it several times. Was she really pregnant? How fun! I had never encountered pregnant locals in a video game before and didn't quite know how to react. How could I leave her like this with the Zatrathi? How far along was she? And most importantly—what did I have to do with all this? I had a specific goal that I felt I was more than halfway to. All I had to do was find out the coordinates of the seven planets and carefully explore each one. At that point, my time in *Galactogon* would probably come to an end.

"I'll let him know," I replied, still wondering why I was taking on all these additional errands. On the other hand, that prize check was unlikely to go anywhere while I took a little trip to the Delvians. I doubted that any of the remaining contestants had even left their Training Sectors yet...Speaking of which!

"Sorry, I have another question for Rrgord. I need to get a recruit out of a Training Sector before she has officially graduated. May I have an access key to Planet Vozban in the Gantanil-3 system?"

START THE GAME

"You want to take a recruit out of the Training Sector before they have completed their training?" the Delvian asked with surprise, making no move to translate my question to the Precian. "That's impossible! You can't release unprepared recruits into the larger world! They will fall easy prey to the Zatrathi!"

"Princess, please just relay my question to Rrgord," I insisted. "It's very important for me to get this person out of the Training Sector because...Well, she is a woman and she and I 'made it' too."

The Delvian blushed all over again, sucked in a large gulp of air to say something, changed her mind, sighed heavily and passed my question on to Rrgord. The Precian raised his eyebrows in astonishment, stared at me like I was some mythical creature and finally shook his head in the negative. The prince was against the idea. The fox girl tried to explain something to him, but Rrgord was as adamant as a cliff—he refused to grant me access to the Precian Training Sector.

"It won't work, pirate," the girl said sadly. "I knew it'd be pointless to ask Rrgord. Recruits are an extremely sensitive topic for any empire. No empire would allow anyone to remove players from its Training Sector. Go now. You can't stay here any longer..."

I flew the two miles separating me from *Warlock* in ten minutes, stopping by the warehouse along the way to stuff my inventory full of Raq. Evidently the developers had planned some kind of epic battle to save the hostages and therefore wouldn't allow me to rescue them prematurely. Otherwise, there'd be no incentive for the players to join the war against the Zatrathi. At least now, the objectives would be clear: Board the station and rescue the VILs without space support. Best of luck with all that! At the moment, I was more concerned with how I was going to escape this place without falling to Zatrathi marines or frying the imperial beau monde.

If I flew out into open space, I'd still be caught in the space disruption field that the station projected. I couldn't simply fly away from the station either—the enemy ships were simply too fast for *Warlock*. Breaking through by giving battle wasn't an option either—outrunning a hundred torpedoes happens once every blue moon. The only remaining option—already tested with *The Space Cucumber*—was to hyperjump from inside the station. I knew that this would result in a 90-foot-thick layer of metal forming around my ship, but couldn't see another way out. At the very least, I had enough powercells on board to ensure my self-destruct once I had jumped away from this place. The main thing was to get away.

"Braniac, plot a hyperspace jump to Qirlats," I said, as soon as the door to my ship dissolved behind me. *Warlock* once again looked like a perfectly smooth metal sphere.

"I must recommend against attempting a hyperjump from inside the station," the computer instantly struck up his Canary song.

"Braniac, that order stands as issued." I cut him off before he could get in the swing of it. "Calculate a jump to Qirlats. I know exactly what will happen. That's a direct order!"

"Understood. Jump will be initialized in one minute and twenty seconds."

"Since we have some time, why don't you tell me what you've managed to haul away from that warehouse…"

Forty tons of Raq, two tons of Tiron, five of Elo—the droids had done their best and still they hadn't managed to fill *Warlock*'s cargo holds even halfway. Considering that the orangutan and marine had regained 100% Functionality, which meant that respawning wouldn't do anything to them, we had really taken a good bite out of the Zatrathi riches. It was too bad that I hadn't managed to rescue the aristocracy but the other players could handle that just as well. My reconnaissance operation had turned out well and now I just had to get the information out to the main world. Or rather sell it.

"Ship is ready to jump to hyperspace!" Braniac said unwillingly and couldn't help adding, "If we jump from inside the orbital station, *Warlock* will become covered in a 120-foot-thick layer of metal."

"I thought it'd be close to 90 feet thick?"

"One hundred and twenty feet. In the worst case scenario, 150."

"Will we be able to break through it?"

Braniac fell silent for about twenty seconds, then reluctantly said, "Using all of the cryptosaur's Functionality, we will be able to make a tunnel in the shell that would be wide enough for the slizosaur to exit. If we feed her with the Raq that we have, we will be able to remove 80% of the metal layer."

"Will the remaining 20% be around the ship or just on some side of it?"

"If we aim the slizosaur at the body of the klamir, she will be able to..."

"Braniac, stop dilly-dallying! Will we be able to remove the outer shell without the ship having to self-destruct or not?"

"Self-destruct?" a note of alarm sounded in the computer's metallic voice. "Why would we self-destruct *Warlock*?"

"Because you keep dragging your legs instead of giving me an answer! Enough talk! If we can't free ourselves from the metal shell, we'll blow ourselves up. Engage jump!"

"Roger," Braniac said in as crestfallen a voice as I've heard a computer use. "For your information, the Zatrathi marines have just broken through the barricaded hallway and will be arriving in twelve seconds...eleven...ten...Hyperdrive engaged. Entering hyperspace now."

I sighed with relief once our surroundings had turned into shimmering lines—up until the last moment, I was afraid that the station's space disruptor would block our hyperjump even inside the station itself. The danger passed. It seemed that the Zatrathi had not anticipated that someone would sacrifice their ship to escape. I guess *Runlustia*'s devs had something to teach their *Galactogon* counterparts after all.

"How long will we be in hyperspace?"

"ETA is twenty minutes. Egress coordinates remain undetermined."

"We'll figure that out. The important thing is not to collide with anything bigger than us. Give me a rundown of the information you managed to steal about the Zatrathi vessels. Speed, firepower, weak points and strengths—in other words, anything that will help us fight them. We need to study our enemy from every possible angle."

"Transmitting data to the screen now," Braniac replied after a short pause. "According to the preliminary analysis, the enemy ships may be divided into several categories..."

The twenty minutes of hyperspace travel passed unnoticed in the study of the stolen data. The best way to characterize my sense of time was with a phrase I heard someone say somewhere once: "One and the same minute passes in different ways for a person on a date with someone they love and a person who's rushing to get to the bathroom." Braniac did such a good job of presenting the crucial moments of the battle, the battle characteristics of the Zatrathi ships, their tactics, the speed of their torpedoes and so on that I couldn't help but rub my hands in anticipation—this kind of data would garner good money from a number of *Galactogon*'s guilds. I just had to make sure to sell it the right way.

"Ten seconds before we emerge into real space," Braniac jarred me from my reading. "What are your orders?"

"Prepare the crew for breaking through that outer layer." Unwillingly, I put aside the report about the Zatrathi for a better time. "The main objective is to create an opening in the outer shell. Also, I need the coordinates for our whereabouts. Braniac, what condition does *Warlock* need to be in to be capable of jumping to hyperspace?"

"I don't understand the question."

"Can the ship jump to hyperspace if it is partially covered in a layer of metal? That is, will you be able to calculate our destination coordinates accurately or will they remain random?"

"Request understood. Processing now…"

"Cappy, this may be a dumb question, but why do you care?" the engineer asked over the comm. "The marine will make a hole, I'll destroy the outer layer and then we can be on our merry way. All we need is ten hours—and even that gives us room for error."

"That's assuming our errors won't be forced onto us," I replied. "What if we pop out in the center of another Zatrathi fleet? Or in the middle of an empire? We might not even get thirty minutes."

"I agree, at least as far as the Zatrathi are concerned, and yet the chance of that happening is so insignificant that it's not even worth considering. As for imperial space, I wouldn't be so quick to judge. If we tell them that we have information concerning their beloved princes…At the very least they'll be willing to talk—by the time we arrange that, I'll be done with that shell."

"Egress imminent!" Braniac interrupted, as *Warlock* began to shake. In earthquake terms, the shaking felt like a 7.0 on the Richter scale, no less! *Warlock* sank into a frightening silence and all the lights dimmed as if someone had cut the power—the intercom was the only thing still telling us that we hadn't been destroyed. Not entirely, at least. "The primary reactor is out of order, power has switched to reserve powercells. We have approximately twelve minutes of reserve power remaining. The cryptosaur has begun to make a passage through the outer shell. He has been granted access to all onboard Raq. Ship Durability is down to 30%."

"Engineer, fix that reactor," I instantly commanded. We simply could not remain without power. "Do what you have to— but I need it back on line."

"Roger that!" the snake replied and I saw her body slither past the main deck. I guess she could no longer get around along the surface of the ship. She reported back a second later: "I need about ten minutes to make repairs."

"Braniac, what can you tell me about the metal shell?" I asked with some relief. If we had power, then the ship could hold out for a while. And if we hadn't been destroyed as soon as we'd left hyperspace, then we had a chance of surviving. And if…hmm…There was starting to be too many ifs.

"Drilling depth is currently fifteen feet. Estimated time until completion is seven minutes."

"Roger. Do we have any idea where we are?"

"The ship's sensors are currently unpowered. Do you wish to redirect reserve power to the sensors? Be advised that in that case, we will have only ten minutes of reserve power for other ship functions."

"Engineer, will you manage?"

"I need nine minutes, thirty seconds!" came the reply. "Go ahead and connect whatever you need."

"Turn on the sensors, Braniac," I decided and instantly one more screen came to life before me. "And so—where are we?"

"...leave this system immediately! You have two minutes to comply. I repeat—unidentified vessel, leave this system immediately! You have one minute and fifty seconds to comply!"

"Braniac, where are we?" I almost yelled into my comm.

"Calculating now," replied the computer. "We are in the Lentar System, Precian space. This is where the Precian Raq mines are located."

Great. Just great. The only surprising thing was that they had given us two minutes at all.

"Can we transmit?"

"The sensors are working in passive mode at the moment. If we turn on the transmitter, we won't have enough power to repair the ship."

"Engineer?"

"Braniac is correct. I am of course a pretty singular creature and all, but I can't make repairs without the Elo to do it. My tools simply won't work."

"Turn on the transmitter," I leaned back in my seat, realizing that there was nothing left to do. We'd be forced to respawn either way. "We need to buy some time..."

"Unidentified vessel, leave this system immediately! We will open fire in thirty seconds!"

START THE GAME

"This is Surgeon, captain of *Warlock*. I have information concerning the demise of the Qualian prince! I repeat: I have information concerning the Qualian prince's death. He was killed by Rrgord! I have basically no power left and cannot leave this system. We just engaged the Zatrathi and were forced to jump to hyperspace from inside their flagship. Please inform your senior officers that I have information concerning the prince's death, as well as the current location of Zatrathi forces! Do not fire on our ship!"

"*Warlock*! You have ten seconds to leave this system. If you do not submit to our orders, we...Sir yes sir! Surgeon, please transmit the information you have concerning the prince's demise."

"I don't have enough power for the transmission. My reactor's damaged and the ship needs repairs. Please send over a team of engineers. I need to peel this metal layer from my ship. The reserve power is enough only for three more minutes of communication."

"If you entered hyperspace from inside the station, then the metal shell has fused with your hull. You won't be able to save your ship unless it's bound to a homeworld."

"They're not fused! I need assistance. Only then will I tell you what I know about how your Rrgord killed the Qualian—and where he's currently located."

"You are not in a position to barter." A new, much more authoritative voice joined our exchange. No doubt some admiral or, quite possibly, the emperor himself. We were talking about his son, after all.

"I have a minute's worth of power left. After that I'm activating the self-destruct and leaving this place for good. I don't want to lose a hundred levels of experience, but trust me, I would prefer that to freely giving up information that I sacrificed my ship for. You have thirty seconds!"

I was trying my best not to giggle until I'd lifted my finger from the comm's transmit button. What a nice little exchange this had been:

"We will destroy you!"

"Don't! I have information!"

"Okay, hand it over!"

"I won't! I want money and repairs!"

"Are you nuts?"

"If you won't give it to me, I'll destroy myself."

How nice it'd be if that worked every time.

"There are no engineers in this system capable of repairing a ship in open space," said the Precian commander after ten seconds. "Please shut down your equipment. We will transport you to a different system where we will repair you and remove the metal layer."

"Roger!" I barked curtly and ordered Braniac to conserve energy and recall the marine. Why waste Raq on him, if someone else was going to remove that shell anyway? That Raq could be sold for good money...

"Braniac, how much reserve power do we have now?"

"Three minutes, twenty seconds in economy mode.

Without transmissions or sensors."

"We need those sensors," I said pensively. "Engineer, what's up with the reactor?"

"Eight minutes of work. No less."

"Cancel everything. Braniac, activate sensors every five minutes to establish our location. We need to know where they're taking us."

"In that case, effective operating time will be limited to 90 seconds." The pedantic computer could not pass up an opportunity to offer his two cents. "In addition, constant starting up and shutting down of these systems will have an undetermined effect on our remaining power reserves."

"Do it," I ordered, leaning back in my chair wearily. The last few hours of the game had really taken a toll on me. First the station, then the jump, now the transport to a different system. This was not how I had imagined my tranquil search for the check. Speaking of which! I would have to remember to wheedle my way into the Precian capital system—to talk to the emperor. Maybe, it wasn't such a bad thing that we'd stumbled across these Precians.

"We have entered hyperspace," Braniac informed me five minutes later. "We have enough power to start the sensors three more times in order to establish our location."

"Alright, instead of using a five minute interval, use a ten minute interval," I tweaked my earlier order. *Warlock* had entered hyperspace? How? Had we been taken on board a cruiser or a Grand Arbiter? I'd love to have seen that from outside. But then again, the 120 feet of Zatrathi metal would get in the way of that. Hmm…So they managed to load a 300-foot sphere into another ship?

"Braniac, what are they transporting us in?"

"A cargo vessel that is designed to haul Raq. I have no technical information about this type of ship, since no such information was present in the frigate's computer. But in the past, when klamirs such as myself were common throughout *Galactogon*, resource transportation was effected by immense and unwieldy transport ships—their main purpose was to haul their cargo to the trade planets. It looks like the Precians are using a similar transport here too."

We only had enough power to turn the sensors on one more time. We learned only that we were still in hyperspace. After that, *Warlock* became a dark and quiet tomb. Bereft of power, Braniac fell silent, the crew fell silent and—unwilling to use my own power (even though my suit was fully charged)—I too kept my motions to a minimum.

I placed my hand on the self-destruct button—the only remaining functioning device aboard *Warlock* and closed my eyes, hoping to sleep.

The day had been an exhausting one.

"We have guests," the snake's quiet voice brought me from my doze, seemingly, a moment after I closed my eyes. The clock on my armor's HUD, however, showed that I had slept no less than two hours. Once again, I considered time's relativity.

"What guests?" I didn't comprehend right away.

"Someone is drilling through the shell. From outside. Judging by my acoustic readings, they have drilled about thirty feet already. Should we help them?"

"No need," I shook my head, even though my armor did not transmit this gesture. "Who knows how they're drilling. You'll start cutting through on this side and suddenly run right into whatever they're using. We'll wait."

We had to wait half an hour.

"Surgeon?" A marine in full combat armor entered *Warlock* through the opening in the metal. I guess he deserved the achievement for the first local who stepped aboard my ship. In fact, he was the first sentient being to step aboard my ship after my crew.

"The very one. Took y'all a bit," I said, slowly rising to my feet. The soldier made no sudden motions that could be construed as aggressive. He was smoothness personified.

"Please follow me," the marine said, clipping a bandoleer to my armor. Which instantly set the armor's security software howling—the marine had just hung several packs of explosives on me. Judging by the amount—nothing within thirty feet of the blast would survive it.

"I don't expect I'll make a very good Bo-omb," I said, surprised. "What kind of meeting is this then?"

"Please follow me," the marine repeated. "It's the

general's order. That security belt is insurance. Without it, you may not step onto Vozban."

Vozban!

I almost lost my breath. That was the very same planet that Eunice was on!

"I need five minutes," I told the marine and signed out IRL. I had to talk to Eunice immediately!

"Welcome back, Master!" Stan started up—as ever, I had to cut him off:

"Get Eunice out of that capsule ASAP. Emergency sign out."

"I do not have access to the command circuit. Eunice's capsule is controlled by the other unit that you granted access to."

"Stan give that other comp whatever it wants, just get me Eunice right now!"

I gave the AIs three minutes to come to an agreement, after which I said I'd pull her out myself. Of course, cutting off the cocoon manually is not advised and basically reserved for emergencies. Yanking the interface bus abruptly out of the player's nervous system could cause mental and even physical trauma.

"What happened, Lex?" Two minutes later, the cocoon's lid moved aside and the girl's stunned eyes focused onto me. "We've got some kind of alarm going on in our Sector. Unannounced tests and exercises—everyone's being herded into training capsules. I really don't want to be missing this. Just doesn't resemble the ordinary day-to-day in the Sector. I want to figure out what's going on."

"I can tell you that myself. In several minutes, I shall descend to Vozban. I have a meeting with your general."

"WHAT?!"

"What you heard. I'll dump you my comm number. We really should have thought of that earlier. I'll wait for your call. We'll decide how to get you out then."

"How, Alexis?!"

"Stop waving your arms, I'll tell you later. *Warlock*'s been damaged. They're going to fix her up in Vozban's orbit."

"Why not on the planet itself?"

"Because my ship's encased in a shell of metal 120 feet thick. That they're going to try and cut through now."

"You jumped into hyperspace from another asteroid again?"

"That's your hubby! Anyway, I'll wait for your call. I'm going back. I got no time whatsoever. Something tells me that if I don't return, no info in the world will save me from the general's wrath. Or the emperor's."

"Info..." Eunice said pensively and flatly. "Were you involved in the death of the Qualian prince?" She stuck her finger into the air and, noticing the surprise on my face, exclaimed: "Yeah right!"

"I wasn't involved. I was just right there when it happened. Eunice, don't go to the exercises and exams with everyone else. If you get locked into a capsule, I won't be able to find you. Alright, I'll see you in there soon."

"You're mad!" Eunice managed to get out before her cocoon's lid shut over her. He's mad who argues. Would a sane person make the same life choices as me? We are all a little mad—that's the line of work we're in.

"New orders from the general." As soon as I reappeared in *Galactogon*, the marine yanked me about to face him. "If you do not appear down on that planet in ten minutes, the explosives will be detonated. Please follow me. The descent will take five minutes."

Happy that I had guessed right, I followed the marine through the drilled passageway.

"How about those repairs?"

"They will be done. Please don't fall behind."

"My crew is on the ship…"

"They will be accommodated. The general will answer all your questions. Please don't dally. The explosives will go off in nine minutes. You need to get to Vozban's surface."

We walked the rest of the way in silence.

Beyond the drilled passageway stood an interceptor which whisked me away down to the planet. The only thing I saw during the short flight was an incredibly huge ship which was slowly flying away from the planet and a medium-sized repair station which was sending some kind of tentacles out into *Warlock*'s direction.

Besides that, there were several Grand Arbiters and a swarm of smaller ships. Gantanil-3 bore more resemblance to a beehive than a Training Sector. The Qualian Sector had looked completely differently when I was escaping it with Lestran.

"Pirate Surgeon—a dropout from the Qualian Training Sector, an outlaw and an enemy of the Altan Alliance. Therefore, an enemy of the Precian Imperium too," the general said slowly as soon as I stepped into his cabinet. It was like he was savoring this information. Two marines stood behind me, their blasters leveled on me as though I might decide to attack or flee—with a bomb on my armor that no one had bothered to remove yet! The general went on: "A sentient who is wanted dead or alive with a bounty of ten million credits on him. You have no idea how overjoyed I am with your appearance. You should know that the Qualian Grand Marshall—who was in charge of the Qualian Training Sector— was a dear friend of mine. *Was*. The Qualian Emperor had him executed. Now I have a chance to settle scores. We are already downloading all the data we need from your ship. You have nothing new to tell us and I would like to share some good news with you: When you're on a Training Sector planet, your binding to your homeworld is void. If you die here, you will be resurrected here—always here. Welcome to your own personal hell, Mr. Surgeon! Marines: Fire!"

Before I could manage a word in edgewise, the Precians blasted me point blank in the back, destroying my armor with all its ample protection.

Here was the ten minute break before I could respawn again. When that happened, I'd return in my clothes, since my armor and its blasters would fall as loot in the general's cabinet.

The only good news was that my personal inventory

remained on me. In my case, this included a weak assault blaster and two manipulators.

It would have to suffice. If the Precians wanted war, they would get it!

CHAPTER FOURTEEN

THE EMPEROR OF THE PRECIANS

"What's going on here?" said an irate old voice as soon as I signed back into the game. "Even here, there's no peace for an old man!"

I found myself in a small room chock full of pipes, valves, cathode ray tubes and various other mechanical contraptions. At the other end, I saw a wrinkled old Qualian sitting in a soft armchair. I knew right away what his job was by the book he had sat aside, but seeing a Qualain in the Precian Training Sector surprised me nonetheless. Moreover, judging by his uniform, his position was an officially-sanctioned one.

"What're ya staring at, sonny? Here you go—you have been resurrected. Thank your lucky Planetary Spirit! Now get on back up there!" the old man grumbled, seeing that I wasn't about to go anywhere. "Bunch of rabble constantly going in and out of here taking whatever they feel like…"

"Where am I?" I couldn't help but ask. Long pipes puffing with steam—darkness—strange inscriptions—dusty monitors: The atmosphere here seemed so post-apocalyptic that I even opened the menu to make sure that I was still in *Galactogon*.

"Where-where? Where-where? I'd tell you a dirty joke, but you're too young to hear it. Oh! More guests are coming," added the old man, glancing at the lone working monitor. "Soldiers? What do soldiers need underground? Ah! They're coming for you! I see this order here: 'Apprehend a certain Surgeon and deliver him to the General.' You wouldn't happen to be that Surgeon, now would you, sonny?"

"I am." It was pointless to argue.

"Then get on up there. They're waiting for you." The old man pointed at a rusty lift, directing me away from him.

"I'm going as fast as I can," I muttered in reply, got out my blaster and aimed it at the elevator's gears. "Warm greetings to everyone! Make sure to write!"

"What are you doing?" yelled the Qualian once I'd dumped a powercell's worth of bolts into the lift.

"Welcoming our guests," I said spitefully, as Precian swearing came blaring over the old man's intercom. I couldn't understand a word, but you don't have to be a polyglot to tell the difference between civil conversation and cursing harangue—even in alien. Getting another powercell from my inventory and reloading my blaster, I asked the old man a single question: "Where's the exit?"

The Qualian looked at the blaster pointing at him fearfully, looked back at the demolished lift mechanism and started talking...

The Training Sector's respawn area was buried deep underground. The reasoning behind this was that if war started, any killed recruits would be able to respawn in a safe place and head up to defend the Sector. An ordinary, narrow lift would take them up to the surface, about half a mile above. The old man had begun working for the Precians only several weeks ago and during that time, no player had had occasion to respawn. To my astonished question of where the old man had worked before, I was told that he had been at one of the Qualian Training Sectors. For many years there had been no incidents there—and then suddenly crowds of enraged players started popping up and fighting for a place on the lift—which could only accommodate two at a time. That was when the old man decided that he would find a better job. He contacted an acquaintance of his, who contacted someone else, who contacted someone else and in the end, the old man was given a cozy position as Recruit Resurrection Facilitator at a Training Sector where nothing had ever happened. Although the new position was in a different empire, at least he could now read his books in peace.

The old man explained that there were two exits leading

---

to the surface. The first and most popular was the lift. The second, which the old man hadn't used once during his career—whether with the Qualians or the Precians—was a multi-level labyrinth of pipes, hallways, iron stairwells and chambers. The old man had neither a map nor information about the official exit points to this jumble of steel and rock. Neither was there any information about the monsters that would surely inhabit that part of the Training Sector. Basically, he knew nothing about it at all, aside from how to open the door to it.

Pushing away the last crate that blocked the passage and entering the access code, the old man hunched his shoulders and closed his eyes. He was expecting me to shoot him.

"Best of luck with the repairs," I said, getting a better grip on my blaster and exiting through the door. To be honest, the idea of killing the Qualian had come to me in the first few seconds, but I quickly abandoned it. It was one thing to eradicated packs of soldiers and monsters. It was something else entirely to kill a defenseless old man. I couldn't care less about the moral aspects—I simply had no idea how the system would react to this kind of act. Considering the way the rest of the game had been designed, such a murder would come back to bite me somewhere and sometime. For example—what if I'd discover later on that I'd need grandpa's help to get off the planet? I mean, who knew what would happen?

Welcome to "Trial of the Lost Recruit."
You are on Labyrinth Level 1 (of 333).

START THE GAME

Lol! I guess this thing had been designed specially to test recruits! And yet neither the Qualians nor the Precians seemed to make use of it. Strange. I waited until the old man closed the door behind me and piled up the crates on the other side and then, still unable to believe my salvation, called Eunice.

"What's up! Finally got a chance to ring you up. Where are you right now?"

"In jail," the girl replied. "When I refused to go to training, they simply threw me behind bars. And I took a hit to my Rapport with the Precians. Where are you right now? On the planet's surface already?"

"Even better! I'm beneath it!"

In a few words I related to Eunice the pretty dull story of my meeting with the general.

"Now I see why they're running around up here," mused Eunice. "They've seized *Warlock*. If you don't get back to the ship within 24 hours, they'll be able to confiscate it officially. And that's IRL hours, not game hours."

"I know," I winced. "That's why I haven't signed out. How much longer do you have to stay in jail for?"

"Two hours. After that it's either back to school or another two hours of jail."

"Go back to school then. I blew up their lift. There's half a mile worth of pipes and hallways above my head with the-Planetary-Spirit-only-knows how many monsters lurking along the way. I may have to respawn several times. And I don't have my armor anymore…"

"Alright. Get out of there as fast as you can. I'll be playing the good girl up here."

I never much liked first person shooters. As a rule their designers place you in some grim, dim place with narrow hallways, a low ceiling and plenty of steam. It's like they can't imagine that anything bad could lurk in a normal open area with plenty of light. Given the narrow hallways here, as well as the strange sounds, screams and moans—even if there was nothing dangerous in the labyrinth's beginning, I would bet my life that after a few more steps I'd be shooting anything that moved. Or rather, shooting anything that moves twice, just to make sure.

As I understood it, the first level had been designed to introduce the player to the labyrinth ahead—a hallway about 200 feet long with walls made of pipes that interwove with one another like mating snakes. At the far end, I could see an iron ladder that would allow me to go up nine feet. That was where the next level was, so I would now have to do this 330 times…Something told me that I wouldn't be making it to *Warlock* in 24 hours—and I had no way of getting in touch with Braniac without my armor. I would be proper pissed if those Precian jerks confiscated my ship.

When I got to the ladder, I stopped and stared at the wall, perplexed. The pipes had ended about sixty feet back and given way to an ordinary plastered wall. Right before the ladder, however, a piece of the wall stood out from its surroundings. It was like someone had hurriedly covered a small passageway and painted it over with whatever paint was at hand. If I saw this in the real world, I wouldn't think twice, assuming that some careless workers had simply cut corners. But I was in *Galactogon* and things like this didn't just happen without good reason. Based on my experience in other games, as well as the fact that I was currently working through a labyrinth, I could safely conclude that this patch of wall concealed either something useful or something dangerous. The former was more likely than the latter, since respawned recruits (there was no other way to get here) would have no weapons or means of self-defense. I'd need to check.

Understanding that I was losing valuable time, I hoped back off the ladder and approached the obviously mismatched part of the wall. I didn't want to ruin my last blaster, so I drew back as far as I could and slammed my fist into the wall. Better I lose some health than ruin my only means of convincing the Precians what was good for them. The manipulators would be my last resort.

Found Secret: 1 of 1 on this level.

You have passed Level 1 of the Labyrinth.

You have received the following items: Precian Assault Boots. Item class: E-1.

I didn't lose any health at all—the wall gave way like papier-mâché. A green light illuminated the hallway and a pair of steel-toed boots fell to the floor.

Oh come on! Any middling player would notice this part of the wall. It followed that the Labyrinth's designers had decided to show right there on the first level that their creation was stuffed full of various secrets. On one hand, these boots would be useful for an impoverished recruit—on the other hand, I had absolutely no need for them. As soon as I'd make it to the outside world, I'd buy myself an A-class marine armor and forget all about the other clothes. So, it didn't make sense wasting time to explore each level of the dungeon only to…

WAIT!

The idea that suddenly came to me forced me to instantly pull up the main menu and sign out of the game. Those Precian Assault Boots should be the first part of a set of marine armor. This set would include gloves, a suit, a blaster, pants and who knows what else—but the main thing that excited me was that this set would have to also include some kind of communications device. If I could get that, then I could get in touch with Braniac and order him to self-destruct! I still had the access codes to *Warlock* in my PDA, so Braniac would have to follow my orders. I didn't mind losing one hundred levels, an entire class, if I could retain possession of my ship! But I had to first make sure that the marine set would include a comm to begin with…Did it make sense to waste time looking for it at all?

Secrets found: 3 of 4 on this level.

You have acquired the following items: Precian Assault Boots. Item class: E-1

I swore and tossed aside the loot I'd discovered behind a pipe belching steam. Out of the 32 items in the Precian marine set, I was missing the one thing I actually needed—the communicator. Over the last four hours I had only managed to ascend eighteen levels of the Labyrinth, at which point—as luck would have it—the items in the set started to repeat. It was like they'd decided to outfit another recruit. I walked through the five hallways and six rooms of the current level but didn't manage to find the fourth and last secret spot. It was like it didn't exist! Realizing that I was beginning to lose time, I signed out IRL again. I still had the level recorded in my PDA and so I decided to ask Stan to parse it in search of the final hidden item. There was no point in reinventing the wheel—I had access to a computer, so why not use it?

"Show me the map," asked Eunice, sitting down beside me. Stan was huffing and puffing like a steam engine, trying to solve the problem—yet I hadn't heard anything from him for ten minutes already.

"Let's go through this one more time—you walked down all the hallways and rooms. You didn't notice anything suspicious anywhere. Right?"

"Right," I said, feeling like Captain Obvious.

"You're missing the comm," Eunice stated the obvious yet again.

"That's right."

"Stan, throw up a map of the eighteenth level on the screen," the girl commanded my smart home for some reason. I had no idea what she was trying to do. What did the map of the level have to do with the remaining secret spot?

"Master?" Stan asked me for confirmation. Just because Eunice lived with us didn't give her the right to issue commands.

"Do it."

"There! Look!" the girl laughed happily, pointing at the map. "I knew it!"

"Erm..." I said emphatically, looking on the same image as she and still not comprehending. "Why don't you break it down for us slower ones."

"I came across a similar puzzle in my last game," Eunice began explaining. "The gist was simple—I had to enter a certain combination. But there was no place to input them into. The level had nothing but rooms connected by hallways."

"Are you trying to say that the rooms and hallways—that is, the level itself—are like a huge communicator?" I asked baffled.

"Bingo! Look—*Galactogon* uses decimal notation. The level has eleven different areas. That is—ten rooms for ten digits and one more to freely pass from one room or hallway to another. Look here—this hallway alone," Eunice traced her finger along the screen, circling the largest and longest hallway, "connects all the other rooms and hallways together. All the rest have three exits or entrances. One with the common hallway and two with the neighboring rooms."

"Alright, let's assume you're right. How am I supposed to use this information? Where is room number one? Two? Three? How do I 'press' the number I need?"

"I have no idea," the girl admitted sincerely. "You

---

wandered through the level so chaotically that you must've entered some kind of combination strictly by chance. But nothing happened. It follows that you have to do something in the rooms. But *what* exactly—is already a question for you to answer."

"What do you say, Stan?" I asked my second brain.

"Eunice's hypothesis is plausible. Considering the layout of this level, the common hallway that connects all of rooms, and the small circles that may be found on the floor of the rooms, the conclusion that there is a gigantic communicator here makes sense. However, there is one detail you and Eunice have overlooked—there is a circle in the common hallway as well."

"What circle?" Eunice and I said almost simultaneously.

"I will show it on the screen. As we know, each room and hallway has a small circle, about twenty inches wide. The circles' locations correspond to the intersections of virtual diagonals. In the common hallway, the circle is located at the far wall without any regard to the overarching geometry formed by the placement of the circles in the rest of the level. The circle in the common hallway stands out from the floor by virtue of a darker shade of paint, which makes it basically invisible in the Labyrinth's low lighting. If we follow Eunice's hypothesis, we may conclude that the circles are all buttons corresponding to different number values. And the call button itself is located in the common hallway. I can calculate no other possible solutions at the moment."

"So all we have to figure out now is where the beginning of this convoluted keypad is located," mused Eunice.

"That's actually the easiest thing to solve," I realized. "All

---

the rooms are linked together sequentially. Consequently, we assign '1' to a room, and use it to calculate the other digits. Then we make the call. If it doesn't go through, we'll assign '1' to the next room and repeat the operation. *Warlock*'s number only has thirty digits. The level has ten rooms—in a few hours I'll be able to go through all the combinations. Then I'll keep my klamir!"

I was a little off in my estimate. It took me an entire hour to walk through thirty rooms in the correct sequence and finally press the "call" button.

That was just for one call! After waiting a couple minutes to make sure that there really was no result, I switched to the next room-sequence in my PDA and began entering the next call. If Eunice's theory was correct, it would take me no more than ten hours to try every possible combination. If, on the other hand, she was wrong…Well, I didn't even want to entertain that possibility.

Secrets found: 4 of 4 on this level.
You have gained access to the stationary communicator.

I almost jumped, seeing the notification that popped up after my fourth run through. It was that unexpected. I was already beginning to doubt Eunice, since I'd gotten no response to the first three "dials." And here suddenly I was granted access to the stationary communicator! Please, please let it be Braniac!

"*Delranos keltake ugranda de*!" said a man's voice from the wall beside me as soon as the notification had faded. It looked like the speaker and mic had been built right into the wall. I was not familiar with the language being spoken by whatever creature was on the other end. He could've been a Delvian or an Anorxian or even some Zatrathi—cleaning toilets on the very station I'd recently escaped from. Surely the devs had furnished them with the same means of communication as the rest of *Galactogon*.

"This is Surgeon, captain of *Warlock*!" I said, checking to see if I could be heard. It'd be a heck of a thing if I'd finally reach Braniac only to discover myself unable to actually tell him anything.

"Qualian?" the man on the other end asked in a language my character understood. "How did you get this number? Who gave it to you?"

"I repeat, my name is Surgeon. I am the captain of the ship *Warlock*. I dialed your number entirely by accident. Whom do I have the pleasure of speaking with?"

"My name is Grandar. I am the junior advisor to the deputy weeding assistant to the gardener of the Third Palace of his Imperial Highness, the Emperor of the Precian Empire (hallowed be his persona). Please do not call this number again, as I have not the time to speak with various…"

"Wait!" I yelled, before Grandar could hang up. "I have information about the kidnapped prince! I know where Rrgord is being held! I know why the Qualian prince died!"

"WHAT?!" curiosity reared in the voice of the twelfth advisor. "Speak! I need to know this information urgently!"

Uh-huh. Allow me to fall all over myself to tell you. I'm being persecuted by a Precian general who's taken my *Warlock*

---

and stranded me inside "my own personal hell," and I'm going to give this random gardener's assistant this info for nothing? Thanks but no thanks.

"Grandar, you have," I glanced at my PDA, "three hours to find someone authorized to negotiate for this information. I will call you back in exactly three hours and I beg you—make sure that whoever's beside you at that time is someone who is capable of making serious decisions. Not some advisor to the junior deputy et cetera et cetera. The information that I have is much too serious to be disclosed to unauthorized parties. Do you understand me? Three hours! If in three hours you don't find someone, then I will publicize what I know about Rrgord to all of *Galactogon*. And trust me, your boss won't like that one bit. Three hours!"

Without giving Grandar a chance to respond, I stepped out of the "call" circle. Funny how things worked out. I had unwittingly managed to contact someone from the Precian Emperor's administration. I now had an ever so slight chance to save *Warlock*. Just over ten hours remained until the Precians could take control of it, so I decided to use the next three hours in finding the number to the ship. If Grandar produced another deputy to a junior advisor, I'd have nothing to say to him. I wasn't about to surrender my info about Rrgord for free. War between the Precians and the Qualians didn't bother me one bit. All I cared about was gaining access to the Precian prince's ship.

"This is the command circuit for the klamir *Warlock*."

"Braniac is that you?" I yelped joyously, having entered

the next sequence of buttons.

"Boss?" the computer asked with surprise. "Why are you calling from an unknown number?"

"Braniac, they've taken away my comm. Block it before it's too late."

"I am sorry but I am unable to fulfill your request. The current comm number is not registered in my database. I am therefore unable to execute any orders issued from it. Be advised that the previous comm has already been blocked. I received a command from it to provide full access to protected system resources from it—in contradiction to my earlier instructions."

"Braniac, how can I prove to you that I am me?"

"That is an invalid question. You are by definition you."

"Okay, how do I prove to you that I am the captain of *Warlock*?"

"You must import data about the current communications device into the ship's internal database for authorized command numbers. You may do this only from the captain's deck inside the ship…"

"Braniac!" I yelled wrathfully. "Have you lost the plot? What captain's deck? We don't even have a captain's deck!"

"If you continue your aggressive conduct, your number will be blocked," the computer rebuked me. "Access to the ship's configuration is possible only from the captain's deck. The area that you (if you really are Surgeon) piloted the ship from is called the captain's deck."

"Braniac," I explained slowly, trying my best not to raise

my voice, "if you don't activate the self-destruct procedure in seven hours, the Precians will assume control over you and they will do whatever they feel like with the ship. You have only seven hours! I need you to activate the self-destruct and return to Blood Island. Understand that I really don't want this…"

"I cannot accept a self-destruct order from an unregistered number," rattled Braniac. "Your number will now be blocked. Have a good day!"

The call dropped. It took all I had to keep myself from slamming my mighty fist into the paltry wall and thereby breaking the communicator to pieces. I needed to talk to Grandar. But how about that Braniac, huh?! A real digital bitch. I told him in natural language—blow yourself up! Why wouldn't he listen to me? If I managed to retain possession of *Warlock*, I would do such a number on that stubborn, brainless tin can…

"Surgeon?" Grandar's tinny, deferential tone was so sharply different from earlier that I was stumped momentarily. Why the change all of a sudden?

"That is correct. Did you find someone who can make decisions?"

"Is the Emperor of the Precian Empire enough of an authority to make important decisions, as you say?" said a voice so authoritative and powerful that I unwittingly straightened to attention.

"Absolutely, your imperialness," I retorted, mentally giving Grandar a grade of "Excellent." I had no idea how the junior advisor to the deputy weeding assistant to the gardener of the

Third Palace managed to reach the emperor himself, but the fact remained—I was speaking with the head Precian. In *Galactogon*, this was not a joking matter.

"Why could I not reach you on your number earlier?" The emperor instantly went on the attack.

"Because this is not my number. At the moment, I am on the planet Vozban in the Gantanil-3 System. I was forced to flee here from the Zatrathi station where I witnessed the death of the Qualian prince. The general in charge of Vozban killed me and is planning on taking my ship, despite me telling him that I have information concerning the abducted princes."

"You are calling from the Labyrinth?" the emperor showed his familiarity with the game. "What level?"

"The eighteenth," I replied, trying to conceal my surprise.

"You said that the Qualian prince was murdered. By whom? The Zatrathi?"

"No your imperialness. Rrgord killed him."

I could hear Grandar gasp in surprise and this was followed by silence descending on the other end of the comm.

"Who else witnessed this?" the emperor asked at last.

"The other ten princes and princesses. They were all there when it happened."

"Why did Rrgord kill the Qualian?" Despite the fact that the emperor's voice was authoritative and neutral, I could hear a barely concealed irritation in it.

"Because I told him that the KRIEG had been built."

"WHAT?!" roared the Precian and I thanked my lucky

stars that I was in a different place. He sounded like he could've killed me. "How do you know this?"

"Two months ago, I was an ordinary recruit in the Qualian Training Sector..."

Over the next hour I told the emperor (who kept interrupting me to ask various questions) about how I learned about the KRIEG's creation. How I was thrown in solitary, how I exchanged knocks with the unknown creature, how I told Rrgord about the KRIEG, and how he destroyed the Qualian prince—throwing him past the boundaries established by the Zatrathi. It didn't make sense to keep this information from the emperor—you don't haggle with locals of his stature. Either you get an imperial reward or you get an imperial kick in the butt (one that'll send you flying clear across all of *Galactogon*).

"Remain on the eighteenth level," the emperor ordered, once my testimony and his cross-examination came to an end. "In three hours, someone will come for you. Do you have any other requests of me?"

"Yes, three," I decided.

"Speak." It sounded like the emperor had furrowed his brow, since the static in the comm suddenly vanished. There are not many who would venture to ask an emperor for a favor.

"I don't know who Grandar is or what he does, but if it weren't for him, we would not have been able to speak. I have no idea how a Precian of his level managed an audience with your imperialness, but his effort is worthy of praise and a reward. I ask that you treat him graciously and generously."

START THE GAME

"That's your first request?" the emperor asked surprised. "You ask a favor not for yourself but for a Precian you do not know?"

"If I get my ship back, then I'll need little else in this life. I am trying to acquire what I want on my own."

"This is worthy of praise. Your ship is your second request?"

"Yes. At the moment it is in orbit around Vozban. In seven hours, the Precian Empire will take control of it. I really do not want to lose it."

"The ship will remain yours. You have the word of an emperor. What is your third request?"

"Rrgord gave me the access key to the capital system. I would like to receive your personal permission to explore one of Zalva's three moons."

"One of the moons?" the emperor asked surprised. "For what?"

"According to my information, there is an Uldan base located on it."

"The Uldans are a legend," the emperor cut me off.

"My ship is a legend then too. She is a klamir."

"You are the owner of a klamir?" the emperor said slowly, as if spelling out each word. "Very well, I gave you my word that you shall have your ship back. All your requests will be granted. You have an emperor's word!"

Your Rapport with the Precian Emperor has increased.

GALACTOGON BOOK ONE

Current Rapport: 10.

Mission Unlocked: "Ancient History." Description: For all of Galactogon, the Uldans are nothing but a legend—without any basis in fact. You can begin the search for this vanished civilization. Do you wish to accept this mission?

YES! Regardless of how my search for the billion-pound check turned out, I really wanted to have a hand in solving one of the great mysteries of this game. The Precian Emperor seemed to know something about the Uldans; therefore, my search would begin with him. If this was just an in-game legend, then there had to be a way to prove this legend real. The devs wouldn't have done it any other way.

"I will grant you audience in my palace," the emperor continued. "We would like to hear how you managed to obtain this ship. Remain in your place. My soldiers will come for you."

"But the general said..."

"Forget about that poor creature. On behalf of the Precian Empire, I officially beg your pardon. You will be awarded any material damages upon your visit to Zalva. End transmission."

In a shocked daze, I stepped out of the calling circle and sat down on the floor. I wondered how often players in *Galactogon* had the chance to speak with an emperor. What would one normally have to do to make this happen? As far as I could recall, this persona was like some unreachable goal for an enormous number of people. The emperor really did provide imperial gifts but as I mentioned above, he also dispensed

---

imperial punishments. No doubt, that general who had trapped me on this planet had already been destroyed—quickly and to the point without any superfluous ceremonies.

What a cool game this was.

"Please follow us, Surgeon." Twenty minutes later, as I was dozing off, the wall containing the comm mic slid aside. I saw three Precian marines in a large cargo lift, clearly built to the best safety specifications. Well, well. So the Precians had access to every level of the Labyrinth? Why didn't they come on down earlier then? It didn't much befit a general to allow a criminal to wander around on the lam—and with a blaster too boot. Well, the ex-general, I guess. The only excuse I could see was that he'd been unaware of the lift. How that was possible, I had no idea—it was simply the only possible explanation. Of course, there was also the possibility that I was in a game and the locals were only playing out their role in it, but for whatever reason I didn't really want to think about it this way.

The second exit (or entrance—everything depends on how you look at it) to the Labyrinth was located a few hundred yards beyond the premises of the Training Sector. I was stunned by the huge stone walls that towered high above us, marking the limits to where the recruits could go. During my time in the Sector, I had never considered what lay beyond them. I never got much of a chance to. Now that I was outside the system so to speak, I began to appreciate the scale of *Galactogon*'s worlds. The developers had even designed this nursery—the place where all newbies would start—to include multiple levels, multiple components and all kinds of options for developing and leveling one's character. What could you say about the world that lay beyond these walls after that? It was not so surprising that less ambitious games like *Runlustia* had gone extinct. Who could compete with a giant of *Galactogon*'s magnitude?

"Surgeon, as the acting commander of the Training Sector, I wish to apologize for any inconvenience you have experienced." As soon as we entered the walls, I was met by a squad of soldiers. One of them addressed me in Qualian. "By way of preliminary compensation we have taken the liberty of filling *Warlock*'s cargo holds with forty tons of Raq. We have also fully repaired your ship. The external shell of metallic debris has been stripped. The crew's Functionality has been restored to 100%. All confiscated items have been returned to your holds."

"What about my armor?" I couldn't help but ask. I just didn't feel normal in *Galactogon* without this second skin. In fact, I felt naked. You couldn't just buy an A-class marine armor in *Galactogon*. You needed connections like Marina. Losing an item like that was the last thing I wanted.

"Pardon?" the Precian asked uncertainly. "What armor?"

"I was sent to my resurrection in the general's office," I explained calmly. "Everything that I was wearing remained in that office. I'd like it back please."

"Erm..." stammered the Precian. "You see, we have a situation at the moment...Erm...The general's office is inaccessible. No one can get into it at the moment. If your armor suit is still there, then..."

"The general is still alive?" I asked with surprise and watched fear flicker across the acting commander's eyes.

"A temporary misunderstanding. The emperor has no need to know about this," he began yammering. "The office of the Training Sector's commander is located in a place where heavy weapons simply cannot be employed and we do not have any specialized cutting equipment on this planet at the moment. We have requested it, but it will take another three hours before this misunderstanding can be resolved. It goes without saying that all of the emperor's orders will be followed to a T."

"It doesn't matter to me," I shrugged my shoulders, calculating how I could turn this situation to my advantage. "But when the emperor inquires why a mighty pirate like myself would walk around without any armor, I will be forced to tell him the truth. I would never lie to an emperor, you see."

"You could consider waiting a little..." the Precian began.

"Emperor's orders!" interrupted one of the marines who'd escorted me from the Labyrinth. "We are to deliver him immediately!"

"So my favorite item in the whole universe is lost to me," I sighed bitterly. "What can I say..."

"Nothing is lost! We will send it to you on the next flight out. You will have your wonderful, mighty item before you can blink twice."

"I don't even know how I'll be able to go on without it..."

"We are prepared to make it up to you, oh mighty pirate. What is your wish?"

Finally!

"There is a recruit in this Training Sector. Her name is Nurse," I said, using Eunice's in-game name. I'd lost it when she had told me—the betting masters obviously had some kind of fixation with medical occupations. "By way of compensation, I would like to invite her to my meeting with the emperor—if she agrees, of course."

"You wish to remove a recruit from the Training Sector?" the Precian asked surprised. "That's impossible."

"Lying to the emperor—that's what's impossible. Temporarily taking a recruit on a trip is extremely possible."

"But she has no clearance to go to Zalva."

"Yes, but I do—isn't that right?" I turned to my escorts who were waiting with us for the shuttle to land.

"The emperor has granted a sentient named Surgeon permission to land on Zalva," the marines confirmed.

"You must understand..." the Precian began.

"I request once more that you give Nurse permission to travel with me." I cut him off. "I have an additional access key to Zalva, which I will be happy to transfer to her. Is this key valid? Can a recruit use it?"

I opened my PDA and showed the access key that Rrgord had given me to the marine standing beside me.

"That key grants one sentient access to Zalva. There are no limitations on what type of sentient the sentient is," came the laconic reply. "The key may be used by a recruit to make landfall on Zalva."

START THE GAME

"My friend," I turned back to the Precian, "I am seeing several options here. Either I'm flying to Zalva with Nurse and not saying a word to the emperor about your little situation with the general, or I'm flying there on my own and hanging you out to dry. Let the emperor decide whether or not you could smoke the general out of his lair or not. In the end, this is just not my problem to deal with."

"Alright!" the acting commander almost yelled. "She will be given permission to leave the planet—but only if she agrees to do so. I won't force her to go against her will!"

"Call her," I replied, barely containing my smile. "We'll see shortly what she wants…"

"Welcome back, Captain," said Braniac as soon as I entered *Warlock*. "The ship's status…"

"Braniac, why did you ignore my direct order?" I cut off the computer.

"The number that you called from did not correspond to the authorized ship command numbers. The number that was authorized had been blocked due to…"

"Leave off the malarkey!" I interrupted again, raising my voice a bit. "I will repeat my question—why did you ignore my direct order?"

"Because he didn't feel like getting respawned," said the engineer, popping her head out of the wall. "Not so fun to lose a whole class."

"More fun to get a new captain, eh?"

"No one was going to change captains! If we didn't hear from you, we were going to blow ourselves to kingdom come and that's all. A few minutes before we lost the ship. We had a whole think session here—and here you are flaming Braniac."

"Where'd you learn all these words?" I asked the snake. "'Not so fun,' 'think session,' 'flaming.' You didn't speak that way earlier."

"I didn't get out much earlier either. I have no idea what it means, but that's the way people talk on the web I've been reading. So don't get all butthurt about Braniac—no one wanted to self-destruct. It's no pleasure to blow yourself up."

"Braniac?" I asked the computer.

"Ignoring the official side of this question...It is true—I really did not want to lose a hundred levels—a whole class..."

"Lex, are all your AIs like this?" Eunice asked me quietly. "Stan, Braniac, the snake...All of them have personality matrices, but you talk to them as if they're real people...I mean, I understand them—but, I swear, they seem to be arguing with you."

"You know, everyone you just listed is much dearer to me than most of the Earth's population. What difference does it make *who* created sentience—whether it was us humans or some almighty? If a consciousness is subtle enough, why not treat it on equal terms?"

"What are our plans, Cap?" asked the snake. "Where we off to now? Are we going to go troll some Zatrathi?"

"No. And look up how to use 'troll' properly. The Precians

---

are about to load us into a cruiser and then we'll be off to their capital, Zalva."

"*Warlock*," the dispatcher's voice came over the comm. "You will now be transferred to a transport ship. Please do not engage your engines. We will arrive in Zalva in thirty minutes."

"Braniac…"

"Understood, engaging sleep mode. Captain, I really did my best to follow your orders…"

"Alright, forget it. Actually, I should say thank you for not self-destructing immediately. I really don't feel like traveling around *Galactogon* without *Warlock*," I said and turned to Eunice. "Listen, we have thirty minutes of flight time ahead of us. Want to pop back IRL? I don't see any point in staying in-game. What do you say?"

"I'm all for it! I was going to mention it myself. My head feels like it's about to explode. I'm exhausted. Want to race to see who can get out of the cocoon faster? Loser has to order dinner."

"Roger that. Ready, set, go!"

Sign out.

I had never opened the cocoon's lid so quickly. It was silly of course, but Eunice had gotten me into it. Could a girl really beat me out of a game? Never!

"Look at that," I heard an oddly familiar voice as soon as I jumped down to the floor and threw up my arms in triumph. Eunice had only just begun to descend from the platform. "Why, you popped out of that cocoon like a cork out of a bottle. It's like some kind of race or something. Oh no, no—keep those arms up.

GALACTOGON BOOK ONE

You should raise them too, little darling. Oh and it's not a good idea to make any sudden movements right now. It's really not. Who knows, my trigger finger could slip…"

Without putting down my hands I turned around and saw Constantine, smiling spitefully. The very same Constantine I met on the first day of the bet. The very same one I thought was dead. Sprawling in an armchair with a blasé air, he was sipping some kind of beverage through a straw and holding a gun in his other hand. The gun was aimed in our direction. Perhaps the strangest thing however was the absence of Stan's voice.

"Since we are all together again and at last, I propose we have a conversation. We will begin with the most important thing—which of you two will bring me that billion?"

CHAPTER FIFTEEN

THE DECISION

"**Y**ou two look like your mom just caught you smoking and you have no idea what you're gonna tell her," laughed Constantine, lowering the gun. "Reminds me of a famous painting by Goya called *The Third of May*."

"What is the meaning of this?" Eunice asked angrily, dropping her hands. "We were told that you'd been killed."

"Hands up," our guest barked, raising his gun again. "Let's all be real clear about what's going on here. I'd rather you not get any brilliant ideas. Eeny, meeny, miny, moe," Constantine moved his gun between me and Eunice as he read out the counting rhyme. He ended on the girl and said, "Perfect. This way we'll be even for that first day too. You didn't give me any…"

A silenced gunshot sounded. Eunice jerked and looked at Constantine with astonishment. A red spot appeared on the girl's shoulder—my wife collapsed to the floor.

"Are you completely nuts?" I yelled and darted over to the

---

girl. That idiot had shot Eunice! "She's pregnant!"

"Shut your hole," our visitor said tersely, tossing me a small white object. "Press it to the wound. It'll stanch the blood. Only the fact that she is pregnant saved her life just now. Hey! Princess! Can you hear me? Can you talk?"

"You piece of…! Go to hell!" Eunice whispered.

"I'll assume that's a yes. Excellent! We understand each other clearly now. I am here neither for your edification nor your entertainment. As soon as either one of you gives me a reason, I'll be shooting to kill. Are we clear?"

"If you do that, you won't see that check any more than you can see your ears!" the girl growled through her teeth. The bullet had passed clean through her shoulder, so the wound did not seem too serious. The object that Constantine had tossed me turned out to be a miniature first aid kit. As soon as I pressed it to the wound, some kind of mechanism whirred up inside, Eunice received several shots and the blood ceased to flow from either end of the wound.

"And that is precisely why I'm here. We are now going to negotiate an agreement," smiled Constantine, lowering the gun again. "Isn't that right, guys? Guys…?"

"About what?" I replied, standing up.

"Well, here's the deal. I want the coordinates to the prize planet. Yeah, yeah—I know that you've basically got them in the bag by now. I'll admit that I didn't expect you to pop out before your meeting with the emperor, but…well, since you're out, you're out. You could have died peacefully and painlessly."

START THE GAME

"Died?"

"Yup," laughed Constantine. "Died! Did you really think I was going to let you live? So naïve...What're you getting all tense for? Want to try and tackle me? Well, well...You know, you can use the capsule just as well without your legs. You don't actually need them in there."

Another silenced gunshot followed. My right leg was pierced with a sharp and fiery pain. Or did the pain come first—before the gunshot? I can't remember anymore.

"Press the kit to your wound. We wouldn't want you to bleed out." I heard Constantine say through a layer of fog.

A moment passed and I felt a cold numbness pour over my leg, extinguishing the blazing wound.

"There you are. Now that no one is in a hurry to go anywhere, we have twenty minutes before you two sign back into the game. I suppose we should use this time to chat. I will begin—let me reiterate: You will die. That's a fact. But! There are some details."

Without looking away from Constantine, Eunice gripped my hand anxiously. Judging by her evident trembling, the girl was on the edge of complete panic.

"It turns out," went on our tormentor, frowning a little, "that one of you is pregnant. Now, I don't kill kids. So instead of killing you two right away, I can give you one small chance. We can help each other."

A pause followed. Constantine was looking at us and we were looking at him, neither of us saying anything.

"Eh…it's not very interesting this way," our visitor spoke up first. "Where are the inevitable questions? 'How?' 'Why?' "What?' Where are the lamentations and the begging? The others were more talkative. Alright, let me tell you the whole story. Allow me to reiterate again—you're both dead meat. You may as well come to terms with this fact. However! I can simply destroy this lovely girl's mind and leave her body whole and healthy. Then, it will be able to carry the child to term and give birth. That would be quite kind of me, wouldn't it?"

"Constantine, why are you doing this?" I asked. In my view, the important thing at that moment was to stall for time. Stan wasn't saying anything and neither was Eunice's smart home—so most likely that jerk had turned them off somehow. And yet we were under surveillance! The old man said that we couldn't even expect privacy in the bathroom. If that was so, the SWAT team should be arriving at any moment. All we had to do was waste time.

"You trying to waste time?" came the cutting answer. "I don't want to disappoint you," said Constantine glancing at his phone beside him in the chair, "but at the moment the surveillance team thinks that you two are sixty-nining. Look at that! Why Eunice, how masterful you are with the…"

"Shut up!" hissed the girl, blushing deeply.

"That's right. The entire surveillance team—mouths agape and hands in their zippers—is watching you two do the deed. No one will disturb us for at least thirty minutes—so we can continue our negotiations in peace. Now, what do you say to my offer?"

"Kill both of us—or kill just me and turn Eunice into a vegetable?" I answered his question with mine.

"And, importantly, save your child's life in the process. Or—if you prefer—all three of you can die here. Then, I'll miraculously come back to life, convince the old fogeys that I was simply in hiding, undergo all the necessary checks (got my alibi ready and everything), return to the game and begin grinding my Rapport with the Precians. I'll meet the emperor and find out the planets' coordinates...You get it. Basically, I'll return and peacefully play on my merry way since I'll have no competitors left."

"WHAT?!" I exclaimed. "No more competitors?! You killed Lucille?"

"Lucille?" Constantine furrowed his brow. "Oh! The cute uppity girl? Yesterday. Her and her retarded husband. I'll admit that I couldn't help myself and just had to see what those titties looked like...But—let me be crystal clear—I did not touch the little boy. So, believe me when I say that you really *do* have the opportunity to leave the fruit of your perverted tryst to this world."

"You bitch," I hissed like Eunice. Alonso and Lucille were dead! If he had simply said "yes," there'd still remain a doubt in my mind, but in mentioning their son, Constantine had shown that he was not bluffing—you couldn't make that up. My best and only friend in this reality was dead!

"We don't have much time," the killer smiled again. "We've only ten minutes left, so I will repeat my terms—you will return to the game, meet the emperor, find out the coordinates from him and then die a painless and peaceful death. In the process, you make no unnecessary movements or notifications. If you do—if you try to play the hero—you will become the reason that your unborn child dies."

"You never answered me—why are you doing this?"

"Can you not think of a dumber question to ask? We all know the answer—a billion pounds. They'll be all mine. You two are all that stands in my way. Accordingly, you must cease to be…"

"How about an option in which we remain alive," I began to improvise. My thoughts were darting in my head faster than a flyer gone supersonic. I needed to think of a way to survive—but all the while I kept stumbling over the idea that this was all just some kind of dream. Eunice's wounded shoulder and my wounded leg said otherwise. That kind of pain didn't happen in dreams. "We made a new contract with the old guys, under which instead of the original prize of one billion, we would get two billion pounds. A billion apiece. They're yours if you let us live."

"Yes, I already considered this," Constantine scratched his head with his gun pensively. "That's why I left you two until the very end—I wanted to see the bettors' reaction to you guys almost reaching the finish line. I can confidently say that I didn't like this reaction one bit. Specifically, I have seen an internal document stating that you will not be given the two billion. In the organizers' view, only Alexis found the planet, whereas Eunice joined him only at the very end. So, thank you—but no thank you. This option

START THE GAME

---

is just too risky for me. Plus, it's much easier to kill you now than worry about you two paying up later on down the road."

The room grew quiet again. I tried to wiggle the toes on my numbed leg but nothing seemed to happen—either the anesthesia was too strong or the bullet had hit some nerve. A video game would normally use debuffs to simulate such injuries. In reality, everything was much more complicated.

"Okay. I agree," Eunice whispered in a deathly voice, "But I need a guarantee that my child will survive."

"I repeat: I don't kill kids. Have you heard of a thing called a lobotomy? I'll admit—I am very skilled when it comes to this little procedure. You will cease to exist as an individual—but remain a fully functional vessel for your child. Alexis, what do you say? Are you with us, or are we sending Eunice back on her own? Though, as I understand it, all the missions are yours—so there's no point in sending her without you. Without you, this deal won't work."

"Lex, please..." Eunice screamed wordlessly. "He will live..."

Goddamn! What the hell was going on?! When agreeing to participate in the wager, I never imagined I'd be faced with the choice of either helping some bastard and dying but saving a child in the process—or helping no one at all and dying with my head held high. But dying either way! That *bitch*!

"But you repeat yourself," smirked Constantine—it seemed that I had said that last word aloud.

"Let's say we agree and give you the planets' coordinates," I went on stalling for time. "Then you'll be the last one left—you'll reappear in the world and instantly become the main suspect. The betting masters will pick you apart molecule by molecule—and they'll find out everything. On the other hand, we are ready to give you our money. It'll be much less of a headache for you."

"Well, look. Officially, it is the fourth week now that I am bedridden in a coma in my city's hospital. After the failed attempt on my priceless life, I suddenly didn't feel right—and my mind suffered some kind of breakdown. The contest organizers visited me several times and checked my DNA to make sure that it was really me. So my alibi really is ironclad. But thank you for your concern," Constantine quipped. "I find it touching. You have seven minutes before you have to sign in again. Are we choosing the long way or the short way?"

"The short one," I barked once I realized that he was talking about himself. "Before we get back into the capsules—tell me—how did you do all of this?"

"Do you want me to play the movie villain and tell you all my plans?"

"You already told me about your alibi," I shrugged, "why not explain how it all started as well?"

Time—I needed time to think of something. Surely Eunice and I wouldn't make love eternally on the screens of the surveillance agents. At some point they would have to notice that the video was looped.

"Well...I guess, you're right. I told you the first part, so I may as well tell you the second too. Everything started that first day when they brought us to the palace with the old men. I did a good job of playing dead drunk that night. You think I don't remember how you two left me alone on the floor? In the middle of the hallway? You two went off to make your baby—while I remained lying there. Even the servants refused to touch me, since I had vomited and pissed all over. All they did was cover me with a sheet to keep me out of sight and left me lying there until morning."

"You hacked into their system?" Eunice spoke up.

"Yup! Carefully, delicately and—most importantly— stealthily. I dug around their network and discovered many interesting things about who the bettors were, about the rules and about the prize. For example, did you know that you don't actually have to find the check? It's enough to simply step on the correct planet! That's why I showed up today—victory must be mine. I uploaded a Trojan of my own concoction onto their network and then spent several days planning how I would acquire my billion pounds. All I had to do was 'dispose' of myself and then dispose of any competitors. We three are the last of the twelve. Sabotaging a personal flyer and then a transport flyer, changing the temperature in a sauna—I did my best to be creative in my methods. Alright, there are only three minutes left. Please take your places in the capsules. Any last wishes?"

"Die," hissed Eunice getting to her feet.

"You're a mean one," smirked Constantine and raised his gun. A series of gunshots followed and Eunice collapsed to the floor with wounds in her legs and arms. Four shots—four limbs.

"You have half an hour to get me those coordinates," the lunatic said spitefully. "After that, I tear up our contract. As for this bitch," he looked over at Eunice who was lying unconscious on the floor with a puddle of blood spreading beneath her, "she's got no business in *Galactogon* anymore. While you work for me, I'll have some fun with her. I prefer them when they don't resist."

The shock of everything that had happened dampened my fear of dying so much that I actually began to see things much more clearly. The life of our child suddenly ceased to be some kind of obstacle for me.

Who could guarantee that this psycho was telling the truth? It didn't cost him anything to shoot Eunice one more time and end her life for good.

I needed to act and do so now without waiting for outside help.

Suddenly, I began to perceive everything like a game: Constantine was the final boss and I needed to take him out. Eunice was the medic/tank/barbarian and I needed to save her.

The boss cast bolts of lightning that could basically one shot me. But!

If I turned one of my flanks to the boss, then the lightning bolts would only strike that side of me! Then, the other side would remain okay and I could go on fighting!

But how?

What could I do against this boss? I wouldn't be able to respawn, so I had to act only if I was sure of what I was doing. And, all the while, I'd have to take into account that the boss was very smart and fatally dangerous.

The first thing then was to look shocked and freeze—as if I was paralyzed with fear. I'd have no problems doing that—I was at the edge of consciousness as it was.

"What'd you freeze like a statue for?" smirked Constantine. Perfect! The boss was now following my rules. I didn't answer him, remaining silent and still. I had to keep thinking...

"Hey! Ground control to Major Tom! Come in!" the killer said with mounting mirth. Seeing no reaction from me, he added, "What a sad bunch of enemies I have. Buddy—don't croak prematurely on me, alright?"

Constantine's attention switched to Eunice, then to me, then back to Eunice and his smirk vanished from his face.

"The bitch! She's about to die! Why do I have to do everything myself?"

The second thing was to force the boss to switch his attention from me to my injured partner, so I had time to act. Done!

"Eh, old age is no blessing," Constantine grunted like an old man, bending down to Eunice and pressing the first aid kit to her wounds. When he turned away, I had my opportunity. I felt my body spring into action.

The third thing is that it's pointless to attack the boss directly. He is stronger than me, he has better armor, a stronger attack and is in better health than I am. Despite the fact that the capsule has turned me into a well-toned young man, my muscles

---

and reflexes are not trained for close combat.

But I do have something that can give me a slight chance of winning.

Weight plates from my barbell.

Fifteen pounds of iron shaped like a giant token.

Everyone who knew about my love for working out IRL always laughed at me. They thought that losing an extra hour of gameplay only made me weaker. After all, while we sleep, our enemy grows stronger.

In my case, they said that while I pump iron, my enemy levels his character—and gets the loot that I should be getting. Yet I remained unmoved. Working out in reality was mandatory. Full stop. That's what my father had taught me.

I dart to the plates and instantly something singes my arm—the bullet has just nicked it. Damn! The boss has turned out more agile than I expected.

To hell with it! My target is too close to stop now.

I grab the disc and show the boss my side—which is instantly pierced by two lightning bolts. Both hit my shoulder, throwing me backward.

I turn the force of the second bolt into angular momentum and rotate my body. I extend my arm with the plate, feel another lightning bolt strike my leg (thankfully, not the one supporting my weight), complete my rotation and release the disc. Just like in practice (and who cares if that's the first time I've practiced the discus throw…)

Another bolt pierces my chest. I am stamped into the wall

by its inertia. But before I meet the coming darkness, I catch a glimpse of the disc as it smashes right into the boss's head.

A critical hit!

I've leveled up!

Where's my loot?

END OF BOOK ONE

Want to be the first to know about our latest LitRPG, sci fi and fantasy titles from your favorite authors?

Subscribe to our *New Releases* newsletter:
http://eepurl.com/b7niIL

Thank you for reading *Start the Game!*
If you like what you've read, check out other sci-fi, fantasy and
LitRPG novels published by Magic Dome Books:

Reality Benders LitRPG series by Michael Atamanov:
Countdown
External Threat
Game Changer
Web of Worlds
A Jump into the Unknown
Aces High

The Dark Herbalist LitRPG series
by Michael Atamanov:
Video Game Plotline Tester
Stay on the Wing
A Trap for the Potentate
Finding a Body

Perimeter Defense LitRPG series by Michael Atamanov:
Sector Eight
Beyond Death
New Contract
A Game with No Rules

League of Losers LitRPG Series
by Michael Atamanov:
A Cat and his Human

The Way of the Shaman LitRPG series
by Vasily Mahanenko:
Survival Quest
The Kartoss Gambit
The Secret of the Dark Forest
The Phantom Castle
The Karmadont Chess Set
Shaman's Revenge
Clans War

The Alchemist LiTRPG series by Vasily Mahanenko:
City of the Dead
Forest of Desire
Tears of Alron

Dark Paladin LitRPG series by Vasily Mahanenko:
The Beginning
The Quest
Restart

Galactogon LitRPG series by Vasily Mahanenko:
Start the Game!
In Search of the Uldans
A Check for a Billion

Invasion LitRPG Series by Vasily Mahanenko:
A Second Chance
An Equation with one Unknown

World of the Changed LitRPG Series by Vasily Mahanenko:
No Mistakes
Pearl of the South

**The Bard from Barliona LitRPG series
by Eugenia Dmitrieva and Vasily Mahanenko:**
The Renegades
A Song of Shadow

Level Up LitRPG series by Dan Sugralinov:
Re-Start
Hero
The Final Trial
Level Up: The Knockout (with Max Lagno)
Level Up. The Knockout: Update (with Max Lagno)

Disgardium LitRPG series by Dan Sugralinov:
Class-A Threat
Apostle of the Sleeping Gods
The Destroying Plague
Resistance
Holy War

World 99 LitRPG Series by Dan Sugralinov:
Blood of Fate

Adam Online LitRPG Leries by Max Lagno:
Absolute Zero
City of Freedom

In order to have new books of the series translated faster, we need your help and support! Please consider leaving a review or spread the word by recommending *Start the Game!* to your friends and posting the link on social media. The more people buy the book, the sooner we'll be able to make new translations available.

Thank you!

Till next time!